PERDI
DAUGHTERS

PERDITION'S DAUGHTERS

A Dan Temple Adventure

DARREN RODELL

Copyright © 2013 Darren Rodell

The moral right of the author has been asserted.

Apart from any fair dealing for the purposes of research or private study, or criticism or review, as permitted under the Copyright, Designs and Patents Act 1988, this publication may only be reproduced, stored or transmitted, in any form or by any means, with the prior permission in writing of the publishers, or in the case of reprographic reproduction in accordance with the terms of licences issued by the Copyright Licensing Agency. Enquiries concerning reproduction outside those terms should be sent to the publishers.

Matador
9 Priory Business Park,
Wistow Road, Kibworth Beauchamp,
Leicestershire. LE8 0RX
Tel: (+44) 116 279 2299
Fax: (+44) 116 279 2277
Email: books@troubador.co.uk
Web: www.troubador.co.uk/matador

ISBN 978 1780884 493

British Library Cataloguing in Publication Data.
A catalogue record for this book is available from the British Library.

Printed and bound in the UK by TJ International, Padstow, Cornwall
Typeset in 11pt Minion Pro by Troubador Publishing Ltd, Leicester, UK

Matador is an imprint of Troubador Publishing Ltd

For my Girls

ONE

"Brute force, no matter how strongly applied, can never subdue the basic human desire for freedom."
Dalai Lama.

It was the usual weekday morning; chaotic. Jennifer Mead dashed from bathroom to bedroom to kitchen, a whirlwind of youthful activity. It was the first day back at college following the autumn half-term break and her A-level mocks beckoned. Hurriedly, she crunched a mouthful of butter smothered toast and gulped down her tea. Pulled her striped, brightly coloured sweater on over her T-shirt, wrapped her scarf around her neck, threw her books in her bag and bounced out of the door.

'Bye, Mum,' she shouted as the door slammed behind her.

Briskly, she walked down the broad suburban avenue, as she had done every term day for the last year. The weather was bright and cool and the northerly breeze felt distinctly chilled as it blew across her face and small expanse of exposed midriff.

Switching on her iPod, she flicked through to her latest favourite album and turned up the volume. Cocooned in her thoughts and music, the chill of the autumn morning dissolved around her.

The men watched her go.

The van cruised anonymously along the avenue, the neatly stencilled lettering on its white side panels proclaiming the skills, trustworthiness and contact details of the local building and house maintenance services on offer. The two men looked at each other, smirking as they watched the girl. Her firm, rounded bottom swayed provocatively in her tight, sprayed-on jeans as she walked quickly along the pavement, oblivious to her surroundings.

The van slowed and pulled in close behind.

*

The man at the bus stop looked up, his interest and imagination captivated by the young girl's attractive face and curvy figure, accentuated by her low-cut hipster jeans and tight, colourful sweater. Her wavy long blond hair flowed behind her on the fresh morning breeze and her cheeks glowed pink in the crisp autumn air. He watched appreciatively as she drew level with him, kicking her way through the autumnal carpet of brown and gold leaves on the opposite side of the road. Her perfectly formed teenage body made a warming, welcome distraction to his otherwise cold and uneventful wait. The girl glanced over as she always did, smiling self-consciously, seemingly appreciative of his admiring looks, then slightly, almost teasingly, accentuated the sway of her hips.

The van crawled slowly by, momentarily blocking his view.

The girl walked on.

He waited, eager to catch one last glimpse of the girl before she turned out of the avenue and out of his view for another day.

Suddenly, the van accelerated.

The man's eyes and brain disconnected, momentarily unable to comprehend the visual deception.

The girl was there.

The van passed slowly.

Then she was gone, vanishing like a beautiful apparition.

He stared at the empty pavement. He looked left, to the rear of the van, then back to the void where the girl should have been. The space now filled by swirling leaves which hung in the air, then floated gently, innocently to the ground.

His eyes knew what they had witnessed, but his mind delayed the connection. He stood paralysed, temporarily frozen, locked in a cold, still and silent vacuum, waiting for the world to restart.

A girl's scream jarred his senses. His mind reconnected with full sound and vision. Comprehension returned. He reached into his pocket, grabbed his mobile phone and dialled 999.

*

The music ended abruptly as Jennifer Mead's feet involuntarily left the pavement and her legs walked briefly in the air, leaving a flurry of scattered leaves dancing on the breeze.

She kicked and struggled, scratched and bit as rough hands gripped her, firmly pinning her to the cold, harsh metal floor of the van.

She saw the needle, stared wide-eyed, then screamed an ear-piercing, panic-stricken scream. Icy terror and adrenalin raged through her body and she fought with all the strength and courage she could find.

The needle scratched painfully into her arm.

Her head swirled and her vision blurred as the drugs rushed her to dark unconsciousness.

The van drove on, turned out of the avenue and melted innocuously into the rush-hour traffic.

*

The young couple made love slowly, their bodies intertwined, each totally absorbed in the other. Every look, every touch, every caress, responded to with increasing desire as their passion grew and their body heat warmed the chill of the morning.

The girl spread her legs wide, then lifted them, wrapping them around her lover. Her pelvis moved in rhythm with his increasingly urgent thrusts and she moaned softly, her orgasm building. The young man pushed himself up on his arms, staring lovingly in to her glistening, soft brown eyes. Unable to hold his rapidly approaching climax, he threw back his head, thrusting deeper and harder until they climaxed together in strong pulsating waves of all-consuming passion. They lay wrapped together, still and silent, hearing nothing but the sound of their breathing, enveloped in the warm afterglow of their love.

The sound of a slow, derisive hand clap from their uninvited audience tore through their warm, contented world.

Startled, Elizabeth Mead looked across to the open bedroom door, her eyes opening wide as uncomprehendingly she gasped with fear – she screamed.

Her boyfriend leapt naked from the bed. Fit, strong and agile, he moved quickly; no thought of asking questions, no concerns for his own safety.

Elizabeth looked on, transfixed and frightened. The two men seemed undaunted as her boyfriend sprang from the bed and launched himself across the small bedroom. Time and motion slowed as in unison the men raised their arms and silently fired.

Her boyfriend's forward momentum ended as abruptly as it began. Hit by the invisible, mid-air projectiles, his body violently recoiled back onto the bed with two ragged, bloody holes puncturing the centre of his chest.

Elizabeth's screams stuck in her throat; her initial fear savagely replaced by total, mind-numbing terror.

The two men approached the bed and tore the sheets from her naked body.

Instinctively, she fought, thrashing her arms and legs, kicking and punching in vain, but the strength in her small, slender frame was no match for the powerful hands and arms pinning her to the mattress.

A huge, rough paw of a hand clamped harshly over her mouth.

A needle stabbed sharply into her buttock.

The room span.

Her vision blurred.

Her eyes fluttered and closed.

Muted sounds rushed through her ears.

Her terror subsided and vanished, replaced by

silence and the cold hard blackness of complete unconsciousness.

*

'It's done,' said the man sombrely, walking toward the desk in the small, dimly-lit room.

Zoran Durakovic momentarily looked up from his desk, then nodded once; his pale-grey eyes, as cold and hard as steel, conveyed no emotion.

'Are you certain, Jan?'

'Positive. They're on their way.'

'Any problems?'

'None.'

'Excellent,' Durakovic replied, reaching for the telephone.

TWO

The telephone on Richard Mead's desk rang at exactly 9:00am. It was nothing unusual – he was a busy man; his services were always in demand. Since retiring from the SAS to start his security consultancy business, his telephone had been ringing constantly. He waited a few moments before he answered, then pressed the record button and lifted the receiver, ensuring, as always, that he had a pen and pad at the ready.

'Richard Mead,' he stated confidently.

He was greeted by a lengthy pause and listened intently to the static silence.

'Richard Mead,' he stated again.

'Good morning, Colonel Mead,' replied the heavily accented voice.

'Good morning,' Mead acknowledged in a polite, business-like fashion. 'How may I help you?'

'You know what it is I want, Colonel. You know there is only one way in which you can help me.'

'I'm sorry, I don't understand. Do you wish to discuss my business services?'

'In a manner of speaking. But first I want you to listen.' The words were delivered simply – the voice hard and edgy.

'I don't mean to be rude, but I do have a nine o'clock appointment. Perhaps I could take your details and get back to you?'

'You don't need my details, Colonel. Your appointment *is* with me.'

'I'm sorry, who is this?' Mead asked, already irritated with the unnecessarily cryptic conversation.

'Do you not recognise my voice, Colonel? Surely you haven't forgotten me already? After all, you put so much time and effort in to pursuing and capturing me –' the man paused for a moment. 'We never did finish our last conversation, Colonel. We still have many things to discuss, you and I,' the voice stated, firm and insistent.

Richard Mead slumped back in to his chair. The voice registered and alarm bells sounded like claxons in his head.

'Durakovic,' he responded quietly.

'Well done, Colonel. You see, you do remember.'

'What do you want?'

'I already have what I want, or should I say, who.'

It was a cold statement, laced with callous, malicious intent.

'You didn't honestly think I would let the matter rest – let our business go unresolved – did you, Colonel? It is time for you to pay. There is no get-out clause, Colonel Mead, not in this relationship.' Durakovic venomously spat down the phone.

'I cannot help you, if you will not help me, Colonel.'

Richard Mead switched off the voice recorder, gathered his senses and his composure and listened carefully, waiting for the punch line.

'What do you want?' he asked again.

'Insurance, or more accurately an incentive –' Durakovic paused again, leaving a long, drawn-out silence. 'Have you seen your daughters lately?' he asked icily.

The words ominously bore down in Richard Mead's mind; the reality and purpose of the question registered immediately.

'If you hurt them, I'm going to hunt you down and kill you with my bare hands.'

Durakovic laughed.

'Save your theatrical words, Colonel. You're a smart man – I am sure you have already switched off the voice recorder.'

'I mean it, Durakovic; I'm going to find you and I'm going to kill you.'

'If only it were that easy, Colonel. You know what you need to do. Your daughters are my insurance. Their only hope of redemption rests with you. Fail and your life, and theirs, will be over. You will suffer the never-ending pain and torment that I have suffered, and your children will suffer with you. However, we are both business men, despite what has happened between us – so, please, Colonel, do we have agreement?'

'I've told you, I can't do it.'

'Maybe not, Colonel, but I am sure you know someone – can arrange for someone who can. You can do that, can't you, Colonel?'

Richard Mead closed his eyes.

'Yes,' he replied, his voice no more than a harsh whisper.

'Good, then we have an agreement?'

The pressure of another protracted silence felt long and heavy. Thoughts and options span through Mead's mind; there was no choice. He cleared his throat.

'Yes,' he confirmed, reluctantly forcing out the solitary word through gritted teeth.

'Excellent. Switch on the voice recorder, Colonel; let me help you get started.'

Richard Mead sat forward.

'Go on,' he said, pressing the button.

Durakovic continued. 'I'm going to bring you

into my world now, Colonel. There are matters you and I need to conclude. Until that is done, you're going to live in hell. I just wanted you to know what was going to happen to your precious girls. You know what I do, don't you, Colonel? What goes on here? I am the door to the white slave trade; you understand what will be done, what their lives will be like, don't you? I am going to make a gift of your daughters. They will be forced into sexual slavery, into a world of abuse, torment and degradation, and I will revel in every agonising moment. Who knows, I might even take some pleasure with them myself. More satisfying, though, will be the knowledge that there is nothing in your power or control that you can do about it. If you come for them, they will be killed. If you contact the police or any other law enforcement agency, they will be killed. Your daughters will be in your nightmares. You will be together in hell. They will be perdition's daughters.'

The phone went dead and Richard Mead's life plunged into purgatory.

THREE

The call came at 2:00am; the sound of the telephone was loud and harsh in the cold silence of the night. By 2:30am, Daniel Temple was racing through narrow country roads, his battered green Land Rover power sliding through bends and galloping down straights. The big V8 engine roared as it accelerated, sending rain and mud spitting from the tyres as Daniel expertly pushed the vehicle to its limits, careering at breakneck speed down the country lanes, then pushing hard and fast along the near empty motorway.

Daniel skidded to a stop outside Richard Mead's house in the leafy avenues of Royal Tunbridge Wells. It was 5:00am.

Daniel's philosophy was as straightforward and honest as the man himself. If someone you consider a friend calls for help, you respond, no questions asked.

Richard Mead's call had been one of desperation. Daniel didn't need to ask – it was simple deduction. Anyone who calls at 2:00am is usually one of three things – mad, drunk or desperate. Daniel knew Richard very well. He was Daniel's friend, business partner and ex-Commanding Officer. SAS trained, shrewd, experienced and as good as they came. The call could mean only one thing: trouble, desperate trouble.

Daniel rang the doorbell and waited in the cool dark of the autumnal morning. Richard Mead answered the door. A usually tall, strong and athletic figure, he looked stooped, tired and shaken. Worse – he looked afraid. Daniel didn't waste time with small talk; he wasn't the type.

'What's wrong, Richard, what's happened?' he asked with genuine concern.

Richard looked at him through bloodshot eyes.

'Thanks for coming, Daniel. There was no one else I could turn to. No one else I would want to turn to,' he said, stepping aside to allow Daniel's huge frame through the door.

They walked across the hallway and stepped into the lounge. Daniel could see Jane Mead sat on the sofa. She was crying; she looked as if she'd been crying forever.

'Hello, Jane,' he said softly as he glanced around the room.

It was a warm and welcoming lounge. Two large armchairs sat facing a long, comfortable looking sofa, either side of a rectangular coffee table. Ornaments, keepsakes, pictures and memories adorned shelves and bookcases. It was a real family room, just as he remembered it. Daniel looked at the display cabinet standing against the wall behind the sofa. Numerous photographs sat behind the glass-fronted doors. He saw himself in one or two, uniformed and otherwise; all seemingly happy occasions. His gaze fell on the central picture – a family portrait, taken recently by the look of it. Richard and Jane sat, slightly angled toward each other. Their two daughters, Elizabeth and Jennifer stood behind, smiling, each resting a hand on their parent's shoulder. It was a cheerful picture. A happy family, just as Daniel knew them.

Jane looked up, her eyes bloodshot and tearstained.

'Please help us, Daniel,' she pleaded, collapsing back into the sofa and sobbing uncontrollably.

Richard sat down next to her, awkwardly but gently stroking her hair.

Daniel sat and waited, calm and patient. They would talk when they were ready. It was a full ten minutes before Jane sat up, wiping the tears from her eyes.

'I'm sorry,' she said, a little more composed.

Daniel looked at her sympathetically.

'It's OK,' he replied gently. 'Perhaps we could have some tea? I think it best Richard and I speak alone, at least for the moment, Jane.'

She nodded. She understood, as Daniel knew she would.

Daniel waited for the lounge door to close, then refocused his thoughts. He looked across the coffee table to Richard.

'Why don't you tell me what's wrong and how I can help?'

Richard nodded, took a deep breath and launched straight into his explanation.

'Please don't interrupt whilst I tell you this. I need to get it all out. Then we'll talk it through again and I'll answer any questions you have, OK?'

'Fine. It's OK, Richard, there's no rush, just tell me everything you can.'

'Back in the nineties I served in Bosnia. I was still a Major at the time. Whilst I was there, I witnessed some absolutely horrendous atrocities; genocide and other war crimes. One of the main perpetrators was a local Serbian Commander named Zoran Durakovic. Toward the end of the war I was tasked, along with others, to track him down and bring him to justice. As the war came to a close and the official conflict ended, he managed to disappear. We continued to hunt him, eventually catching up with him towards the end of the summer of 1997. My SAS unit was ordered to take him. He was hiding out in a remote country house in the Carpathian Mountains and still had a small band of loyal men with him. We knew he wasn't going to come without a fight, so we went in with a full assault team. There was a brief, but intense firefight. We took the house but Durakovic wasn't there. I don't know how he got out, but he did. When we searched the house, we found seven men. We also found his wife and young son; both had been shot once through the back of the head – assassinated. I knew none of my team killed them, but I couldn't explain it – I still can't – although I have my theories. When Durakovic found out, he surrendered – just came in of his own volition. He went to trial for a number of war crimes, but it went disastrously wrong. The witnesses disappeared one by one – most of them without a trace. In the end, we were down to two key witnesses. We moved them to a safe house, under Bosnian protection. Then, the day before the trial was due to start, the witnesses and their guards were found dead – executed. The case collapsed. Added to this, all throughout the trial, Durakovic blamed the British for persecuting him – wrongly accusing him – pursuing him for crimes he didn't commit and murdering his family. He blamed me and swore his revenge. I ignored it naturally – you have to. Shortly after, I was ordered out and that was the last I saw or heard of him.'

'Until now,' Daniel perceptively stated.

Richard nodded slowly, almost hesitantly.

'Yes, until now. Until 9:00am yesterday morning, in fact. He called me at the office,' Richard explained, struggling to maintain his composure.

Richard stopped talking, fighting his emotions, unable to say the words; his left hand shook slightly as he gripped it in his right and his eyes wandered around the room.

Daniel's eyes narrowed. The words were fine; the manner in which they were delivered, less than convincing.

'You're certain about that, Richard?' Daniel asked, looking directly into Richard's face.

Richard looked away, then down to the floor.

'Yes, I'm certain.'

Daniel let it ride. It wasn't the time to doubt what he was being told. He looked past the haunted shell of the man sat on the sofa, up to the family portrait, then back to Richard.

'He's taken Elizabeth and Jennifer hasn't he?'

Richard nodded again but didn't speak.

Daniel relaxed back into his chair, letting the silence work; letting Richard recompose himself and prepare to continue.

'Yes, he's taken them.'

Daniel sat passively, discretely assessing Richard as he assimilated the information. The man was upset, that was obvious, but there was something else, something in his body language – it wasn't right. He seemed angry and agitated, somehow preoccupied, as if he were fighting some inner torment. Daniel registered his uncomfortable demeanour; his posture, the movement of his hands when he spoke and the rapid, constant movement of his eyes. Then he set it aside, accepting it was probably the shock, undoubted tiredness and emotional stress.

Jane Mead returned with two mugs of tea and set them down on the table.

'I'll leave you both to talk for a little while longer, but please don't leave without saying goodbye, Daniel,' she said.

Daniel smiled. 'Thanks, Jane, I won't,' he replied warmly. 'There's more, isn't there?' Daniel asked as soon as Jane left the room.

'Yes,' Richard confirmed. 'He said he wanted his revenge for what I had done to him. Said he was going to put the girls into white slavery – sexual slavery. If I tried to get them back, went to the police or told anyone, they would be killed. He said they would be perdition's daughters and that I would live the rest of my days in hell. I taped the call; I tape all of my calls, just in case. It's a prudent measure in our line of work.'

Richard set the tape player on the coffee table in front of Daniel and pressed play.

Daniel listened to the tape, frowning as he did so. The conversation seemed to be as Richard described, and then it wasn't. Daniel couldn't quite put his finger on it, but his instinct told him this wasn't the whole story – something was out of place; the voice, the words, the responses – something.

'Can I take this?' Daniel asked, ejecting the tape. 'It would help if I could listen to it again when we've finished.'

'Yes of course, that tape's a copy,' Richard confirmed before continuing. 'I need your help, Daniel. I can't go after them and I can't – won't – consider going to anyone else, especially the authorities – I just can't take the risk. Please find them, Daniel. Bring my girls home.'

For the first time ever, Daniel could see that Richard Mead was close to tears. His desperation echoed in every pleading word.

Daniel sat without a hint of emotion, but his thoughts were dark and disturbing. There was no need to think it through; Richard was his business partner, but above all, his friend, and the girls as close his own family. His response was strong and unequivocal.

'I'll find them, Richard, and I'll bring them home.' He left a short pause, then continued. 'Jane doesn't know the full story, does she?'

Richard shook his head.

'No. I thought it best to spare her the details. She just knows they have been abducted. I told her it was something to do with my work. That they would be fine as long as I co-operated. I can't tell her the rest.'

'Good, keep it that way; imagination can be a terrible thing,' Daniel added and continued. 'One last thing, Richard, before Jane returns, although I'm sure I know the answer. What do you want me to do with Durakovic?'

Richard looked at Daniel, the answer plain and clear as his expression hardened.

Daniel nodded his silent understanding and approval.

Jane returned, joining Richard on the sofa. They sat hand in hand, staring expectantly at Daniel.

'OK, we need to talk this through together. I will need the most recent details on the girls. What were their regular movements, friends, especially any new ones, college and work details? You know the sort of thing. I obviously don't need photographs; I know the girls well enough. After today, we don't speak or contact each other in any way. Do not tell anyone what has happened and do not tell anyone you have seen me – clear?' Daniel asked, his tone firm and business-like.

The Meads nodded.

'Clear,' they confirmed together.

Daniel thought again.

'Jane, I'm sorry, I don't mean to be rude or unsympathetic, but please leave. I need to talk to Richard alone, for just a while longer.'

Richard looked at his wife and half-smiled.

'Please, Jane. There are things you don't need to hear.'

Daniel waited and watched as Jane Mead left the room. He knew she understood; she had been a soldier's wife long enough. There were always secrets in Richard's line of work and she had known Daniel long enough not to take offence at his emotionless, direct style.

He turned back to Richard as the door closed.

'You said you had a theory?'

'About Durakovic's family? I do, but that was a long time ago. I can't see what it has to do with this.'

'Humour me. Tell me everything you can, however trivial or unconnected you think it is.'

'OK. As I said, my unit was ordered to take Durakovic after we had traced him to where he was hiding.'

'How did you trace him?'

Richard shook his head. 'I don't know. It may have been intelligence data, but most likely a tip-off, you know how it is. I didn't get told how we found him, I just got told to go and get him.'

'OK, carry on.'

'We moved in. It was rugged, mountainous

country, heavily forested, lots of cover. The house was in a level clearing, close to the banks of a river. There were three teams, twelve men in all. The information we had was that Durakovic was definitely there with his wife, son and eight other men, including his second in command, Jancic.'

'You said seven earlier?'

'I said we found seven. I can't be sure if there were any others. That's where my theory comes in.'

'Go on.'

'The team moved in, early morning – 4:00am. It was summer, just turning light. I thought at the time they weren't expecting us.'

'But now?'

'Now? Now I think different – they knew we were coming.'

'How?'

'Nothing concrete, nothing I can evidence – just gut feeling.'

'Good enough for me, your instincts were always good.'

'Anyway, we moved in and hit them hard, expecting to catch them totally cold. They were waiting. Not that well organised, but they were hardened men, completely loyal to Durakovic – they fought to the last.'

'I have to ask this, what were your orders, exactly?'

'To take Durakovic, that's it, plain and simple.'

'Come on, Richard, I know the score, I know how these things work. Were you told to leave no one alive?'

'The family, you mean? No, absolutely not. Quite the opposite. The orders were to take Durakovic, alive if possible; certainly not to kill non-combatants. My men didn't kill his wife and son. You were in the regiment. Do you know anyone who would execute a woman or small boy like that? I don't.'

Daniel stared at Richard, clinically surveying his face. He reflected for a moment, but didn't answer the question.

'So what happened when you moved in?'

'As I said, they were waiting. There was a brief but bloody firefight. We lost two men taking the house. Once inside, we swept through, clearing it room by room. When it was over, we found seven bodies. Durakovic's wife and boy were in the cellar; both had been shot once through the back of the head.'

'Definitely executed?'

'No doubt about it.'

'And you never found Jancic?'

'Not to this day. He just vanished.'

'What's your theory?'

'Jancic rather than Durakovic was behind many of the atrocities attributed to Durakovic. Not that

Durakovic was clean by any means – he wasn't. Equally, he may not have been as evil or as ruthless as we believed – at least he wasn't then. The truth would have come out at Durakovic's trial and Jancic knew that. I think someone tipped them off; someone senior in the Bosnian army, and either Jancic or Durakovic's men spirited him away. My theory is that Jancic offered to stay to protect the family – a show of absolute loyalty – a sham. I would say the first people to die that day were Durakovic's wife and son – I'm certain of it.'

'That leaves a hell of a lot of other questions, starting with why?'

'I know. I don't have the answers, just personal theories, which until now I've kept to myself. I'm sorry, Dan, I can't see what any of this has to do with my girls.'

'I need to know everything, Richard. Who and what I'm up against. What are their motives? Keep going, please.'

'Alright, we're coming to the crux of it. You asked why? During the war, mistakes were made – that's obvious – and some of these only became apparent very late on. One significant piece of information to come out was that Durakovic had ordered the destruction of a small village, right on the border between what is now Bosnia and Serbia, but in those days that distinction didn't exist. Jancic carried out that order.'

'So?'

'So, it was the village where Jancic had lived. He thought his family had left and were already away and safe. It may have been that Durakovic told him they were; either way, he was wrong. The village was heavily shelled and Jancic's family were killed. He found them himself when the army swept through to complete their "cleansing".'

'So Jancic returned the favour?'

'I think so, but there is more. As the war came to an end, a number of senior army figures and government officials disappeared. Some were found dead – executed. Some did us a favour and committed suicide, whilst others just fled. One of the theories at the time was that the smart ones had already lined up powerful and very lucrative positions in the emerging mafia-related operations in the Balkan states. You know what it's like. War presents opportunities – peace presents even more.'

'You think that's what Durakovic and Jancic did?'

'I'm sure of it. I also think they now run rival organisations, but again I can't prove that. Jancic has never been found, as far as I'm aware.'

'OK, that might be a dead end, but it's good to know. What about the girls? Tell me about them – their schools, college, work, friends?'

Jane returned to the lounge, bringing fresh mugs of hot, strong tea. Daniel let her stay. She would know more about the girl's lives than Richard, it stood to reason; he was often away on business. They talked for another two hours as Daniel gleaned all the information he could. He asked questions, covered every aspect of their lives then covered it again, leaving no stone unturned and no subject unexplored. It was raw and distressing and they paused regularly, letting emotions run their course before picking up the painful threads of conversation again.

'One last thing, and I am sorry, but there is no easy way to say this. You have to be prepared for a few things. First, I may not get them back; you have to accept that. Second, you may not get the same people back.' Daniel looked at Richard before continuing. 'Whoever has abducted them may not treat them well. They may be traumatised by what happens to them – you also have to accept that. Lastly, this may not be quick and it certainly won't be easy. Don't expect them back in a few days, maybe not even a few weeks. As time passes, you will wonder what's happening. You will imagine all sorts of things and you will want to contact me. Whatever you do, don't do that,' he emphasised.

The Meads looked at each other, then nodded again.

'Right, I have what I need and you have my promise. I will do everything I can to bring them home,' Daniel said without emotion.

He stood and firmly shook Richard's hand as their eyes locked; his friendship and promise absolute.

Jane stepped forward, hugged him then kissed him softly on the cheek.

'Thank you, Daniel,' she said quietly.

Daniel left the house and climbed back into his old green Land Rover. It was 9:00am on a cold, grey and dismal November morning. He knew the most critical element, time, was against him, but he was back, doing what he did best and on the hunt again.

FOUR

Elizabeth Mead lay, cold, frightened and naked, tied to a folding metal bed in the dim and squalid room. Her head throbbed as she opened her eyes and tried to focus in the shadowy light of the large, austere room. Slowly, she took in her surroundings. The walls were streaked a dirty brown and covered with mildew, mould and damp. The once-bright wallpaper, now tattered and faded, peeled away in long strips which hung bowed and torn, forlornly reaching for the bare wooden floor. There was nothing else to see. She pulled hard at her bonds, but the bed just wobbled and creaked loudly as she struggled. Her efforts were futile – she was held fast.

She started as behind her a man stepped menacingly from the shadows, laughing cruelly at her pathetic struggle. Slowly, he walked to the bed and stood over her, leering depravedly at her body.

Menacingly, he sat next to her. Reaching out, he stroked her naked breasts, letting his rough hands linger on her soft, smooth skin.

Terrified, she tried to cower away, but couldn't.

His fingers brushed lightly over her nipples.

She turned her head away, not wanting to look; not wanting to see.

The man pawed at her exposed body and her breath caught, then quickened. Fearfully, she closed her eyes, letting the tears roll down her face.

The man reached over, gripped her face in his short, fat, nicotine-stained fingers and turned it roughly toward his own.

'Open your eyes,' he growled, his voice laden with a heavy central European accent.

Fear held her in its icy grip. She did as she was told. The man was brutishly ugly. His bloated, pockmarked face, unclean and unshaven, stared down at her, his look conveying a thinly veiled threat of sexual desire. His hand moved again, roughly grasping her small, pert breast and pinching the nipple hard.

She gasped in pain and closed her eyes once more, feeling sick to the pit of her stomach as she tried desperately to pull away.

'Soon,' he said exhaling a breath that reeked of stale alcohol and cigarettes.

He let her go and stood up, smiling cruelly,

exposing stained and rotten teeth, then walked back to the corner of the room, returning with a plastic supermarket carrier bag. Untying her bonds, he threw the bag onto the bed.

'Put these on,' he ordered, pointing to the oversized, plain grey jogging bottoms and sweatshirt which had spilled onto the bare, stained mattress.

The man left, locking the door behind him.

Elizabeth curled into a ball. Pulling her knees tightly to her chest, she clasped her hands firmly around them and sobbed as if her heart were breaking, never to be mended.

'Daddy,' she cried softly to herself.

She was just thirty miles from home.

*

At the opposite end of the same large, derelict house, one floor away from her sister, Jennifer Mead sat blindfolded and tied to a chair, shivering in the cold blackness of her terror.

Her head turned, nervously following the sound as someone moved closer.

'Who's there?' she asked anxiously, her voice conveying every ounce of her fear.

She listened hard. There was a faint rustle and a metallic snick, then footsteps drew closer to her chair.

Anxiously she waited, then started as a hand gripped her shoulder.

'Don't move,' a man growled.

She held her breath.

The ropes binding her hands to the chair tugged and tightened, then fell away, followed by her blindfold. She blinked as the light filled her eyes. Her vision blurred, then slowly focussed on a man's hideous face and she screamed, a terrified, high-pitched, ear-piercing scream.

'Shut up, bitch,' the man spat angrily.

Her scream ended as abruptly as it started as the man's hand slapped her hard, stinging her face and producing a trickle of blood from her nose. Hardly able to breathe, she stared at the man and fearfully sucked in her sobs as her heart pounded so hard that it threatened to burst through her chest.

The man leered at her.

Jennifer stared back, her eyes blinking with shock and pain. Her mouth moved but no sound came forth and her gaze fixed on a long, ugly scar that curved from the centre of his left ear across his angular face and ended in the middle of his chin.

The man rubbed his unshaven skin, stroking the scar through the greying black whiskers as they rasped against his huge rough hand.

'Stand up,' he ordered.

She stood slowly, hesitantly, her fear making

every movement a conscious effort. Jennifer watched the man, his eyes wandering lustfully over her young body as his tongue slightly protruded and involuntarily, he licked his lips. Her eyes moved to the knife. The blade shone, long and sharp.

He pointed it, his breath quickening.

'Take off your sweater,' he instructed.

She reached down as if in a trance, grasped the bottom of her sweater and pulled it slowly up over her head. Her T-shirt rode up with it, exposing her smooth, flat stomach.

The man licked his lips again as Jennifer stood nervously and self-consciously before him. He stared at her chest. Her nipples prominent, hard and erect in the cold, pointed through the thin material of her bra and tight T-shirt.

'Take off your T-shirt,' he growled, his voice dry and croaky.

Horrific realisation exploded in her mind. She knew what he wanted. She shook her head and tears rolled down her face as she watched the knife wave in front of her face.

'Do it,' he snapped harshly, her fear obviously arousing him.

She reached down, reluctantly pulled the T-shirt over her head and stood still and silent, terrified and provocative, her hands moving to cover her breasts.

'Move your hands,' he ordered, his excitement growing.

Her hands dropped slowly and unwillingly to her sides.

The man stared.

'Take it off,' he commanded in a hoarse, excited whisper.

Jennifer shook her head and stepped away until her back pressed against the cold, damp wall. The knife flashed in front of her face.

'Take it off,' his voice rasped.

She reached behind her back, undid the clasp and let her bra fall to the floor.

The man stood before her, breathing hard, seemingly mesmerised by her full, firm breasts. She could hear his rasping breath and smell his foul odour.

He touched himself, his erection straining hard against the front of his trousers, then he reached out, cupping her breast in his hand and stroking the soft skin as a small groan escaped his lips.

Jennifer closed her eyes and shook her head again.

'Please don't,' she begged.

The spell broken, he let her go and turned away.

'Get dressed,' he ordered. 'Leave your bra off.'

Jennifer stooped, picked up her T-shirt and sweater and hurriedly put them on before gasping in pain as the man grabbed her by the hair, dragged her through to another squalid room and threw her onto an old sofa. It was torn, stained and damp and smelled of human depravity, stale sweat and urine. Jennifer collapsed, bursting into tears as fear and shock wracked her trembling body.

*

Elizabeth wiped a layer of grime from the small, solitary window in her room and stared out. The early November day which had started dull and grey had grown darker and colder as the weather closed in. The wretched house now seemed ever more foreboding and sinister, its atmosphere changing with the climate. Inside, the air was dank and cold, the room dim and desolate, its appearance and mood descending by the hour. She shivered. This was a colourless, sordid place, where life itself seemed to have drained passively away.

Outside, there was nothing to see. The clouds hung low, solemn and grey, obscuring any hint of sunlight. Rain hung in the air, forming a thick chilling mist which oozed and swirled into every space like cold wet smoke.

It had been twenty-four hours since she had been abducted. At first, afraid, cold and alone, she had called out, crying for help, desperate to raise the alarm. Her voice went unheard and her initial fighting spirit was subdued by threats of rape and vile acts of perversion. Frightened and alone and with the exception of occasional sobs and whispered prayers, she fell pitiful and silent.

*

The transport arrived at 10:00pm. A Ford Transit van, white, plain and nondescript; identical to thousands of other vans anonymously driving the roads of Europe every single day.

The weather had changed. A biting wind had cleared the soft clinging mist and now whistled icily across the open, desolate ground, driving the fine drizzle into hard, stinging rain. The man with the scarred face stepped out of the house, wrapped against the weather in a black, full-length waxed cotton drovers coat. He marched across the sodden ground, splashing heavily through the growing puddles, and greeted the driver with a curt nod and grim silence. The two men worked quickly; neither pleased to be working outside in the miserable weather. Hurriedly they prepared the van's interior, sliding away the false metal floor to reveal a long shallow chamber, just deep enough to hold two bodies, one next to the other.

The scar-faced man ran back to the house as the

driver climbed, sodden-clothed, into the cab. He started the engine and turned up the heater full blast to dry his clothes and hair.

Gagged and hooded, the girls were lead from the house, their terrified cries barely audible beneath thick canvas hoods. The men dragged them, stumbling through the rain. Growling and barking, slapping and pushing, they forced the girls down in to the deviously converted transport.

Subdued, the girls lay meekly, side by side, not daring to move. Concealed in the coffin-like floor compartment, they sobbed quietly as the floor slid slowly back into place and was invisibly sealed.

Solemnly the men worked on, loading the van with its legitimate cargo until the innocent boxes of automotive components filled the cargo space to capacity. The loading complete, the two men climbed into the cab with the driver, their heavy wax coats running with water. An hour after it arrived, the van drove from the isolated house and headed for the Dover ferry terminal, following the route and timetable they had travelled a hundred times before.

The men sat cold, dour-faced and humourless as, one by one, the line of assorted vehicles was ushered aboard the waiting ferry.

Terrified in the darkness, the girls listened. They could hear and feel the stop-start motion of the van and traffic all around. The van pulled to a stop.

Outside, rain clattered heavily against its thin metal panels and muted voices spoke. Questions were asked and instructions given. Then they were moving again. In vain, the girls tried to call out, but their voices were muffled and inconsequential. No one heard.

The van climbed the ramp and disappeared into the dark bowels of the ferry.

The crossing to Calais took just ninety minutes; the sailing was smooth and uneventful. The men locked and left the van, moving to the comfort of the ferry's restaurant and lounges where they dried their clothes and drank coffee in grim, morbid silence.

The ship docked on schedule. The huge bow doors opened. The van rumbled down the ramp and followed the signs for the port exit.

The girls lay next to one another in the darkness, shared fear and horror creating a natural bond as they bumped and jostled in the cold, claustrophobic and uncomfortable confines of their hidden compartment. Unable to communicate, their hands reached out for the other, gently touched, then locked softly together, each providing and taking what comfort they could.

FIVE

Daniel drove through the thick, grey veil of clinging mist and rain. The morning commuter traffic was heavy and his progress slow. His thoughts dark and sombre, he peered ahead through the morning gloom.

Rain-blurred tail lights flared red as cars and trucks braked, one after the other, to a stop. Daniel lifted off the accelerator, pushed the brake and slowed to join the three-lane tailback. Queuing behind the blue flashing lights and orange cones warning of an accident ahead, he hit his fist on the steering wheel in frustration. The wipers swished back and forth across the windscreen, squeaking incessantly as they scraped away at the constant film of water. It wasn't a dynamic start; time was of the essence. He needed to be moving – he had to be in time. He swallowed hard and dispelled his worst thoughts, suppressing his feelings and burying them deep. Imagination, he reminded himself, could be a terrible thing.

*

It was just after noon when Daniel arrived back at Temple Farm. Mrs Hall, his housekeeper, was busy as always, cleaning and tidying the farmhouse. She looked up from sweeping the stone-tiled hall floor as he entered through the front door, wiping his feet methodically on the heavy mat.

She watched him trudge silently through to his study, his face solemn and his brow deeply furrowed. He looked like he was carrying the weight of the world on his shoulders. She stopped her work and went to the kitchen, reappearing minutes later in Daniel's study, a hot mug of tea in hand.

'Strong, one sugar, just how you like it,' she said, handing him the mug. Daniel looked at her, managing half a smile.

'Thanks, Mrs H,' he replied.

'What's wrong, Daniel?' she asked with motherly concern, surveying his face.

'That obvious, huh?'

'As the nose on your face.'

'A friend in need,' he replied cryptically. 'Or in this case, friends –' he paused, a moment of self-doubt or second thought seemingly entering his mind. 'I'm sorry, Mrs H, I can't tell you any more, other than I have to go away for a while. A week or two, hopefully no longer. I'm going to grab a few things, make some arrangements, then head off.'

'Head off where?'

'I'm sorry, I can't say.'

She frowned; it wasn't like Daniel to be so serious and secretive. Not since their very early days together, shortly after Daniel had left the army, when those awful men had come and taken his then-girlfriend, Caroline, had she seen Daniel's mood so dark.

'It must be desperately important for you to take off like this?' she said, leaving the implied question hanging.

She waited as Daniel stared into his mug, then out of window, watching the rain swirl in the chilling wind and lash against the pane.

'It is,' he said at last, his voice tinged with sadness and concern.

'You know you have a meeting tomorrow. The architect and builders are coming.'

'It will have to wait. I'll call them and cancel.'

'But you've been waiting ages. I thought you wanted to get things moving now that your business with Mr Mead is starting to grow?'

'I said it'll wait. Please just leave it, Mrs H,' Daniel snapped.

Mrs Hall nodded.

'Alright,' she said, 'I can see that it's important. I'll leave you alone and stop my prying. You know you can talk to me whenever you want to.'

Daniel reached out and took her hand.

'I know. I'm sorry, I didn't mean to be abrupt. I have to do this. The meeting will wait until I get back,' he said, managing another half-smile.

She understandingly patted his hand and left, closing the study door behind her.

Daniel turned back to his cluttered desk, cleared a space, reached for a pad and pen and pulled the telephone closer. He dialled the number, calling the first of only two people he was going to trust.

John Shaw picked up the phone on the third ring.

'Shaw,' he stated firmly.

'John, it's Dan. How's things?'

'Dan, great to hear from you. What's wrong?' he added, detecting Daniel's obviously subdued tone.

'I need your help.'

'Not again! What is it this time?' John cheerfully joked.

'John, it's serious, deadly serious,' Daniel replied, a hardened edge to his voice.

'Christ, Dan, it must be, sorry. Anything, you know that. What do you need?'

'I can't tell you all the details, not over the phone. I'm going to come to London, can we meet?'

'Of course, when are you coming?'

'I'm leaving in about an hour. Meet me at the Benjamin Hotel in Bayswater, 7:00pm tonight, OK?'

'Sure, no problem,' confirmed John, his voice matching Daniel's firm, level tone.

'Can you do something for me before you come?' Daniel asked.

'Yes, what do you need?'

'Information – everything you can tell me about a guy called Zoran Durakovic. Can you do that?'

'Dan, don't worry, consider it done. I'll see you later.'

'Thanks, John.'

Daniel hung up and stared thoughtfully back out of the window to the mist-shrouded hills in the distance. His eyes wandered, then focused on the droplets of rain as they ran down the glass pane and collected in a small puddle on the white painted sill. His frustration was growing. He had to move faster. The girls had already been in hell for nearly thirty-six hours. Every minute that passed would only prolong their suffering.

Throwing off his negative thoughts, he refocused and reached for the phone once more. A few minutes later, he had booked a taxi to the station, a first-class rail ticket to London and one night at his favourite London hotel, The Benjamin.

His immediate arrangements made, he ran

upstairs, showered, shaved, changed and packed in record time.

Mrs Hall was waiting for him by the front door. He put down his leather weekend bag and placed his hands gently on her shoulders.

'I'll see you soon, Mrs H,' he said.

She pulled him close and, not hiding her feelings or concern, hugged him like a mother would a son.

'Please take care of yourself, Daniel,' she said.

He stooped, kissing her forehead.

'I will, Mrs H. I promise,' he replied, stepping out of the door to the waiting taxi.

*

The journey from Salisbury to Waterloo took just under ninety minutes. The time passed quickly, the countryside flashing by in a blur of dull grey and muted autumnal colours. He thought about his conversation with Richard and Jane Mead and the information they had given him. Something about Richard's demeanour nagged and gnawed at the back of his mind. He closed his eyes and rested his head back against the seat. His thoughts drifted back in time to his final, near-fatal mission. To his anger, resentment and retirement. The artefacts from the museum in Kabul. The abduction of Caroline, his girlfriend, the murder of his brother and death of his father. To Malik, the assassination squad, Mr Khan and Salim. How they had torn through his life and forced him, reluctantly, to re-enter the hard and lonely world he had known for so long. Doubt and second thoughts edged back into his mind. The normal life he had craved since his retirement was never going to come. He remembered Richard's words when he came to help. "You got shot and you got shafted – what are you running from, Daniel? This isn't you, not the Daniel Temple I know. Doubt and uncertainty never used to enter your mind – all that money turned you soft? You can be what you want to be, Daniel, but also accept that you are what you are. You have an ice cold, ruthless capability that few men possess. Lay your ghosts to rest, or one day you may live to regret them."

The words had been delivered bluntly, but sincerely, out of true friendship. He mulled them over again. They had broken down his mental barricades and turned him around. Richard had calculated and cleverly brought him back, sending him after Caroline and Malik, as cold and ruthless as he'd ever been. Now he had to be the same again.

His concentration broke as the train clattered its way through Clapham Junction, rolling slowly through to its designated platform at Waterloo. He opened his eyes, and in that moment, normal life disappeared for good. All doubts evaporated and he felt the surge of adrenalin, tempered with an icy resolve to get the job done. He was never going to let Elizabeth and Jennifer down.

Daniel stepped off the train and walked toward the exit, his long stride rapidly taking him across the platform. A young man dressed in his pinstripe City suit careered into him as he rushed to board his train, desperate to escape the drudgery for another day. He hit Daniel with a juddering impact, bounced straight off and fell in a crumpled heap on the dirty, wet platform floor.

'Arsehole,' the guy shouted before taking in Daniel's size or demeanour.

Daniel turned, his cold blue-green eyes flashing a momentary warning. It was the sort of look that would dissuade all but the insane from taking the issue further. The young man hauled himself to his feet and scurried away, obviously deciding that discretion was the better part of valour.

Daniel marched on through the platform gates, striding purposefully across the wide expanse of the station. The heaving mass of early evening commuters herded together beneath the electronic display boards, then bumped and jostled their way to waiting trains as platform numbers flicked into view, desperate to be the first on board, claiming that all-important seat at the end of another long, dull day.

Daniel reflected, as he always did, why would anyone want to do this? Central London was a drab, depressing place. Every time he visited he couldn't wait to get away – he hated the place.

The inclement weather doubled the usual length of the queue at the taxi rank and he waited a chilly twenty minutes before climbing into a cab. The London traffic was proportionally heavy and slow. The cab moved in stop-start fashion, seemingly inching its way toward Bayswater and the comfortable refuge of his hotel. Occasionally, he cleared the condensation from his window and watched the rat race scurry past. A myriad of tired, miserable-looking people hurried through the blustering rain, their faces pale, heads bowed, their umbrellas pulled low and collars turned up.

His cab slowed and pulled up a short way out from the pavement, the driver thoughtfully avoiding the large puddle which had formed at the kerb side and was spilling in a wide arc into the road. Daniel stepped out, holding a copy of *The Times* over his head as he paid the fare and tipped the driver. Then he turned, bound over the puddle, ran up the wide marble steps and into the hotel lobby.

The receptionist saw him enter, watching appreciatively as he approached the desk. She smiled a warm, bright and alluring smile.

'Good evening, Mr Temple, how lovely to see you

again,' she purred, gazing into his eyes.

Daniel returned her smile. She was an attractive woman, mid-thirties maybe, with long dark hair and warm, golden-brown eyes. Her flirting and attentive style always made him feel good. Perhaps another time, he might see how serious she really was, but for now he contented himself with signing the register and handing over his credit card.

'Let me know if you need anything,' she smiled, handing Daniel his key.

'Thanks, I will,' Daniel said, turning for the elevator.

Daniel found his room, dumped his gear and checked his watch – it was 6:00pm.

*

John Shaw checked his watch – it was 6:00pm. He switched off his computer, packed the documents in his briefcase, switched off his desk lamp and locked the door to his office. He hurried down the corridor, shrugging into his coat as he stepped into the elevator.

'Great,' he said, looking to the skies as he stepped out of the lobby and into the pouring rain.

He turned up his collar, held the briefcase over his head and ran for the tube station. The underground was packed. The seething herd of commuters stood five deep, shoulder to shoulder, running the length of the platform, every passenger intent on squashing and squeezing their way into every available space on the train. The train squealed to a halt and the doors swished open. Nerves and tempers stretched and frayed as the condensed mass of human madness surged forward, cramming into the carriage. John went with the flow as the bodies crushed together. Hot, damp and uncomfortable, he stood passively in the middle of a three-way sandwich, pressed pleasingly tight against an attractive young woman, her wonderful perfume and impressive bosom. The wonders of modern science, he thought, unavoidably staring down into her ample, silicon-enhanced cleavage. He smiled to himself; the view passed the time.

The Bayswater stop finally came, and with some relief, he pushed his way out of the carriage. Five minutes later, he walked into the Benjamin hotel to find Daniel sitting in the bar with a glass of his favourite whisky already waiting.

'Cheers,' John said, raising his glass to Daniel. 'It's good to see you again, Dan.'

Daniel nodded and smiled.

'Cheers, John, same here. Thanks for coming; I know you must be swamped.'

'There's nothing on my desk that won't still be there tomorrow,' he said. 'Anyway, a friend in need –'

'Yeah, I know. Is a pain in the arse,' Daniel finished the sentence.

They both laughed.

'Do you want another?' John asked, draining his glass and pointing at Daniel's.

'Sure, Jameson's and ginger, thanks.'

John returned with fresh drinks and they sat in the corner of the cosy wood-panelled bar, talking about old times, before Daniel brought the conversation into the present.

'Did you get the information I asked for?'

'Of course. I knew the name as soon as you said it, but I wanted to get all the background, so I didn't say anything else on the phone. Durakovic is bad news, Dan, very bad news and very well connected with people you just don't wanna know. Please tell me you're not caught up in something with him.'

Daniel looked at him and shrugged his shoulders.

'Shit, Dan. What? How?'

'It's like you said. A friend in need.'

'Must be a bloody good friend.'

Daniel nodded. 'Richard Mead,' he said.

'Colonel Mead?' John asked, raising his eyebrows in surprise. 'Thought you two were running that new security business together? I bet that's bloody lucrative.'

'We are. It is. You turned down the offer to join us, remember?'

'So? What's happened? Don't remind me!'

'A ghost from the past.'

'Durakovic?'

'Durakovic,' Daniel confirmed.

John frowned. 'Bosnia, wasn't it?'

Daniel nodded again. 'It seems he holds Richard responsible for the death of his family and now he wants his retribution.'

'Bastard, what's he doing?' John asked.

'Not doing – done. He's taken Richard's daughters; says he's sold them into the white slave trade,' Daniel replied, his voice low and solemn, his expression severe.

John just stared at him in disbelief.

'Jesus Christ,' he said slowly, his head bowing to the floor.

His head jerked up abruptly, looking Daniel in the eye.

'Tell me you're not going to do what I think you're going to do.'

'I'm going to get them back,' Daniel confirmed, holding John's gaze, his piercing, ice-cold eyes not reflecting a single trace of doubt.

'Oh no, no, no, Dan, you can't, its madness. You don't know anything about this guy. You're not going up against one man. You're going against an army, a fucking nasty army. This is Russian mafia – major league organised crime. Dan, you can't do it.'

'I promised,' Daniel said simply.

'Dan, it's insane. I thought you wanted to leave all this behind. We've been friends a long time. Dan, please don't do this, not on your own – let me help. Human trafficking and organised crime is one of MI5's highest priorities. More and more girls are flooding into the UK every year.'

'No,' Daniel snapped, before dropping his voice to whisper. 'Not a word. Not a word to anyone. Promise me, John. The slightest whiff of this gets out before I get to Durakovic, and those girls are dead. It has to be me, my way – nothing else.' Daniel's eyes locked on to John's, demanding agreement.

John held up his hands.

'OK, Dan, you have my word. This is just two friends talking, nothing more. Guaranteed – it goes no further –' He paused, considered his next statement. 'Look, Dan, please take this in the way it's intended. I know what happened to you and why you wanted it, but it's not you, this normal life thing. It never has been – never will be. Whatever you do now, you should take a more active role in the business with Richard. Look at you, you're buzzing again. That nasty cold stuff in your veins is pumping, your mind is calculating – it's what you're good at.'

Daniel nodded. 'Thanks, I know. It's taken a while to realise that, to fully come to terms with it. I had so many self-doubts after Chechnya. Not because I got shot, but because of how I was being used – I was angry. I don't regret leaving the SAS, but perhaps I made some hasty decisions.'

'You did. I should have said that to you before. Last year after your father died and that business with Salim and Malik. Richard turned you around, helped you do the right thing, but don't make a mistake now, don't do this alone. Let me help.'

'You are helping. I know what I'm doing, John. I have thought about this, believe me. I'm doing the right thing and I'm doing it for my reasons. Durakovic contacted Richard yesterday morning; his instructions and intent were explicit. If he even thinks Richard has asked for help or gone to the authorities, their lives are over. Not just Elizabeth and Jennifer, but all of them. I have to go alone; I just need to know where to find them.'

'Alright. At least I can help you with that. If Durakovic has them, they'll most likely be in Sarajevo, but if he's moved them on, then God knows. There are numerous places you would have to start looking, Russia, Ukraine, Lithuania maybe. But after that they could be shipped any place – South America, the Far East, Africa, literally anywhere. It also depends on what they look like – blonde, brunette. You know how it is – different places, different people, different tastes.'

John watched Daniel as he spoke, his sharp mind

clinically processing the information.

'This is different – this is a personal vendetta. I think Durakovic will keep them close, but not necessarily with him; they'd be too easy to find. He must know deep down that Richard will try to get them back – what parent wouldn't?'

'Maybe that's what he wants, have you thought of that?'

'Yes, I've thought of that. I also think whatever Durakovic does, he will want to know where they are and what's happening to them. He will want to know they are suffering.'

'If that's what he really wants.'

'How do you mean?'

John shrugged. 'Just another theory. Is it possible he doesn't really want the girls at all? Perhaps they're a decoy, the bait – a way of getting something else?'

'You have a devious mind, Mr Shaw,' Daniel smiled.

'It helps in this game.'

'You might be right, though. Maybe Durakovic wants both – the girls and something else?' Daniel added to the conjecture, his thoughts switching back to his meeting with Richard.

John nodded. 'Hold that thought,' he said, opening his briefcase and pulling out a number of files. 'Durakovic,' he added, passing over half of the files to Daniel. 'Let's see what we can find out.'

'Are you OK with this, John? Staying, I mean?' Daniel asked, checking the time on his watch.

'Well I did have a hot date – no, seriously, Dan, its fine; I'm here as long as you need me.'

Daniel glanced at his watch. 'Thanks, John. I'll book you a room.'

'Great, thank you. Haven't you got the glass on that old thing fixed yet?' John asked, pointing at Daniel's battered Rolex Submariner.

Daniel glanced again at his wrist.

'No, not yet. I'll get round to it.'

'Give it here. I'll get the boys in the lab to fix it. You can pick it up tomorrow if you need it back quickly.'

Daniel undid the clasp.

'That's misappropriation of taxpayers' money,' he said, handing the watch to John.

John smiled. 'If they only knew what else we spend it on.'

The two friends turned their attention back to the Durakovic files, scanning their way through pages of interesting but irrelevant information and pausing every few minutes to note or extract a detail that might prove useful.

'I have a theory based on what you said, Dan,' John declared after another thirty minutes of intensive reading.

'Go on.'

'Durakovic is the head of the Russian mafia in Bosnia, the local commander, if you like. The real boss, the man he answers to, is a guy called Sergei Kozlov, often referred to as "The Beast" – and not without good reason. He really is a nasty piece of work. He's also known to have some pretty weird and sadistic sexual tastes – basically your complete pervert,' John explained.

Daniel frowned, glaring at him for a moment.

'Sorry, Dan. I just wanted to explain my theory.'

'It's OK, carry on.'

'If Durakovic wanted to put these girls and Richard through hell, but also keep them where he knew what was happening to them, where better than with Kozlov? And if he also wanted to ingratiate himself, maybe work his way up the ladder a little further, how better than to make the girls a present to his boss?'

'Plausible,' said Daniel.

They sat in quiet reflection for a moment.

'If he has them, Kozlov could be another way in. Do you know where he is?' Daniel asked after a few minutes.

'I don't know for sure, but Moscow probably. Failing that, he can usually be found in St Petersburg. I'll see if I can find out by tomorrow – good enough?'

'Good enough.'

'This might be a dumb question, but finding the

girls is one thing. Getting in and getting them out will be something else. How are you going to do it?' John asked.

'Simple. I'm going to take a gamble, go straight to Durakovic and ask what he wants.'

'You sure that's wise?'

'The alternative is to work a way in through Kozlov.'

'How?'

'Easy. They're always looking for good men, right? I can speak Russian like a Russian. I'll just turn up on his doorstep and ask for a job,' Daniel said with an easy smile.

'You're fucking mad,' John started to laugh, then stopped, his smile evaporating as he realised that Daniel was deadly serious.

SIX

The nondescript van exited the dock gates and drove at a steady pace; not too fast, not too slow. Nothing out of the ordinary. Nothing to attract attention. It just followed the signs, obeyed the signals and drove. They left the city and continued to follow the quieter country roads, heading south.

The night was black. Heavy clouds hung low and sullen, obscuring whatever moonlight there was as the rain poured down. The van made slow progress, eventually pulling in to stop, like so many others, at a small roadside café and lorry park on the outskirts of Lens.

The men climbed out of the cab, stretched briefly to relieve their tired limbs, then ran for the small makeshift shelter beside the coffee hut.

The girls listened nervously, expectantly, as the doors slammed and feet crunched through gravel.

But no one came and the compartment remained closed. The sound of feet in gravel faded away and they lay still and quiet, encased in their blackened mobile tomb, shivering with fear and cold.

The men ran across the wide expanse of the parking lot and ducked beneath the cover of the small wooden building from where cheap food and poor coffee were served twenty-four hours a day, seven days a week. They stood, huddled under the faded blue and green awning, sheltering from the rain that poured incessantly from the black night sky. The water collected in the bowing canvas cover and cascaded over its sides, splashing into the ever-growing puddles at their feet. They smoked cigarettes, drank coffee and spoke quietly whilst they waited.

The lorry arrived at 3:30am. It turned in, swinging round in a wide circle, spitting out gravel, mud and water as it splashed heavily through the deep, rain-filled potholes. The air brakes hissed loudly as the driver pulled to a stop directly in line with the van, then backed up carefully, leaving just enough room for the rear doors of the van to open against the rolling shutter of the lorry. The driver, obscured in shadow, remained in the darkened cab. He flashed the headlights once. The three men finished their coffee, threw the polystyrene cups on the ground and walked back into the torrential rain.

Exhausted, the girls had drifted into a hazy sleep in the tight confines of the cold and insufferable van. The small holes perforated in the floor panels allowed them just enough air to prevent suffocation. They came to as the sound of a reversing lorry slowly registered in the blackness. The harsh beep, beep, beep of the alarm indicated and warned of its backward direction. There was a moment of silence, then quick feet came crunching back through the gravel. Doors opened and closed. Bolts and clasps were undone and a shutter rolled up.

The men worked quickly, undoing the fastenings at the rear of the lorry and rolling up the metal shutter. One man jumped inside and switched on the trailer's internal light, illuminating a seemingly half-full container of cardboard boxes, stamped "fair trade coffee". He walked to the centre of the trailer and pulled away the first heavy layer of boxes, revealing another, apparently identical layer. Kneeling, he felt the now-exposed metal floor at his feet, found the small flap, lifted it and pressed the button. There was a muted metallic clunk and the second layer of boxes parted and swung slowly open from the centre, revealing a narrow steel door. He opened the door. It led into a small steel-walled cell, clinical, bare and cold, like a meat locker. He turned and nodded to his accomplices.

'Get them,' he said.

The other two men opened the rear doors of the van and transferred its cargo of boxes across to the lorry. Stacked down each side of the trailer, they formed a narrow corridor, that led to the open cell. Returning to the van, the men slid the floor panels open and unceremoniously hauled the girls from their compartment.

*

Hauled to their feet, the girls stood unsteadily, their fear and uncertainty increased exponentially by their artificial blindness.

Elizabeth listened. She could hear the other girl crying softly beneath her hood, the sound all but silenced by her gagged mouth and covered face. She moved slightly toward the sound, feeling in the darkness and taking the girl's hand. She gasped as rough hands pushed her from the van and she tripped and stumbled her way forward.

She staggered on behind the other girl. Her bound hands reached out through the blackness, desperately trying to hold on, to retain the small, pathetic remnant of comfort.

Blindly, she crossed the uneven threshold into the lorry, then stood, trembling in black, terrified silence. Through her hood, she could smell the foul body odour of the man holding her. Her body tensed as sickening sounds cut through the blackness. There was the sound of a thud – a body hitting the floor.

'Get up, bitch,' a voice growled.

Elizabeth waited. The other girl cried in pain.

'Be quiet, you whore,' a man snarled spitefully.

Hands pushed Elizabeth forward again and she shuffled blindly down the unseen corridor and unknowingly entered the cell.

'Sit,' a voice snapped, pushing her down to sit side by side with the other girl on a hard steel bench.

A door slammed closed.

They felt the engine start and the lorry gently vibrated, turned and rumbled forward.

*

The girls sat in dark silence, chilled to the bone. Time and space were merely vague concepts in their tired, fear-dulled minds. Hour after hour, mile after mile passed them by until eventually they came to a stop.

They felt the lorry slow, turn, then ease to a stop. They listened hard, but could hear nothing. Their steel-walled cell insulated them from all external noise. They heard the door to the cell unlock and open. Invisible, rough hands pulled them to their feet, guided them slowly down the length of lorry and lifted them to the ground.

They stood perfectly still, listening to the sound

of footsteps and growling voices as the men separated them once more.

'Don't move,' said the voice.

Elizabeth stood like a statue as a small hole was cut into her hood and fingers delved in to ease her gag. Seconds later, her hands were untied, pulled in front of her body and a cold bottle was thrust into her grasp.

'Drink,' barked the order as the bottle was lifted to her face and a plastic straw pushed into her mouth.

She drank gratefully, savouring the taste of the chilled mineral water, then carefully placed the bottle between her feet and raised her hands to ease her gag a little further.

'May I use the toilet?' she asked meekly.

The men laughed.

'Go if you want to go,' said one.

'Where?' she asked.

Unable to see the hardened, emotionless faces through her hood, her spirits temporarily lifted at the apparent agreement.

'Where you stand, bitch. Just squat or piss your knickers, we don't care,' said another.

'She's not wearing any,' laughed the third.

Her spirits plunged to new depths. These men had no sense of decency or human kindness. The tears rolled unseen down her cheeks. She swallowed hard, wanting for all the world to hold it in, to not give them what they wanted, but she couldn't – she was bursting. She had no choice. She agonised for a minute, then slowly pulled down her grey jogging bottoms, squatted down over the sodden earth and peed.

She sensed the men leering at her nakedness as they called to her, cruelly and crudely. Finished, she stood and self-consciously pulled up her trousers, strangely aware of the perverse, leering stares. She shivered in cold, relieved silence.

She jumped as one of the men gripped her shoulder hard, re-tightened her gag and forced her arms behind her back, re-binding them as before. Then she was led back into the lorry to re-join the other girl in the chilled steel cell.

Enveloped in absolute darkness, the cold and fearful silence gnawed constantly at the her senses. Unable to tell whether it was day or night, time became an irrelevance, the nightmare journey an eternity. Shrouded in her black, claustrophobic, soul destroying world, she wept.

*

Early in the morning on the third day, the lorry crossed the border into Bosnia and picked up the road to Sarajevo. The rain had stopped and a thick mist swirled in the air, enveloping everything in a chilling, soft, wet clinging film of white. The driver waited patiently as the men checked and prepared the transport which had been left, ready for their arrival.

The men didn't take long. There were no more concealed compartments or hidden cells. The van was small and simple, it's windowless, white painted panels, more than adequate to conceal the contents inside.

Satisfied everything was in order, the girls were transferred in quick succession. Their journey was coming to end. Their true nightmare was only just beginning.

SEVEN

The house had been found and recommended by Jancic. Large, old and very remote, its dark-grey flagstone walls, built under a black slate roof, gave it a grim, foreboding appearance. It was set at the end of a long, single-track road which twisted through dense woodland for several miles before opening out to a broad area of grass and black gravel in front of the house. Even on a brilliant summer's day, the house looked dark, sinister and unwelcoming; its appearance and atmosphere somehow absorbed and reflected the evil and despair it held within.

Zoran Durakovic paced the grey-stone floor, agitated and impatient. His men watched him nervously. Unpredictable at the best of times, they knew in this mood that he was unreasonably volatile – unreasonably violent. Those that had known him since the war, since the death of his family, had witnessed his steady decline. He was once considered to be a good man and a good leader, fair and just – an exemplary soldier, who had served his country, done his duty and well by his men. Then everything changed. He had been pursued relentlessly by the British and his family murdered. If it hadn't been for the loyalty of Jancic, his second in command, he would have been killed himself that day.

Dian Jancic had persuaded Durakovic to leave under cover of darkness, pledging to protect his family, but Jancic couldn't hold them. He had fought hard and barely escaped with his own life. Everyone knew the story. They had tried to surrender when the soldiers came, but they just opened fire, assaulted the house and swept mercilessly through, killing everyone inside.

Jancic, despite being shot and wounded, had managed to hide, avoid detection and escape. He was the only one left alive, and it was he who found Durakovic and told him the news; his family were dead, murdered by the British major leading the assault team. Thereafter, Jancic changed his appearance and remained anonymously at his commander's side, providing his counsel and doing his bidding. He had been the one who arranged for every witness at Durakovic's trial to disappear, until the case against him had crumbled and the authorities were forced to release him.

Jancic watched Durakovic now. He was a pale shadow of the former man, wracked and tormented by his loss, by the vengeance he had sworn, and driven by his new-found desire for absolute power.

The double wooden doors of the room opened and two men walked in. One, small and wiry with long, lank and greasy black hair that straggled down over an insipid, narrow face. The other, slightly taller with a stockier build and short reddish-brown hair. Both wore black denim jeans and black sweatshirts. Neither would win any prizes for appearance or style. Each respectfully acknowledged Jancic before smiling obsequiously at Durakovic.

'The shipment from Ukraine has arrived, Sir,' said the smaller man nervously. Durakovic glared at him.

'I didn't hear you knock,' he said.

The two men bowed their heads apologetically.

'Sorry, Commander Durakovic,' they replied meekly.

Durakovic strode purposefully across the room.

'Show me,' he ordered.

The men led Durakovic out of the room. Jancic didn't follow; he wasn't interested. They walked across the gloomy, cavernous hallway to a broad opening where a set of stone steps dropped from its centre. The stairs descended into a dim, foreboding labyrinth of rough-walled corridors and cellars hewn out of the black rock beneath the house. They walked, turning left then right down the dimly-lit passages. The sound of their footsteps echoed and blended with other more sinister noises – muffled cries and eerie groans, the sounds of soft skin being harshly slapped and of women yielding involuntarily to the forceful will of sick and twisted men.

They arrived at a wide, black wooden door that looked solid and impenetrable; a sinister threshold from which there could be no return, once passed from the other side. The stocky, brown-haired man unlocked the door and swung it open. The hinges creaked loudly, as if they knew the evil script, and Durakovic stepped inside.

The austere room was large and square, devoid of any features, except for another identical door on the far side. Inside, there were ten young girls. They huddled together in the centre of the room, holding one another for comfort. Some were barely dressed, whilst others were fully clothed. All were terrified.

Durakovic looked them over carefully, cruelly assessing each one in turn. He singled out two girls, both about nineteen. One was tall, about five feet ten inches, the other a little shorter. Both were slim and attractive, with long dark hair and large round breasts. Ordering them to separate from the others, he watched them appreciatively as they moved slowly away from group.

He moved menacingly closer.

They cowered away.

'Stand still,' he roared.

The girls stood, gripped by fear.

He looked them up and down. One wore a short denim skirt and a sweater; the other, nothing more than a flimsy silk nightdress. He pulled her away and stood her under the light.

She cried, shivering with cold and dread.

He reached out and ripped the nightdress from her body.

She stood trembling and naked, moving her hands, vainly trying to cover her breasts and pubic region.

'Move your hands,' he growled.

The girl didn't move.

Durakovic slapped her hard across the face. Her cheek reddened fiercely as blood trickled from the corner of her mouth.

She moved her hands and his eyes consumed her body.

He turned to the other girl.

'Strip,' he snarled.

She stood still and silent, paralysed with fear, tears rolling down her face.

Durakovic turned to his men.

'Strip her,' he barked.

The men moved forward.

She watched them coming and shook her head, unable to move.

They tore the clothes from her body and left her standing bare and sobbing, exposed to Durakovic's depraved examination. He took his time, his eyes and hands wandering over her body, touching, feeling, devouring. He stepped away.

'Keep these two clean. Break the others in, then send them on for sale,' he said, with a vile lack of compassion.

*

The small van wove its way along the narrow gravel road then passed around the side of the grey stone house, parking opposite the set of double wooden doors that were set in the dark flagstone floor. The doors were already open, awaiting their arrival as the two men climbed out, stretched away their discomfort and opened the rear of the van.

Oblivious to their surroundings, Elizabeth and Jennifer were pulled from the van and marched, tripping and stumbling, down the steps.

They entered a short corridor which ended at a black wooden door and waited. There was the rattle of a key and the clunk of heavy bolts as the door was unlocked from the inside and they were met by a small, wiry man with long, greasy black hair. The men pushed the door open and walked in, dragging the girls behind them. The men shoved the girls into the centre of the room, cut their bonds and removed their hoods as the door slammed shut and was locked again.

The girls stared in disbelief, then fell into each other's arms, whispering their names.

Unmoved, the men pulled the girls apart, untied their hands and removed their gags.

Free from their bonds, the sisters collapsed back into their embrace, sobbing with joy and relief, fear and foreboding. A tidal wave of emotion washed over them as they held each other tightly.

'Damir, we should take them to Commander Durakovic. He wanted to see them as soon as they arrived,' said the man with the large scar.

Damir stepped forward and roughly pulled the girls apart. His hand clamped Elizabeth's arm in a vice-like grip before shoving Jennifer across the room.

'Here, Mirsad, you take this one.'

They dragged the girls across the room and waited as the small, wiry man unlocked the door.

Elizabeth and Jennifer stared with trepidation at the threshold which conveyed and betrayed its intentions. More than just a door, it was an opening to a world of demonic depravity. The entrance to hell.

EIGHT

Daniel finalised his plans with John Shaw, arranging to meet again at noon the following day at Vauxhall Cross, the home of MI5.

'Thanks again, John. Don't worry about the bill when you leave in the morning, I'll pay it with mine,' Daniel confirmed, warmly shaking John's hand.

'Thanks, Dan. Anytime, you know that. I'll see you tomorrow. Hopefully I'll have some more information.'

'Great. Do me one more favour, would you? Listen to this tape and tell me what you think,' Daniel requested, handing John the tape of Richard Mead's conversation.

'Sure, no problem. Good night, Dan.'

It was late when Daniel returned to his room and he was tired. He lay on his bed and closed his eyes, his head whirling with new thoughts and information. Consciously relaxing his mind, he began to methodically sift the data, mulling over the first rudimentary elements of the plan he had pieced together during the evening. His eyes snapped open and he leant across the bed, picked up the phone and dialled the number.

'Broughton Hall,' the familiar voice of Coleman, his late father's friend and confidant, answered.

'Coleman, it's Daniel.'

'Daniel, how are you? What's wrong?'

'I'm alright, thanks. Does there have to be something wrong?'

'It's late – too late for a social call, and your voice is a little edgy – so tell me, what's wrong?'

'OK, you're right. Long story short – I need to get into Russia, fast. No questions asked. In fact, it needs to be undetected and untraceable; no one must know I'm there.'

'How fast?'

'Tomorrow.'

'Alright, I know I shouldn't ask, but why?'

'You remember Richard Mead?'

'Colonel Mead, yes of course. Good man, lovely family.'

'Well, let's just say he needs my help and he needs it right now. I can't say any more, not for the moment.'

'In Russia?'

'Yes, I need to get in quickly. I can't tell you why. Can you discreetly find out if Temple Stamford has anything going on that might help? If I ask, there will be all sorts of questions. You know the board are a little wary of my activities.'

'You do own the company, Daniel, you can ask what you like, but OK, let me see what I can do. Call me in the morning.'

'Thanks, Coleman. Goodnight.'

'Goodnight, Daniel.'

Daniel rolled onto his back and stared up at the plain, smooth white ceiling of his hotel room as he slowly drifted into an uneasy sleep. His dreams were unwelcome, disturbing intrusions, flashing between vivid images and vague impressions, all of them cutting deep into his subconscious and leaving their unwanted, monstrous imprint. His mind filled with visions of Jennifer's haunting features, looming large and distorted out of the darkness. Her eyes, black and lifeless, stared out from her ghostly white face. She began to cry and crimson tears of blood rolled down her cheeks as she reached out, pleading to him.

'Help me, please, help me.'

Daniel woke with a start, his body covered in a cold sweat, his heart pounding against his chest. He sat up and looked at the clock. It was 4:00am. He slept no more.

He waited another hour, running through his

plan for the rest of his day. The clock ticked slowly round to 5:00am. He padded through to the bathroom and took a long hot shower. Standing with his arms outstretched, he leant against the cream tiled wall with his head bowed under the jet, letting the water and steam seep into every pore, as if they would cleanse away his darkest thoughts. He stepped out, wiped the steam from the mirror, stared dolefully at his misted reflection, rubbed the towel over his short cropped blond hair, then turned away.

He ordered breakfast at six; fruit, cereal, extra toast and tea for two. He ate unhurriedly, watching the clock tick ever slower round to 7:00am. At seven sharp he picked up the phone and dialled Broughton Hall again.

Coleman answered with his usual confident and assertive manner.

'Coleman, good morning. It's Dan.'

'Daniel, right on time. You're in business.'

'You've done it?'

'Of course. I spoke with Michael Eames, the Ops Director. He guessed it was for you, but promised it would go no further. Now, listen carefully as I have assumed when you said "undetected and untraceable", that's exactly what you meant. Temple Stamford has a contract assisting the Russians with some Trans-Siberian gas pipeline work. The company has a team based just outside Vologda. The engineers are due to rotate tomorrow, which means they are flying the fresh team out from Stansted tonight. As it's one of TS's company aircraft, it's all set up for the job. The front section is separated for crew and workers, the rear section for equipment and cargo. You'll be in the rear. Apart from you, there are three people who know the arrangements. Michael, myself and the pilot – no one else. The gear you need will be on board. Once the pilot starts his descent, he is going to open the rear cargo doors and you can bail out.'

'Bail out?'

'Well, you said undetected, didn't you? What better than a small jump? Your chute will be stowed in the cargo hold – it'll be a walk in the park. Is there anything else you need?'

'Yeah, just one thing. Where the hell is Vologda?'

'It's about half way between and three hundred miles east of Moscow and St Petersburg, but don't worry – you're unlikely to see it. The pilot will drop you about a hundred miles out.'

'*Fantastic*,' Daniel replied sarcastically.

'Sorry, Daniel – it's the best I could do at short notice.'

'No, I'm sorry, Coleman, it really is terrific. What time does the flight leave?'

'You need to be at Stansted by 19:00 tonight. The pilot will get you aboard before the engineers arrive. The flight's scheduled to leave at 21:00. All clear?'

'Yes, all clear. One last question, have you ever heard of a man called Kozlov?'

'Sergei Kozlov?'

'Yes.'

'Our paths crossed once or twice,' Coleman acknowledged. 'He was quite an adversary when your father and I worked together. I also had the dubious pleasure of having to pay him off several times when I ran global security for TS Industries. It's a tiring necessity when you negotiate contracts and business in Russia. There's always someone to pay – mostly the local mafia. Oddly enough, Mead Associates have acted as advisors on some of TS's recent deals, providing security services and escorts for some of your executives. I thought you would have known that, Daniel?'

'I don't get involved in all the deals. I'm more a sleeping partner at the moment. Does Richard know him?'

'Yes, Richard met him when he went to Russia. Why?'

'Nothing, just wondered.'

'Daniel, if you're mixed up with anything to do with that man, get out and stay out. I mean it – he is not someone you want to mess with.'

'Alright, thanks, Coleman. I'll call you when I get home.' Daniel hung up the phone before his old friend could say any more.

Daniel dressed in faded jeans, shirt and sweater, then pulled on his old hiking boots and jacket. He packed his smarter clothes into his leather weekend bag and went to check out of the hotel, disappointed not to find the attractive, dark-haired lady at reception.

'I still have some things I need to do. Can I leave my bag with you until later?' he asked the man behind the desk.

'Certainly, Mr Temple, leave it with me. I'll put it in our storeroom,' the man confirmed, passing Daniel a luggage receipt.

Daniel stepped out into the chilled morning air, hailed a cab and headed for the Kilburn High Road. He found the military surplus store he was looking for tucked down a narrow side street and asked the cab driver to wait.

The store was big and square, with long, wide aisles lined by three tiered metal-framed shelves that stood on a thick linoleum floor. The shelves were stacked with good quality surplus clothing, mostly UK, US or NATO issue, in various shades of green, brown, black or combinations of. A long, L-shaped wooden counter ran half the length of the rear wall and a short way across the front window.

Daniel took his time trailing around the aisles, selecting what he needed – two sets of plain army fatigues, 38" waist, long leg, 48" chest. One drab olive green, the other plain black. No badges or insignia, but Velcro strips to add them if required. He added a good winter jacket, also black, thermal socks, a black woollen hat that could be pulled down to form a full-face balaclava and a pair of used paratrooper's boots – German issue, but they fitted the bill well enough. Finally, he picked out a used, plain green, medium-sized kit bag and hauled the lot up to the front of the store, dumping them on the counter.

'How much?' he asked.

The guy behind the counter looked at the pile. He looked like a real military geek. Daniel doubted he had ever been in the forces, but judging by his appearance, he had watched way too many low-budget war films. Daniel watched as he scratched at the clump of thick stubble on his chin, obviously considering the price.

'£250 for cash,' he said, looking at Daniel through nervous, shifty eyes.

Daniel stared at him, his eyes unwavering.

'Discount?' It was more a demand than a question.

The guy looked at the pile and thought again.

'£220,' he asked optimistically, unable to look Daniel in the eye.

Daniel nodded – just one quick dip of his chin.

'Got any badges, insignia?'

The guy smiled, relaxing a little. Daniel appeared to make him very nervous.

'Sure,' he said. 'What do you need?'

'Russian regular army, airborne.'

'Yep, should have. Wait here, I'll be right back.'

The guy stepped out from behind the counter and disappeared through a small, curtain-covered doorway and returned a few moments later carrying a large, plain cardboard box.

'Here we go. Have a rummage. There should be something in there.'

Daniel sifted through the box, found what he needed and added them to the pile.

'£220, did you say?'

The guy looked at the pile again and nodded. He wasn't about to ask for the extra £10 for the badges. He looked at Daniel again, a calculating thought appearing behind his constantly shifting eyes.

'You need anything else?' he asked nervously.

It was the sort of question which could be taken innocently or exactly as it was intended. Daniel took it as intended.

'What have you got?'

The guy shuffled on his feet, his nervousness increasing.

'You the law?'

'Do I look like the law?'

'Hard to tell. You could be. You need to answer,

it's entrapment otherwise,' the guy stated.

'No, I'm not the law. What have you got?' Daniel confirmed and asked again.   'All sorts. What do you need?'

'Firearms. A quality handgun. No crap.'

The guy looked around. There was no one else in the store. He stepped around the counter, flipped the sign in the window to "Closed" and locked the door.

'Step this way,' he invited with an almost theatrical inclination of his head.

He walked to the small doorway. Daniel followed. They entered a rear storeroom that was lined with more metal-framed, wooden shelves, stacked with an array of military surplus from all over the world. The guy kicked the well-worn rubber matting to one side, revealing a large trap door. He stooped down, pulled and turned the ring-shaped catch and hauled the heavy wooden door up and open. A set of steep wooden steps descended into another dimly-lit storage area. They walked down. Daniel stayed a few paces behind, cautious and alert. Reaching the bottom, the guy hit another switch and the lights flickered on, bathing the room in bright fluorescent light.

'This way,' he said, leading Daniel through more rows of dust covered shelving.

At the back of the room, they came to a solid-looking metal cabinet, painted blue, standing against a bare brick wall. It was big – over six feet in height and at least ten feet wide. A broad metal bar ran horizontally across its centre, fixed in the middle by a large, sturdy padlock. The guy pulled a key from his pocket, unlocked it and swung the doors open.

'Ta-da,' he said with an enthusiastic flourish.

There were rows and rows of handguns. Each one, cleaned and neatly housed in its own slot, ready for inspection. Daniel scanned along the cabinet. There were Berettas, Brownings, Colts, H&Ks, Sigs and more, all in pristine condition. One gun caught his eye. It was exactly what he was looking for – a Makarov PM. Daniel took it from its slot and examined it carefully. It was the newer 9mm model with the optional ten-round clip. Expertly, he dismantled it, checked the chamber, the magazine and firing mechanism, then reassembled it and felt the weight. For a small, compact gun, it was reasonably heavy. It was a simple, reliable, effective gun. Most importantly, it was the standard issue sidearm for Russian forces.

'You got ammo for this?'

'Sure have,' smiled the guy.

'The gun, a spare clip and fifty rounds, how much?'

The guy thought. Daniel figured math was not his strong point.

'£220 for the goods upstairs and £500 for our little transaction here, that's um, £720.'

Daniel's eyes narrowed as he looked at the man. The guy looked at Daniel and smiled nervously again.

'Let's say £700, for cash,' he said hopefully.

Daniel nodded. 'Done,' he said.

They returned to the shop. Daniel packed his new gear and the Makarov into the duffle, paid the guy in cash, waited for the door to be unlocked, left the store and climbed back into the cab.

'Where to now, guv?' the driver asked.

'Vauxhall Cross, please. Thanks for waiting.'

'No problem,' the cabby responded with a cheery smile.

Daniel thought again.

'Can you go via the Benjamin Hotel in Bayswater?'

'Go where you like, guv, you're paying.'

Twenty minutes later the cab pulled up outside the hotel. Daniel jumped out, pulling the duffle bag off the seat with him.

'Five minutes OK?' he said, leaving the cab waiting again.

He ran up the steps and into the lobby. The receptionist saw him coming, beaming a smile at him as he approached the desk.

'Hello, Mr Temple.'

'Hi. I know I checked out already but could I store this bag with the other one for another hour or so?'

The receptionist gazed into his eyes.

'Sure you can,' she said cheerfully. 'Let me get you a tag, just a moment.' She tagged the bag and handed him the receipt. 'There you go,' she added, with another dazzling smile.

'Thanks,' he replied, returning her smile.

She flushed pink. 'Any time,' she said.

Daniel jumped back into the cab.

'Right, Vauxhall Cross, please,' he confirmed.

The cab dropped Daniel off at exactly midday. He paid the fare, walked into the main reception area, passed through security, confirmed his appointment and waited.

John Shaw appeared from the bank of elevators five minutes later. They shook each other by the hand before John led Daniel back to his office.

Shaw's office was a small, functional room on the 5th floor of the building. Its décor, plain and neutral, the furniture cheap government issue. A desk, a bookcase, a lockable filing cabinet, a PC, a printer, a telephone and two chairs. No pictures, no plants, no distractions.

'You want a coffee, Dan?' John asked as Daniel settled into the chair in front of the desk.

'Sure, thanks.'

'Be right back,' John said, leaving the room for the coffee machine sat half-way down the hall.

'I got a fix on Kozlov. He's in St Petersburg, or more accurately, just outside it,' John resumed the conversation, walking back in, carrying two white polystyrene cups. 'He lives in what can only be described as fortress, a few miles north of the city, on the road to Sestroretsk. I also did some extra research. It doesn't make good reading. You really need to think again, Dan.'

Daniel sipped his coffee and winced.

'Christ, what is this?' he asked, deflecting the comment before asking another question. 'I meant to ask you this last night. Does the name Jancic mean anything to you?'

'Where did you dig that name up from?' John asked evasively.

'It does, then?' Daniel pressed.

'Officially, no. *Officially*, the guy disappeared and was never traced.'

'And unofficially?'

'He was and still is Durakovic's right-hand man.'

'Durakovic? You sure?' Daniel questioned in surprise.

'Yeah, Durakovic. Why?'

'Nothing, just something Richard Mead said, carry on.'

'When Durakovic resurfaced in Sarajevo a few

years ago, Jancic was right there with him. It took MI6 a while to prove it was the same man. He looks significantly different from when he disappeared.'

'Different? How?'

'Hair, face – that sort of thing. He was clean-shaven with thick brown hair and brown eyes, according to the records. Now he's got a shaven head, a black goatee – dyed I would think – and blue eyes – contact lenses probably. He's also had some cosmetic work done, changed the shape of his face a little, a nose job, etc. But it is him. MI6 are certain.'

'Why hasn't anyone gone to get him?'

'Simple – it's too difficult and politically sensitive, so they just left him. Sleeping dogs and all that.' John Shaw sat back in his seat for a moment, quiet and pensive. 'Look, Dan, please think this through again. I know I said a normal life is not for you, but these guys are animals. None of them will think twice about taking an axe to your head, or other, more sensitive parts of your anatomy. Please let me help you,' he said at last.

'You are helping.'

'You know what I mean.'

'I know what I'm doing, John. I appreciate your concern and the offer, but I can't take the risk. It just has to be me, on my own.'

'OK, but don't say I didn't ask. I don't suppose you've thought about what name you're going to use, or a passport, or papers – or anything practical like that yet?' John asked.

Daniel shook his head.

'No, not yet. I wasn't planning on jetting in from Heathrow, though.'

'No, I'm sure, but nonetheless, they'd be useful, right?'

'Sure,' Daniel acknowledged with a casual shrug of his broad shoulders.

'Good. Here you go then,' John answered, handing Daniel a small package. 'There's a perfect duplicate Russian passport and papers complete with previous travel stamps, plus an old military ID, airborne division.'

Daniel looked at the package with a rueful smile. He looked at John, the question evident in his expression.

John rolled his eyes and answered the question before it was asked.

'Elementary, my dear Mr Temple. Unless Durakovic suddenly decides to just hand those girls back, you're planning to drop in and ask Kozlov for a job. Foolhardy, but I admire your front. You know Kozlov won't just welcome you with open arms. He and his men will be suspicious – very suspicious. You're going to need to be totally convincing. I figure you're gonna say you're ex-military, handy with a gun, which, by the way, you will have to prove. You were in the Paras before the SAS. Therefore, you're going to say you're ex-Russian army, airborne division. Am I right?'

Daniel rose to his feet, clapping.

'Superb, my dear Holmes,' he laughed.

John bowed.

'Goes with the territory,' he said, laughing with Daniel.

'By the way, in case you haven't picked one, your new name is Danil Kuznetsov. You should at least be able to remember the first bit.' John turned, reaching down to open his desk drawer. 'One last thing,' he said, handing Daniel his watch. 'The boys in the lab cleaned it and fitted a new glass. Should be as good as new.'

Daniel slipped it onto his wrist.

'Thanks, John. Thanks for everything,' he said sincerely.

'No problem,' John replied, looking at Daniel pensively.

'What?' Daniel asked, acknowledging the look.

'That tape you asked me to listen to.'

'Yes, what do you think?'

'It's not a complete tape; it's been edited. Even on the first run-through I thought it sounded a bit odd. You don't have to listen that carefully to tell it's been modified in some way.'

'You're sure? It couldn't just be because it's a copy?'

'No, I'm certain. I even had one of the boys in the lab run it a couple of times. They digitally rerecorded and enhanced it. It's definitely not the full conversation. Let me play it for you.'

John pulled the MP3 player on his desk over and hit play. There was a short hiss of static silence from the original recording, followed by the sound of Richard Mead's voice.

'There, you hear it? Two small clicks,' John interrupted over the voices.

Daniel frowned and listened intently as John replayed it.

'Did you hear it?' John asked again. 'The voice recorder was stopped and restarted. What sounds, at first pass, like it might be a full conversation, isn't. There was more dialogue in that conversation than is on this tape. Let me rewind it and play it again. There are two small, very faint clicks as Durakovic speaks. Listen again.'

John hit the buttons, rewound the recording a short way and hit play again. Daniel listened closely as the voices of Richard Mead and Durakovic played out in clear digital stereo.

'There is no get-out clause, Colonel Mead, not in this relationship –' Click.

Click, 'I'm going to bring you into my world now, Colonel –'

'Could be anything,' Daniel said with a shrug.

Despite his own initial misgivings, he wasn't prepared to doubt the word of Richard Mead. He knew the situation was real – he'd seen that for himself.

'No, it couldn't, Dan. That tape was stopped and restarted.' John affirmed.

'Why?'

John shrugged his shoulders.

'I don't know. Only Richard can tell you that. There is something else though, Dan. The boys in the lab listened to the tape cold. They have no context or background; they just analysed the voices and conversation.'

'You let them listen to the tape?' Daniel asked angrily.

'Dan, I'm trying to help. These guys are MI5, they're safe. Not only that, they're experts and they're doing you a favour, so come down off your high horse. Christ, I could get fired for this.'

'OK, I'm sorry. Carry on.'

John fixed Daniel with his own steely gaze before restarting.

'You gave me that tape because your gut instinct said there was something wrong. Am I right?'

Daniel nodded. 'Yeah, you're right. It's not only the tape. It was Richard himself; the way he acted and spoke. Something was wrong; I put it down to the stress of what was happening, but now I'm not so sure.'

'OK. The voice analysis suggests the actual conversation and the suggested topic of conversation were not entirely one and the same thing.'

'What does that mean?'

'It means that whilst Durakovic has certainly taken Richard's daughters, some of the words and statements used, referred to, or were in response to, something entirely different.'

'No, I still don't follow.'

'Alright, let me play it through again in full. This time, listen to the conversation; try to pretend you don't know any of the background. I know that's difficult, but give it a shot. Then tell me your reactions, thoughts, questions – your instant gut reaction to it, OK?'

'Fine.'

John set the recording back to the start and pressed play again. The two men sat in silence. Daniel closed his eyes and listened carefully, trying to take the words at instant face value. The conversation ran just a few short minutes and was over.

'Well?' John asked.

Daniel sat in quiet reflection and gathered his thoughts, rebelling against his immediate reactions. They posed more questions and set further doubts, confusing an already difficult situation.

'Christ,' he said quietly, opening his eyes. 'You want my gut reaction?'

'Yes.'

Daniel took a deep breath then launched into his thoughts.

'What does Durakovic mean, "There is only one way in which you can help me?" or that he can't help Richard unless Richard helps him? That doesn't make sense.'

'It does if you think back to what we discussed last night,' John replied, raising his eyebrows in suggestion.

'You mean he's taken the girls, not for revenge but for some other purpose?'

'Or both. What else do you think?'

'I assumed, when I heard this originally, that when Durakovic said he couldn't let the matter rest, he was referring to the death of his wife and son; that's pretty much what Richard said this was all about. Now I'm not so sure. I don't get why he said he couldn't let their business go unresolved or that there was no get-out clause.'

'Our thoughts exactly. It was a conversation within a conversation. The obvious subject and one more subtle. The important thing is both men knew what was being referred to.'

'Meaning they had spoken before?'

'Almost certainly. Did Richard mention any previous contact with Durakovic?'

'No, I specifically asked him that.'

'You think he was lying?'

'My immediate reaction was yes. If it were anyone else, I'd be certain, but I've never known Richard to lie about anything. In fact, I'd say it was one of his failings – he's too honest.'

'But?'

'But he did seem agitated and angry – distracted almost. Like he was saying one thing and thinking another. But, like I said, I put it down to the shock of what had happened.'

'What else?'

'The first click comes immediately after Durakovic says there's no get-out clause. I think that statement triggered something in Richard's mind. He's a sharp guy. He was thinking ahead. He stopped the recording because he didn't want the next part of the conversation on record.'

'Or to be heard by someone else.'

'Same thing, isn't it?'

'What I mean is, Dan – he didn't want that part of the conversation to be heard by you.' John said pointedly.

'Meaning?'

'Meaning he *was* thinking ahead – he was thinking of *you*. He knew exactly what Durakovic wanted and how to deliver it. Like you said, he's a smart guy, a planner and a strategist. He's partly used this tape to play you. He's your old CO, your business partner and your friend. He knew exactly what you would do before he even called you. You're a good man, Dan; he knew you wouldn't let him down. The tape is edited, at least in part, for your benefit.'

'So what is it? What was discussed? What does Durakovic want?'

'That I can't tell you, but this is far more complicated than you think, or Richard has told you. Whatever it is, Richard is in it up to his neck.'

'That doesn't change the fact that Elizabeth and Jennifer have been taken.'

'No, it doesn't, but it does change the playing field. Think about the last section of the recording, after Richard switched the machine back on. He did that deliberately. Listen to the choice of Durakovic's words, "Matters you and I need to conclude" and "In the meantime". Durakovic has taken those girls partly to punish Richard for whatever he thinks he has done, but also to ensure he now does exactly what he has been asked to do. This is a set-up, Dan. Durakovic is expecting you and Richard knows it.'

NINE

Daniel stood, bunching his fists by his side, as angry thoughts flashed through his mind and his rage simmered just below the surface of his expressionless face.

'I'd best not disappoint him then, had I?' He said firmly.

John threw his arms in the air in exasperation.

'You're still going then?'

'I'm still going. What would you do if it were me – if I'd asked you for help? Whatever the reasons, first and foremost, there are two young girls out there who will have their lives ripped apart unless I get them back. I'll deal with the rest of it later. I know there has to be an explanation, but right now it will have to wait.'

John shook his head.

'OK, Dan, you really are a hard-headed, stubborn

son of a bitch, but I understand. I'm just thankful you're my friend as well. And yes, if it were you calling, I would go too.'

Daniel half-smiled. 'Thanks, John. I really do appreciate everything you've done.'

John shook Daniel's hand. 'My pleasure, Dan. I'll see you soon.'

Daniel left the building with time to kill. He strolled through the bustling London streets, thinking and planning as he walked in the chilling winter air. Half-way back to the hotel he stepped into a small street café and ordered the biggest all-day breakfast he could find.

He sat watching the world unfold outside the cafe window. It was the usual London scene: cars, buses, lorries, motorcyclists, police cars and couriers, all crawling through the congested streets. Their progress made all the more arduous by constant roadwork's and a traffic light system designed and phased to slow it even further.

'Here you go, love,' the waitress said, setting down a monstrous plate of sausage, bacon, mushrooms, scrambled egg, baked beans, two rounds of toast and a huge mug of tea.

He ate the meal, thinking about his plan of action. He needed to work fast but think smart. The information Richard Mead and John Shaw had provided gave him new ideas and a different perspective. If it was a trap, he would need to create distractions and diversions, doubt and uncertainty, then slip in through the maze of confusion. He thought it through and added a new approach. He was used to thinking on his feet, reacting and responding to situations as they unfolded. Now, like Richard Mead, he was planning strategically – thinking ahead. It was an incomplete plan, but enough to get him started. The final solution would come to him; it always did.

He arrived back at the Benjamin Hotel at 3:30pm, walked casually through the front door and slowly up to the reception desk. The attractive receptionist was there, dealing with another customer. He leant on the desk and waited. She caught him out the corner of her eye and her face flushed pink. He watched her, deliberately and obviously. She was very attractive, about five feet six, with a great figure that curved in all the right places. Her long dark hair glowed as it cascaded off her shoulders and tumbled a short way down her back. She smiled at the customer; a warm, genuine smile. Her lips were full and he wondered for moment what they would be like to kiss. Not since he had parted with Caroline, a year ago, had he held a woman in his arms.

The customer left and she turned suddenly, unexpectedly catching Daniel in full appraisal mode. Their eyes locked momentarily, soft golden-brown and piercing blue-green, and her face blushed a deeper shade of red as she maintained eye contact.

'Hello again,' she said, her voice soft and smooth, like velvet.

'Hello, um, I'm sorry, I don't know your name,' apologised Daniel.

'Teresa,' she said, tilting slightly toward him, pushing her name tag forward, along with a perfectly rounded breast which now strained against the fabric of her white blouse.

'Hi, Teresa. Thanks for all your help today and for all the other times I've stayed.'

'It's my pleasure, Mr Temple,' she replied.

'Daniel,' he said.

It was another conversation within a conversation. The true meaning and intent hidden just below the surface of the spoken words.

'Would you like your bags, Daniel?' she asked.

'Please. Well, actually, could I impose just a little more? Could I leave the leather weekend bag with you? I'll be back to collect it soon, I promise.'

Teresa thought for a moment.

'On one condition,' she replied.

'OK?' Daniel asked.

'You buy me dinner when you come back,' she said with a wonderfully alluring smile.

'It would be my pleasure,' Daniel replied with a confident, broad grin.

Teresa stepped in to the storeroom and fetched the green duffle bag, lightly brushing his hand with hers as she handed it to him.

'I'm sorry, there is just one last thing. May I borrow the computer in your office?'

Teresa glanced around.

'Sure,' she said.

Daniel sat at the desk, logged on and started to work. His arrangements completed, he grabbed the two pages of print, logged off and came back past the front desk.

'Thank you,' he smiled as he turned and left.

Daniel hailed one last cab and headed for Liverpool Street station. He bought his ticket, waited a short while, then jumped onto the regular shuttle which ran directly to Stansted Airport. Forty-five minutes later he was leaving the train with his kit bag over his shoulder, taking the escalator up to the ground level of the passenger terminal.

Temple Stamford operated a small, working hangar on the outer perimeter of the airport. The hangar was a modest, purely functional building with plain grey metal sidings under a white roof and a small, TS company logo, painted centrally above the wide, double-doors. A modified Boeing 737 sat silently on the tarmac, half in, half out of the hangar. Daniel watched the engineers working as the bus drove by. He jumped off at the next stop and sauntered back down the road, through an open gate and across to the hangar. An engineer knelt under the nose of the aircraft, working on what appeared to be routine maintenance on the landing gear.

'Afternoon,' Daniel said amiably as he approached.

The man glanced up, then fixed his eyes back on his work.

'You meant to be here?' he asked gruffly.

'I think so. Daniel Temple.' Daniel announced, holding out his hand to introduce himself.

The man looked up, then stood up, wiping his hands on an old rag before shaking Daniel's hand.

'As in Temple of Temple Stamford?' he asked sheepishly.

'In one,' Daniel smiled, putting the man at ease.

'How can I help?' the man replied in a far more conciliatory and respectful tone.

'I just need to find the pilot of the 737 here and I'll be out of your way,' Daniel said, keeping his voice easy and friendly.

'No problem, Mr Temple. He's in the office, far left corner. You can't miss it – it's the only office we got.'

'Thanks,' Daniel said, nodding his head slightly.

He wandered casually into the hangar. Through the glass window of the office, he could see the pilot sat alone, leaning back in a chair, his feet up on the desk with a mug of coffee in one hand and reading documents held in the other. Daniel opened the door and stepped inside. The pilot glanced over the top of his papers.

'Daniel?' he asked.

Daniel confirmed, holding out his hand. The pilot stood up and shook his hand firmly.

'Alex Donald,' he stated in a broad Scottish accent. 'Good to meet you. The Ops Director said to expect you. I understand I need to drop you off en route.'

'Yes, that's one way of putting it,' Daniel said easily.

'Right, we'd better get you aboard – just in case we get any early arrivals. We can talk more on the plane,' Alex said, leading Daniel out of the office, back across the hangar and up the steps to the aircraft.

The 737 had been heavily modified since its days as a holiday charter jet. All of the original seating had been removed and the front end of the aircraft had been refitted with thirty reasonably comfortable seats. They were the sort you might find in a premium economy or low-end business class section in any one of the world's more popular commercial airlines, with ample space and leg room. To the rear of the seats there was a single, functional galley and two toilets. The rest of the plane's space had been assigned as work and cargo space.

The pilot led Daniel on through the aircraft until they came to a solid-looking door. He took a card from his pocket, swiped it through the lock and punched in a five-digit number. The door opened into a general work and storage area. There were a number of racks designed to hold some of the more fragile engineering equipment and a long work bench where laptop computers could be connected, allowing the engineers to work in flight. They walked through, exiting out of another door at the far end and into the empty space of the main upper cargo hold.

'Sorry, it's not the most comfortable of places, but we'll get you settled as best we can. There's a row of pull-down jump-seats you can use over there,' Alex said, pointing to the left hand wall. 'When we get close to the drop-off point I'll unlock the upper, outer cargo door from the cockpit. The light up there will switch from green to red, so that's the opposite of what you would expect on a normal jump, OK?'

'Got it,' Daniel confirmed.

'You can open the door yourself using the buttons to the right of the lights. Your chute is stored in the bins over there,' Alex explained pointing to the lights, buttons and bins at the rear of the hold.

'OK, that's clear,' Daniel confirmed again.

'Consider the red light coming on to be your ten minute warning. At fifteen minutes I will close and lock the outer door and assume you have gone, alright?'

'Fine,' nodded Daniel. 'And thanks.'

'Right, I'm going to lock you in here and get ready for departure. I expect the first of our passengers will be arriving shortly. If you want to use the bathroom, best do it now,' Alex offered in a relaxed, friendly voice.

'I'm fine. I'll just get myself comfortable and keep out of your way. Thanks again for the ride,' Daniel said, shaking Alex's hand.

'Good luck to you, Daniel, whatever it is you are doing.'

Alex Donald left, locking the door behind him. Daniel looked around the empty cargo space. There wasn't a lot to see – just bare metal. He looked across to the storage bins, walked over and pulled one of the two parachutes out from where they were stowed. He checked it over then, set it against the aircraft wall. Turning round, he pulled down the four jump-seats. They were hard, bare metal frames and looked decidedly uncomfortable. He closed them back up, leant his duffle bag against the wall and butted the chute up against it on the floor. Sitting on the parachute, Daniel rested his back against the duffle and settled in as comfortably as he could. Less than an hour later he could hear the sound of voices over the low whine of the engines as the engineering team took their seats and the aircraft prepared to taxi from the hangar. There were no cabin crew or pre-flight safety announcements; just a level of good-natured banter between what appeared to be a friendly bunch of people who had obviously known each other for some time. Daniel shuffled his position, laid back and closed his eyes. The aircraft rolled out of the hangar and taxied for a few minutes. Daniel felt the turns and slight adjustments to the power as Alex manoeuvred the plane onto the main runway. There was a short delay as the aircraft took its final turn, straightened up and waited for permission to take off; then, they were accelerating hard. Daniel slid a short way across the floor of the cargo space before steadying himself with his left hand. Seconds later, they were airborne. Daniel relaxed, closing his eyes again.

It was a little over two hours before Daniel opened his eyes again. Sleep had come surprisingly easy and he felt much the better for it. He stood up, stretching the stiffness from his body, lifted the duffel bag away from the wall and opened it up. Pulling out the set of black fatigues, paratrooper boots, balaclava and coat, he quickly changed, then folded his jeans, shirt and jumper and packed them back into the bag, along with his old hiking boots. The fatigues were a pretty good fit and he stood, feeling a strange, comforting familiarity at being back in a uniform. He slid the commando knife into the sheath on his belt, checked the safety on the Makarov and zipped it into the inside pocket of his coat. Grabbing the parachute, he checked it over again, slid his arms through the straps and buckled up. Then he picked up the duffle bag, squashed the remaining contents down as tight as he could and strapped the bag to his chest as if it were a spare chute. He was ready to go.

In the cockpit, the co-pilot was taking a break, dozing in his seat. Alex Donald reached down, flicked the switch and disengaged the locks on the outer cargo doors.

The light above Daniel's head flashed red. Ten minute warning, he thought, checking his watch. Alex began an easy decent, advising Russian air traffic control of a possible technical fault and their need to decrease altitude slightly earlier than usual. The request was approved without question; it was normal procedure. Daniel waited five minutes, then hit the button. There was a loud mechanical clunk followed by a hiss as the door seal gave and the ramp slowly lowered. Daniel held onto the safety line as the freezing air poured in, buffeting and whirling around the empty cargo space. Daniel looked out as the door opening grew wider and wider, but he could see nothing but black. He steadied himself, held the safety line and walked slowly and confidently to the edge of the now-horizontal cargo door. He pulled the balaclava down across his face, slid his goggles over his eyes and stepped out as calmly as if he were stepping off the kerb.

Alex Donald closed the outer cargo doors exactly fifteen minutes after he had unlocked them and resumed his normal decent into Vologda.

Daniel fell through the freezing, black night sky. He spread his arms and legs, falling in the classic skydiver's pose – controlled and steady. Counting to himself, he calculated his height as he fell. Alex had said he would open the doors at twenty thousand feet. Daniel was free falling at one hundred and twenty miles per hour – one hundred and seventy-five feet per second – terminal velocity. He would open his chute on 102 seconds as he passed two thousand feet, look up, check the canopy and then start looking for the ground, hoping his landing spot was going to be a reasonable one.

The wind rushed past him as he plummeted blindly through the blackness, calm and confident in his ability and experience. It was just another jump; something he had done hundreds of times before. One hundred, one hundred and one, one hundred and two, he counted, then pulled the ripcord. The chute emerged and plumed as the canopy opened to its full extent, jerking him upward. His decent slowed and he looked down, searching for the ground, the moonless night not helping his vision. Looking right and left, he checked his surroundings. There was nothing; no light from anywhere, no buildings, no houses, no cars on roads – just dark empty space. Wherever he was, it was remote. He looked down at his feet. The ground appeared through the gloom, a blanket of pale blue and grey. Snow, he thought. He bent his knees, pulled the toggles, kept his eyes focused on his landing spot and touched down perfectly, stepping forward to gather his chute as it billowed in the light breeze. He rolled it in, unbuckled the rig, dug a hole in the firmly packed snow and buried it along with his goggles.

Daniel checked his bearings using his compass and geographical relief map. He was, by rough calculation, two hundred miles east-southeast of St Petersburg.

Rolling the duffle bag back over his shoulder, he moved out, walking at a steady pace. The open land and fields were covered with a two-feet layer of well-packed snow, frozen hard and crusted with a thick veneer of ice. The snow crunched and squeaked under his feet like breaking polystyrene and the easterly breeze dropped as the night grew still and bitterly cold. The temperature plummeted to well below freezing.

Daniel rolled the woollen balaclava down, pulled

it tight over his ears and turned up the collar of his coat. Thankful he had purchased good quality, military, winter-issue clothing, he marched on, warm enough against the icy embrace of the early Russian winter.

He walked on, checking his bearings every hour. After four hours, he crossed some minor country roads and passed by small rural settlements, giving them a wide berth. Kneeling in the dark, he checked his watch – it was just after 4:00am. A little further ahead, he could see a small crop of isolated buildings – a farm. He moved silently round the side of the first of the buildings – a storage shed of some sort – stopped and knelt again. The farm was deathly quiet. He peered round the side of the shed. The main farmhouse sat a hundred yards to his right, dark and still. To his left, a dirt and gravel track led down and away through snow-covered fields and back to the main road, he figured. Across the other side of the open yard, a large wooden barn stood with its doors wide open.

Daniel ran across the yard, barely making a sound and disappeared through the opening. The barn was pretty similar to the one at Temple Farm. The ground floor was maybe a little busier, cluttered with old farm tools and machinery. He looked around. In the far corner lay a large tarpaulin-covered shape. He moved across and pulled away the covering. An old Lada car sat cold and unused, the keys still in the ignition. Too good to be true, he thought, jumping and turning the key, one click, two clicks. The dashboard lights flickered dimly; the battery was OK, but not charged. He checked the petrol gauge. It showed a quarter of a tank – enough to get started. Climbing out, Daniel pulled the tarpaulin completely away and checked the tyres. They were all inflated; not much tread, but good enough. He walked back to the driver's door, threw his duffle onto the rear seat, reached in and released the handbrake. Bending his knees, he grabbed the steering wheel and half-open door, heaved and turned.

The car rocked forward a little, then rolled back. Daniel dug his feet in, leaned forward and heaved again, pushing hard with his legs and arms. The car moved slowly through the barn, rolled out of the doors and across the yard. Daniel turned the wheel, lined up with the dirt and gravel track, then pushed harder. The car rolled forward, picking up speed as it began to travel quietly down the steady incline of the yard. Daniel jogged a few yards, then jumped into the driver's seat, put the car in gear, waited for the speed to build, lifted the clutch and pressed the accelerator. The car bumped and engaged first time. Daniel smiled.

TEN

The heavy black door closed ominously behind the girls and a resounding thud echoed eerily through the dim, cold corridors which disappeared into the darkness before them. The girls were led single-file through the maze of gloomy passageways until they reached the foot of a broad stone stairway and ascended nervously into the cavernous hall of the main house.

Damir lead the way, roughly pulling Elizabeth along with him. They crossed the wide, grey stone floor with Mirsad following closely with Jennifer, and stopped at a set of more ornate, double wooden doors. Damir knocked respectfully, swung the doors open and pushed Elizabeth inside. Mirsad followed, pushing Jennifer ahead of him.

The two girls fearfully stopped a short way inside the room. Before them, a tall man stood with his back to them, staring in to the log fire which burned in the large stone fireplace, cheering the otherwise dull and sombre room.

Damir and Mirsad closed the doors and stood, one either side of the doorway, waiting in silence.

Elizabeth moved closer to Jennifer. Instinctively, Jennifer reached out, clasping her sister's hand as they waited anxiously, shivering with cold and trepidation.

The man in the centre of the room turned slowly. He was late forties. His complexion was pale, his face solid and his jaw chiselled square, beneath hair that was long and dark, thick and wavy, streaked with grey at the temples. He was tall, but not heavily built. Slim and athletic, he looked like someone who kept himself in shape. Dressed in a charcoal-coloured suit and a black, open-necked shirt, his attire matched his surroundings. He stared at the girls with cold, steel-grey eyes then walked forward, appraising each of the girls in turn.

'I am Commander Durakovic,' he stated. 'You have heard of me, yes?'

The girls looked at each other then back to Durakovic, shaking their heads as they did so.

A look of anger flickered across Durakovic's face.

'It is of no consequence. You belong to me now and I, in turn, am making you a gift to someone else. You will be here for a short while and then you will be collected and taken to your new owner to do with as he pleases,' Durakovic stated with a cold, self-satisfied smile.

The anger inside Elizabeth welled up and overflowed; her courage not yet silenced or defeated.

'You don't own us. We are not animals to be kept or sold. Let us go, you have no right to keep us here.'

Durakovic sighed and stepped calmly forward. He struck without warning. His open hand slapped savagely across Elizabeth's face, sending her sprawling to the floor.

Jennifer gasped and cowered away as Elizabeth lay stunned, sobbing and bleeding on the floor.

Durakovic towered over her.

'You belong to me,' he growled again with added venom. 'And you are a gift for the pleasure of Sergei Kozlov, to do with as he pleases. You will submit or you will die.'

He looked across to his men.

'Take them. Let them bathe. Find them some more appropriate clothes, then put them with the girls I selected this morning. No one is to violate them, is that clear?'

Damir and Mirsad crossed the room.

'Yes, Sir,' they confirmed.

Elizabeth and Jennifer were dragged crying, kicking and screaming from the room.

Dian Jancic walked slowly into the room as the

girls were hauled away, watching them with indifferent eyes as they passed.

'Are you sure you want to do this, Zoran?'

Durakovic's eyes flashed in anger at the question.

'Yes, I'm sure. It's time – I've waited long enough.'

'Why send them to Kozlov? Why not keep them here for you own pleasure?'

'Because it doesn't serve my purposes. I want Mead to do as he's told. I want him to suffer and I want them to suffer. Kozlov is an animal; he will do things you and I could only imagine and he will enjoy every single moment.'

'It makes you happy?'

'It will satisfy my hate and my anger and it will placate Kozlov. He wasn't too happy with the expansion of our operation into Zagreb, or with the fact that we used Mead to do it.'

'He doesn't trust you. You're ambitious and intelligent; it's a dangerous combination. But if it makes you happy, I will see it done.'

'Nothing will make me happy, Dian, but yes, please see that it is done.'

*

Daniel drove until the first shards of cool morning light appeared through the trees. He pulled the car over and surveyed the map. The small country road was running due east. It would eventually run into the main road to Cherepovets where it would divide, turning north toward St Petersburg or south toward Moscow. He thought about the journey. Either way, it was approximately three hundred miles hard driving on icy roads in a stolen car with bald tyres – a bad plan. Deciding on a new mode of transport, he turned the car around and headed back for the city of Vologda.

Driving steadily, Daniel methodically wove his way through the city streets, following the signs for the train station. The station was a building you couldn't miss. Situated on the broad Babushkina square, it was a long, two-storey building with walls painted bright aquamarine and white. He found the car park, parked the car and threw the keys into the glove box. It would be found soon enough and hopefully returned to its owner.

He walked across the heavily-worn and potholed tarmac, crunching through the deep puddles that lay like frosted mirrors on the ground, and entered the station. It was a busy morning. People bustled their way through, wrapped in heavy winter clothing; thick coats, scarves, gloves, hats and boots. Frosty breath filled the air as passengers passed in and out of the entrance, to and from their trains. It was a scene that could be witnessed in every city around the world.

Daniel studied the network map. It was a straightforward journey. Vologda was situated at the crossroads of railways running north to south and east to west. The north to south track formed a spur off of the main Trans-Siberian railway, running north to St Petersburg, then onward, across the Finnish border to Helsinki or south to Moscow. He walked over to the ticket window and waited in line. The queue moved slowly, as if partially paralysed by the freezing air. Daniel stood and shuffled his feet, trying to keep some degree of warmth, for despite his two layers of socks and his thick-soled paratrooper's boots, his toes were starting to go numb.

The grey-haired man behind the window stared at him with a worn expression, his eyes dark and heavy. Daniel asked for a one-way ticket and rummaged in his pocket for the handful of Roubles he had obtained in deliberately small denominations of old crumpled notes and coins. He paid the fare, took his ticket and wandered through to the platform. There was a small waiting room a short walk to his left. Opening the door, he stepped inside. In comparison to the sharp cold of the outside air, the room was hot and stuffy, the atmosphere thick with tobacco smoke. Daniel glanced around; there was no interest in his presence. Everyone in the room seemed old and weary. Their hardy faces were creased and worn. Cheeks and noses glowed red under waves of grey and white hair. Daniel found a corner, dropped the duffle bag to the floor, took off his coat, leant casually against the wall and waited anonymously for his train. Just another transient soldier.

*

Elizabeth's and Jennifer's defiance subsided under a torrent of physical and verbal abuse as they were dragged by their hair across the stone floor and up the main staircase. Pushed along the first floor landing, they were forced into a large bedroom. The interior was cold and unwelcoming.

Damir and Mirsad forced the girls further into the room, then closed and locked the door.

The girls looked nervously at the two men. They knew what was coming. Damir stepped forward.

'Take off your clothes,' he ordered.

The girls stood perfectly still.

The men stepped ominously closer as Damir raised his hand in warning.

'Take them off,' he ordered again, angrily spitting the words out.

The girls moved closer together – neither was going to voluntarily undress.

Damir's slapped Jennifer hard across her face.

She screamed, falling to the floor.

Mirsad grabbed a handful of her hair and dragged her across the room, separating the girls.

Jennifer cried in pain as blood trickled from her nose.

Tears rolled down Elizabeth's face as she stood, shaking her head.

'Please don't,' she pleaded, flinching away as Damir raised his hand again.

He grabbed her face and squeezed her cheeks hard between his fingers, turning her face to his.

'Strip,' he demanded forcefully. 'Or little sister gets some pleasure time with Mirsad.'

Elizabeth nodded weakly.

Damir released her face.

She took two steps back, held the bottom of her sweatshirt and lifted it over her head, standing still for several seconds in the cold light.

Damir and Mirsad stared greedily at her small, naked breasts.

Her mouth quivered as she fought back her tears. Bravely, she pulled the baggy grey sweatpants down, stepped out of them and stood shivering and naked, letting the two men feast their eyes on her slim, athletic body.

Jennifer climbed shakily to her feet and wiped the blood from her face, smearing it across her cheek.

Damir looked at her without an ounce of compassion and nodded.

'Strip,' he said again hoarsely.

The men watched, wallowing in perverse pleasure.

Jennifer obediently pulled her sweater and T-shirt over her head. Her full, uncovered breasts swayed as she moved. She stood for a moment, afraid and self-conscious.

The men stood transfixed as she wriggled out of her jeans and panties, then moved unclothed next to her sister.

The men drank the sight of the girls in, breathing heavily in an obvious state of arousal.

'Bathe. We will bring you clothes to wear,' Damir instructed, gathering up their old garments.

The men left the room and locked the door again.

Elizabeth and Jennifer turned and held each other for a moment, unashamed at their nakedness.

'Daddy will come. It will be OK,' Elizabeth stated as positively as she could to her younger sister.

Jennifer nodded in silence, like she didn't believe she would ever see her parents or home again, then shivered as the cold room, fear, shock and tiredness overwhelmed her.

Elizabeth glanced around the room. There were two queen-sized beds, separated by a single, shared night table. The room contained no other furniture. In the centre of the far wall was a small, barred window. To the right, another door opened into a functional bathroom.

Elizabeth led her sister to the bed nearest the window, gently laid her down and covered her with the thin sheet and blanket.

'Sleep a while,' Elizabeth said, smiling weakly. 'I'll take a bath and wake you when I'm done.'

Jennifer nodded.

'Why are they doing this? Why have they taken us?' she asked, stuttering the words out between heavy sobs.

'I don't know, Jen and we shouldn't ask, not yet – it will only provoke them. We'll keep as quiet as possible. Daddy will come. He'll find us. Sleep now. It's going to be alright,' Elizabeth said again, softly stroking her sister's hair.

Elizabeth went into the bathroom. The room was small, clean and functional. The sanitary ware and tiles were white porcelain, making the room feel cold and clinical. She opened a small mirrored cabinet that contained soap and shampoo and added a little shampoo to the water running in the bath. The bubbles frothed as the steam rose from the piping-hot water.

She bathed, welcoming the feel of a hot bath and being clean again. Wrapped in a warm dry towel, she returned to the bedroom and woke her sister.

'Come on, take a bath. You'll feel better,' she said, leading Jennifer into the bathroom. 'Don't worry.

Close the door; I won't let anyone in, I promise.'

Jennifer looked out of the door nervously.

Elizabeth took her hands in hers.

'I promise,' she said again.

An hour after they had entered the bedroom, the girls were bathed and sat on the bed, wrapped in large dry towels, waiting. The sound of heavy footsteps thudding down the landing pushed them closer together and they huddled on the bed, holding one another for comfort. The key turned in the lock and the door swung open.

Damir walked in and dropped two bags on the bed nearest the door.

'Clothes,' he said in a severe but calm tone. 'Get dressed. I will be back shortly.'

He turned and left the room, locking the door once more.

The girls moved quickly, grateful for the opportunity to dress again and for the deceptive feeling of comfort and safety it gave.

The clothes were deliberately designed to exploit and exhibit the female body. The underwear was small and lacy – bras, g-strings and thongs. The skirts were short. The tops tight and low cut. The blouses, see through, and the shoes, high-heeled. The effect was as Durakovic desired. Even without the addition of make-up, they looked like street corner working girls.

Damir returned fifteen minutes later. He smiled at their appearance.

'Come,' he instructed, gesturing for the girls to follow him.

Damir lead the way down the landing, up another flight of stairs and along to another door. He unlocked it and pushed it open. It was another bedroom, larger and thankfully warmer than the one they had just left. Inside, there were four queen-sized beds c two against the left wall – two against the right. A small bedside table and tall, slim, wardrobe stood next to each. The window in the far wall was larger, but still covered with black iron bars.

Damir pushed the girls in and slammed the door behind them. The key rattled in the lock as the catch turned and closed with a loud metallic click.

Two other girls stood in the room. They were young; more or less the same ages as Elizabeth and Jennifer. Each had long dark hair and was dressed in the same cheap style. The four girls stared at one another in awkward silence.

Elizabeth hesitantly introduced herself and Jennifer.

'Hello. My name is Elizabeth. This is my sister, Jennifer,' she said touching her sister's arm. 'Do you speak English?' she asked hopefully.

The dark-haired girls looked at each other, then stepped a little closer.

'I speak a little English,' said the taller girl quietly, her voice heavily accented. 'I am Lesya and this is Yana,' she said, pointing to the smaller girl, who half-nodded and smiled at the sound of her name. 'We are from Ukraine,' she added.

The four girls stared at each other again.

'Were you brought here today?' Elizabeth asked.

'Today, yes, we come today,' Lesya nodded awkwardly.

Silence and tension fell again, invisibly hanging in the air. Heavy and thick, like choking smog, it enveloped and depressed them. The realisation and horror of their now-shared nightmare becoming all too real. Then, as if right on cue, came the spontaneous release. The girls began to cry; not for themselves, but for their new-found friends. They were tears of sympathy and recognition and strangely, tears of joy. The four girls moved almost in unison. Holding each other, they stood in the centre of the room, crying, embracing, nodding and smiling. The smiles turned to laughter. There were no words; they weren't necessary. Each of them knew they were no longer alone.

ELEVEN

Daniel's train clattered into the station more or less on time. Through the condensation-misted glazing of the waiting room door, he watched the distorted view of the platform as the carriages groaned and squealed to a halt.

Pulling on his coat, he threw the duffle lazily over his shoulder, waited for several of the other passengers to shuffle out of the room, then strolled out behind them. Making his way along the platform, Daniel climbed aboard, sauntered through the carriages and found a near-empty compartment. Choosing an empty row of three seats, he made himself comfortable, stretching out with his back against the window.

The journey was going to take nine hours. Daniel sat and took stock for the first time since stepping out of the aircraft several hours ago. Every hour that had passed since he had left Richard Mead's home had grated his nerves and gnawed at his soul. He knew there was nothing more he could do; he was moving as quickly as possible. The more he confirmed that fact, the more he hated it. Every minute of every hour of every day that passed was a moment too long. He turned slightly in his seat and stared out of the window as the train pulled away, desperately trying to blank out his darkest thoughts and fears.

The sights of the city passed him by, replaced by vague images, subdued colours and muted sounds. He stared vacantly; his thoughts consumed and clouded by concerns and misgivings. His plan was clear, but what if it was wrong? It was high risk and based on guesswork and supposition, not fact. What if Durakovic did something else, something different? What if he was just too late? What if? What if? *What if?* The possibilities just swirled in his mind, crowding and distorting his thinking.

'Tickets, please.'

The call of the conductor snapped his attention back to real time. He delved into his pocket and handed over his ticket. The conductor looked him up and down, then at his muddy boots resting up on the seat. Daniel glared back. It was a look he had perfected over time. It was simple and effective. It made a statement and it answered questions. "Don't go there," it said. "You won't like the response", it confirmed.

The conductor checked the ticket, punched it and handed it back without a word. Daniel nodded curtly, pleased there was no conversation, then stared back out of the window. The city was gone – replaced by a landscape of soft white; plain and nondescript. An ocean of snow, interspersed by the odd village, small wood or isolated house, rolled monotonously by.

Daniel refocused. The voice in his head was firm. He had a plan. He had made decisions. There was no room for doubt, hesitancy or uncertainty. He had made an absolute promise; one he was going to keep. He had better get sharp – bury his feelings and bury them deep. This was just another mission, nothing more. There could be nothing inside him now; no emotion – just cold-hearted, ruthless calculation. He closed his eyes and slept.

Daniel woke as the train rumbled into Moscow's Yaroslavsky station just after 4:30pm. Disembarking, he rode the metro one stop to Savyolovsky Station, bought a ticket for the Aeroexpress and headed for Sheremetyevo airport, north of the city.

The metro and train to the airport were crowded with people. Daniel bumped and jostled his way through, just another face in the crowd trying to get somewhere different to the place he was in. He reached the airport terminal and headed for Sheremetyevo II – first floor, international departures. His flight was already posted; gate twelve. He looked around, found the small airport services counter, walked over and rented a small locker. Taking the orange-fobbed key, Daniel followed the girl's directions to a long row of grey metal cabinets which stood between a parade of cheap coffee shops, snack bars and the start of the airline check-in desks. Discretely glancing around, he opened the locker and deposited the duffle bag containing the Makarov, two clips, spare rounds and his knife. Daniel moved off. His pre-printed boarding card and fake passport in hand, he headed for the departure gate, armed only with his intellect, training and determination. Reaching the gate, he presented his documents and held his breath; this passport had better be good. He waited and watched.

The guy at the gate stared intently at the photograph, then at Daniel. He examined the boarding pass then stared again at the photograph, scrutinizing each closely. Slowly, almost reluctantly, he handed them back.

'Boarding in thirty minutes. Next,' he said.

It was a plain, factual and cheerless statement, followed by an equally staid and officious instruction.

Daniel moved into the Perspex-enclosed waiting

area, found a seat in the corner of the room, sat and waited.

The Jat Airways flight was surprisingly called on time. Daniel joined the queue for boarding, waiting impatiently as the line slowly shuffled forward.

Boarding the aircraft, he made his way down the aisle, through what passed for business class and into the no-frills economy section, which took up most of the cabin. He clambered into his assigned, small, blue-checked cloth seat by the window and sat in quiet discomfort, his knees jammed tight against the seat in front.

The other passengers filed on board, filling the overhead bins with an assortment of carry-on luggage before squeezing into the ridiculously small space allotted. The final passenger boarded. An enormous man, at least in girth, pushed his bulk down the aisle and took the seat immediately in front of Daniel. The seat creaked as it sagged back under the man's weight, wedging Daniel's knees even more tightly into the space.

'Great,' Daniel frowned.

The flight landed at Sarajevo's international airport at 9:45pm. Daniel waited in line. It seemed he had spent the last twenty-four hours either waiting in line or migrating from one mode of transport to another and his frustration began to build again. The main purpose in life for everyone else on the planet, even the whole reason for their existence, appeared to be to slow him down and piss him off. Finally he made the front of the queue. The man behind the counter looked tired, bored and disinterested, like he'd been doing the same job forever. He glanced at Daniel's passport without looking up, stamped it and moved him on. Job done.

Daniel stepped out of the terminal and took a deep breath. The air was clear and frosty. The moon shone full and bright, like a huge polished pewter dish sitting low in the midnight-blue sky. He pulled up his collar, made his way past the near-empty drop-off and collection zone, passed the equally empty taxi rank and climbed aboard the regular shuttle bus to the city.

*

Zoran Durakovic swirled the brandy balloon in his hand, staring pensively into the warm, golden-brown liquid.

'You think I'm wrong, Dian,' he asked, his voice quiet and reflective.

'I think your judgment is clouded, Zoran. There are other ways to get what you want.'

'My vision is clear, Dian; I'm not as driven and tormented as you appear to think. I agree, there may be better ways, but none as satisfying,' answered

Durakovic. 'You think the Colonel will do what he has agreed?' he added.

'Yes, I think so. I would, but then I don't have the decision to make. He knows he cannot come himself – you made that perfectly clear. He's no longer up to the job; he won't take the risk. He will send someone else, someone very good, maybe more than one. It's his background, it's still his job – he makes his living from situations like this.'

'So do we, Dian, so do we.'

'What about Kozlov?' Dian asked, changing the nature of the conversation.

'What about him?'

'Isn't it a bit early to be challenging him?'

'Early?'

'OK, risky then. He's a strong man – ruthless. He may not suspect anything yet, but he is certainly wary. If this goes wrong, he'll have your head on a platter.'

'He'll always be wary and untrusting. Like you said, I'm smart, ambitious, and above all, I'm not Russian – I will never be accepted. We have to take what we want, Dian. The girls will serve their purpose. They will distract him for long enough, they always do – it's his weakness. No one will stand in our path with Kozlov out of the way.'

'Where are the girls?'

'We put them with the others as you instructed.

Do you want to see them again?'

'No. Keep them safe and well. They're a bargaining chip until Kozlov has them, maybe even longer. The next twenty-four hours should tell us which way our Colonel Mead is going to run.'

*

Daniel made his way out of the city on foot, following the directions memorised from the information John Shaw had provided. The road ran steadily up through the heavily-forested mountains, twisting and turning through the rugged terrain north of the city.

He came at last to a wide, sweeping bend in the road and a narrow gravel track which cut off sharply to his right, carving its way on through the trees. Daniel moved off the road, followed the track a few hundred yards, estimated his bearings, then struck out across country toward the house. The forest closed in around him and the light faded to black, slowing his pace considerably as he walked on in darkness.

*

'You don't intend to kill them after Mead's man arrives?' Dian asked.

'No, not whilst they're useful. Why should I? Once they're with Kozlov, their lives won't be worth living anyway – I still get what I want. They're the bait; the absolute and total incentive. As long as they're alive, Mead and whoever he sends will do as they're told,' Durakovic answered with a devious, self-satisfied smile.

*

Daniel emerged from the tree line directly in front of the enormous grey flagstone house. He surveyed it carefully across the wide expanse of grass and black gravel drive. There seemed to be little activity. The house was dimly-lit and deathly quiet. He knelt in the shadows and waited expectantly.

Right on cue, a huge Rottweiler emerged from the far corner of the house, obediently leading his handler. Seconds later, a second guard appeared from the opposing corner, led by an equally large dog. They passed each other in front of the main entrance, exchanged a few short words, then continued, disappearing from view as they followed the narrow path around the house.

Daniel stayed in the shadows and timed their circuit. It was a full minute from the time they turned their respective corners in front of the house, until they re-emerged again.

Daniel scanned the front of the house. A set of broad stone steps led up to the main covered entrance, a deeply recessed, open-sided porch, built from the same grey flagstone. It was topped by a black slate slanting roof and led to a large, single door. There were two, double windows either side. The windows to the left were dark. To the right, a pale, orange light glowed from the farthest window.

Daniel waited until the guards appeared again. They crossed, spoke briefly, then continued on. He watched them go, let them clear the corners to start another circuit, then ran across the gravel, quickly and quietly. He vaulted up the steps, reached the porch and ducked into the shadows. The door was a solid looking barrier, made from thick hardwood, painted deep red and studded with large, pointed brass rivets. The handle was a ribbed, thick brass circular band. He grabbed it, turned it slowly and pushed. It wasn't locked. The door opened silently. Daniel slipped stealthily inside. Closing the door behind him, he stood perfectly still, surveying the vast expanse of the entrance hall.

The centre of the hall was dominated by an enormous wooden staircase. The stairs dog-legged their way up through the house, starting from their origin, next to a broad square opening in the flagstone floor. From the opening, another set of thick, grey stone steps descended into the sinister black depths of the house.

Daniel glanced right, toward a set of ornately furnished wooden doors, and the direction from where he'd seen the light. He listened hard. The sound of footsteps clicking on the flagstone came from the blackened stairway. They grew louder. Heavy feet making a slow ascent of the stone stairway directly ahead.

Daniel moved quickly across the hall and slipped into the shadows beneath the staircase. A man appeared. Daniel assessed him. He was medium height, maybe five feet ten, a stocky build with short, reddish-brown hair, dressed in black jeans and sweatshirt. He cleared the top of the steps, turned left and headed toward the ornate double doors.

Daniel slid out from the shadows and fell silently in behind him.

The man stopped. The inner sense that all humans possess suddenly telling him he was not alone. He started to turn.

Daniel's arm slipped round his neck, squeezed tight and pulled back. The man's feet lifted clear of the floor. Daniel pulled him, struggling, beneath the staircase. Frantically, the man pulled at Daniel's arm, desperate to release the pressure. His legs kicked as his air supply faded and vanished. Daniel squeezed harder, applied the final pressure and listened for the muffled snick and crack as the man's vertebrae gave. The man slithered from Daniel's arms and slumped to the floor, dead.

Daniel flipped him over, searched his pockets, took the gun from his belt and dragged him all the way back into the dark corner.

Once more, Daniel listened carefully. There was no other movement; the house totally silent. He moved forward and pressed his ear to the door; heard nothing.

He eased the door open and moved stealthily into the room. It was dark, quiet and empty. A large log fire burned bright and warm in the black stone fireplace. Daniel scanned the room. There was nothing to see; just an empty reception chamber, austere and cheerless – a place to formally receive business associates or unwelcome visitors. A single door was set into the wall on the far side. A sliver of light, a warm orange-tinged glow, escaped along its bottom edge. Daniel crossed the room, stood by the door and listened again. There were muted voices; two men in serious conversation.

'When do you want to send them?' Jancic asked.

'Soon. Tomorrow, maybe the day after. Kozlov is sending a helicopter to collect them. He seems eager to get his hands on them.'

'And afterwards?'

'They're not my problem. Kozlov can do what he likes with them and I'm sure he will.'

'What if Mead wants them back in exchange for completing what you want?'

'It's all part of the deal, although I must admit I did neglect to mention it,' Durakovic replied with a sadistic smile. 'If he wants them – he can go get them. He's not in a strong position to negotiate.'

'True,' Jancic said, nodding his head in agreement.

Daniel checked the pistol; a Glock 19, a good weapon, with a full nineteen-round clip. Taking a deep breath, he grabbed the handle on the door, turned it, pushed and entered the room, smooth, fast and quiet.

His eyes took in the scene, assessing the situation in an instant. Two men sat facing each other, talking, calm and relaxed, side-on to the door. One man in his late-forties, tall, lithe and athletic. His face was pale and his jaw square, beneath long, dark wavy hair, greying at the temples – Durakovic. The other man was shorter, solidly built. He had a shaven head and a black goatee beard – Jancic. John's information had been correct. Richard had been wrong. They weren't adversaries, they were allies, just as Daniel had hoped.

'Good evening, gentlemen,' Daniel said, calmly announcing himself.

The two men looked up slowly – a deliberate, unperturbed movement. Both surveyed the man at the door. He was big, well over six feet and powerfully built. Dressed in black. Calm and in control.

'We were wondering when you would arrive,' Durakovic replied as Jancic made the slightest of movements.

'I wouldn't do that if I were you,' Daniel advised, pointing the Glock at his head.

Jancic half smiled, inclining his head in acknowledgement.

'Both of you stand up and place your weapons on the desk, slow and easy.'

The two men stood and did as instructed.

'That's better. Now, please sit. Make yourselves comfortable. There are one or two things we need to talk about.'

Daniel stepped closer, keeping his eyes fixed on the two men.

Durakovic stared up at him. Daniel could see his cold, steel-grey eyes searching Daniel's face, carefully gauging the man in front of him. Daniel's expression remained calm, alert and assured. His piercing, blue-green eyes stared back unblinking, equally as cold and devoid of emotion. The look of a true adversary; a ruthless assassin. Durakovic would know Mead had chosen well.

'You have me at a disadvantage. I assume you know who I am, Mr–?' Durakovic enquired.

Daniel ignored the question.

'I know who you both are,' he stated. 'I assume you know why I'm here?'

Durakovic nodded in agreement.

'I do,' he said calmly. 'I am disappointed Colonel Mead couldn't come himself. I was rather looking forward to meeting him again. Do you know the Colonel well?'

'We're acquainted. Where are the girls?'

'Straight to the point! I like that.'

'Where are they?' Daniel asked more assertively.

'They're safe. For now.'

'They'd better be.'

The sound of many heavy steps running through the house echoed down the corridor. Daniel stared at Durakovic.

Durakovic stared back and raised his eyebrows, looking for a reaction, looking for the sudden realisation and for the panic to set in. There was nothing. Daniel merely sighed in acknowledgement, span the gun in his hand, stepped forward and handed it to Durakovic.

'Intelligent move,' Durakovic confirmed. 'Please sit down. We still have matters to discuss,' he added gesturing to a chair.

Daniel pulled the chair across the room and deliberately sat with his back to the door.

The door burst open and several heavily armed men crammed noisily into the room.

Durakovic held up his hand.

'Thank you, Damir, there is no emergency, but well done, an excellent response,' he said to the man obviously leading the small band of guards. Then he stood and retrieved his gun from the desk.

'Silent alarm,' Daniel stated.

'Yes, rather effective, don't you think?' Durakovic replied.

'Very,' Daniel reluctantly agreed.

'Now where were we?'

'You were about to tell me where Colonel Mead's daughters were before handing them over and letting us go safely on our way,' Daniel stated confidently. His words tinged with sarcasm.

'Now why would I want to do that?'

'It might save your life.'

'As I see it, you are the one in danger, Mr–?'

'Alright, information,' Daniel replied more seriously, levelling his eyes on Jancic.

Jancic's eyes narrowed as a slight frown creased his forehead.

'What information could you possibly have that I would be interested in?' Durakovic asked.

'Who really committed the majority of the war crimes you were accused of?'

Durakovic looked at Jancic and laughed.

'You think I don't already know that? You think I don't know what Dian did?'

'You could clear your name.'

'For what? There's no one left to testify against me. You think I don't know how Dian made sure I didn't stand trial? You think I don't know how he made sure the truth didn't come out? Oh no, you'll have to do much better than that.'

'The truth?' Daniel queried. 'Do you mean all of the truth or just some of the truth?'

'Meaning?' Durakovic pressed.

'Meaning, who really killed your family? Meaning how they were cold-bloodily executed – shot in the back of the head.'

Durakovic's expression changed in an instant. Confusion and anger flared in equal measure. Daniel's statement reignited his smouldering hatred, reopening old wounds and festering thoughts that cut deep into his soul.

'Mead did it. That's why I have his precious daughters. That's why they're going to Kozlov. That's why the man must pay,' Durakovic spat venomously.

'That's what you were told, wasn't it? By your friend and comrade here?'

Durakovic fell silent.

Jancic shuffled uncomfortably in his seat.

'He knows nothing, Zoran. Can't you see what he's trying to do? He's trying to unsettle you – play mind games, create a little doubt. Kill him and have done with it,' Jancic argued.

'You know, don't you? Deep down, you know it wasn't Mead.'

Durakovic remained silent. His eyes flicked from Daniel to Jancic and back again.

Daniel continued pushing.

'Yes, you know. Wasn't it Jancic who warned you the SAS were coming that day? How did he know? You were his commander – you didn't know. Did he persuade you to leave? Tell you he would protect your family? That no harm would come to them? Did he tell you how he fought bravely and barely escaped with his life – the last man to get away after all the others had died?'

'This is ridiculous. Zoran, we don't need to listen to this. Kill him,' Jancic urged, his voice raised and anxious.

Durakovic listened, his head bowed, his gun held firmly in his hand. One finger lightly stroked the cold black metal.

'You have a wound to prove your bravery, don't you, Jancic?' Daniel mocked.

Jancic glared at him.

'Zoran,' he pleaded. 'Kill the man.'

Daniel took the gamble and went for broke.

'A flesh wound under your left arm, where the bullet grazed your ribs. A thick ugly scar speckled black. The sort of wound you get when you shoot yourself, holding the gun up close. The bullet rips the flesh and the powder burn gets under the skin. You can't mistake it.'

The look of recognition and realisation flashed across Durakovic's face.

Jancic launched out of his seat, grabbing for his pistol that still lay on the desk. Durakovic aimed his gun.

'Let the man speak, Dian. I'm interested in what he has to say,' he said coldly.

Jancic dropped the gun to the floor.

'Sit down, Dian,' Durakovic ordered with menacing authority.

Jancic sat. His eyes shifted nervously from one man to the other. He knew the story; knew what was coming.

'You knew exactly who was coming, when and from where, didn't you, Jancic. You persuaded Durakovic to leave, had him slip away in the dead of night. Then you waited. You took the woman and the boy down into the cellar for safety. They knelt to pray when the assault started. You mercilessly shot them in the back of the head and left them for Colonel Mead to find. You made good your escape via the river and shot yourself only when you were sure you were safely away.'

'This is insane. Why would I do that? Zoran is my friend – my commander.'

'Because you held him responsible for the death

of your own family, didn't you, Jancic. He ordered the destruction of the village where you grew up and lived before the war. You carried out the order. You killed hundreds of innocent men, women and children, and thought nothing of it. You thought your own family were safe. He told you they were, didn't he? But they weren't. You found them in the rubble of your own home, killed by the shelling you yourself ordered.'

Durakovic and Jancic stared at each other, unable to hide from the truth both had known and suppressed deep inside. Their bonds of comradeship and friendship, held for so long, unravelled and snapped in the silence. Durakovic raised his gun and fired.

Jancic sat, his expression frozen in shock as blood poured from the hole in his chest and his eyes slowly closed. He was dead.

Footsteps thundered back through the house as the guards came running to the sound of shot.

Daniel sat passively in his seat. He had taken the gamble and played his last card. All he could do was wait.

'How did you know?' Durakovic asked.

'I didn't – not for sure. I had an assortment of facts and a theory. I just put them on the table; Jancic did the rest. You can't escape the truth if you're guilty.'

Durakovic nodded mournfully.

'You're obviously a gambling man, Mr–?'

'Temple,' Daniel answered. 'Sometimes, it depends on the odds,' he added.

'It's not over, Mr Temple. I could have you killed, right here, right now.'

The door burst open again as the guards ran into the room.

'Thank you, Damir. Please wait outside.'

'I'm listening,' Daniel replied as the door closed once more.

'I will give you a sporting chance to get what you came for, if you do something for me.'

'Go on.'

'The girls will be collected by Kozlov's men the day after tomorrow. They are to be taken by helicopter to Kozlov's retreat in St Petersburg. It's a long journey – twelve hours flying time. I will let you go, right now, if you agree to my proposal. You will have a considerable head start. You can get to Kozlov before they arrive. If you can kill Kozlov, free the girls and escape, you have my word that this is over. You will never see or hear from me again. Colonel Mead and his family will be safe.'

'Is that what you asked Richard to do? Is that why you took his daughters, to get his cooperation?'

'In a manner of speaking, but unfortunately Colonel Mead was not up to the task. He still has the speed of thought, but not of body. He's not a well man, but then of course you know that, don't you?'

Daniel ignored the question. He didn't know, but for now, it was immaterial. 'And if I don't agree?' he asked.

'Then you will die. The girls will be Kozlov's to do with as he pleases. Colonel Mead will live in hell – he's going there anyway, and I will still get what I want eventually. Do we have a deal?'

'How do I know you'll keep your word?'

'You don't, Mr Temple. That's just part of the gamble,' Durakovic smiled.

Daniel sat for a moment. There was no choice.

'We have a deal,' he said.

'Damir,' Durakovic shouted. The door opened and the guards stepped back into the room.

'My guest is leaving. Please escort him to the door.'

Daniel stood and walked away without another word.

'Goodbye, Mr Temple,' said Durakovic with chilling finality.

Daniel walked out of the house escorted by Damir, several guards and the snarling Rottweilers. He strode out across the gravel drive, ducked into the trees and began to run. The clock was ticking. The race was on.

TWELVE

Sergei Kozlov looked at the man kneeling before him through black, dispassionate eyes. The man did not dare look up. He had failed his assignment – failed badly – and he knew the consequences. He stared at the floor, flanked by two of Kozlov's security guards.

'Look at me, Pavel,' Kozlov demanded.

Pavel looked up slowly, timidly meeting his master's gaze.

Kozlov's eyes stared back, lifeless, like a shark's, black and unfeeling, yet full of menace.

Pavel's eyes were bloodshot. The eyes of a weak and feeble man, made all the worse for the abject fear they now reflected.

Kozlov placed his left hand on Pavel's head. He was a bull of man; strong and powerful, with huge, rounded shoulders atop a solid body, as broad as it was long. Yet, it was an unusually gentle, almost fatherly touch. A deceiving touch. He half smiled, gazing down at his trembling servant.

'It was a simple task, was it not, Pavel?' he asked.

His voice, quiet and level, carried a sinister, thinly-veiled threat of violence and retribution.

Pavel nodded, his hair brushing against Kozlov's hand.

'Yes, Sir,' he answered in a voice rising barely above a whisper.

Kozlov's calm demeanour changed in an instant, erupting like a breaking storm. He moved swiftly, grabbed a fistful of hair and yanked violently, forcing Pavel's head up and back.

Pavel gasped in pain, breathing hard.

'Please, Sergei,' he begged. 'I will not fail you again.'

Kozlov looked down at him with distain. Pavel had already failed him more than once. He was a weak man of sadly little intelligence. He wouldn't be missed; not by his ugly wife or the skinny little waifs they had somehow managed to spawn, and certainly not by Kozlov.

'I know,' Kozlov stated.

The two short words had a resounding, bone-chilling, echo of permanence about them. Kozlov's right hand bunched into a tight, bowling ball of a fist. Without warning, it slammed into Pavel's face. His nose smashed with a sickening crack and blood gushed down his face. Kozlov's breath quickened, his mind seized by wild, demonic retribution. He gripped Pavel's hair tightly and pulled it harder as his fist hammered remorselessly into the diminutive man's face. Again and again it smashed into its unconscious target. Pavel's face shattered and contorted until he was unrecognisable; savagely bludgeoned to a bloody pulp. Kozlov released his grip and let Pavel's limp body drop to the floor. Kozlov looked up, smiled like the devil and drove his heel into the dead man's skull.

A security guard stepped forward and handed Kozlov a small towel.

'Take him away. Dispose of him,' Kozlov ordered, wiping his hands of blood.

The two men nodded and dragged Pavel's pitiful body away.

Kozlov looked down at his blood spattered suit and shoes. His murderous fervour abated and he frowned, dabbing at the crimson spots as he left the room.

Kozlov changed every item of clothing then placed the towel and blood-stained garments in a bag. After showering and dressing in fresh clothes, he walked down to the basement and threw the bag into the incinerator.

*

Daniel made it to the airport a little after 6:00am. It would be a long wait; the return flight to Moscow didn't depart until almost 4:00pm. Stopping at the first small coffee shop he came to, he ordered breakfast and ate, thinking carefully, planning ahead, reconfirming his actions and mulling over Durakovic's words.

He ordered more coffee, sat back and watched the usual array of airport activity. The clock ticked slowly round.

11:00 am. Daniel trawled through the airport and found a bank of payphones. He dialled the number and waited as the reverse charges were accepted and his call was connected via the operator.

'Shaw,' the distant voice stated through the faint background hiss.

'John, it's Dan. I'm glad you're in early.'

'Dan. Where the hell are you? What's happening?'

'I found them, still with Durakovic – at least until tomorrow. I need to know everything you can tell me about this castle Kozlov lives in.'

'You're going in, then?'

'Yes, there's no time to explain – no questions, just tell me what you know.'

Daniel listened as John Shaw tapped on his keyboard.

'OK, Dan, here we go. You listening?'

'All ears. Fire away.'

John spoke for thirty minutes. Daniel listened and absorbed the information.

'You got all that?' John asked as he finished describing every detail he had.

'I've got it.'

'Good, now tell me what's happening.'

'For what it's worth, you were right. Richard has been caught up in something – I was expected.'

'So does Durakovic know you're going to Kozlov?'

'*Know!* He's sending me.'

'I don't get it. What do you mean, he's sending you?'

'That's the deal. To get the girls back, I have to kill Kozlov.'

'And then what?'

'The girls are being sent to Kozlov. If I can kill Kozlov and get the girls out, Durakovic will consider the deal done.'

'What deal?'

'The deal he had with Richard, I guess.'

'You don't honestly believe that, do you?'

'No.'

'For Christ's sake, Dan, be careful. What if Kozlov knows you're coming too?'

'Too late for that. I've gotta go. Talk soon.

Thanks, John. Sorry about the phone bill,' Daniel said, hanging up the phone.

*

John Shaw replaced his handset and continued to stare at the phone in disbelief.

'Pig headed, stubborn, son of a bitch. For Christ's sake, be careful,' he whispered to himself.

He picked up the telephone again, dialled the number and waited.

*

Daniel's flight touched down in Moscow at 9:20pm. He spent thirty minutes queuing in yet another line, cleared the Russian citizen immigration, then raced through to the first floor of the main terminal. Finding the lockers he grabbed his bag, ran to the bus stop, reversed his journey back into the city, heading for the Leningradsky railway station and the overnight train to St Petersburg.

Daniel ran through the sparsely populated station, stopping briefly to snatch sandwiches, chocolate and coffee.

Boarding the train, he found his small, two-berth compartment and dumped his bag on one of the beds. He kicked off his boots, laid out on the other bunk and ate his sandwiches between gulps of the surprisingly good coffee. He finished his meal by eating half of the large bar of dark chocolate, placed the remainder in his pocket and mentally reviewed the next stage of his plan.

John Shaw had provided as much information as he could about Kozlov's retreat. The castle was more like a fortress. Set high on a rocky outcrop, several miles north of St Petersburg, it was remote, secluded and surrounded by dense woodland. Getting there unseen was going to be the easy part. Thereafter, things would get increasingly tougher. Avoiding the defences and entering the castle, manageable. Being accepted into the fold, tricky. Finding the girls and getting out, just plain bloody difficult.

Daniel mulled the defences over in his mind. Kozlov had obviously decided the disadvantages of numerous hidden approaches were outweighed by the location and difficult terrain his surroundings offered. Therefore, Kozlov had focussed on creating a highly effective, invisible, automated electronic perimeter.

There would be a combination of intrusion detection systems that worked day and night. Cameras, heat sensors, wireless motion sensors, pressure detectors, pads, infrared beams and flood lights; all were designed to work individually and in unison and were incredibly difficult to beat. Daniel thought through the approach. He could move at speed, unconcerned about noise for most of the way in. The first line of defence would be situated no further than fifteen hundred feet out, pretty much maximum distance for any of the systems likely deployed. History and experience had taught him that often the simplest of approaches can overcome the most complicated of obstacles. His plan was therefore simple but, he hoped, effective. The defences were designed to primarily combat multiple hostiles. One man, with a little skill, guile and luck, could infiltrate them. Daniel knew others had tried and failed. They had made the mistake of trying to be too clever. He was not going to beat the system, but the human interpretation of it. The system would beat itself. There was nothing more he could do. He settled back, closed his eyes and rested.

Daniel rose, refreshed and alert as the attendant walked through the carriage, knocking on doors, announcing the stop a few minutes before the train rolled into St Petersburg's Moskovsky station. It was just after 9:00am. He had time to kill.

Daniel left the station and walked out on to the broad avenue of Nevsky Prospect. Finding a cheap hotel, he paid the day rate in cash and climbed the narrow, creaking stairs to the top floor. His room was small and bare, containing nothing more than an old, iron-framed bed, a single bedside cabinet and a rickety wooden desk which leant at an awkward angle toward the wall. There were two narrow doors set into the left hand wall. The floor creaked loudly beneath the thin, threadbare carpet as he walked across and opened them. The first was a shallow, empty closet. The other lead into an equally compact bathroom. A shower head hung over a half-bath and the water dripped from the tap at a constant, irritating rate.

Daniel closed the door, turned and stalked round the room, the knot tightening in his stomach, every nerve on edge. Still twelve hours to go.

He stripped out of his clothes, walked back in to the bathroom, turned on the shower and let the water run hot, filling the small room with steam. He showered, standing under the splattering water, deep in thought. He'd met Durakovic and seen Jancic die. He had confirmed and learnt some disturbing facts about Richard Mead and, most importantly, he had found the girls, come out alive and had his Russian passport stamped. So far, so good. Phase one complete. He was ready to move on.

Daniel left the hotel, bought a map of the city and wandered down the avenue to a small restaurant. Following the basic soldiers rule – eat wherever and whenever you can – he ordered a large meal, maintaining his calorie intake and energy levels. He ate slowly and studied the map intently, committing every street, side road and alley to memory.

Leaving the restaurant, he began to walk, taking a crash course in St Petersburg navigation. He walked slowly, taking in the main streets, avenues and thoroughfares. Then he strolled the side streets, confirming and noting every alleyway and cut-through. Finally, he walked a full circuit, then did it all again, circumventing the city, east to west, then again, north to south.

The short winter day started to draw to an end as the pale afternoon sun faded into an even shorter twilight and another freezing night.

Daniel returned to the hotel room and sat on the sagging bed. He stared at the map, closed his eyes, ran a route in his mind, then opened his eyes and checked it. He repeated the exercise over and over until his brain could process no more and he slept.

Daniel woke. The brief nap had re-energised his mind and body. Quickly, he dressed in his black fatigues and winter coat, left his room, descended the stairs and stepped into the freezing night air.

The night was dark and the sky thick with cloud. The air was bitterly cold and a biting wind blew out of the north, sending light flakes of snow flurrying and swirling on the freezing gusts. Daniel fastened his coat, turned up the collar and pulled his woollen hat low over his ears. He walked briskly. Using the road signs and mental map, he set his direction and followed the road to north to Sestroretsk.

THIRTEEN

St Petersburg was dark, its appearance and atmosphere growing more sinister and intimidating the further away from its centre Daniel travelled. The city had declined over the years, decaying steadily from its sophisticated heyday, before the fall of the old Soviet Union. Now, away from the tourist centre, it was a more wild and dangerous place; notorious for gang fights, neo-Nazi factions, mafia territorial wars and a spiralling crime rate. Daniel marched through the narrow back streets, alert and aware of his surroundings. Cutting through an alley, he turned into a busy, gang-controlled thoroughfare as shouts and screams filled the air.

Suddenly, a blood-spattered man crashed out of a door, sprawling headfirst onto the cobbled street. He was rapidly followed by a dozen other men spilling out of a back street bar; fists, feet and bottles flying in all directions.

Daniel calmly assessed the melee.

A large, skin-headed man with swastika tattoos covering his bare, heavily muscled arms span out from the mass brawl with no one left to fight. He turned, angrily fixing his eyes on Daniel.

Daniel moved to side-step the scrapping throng.

The guy stepped with him.

Daniel noted the movement. The guy was sizing him up.

The guy walked forward, a broken bottle in hand.

Daniel wasn't in the mood to fuck around; he had no time to dance with the locals.

They closed together.

The guy stopped and stood square on, throwing down his challenge.

Daniel closed, two more paces, then quickly and deliberately stepped in and, in one fluid movement snapped his head forward. The head butt crunched into the guy's face, his knees buckled and he dropped like a building being demolished. Daniel strode on, his hands still in his pockets.

Daniel marched on, passing through streets of ageing, tired and decrepit concrete tower blocks which in turn gave way to towering factory chimneys and rows of low-rise industrial units. Daniel moved further toward the edge of the city, passing by a long, windowless, single-storey building. The noise of heavy machinery and men working the night shift droned through its walls. The building was surrounded by high metal railings; iron that had long since lost its covering of paint now sat rusting in perfect harmony with the rest of the old, decaying buildings in this part of town.

Daniel slowed as he approached the main gates of the factory. They were open and unmanned. He glanced left. There was a broad expanse of crumbling tarmac and a few sparsely parked cars which had all seen better days. His eyes swept right, closer to the building, to where a long bicycle shed stood, crammed full.

Daniel stopped and looked around. There was no one in sight. He moved swiftly through the gates, keeping away from the dimly-lit security lights that shone weakly over the open area of tarmac. He walked along the rows of bicycles, selected the largest unlocked cycle he could find, pulled it from the tangled rack, and throwing his leg over the frame, cycled casually out of the gates.

With his new-found transport, Daniel made faster progress. He peddled hard, whisking through the last remnants of the city outskirts. The freezing wind bit into his face, making his eyes stream with water. He pulled the balaclava down and cycled on, his long, muscular legs pumping the pedals round like engine pistons, covering the remaining distance in rapid time.

Seven miles out of town, he reached a turning which led off of the main road and onto a narrow gravel track. Daniel stopped, moved cautiously up the track a few hundred yards, then abandoned the bicycle, pushing it into a clump of thick bushes.

The trees closed in around him as he set off through the forest. What light there had been faded to pitch black and the terrain became rough and hard going as the ground undulated beneath his feet. Sudden rises, steep drops and large rocks appeared unannounced. Slipping and stumbling, his pace slowed to a crawl as he made his way almost blindly through the dense, frozen forest.

Daniel stooped regularly as he walked, collecting the larger, heavier fir cones and small rocks from the forest floor and stuffing them into the top of his duffle bag.

A dim light emanating through the trees told Daniel that he was getting close. He slowed his pace, taking one cautious step at a time, carefully gauging his distance. Then he stopped and carefully looked around. Everything appeared to be just as it should be. There were no visible beams, no wires, no antenna – nothing. His caution grew. The sensors were there, waiting for the unsuspecting or unguarded approach. It was time to put his plan into action. He looked at the trees, selected a place to start and stepped forward, confident that he was not yet inside the perimeter defence systems. Selecting a suitable tree, he grabbed the first branch and began to climb.

Daniel climbed easily. The forest was old and unmanaged; a multitude of pine and fir stood in close proximity, their branches overlapping and forming a dense, tangled framework of wooden limbs. Twenty feet off the ground, he began to use the largest branches to move horizontally, well above the forest floor, closer and closer to the forest edge.

The castle stood isolated, black and ominous, staring down over the treeline which surrounded it. Daniel stopped and stared through the gloom. A few yards ahead, the trees gave way to open ground which rose steadily toward the rocky plinth, where the castle walls rose, dark and foreboding.

In the dim external lighting, Daniel could see guards patrolling, walking slow, constant circuits of the open ground. Another guard remained at what appeared to be the main entrance, located left of centre, directly facing him.

Daniel watched and timed the guards route; three minutes for a full circuit. He looked to his right. The grounds were dark. He looked up at the guards, then back to the right. There was a blind spot. He timed their circuit again. The blind spot was easily reachable in the time window from when the guards started their circuit to when they reached the point where they might see his approach. He climbed down, dropped silently to the forest floor, ran around the tree in a wide arc, then climbed again.

High in the tree, Daniel watched. The guard at the main door lifted his radio, listened, then looked directly across to where Daniel had been moving, just a few seconds earlier.

Nothing happened.

Daniel climbed down and repeated the process with the same result. They were already confused – so far, so good.

Daniel repeated the process for a third time, adding forward movement to gain another few yards.

The floodlights around the castle flared, splashing out a pool of brilliant white light which reflected and dazzled off the thin layer of snow that covered the expanse of open ground.

Daniel climbed higher, moulded his body tight against the trunk and watched the guards. Three men converged at the front of the house and joined the other at the main door. Two of the men remained by the door, whilst the other two drew their weapons and walked slowly across the open ground toward the trees.

Daniel watched them all the way. They were hesitant, puzzled and cautious. The alarm system was working, but not in the way they would expect; not in a way they would have experienced before. They edged forward into the trees, one in front of the other, struggling to adjust their vision from the bright floodlights to the darkness of the forest. Daniel watched as they passed directly beneath him, moving further into the darkness, until they stopped exactly where Daniel had triggered the first pressure pad and inspected the ground by torchlight. Concentrating on the immediate area, the men swept left and right, forward and back in a typical two-dimensional search pattern, nervously peering through the trees. No one was there – no tracks, no movement; a false alarm.

The two men shrugged and began to walk back to the castle.

Behind them, Daniel dropped silently to the ground and walked stealthily in their tracks, his movement masked by theirs. He stopped at the tree line, climbed and waited.

A moment later the floodlights went out, returning the castle to its black and sinister appearance.

Daniel paused, waited for the guards to resume their normal routine, then moved cautiously along the outer line of trees, working around to his right. He stopped directly in line with the blind spot he had noted earlier, then climbed high into a tree.

Settled on a thick branch, Daniel began to throw the heavy fir cones, rocks and small broken logs he had collected in all directions. The fir cones were not dry and brittle, but full of frozen moisture and weighty. They carried far as Daniel launched them with hefty sweeps of his thickly muscled arm. Sensor after sensor tripped as the cones, rocks and small logs thumped into the castle walls and landed in the open ground from all sorts of unexpected angles.

The castle's floodlights flared back on, once more bathing the grounds in brilliant white light. Heavily armed men ran out of the house and moved forward in unison to meet the incoming assault.

There was nothing.

Daniel watched them come, his black swathed body wrapped around the trunk of the tree, and became almost completely invisible. He waited – everything was working to plan.

Guards searched and patrolled, covering the grounds and castle perimeter.

Daniel waited.

Directly beneath him, a guard stopped and leant against his tree. Daniel stared down as the guard lit a cigarette. Daniel shook his head – amateur, he thought, watching the small spot of bright orange glow in the dark.

The guard's radio hissed. He lifted it and listened as a monochrome voice ordered everyone back to the castle; it was a false alarm, a system malfunction. The man stepped away from the tree and walked back across the grounds.

Daniel smiled.

He waited fifteen minutes. The castle fell dark and quiet. Fir cones, rocks and small logs rained down once more. The floodlights flashed on. Daniel melted against the tree as the guards poured out of the door, swept through the grounds and found nothing.

*

Sergei Kozlov stormed into the security control room, barely containing his rage.

'What the hell is going on?' he roared.

'It, it must be a malfunction or something. There is nothing out there,' Kozlov's Head of Security assured him, in a nervous, hesitant fashion.

Kozlov looked at him, then at the flashing flights on the control panel, and grunted.

'Fix it,' he demanded gruffly, sweeping back out of the room.

The Head of Security looked at the two other men in the room.

'Get everyone inside. Reset the system,' he ordered.

'Yes, Oleg,' the men confirmed.

Radios buzzed and hissed all over the grounds. The men responded affirmatively, made their way back to the main entrance and disappeared through the doors.

*

Daniel climbed down from the tree, waited for the floodlights to go out, then plunged out of the trees and sprinted across the open ground. Thumping his back against the castle wall Daniel, dropped to his knees, deep in the shadows, and looked along the wall. To his left, a thick, black iron pipe rose from the ground and up to the roof guttering. He followed it up to where, thirty feet above his head, a broad stone balcony jutted into the air.

Daniel moved forward, took hold of the pipe and pulled hard. It was solid. He took a firm grip well above his head, placed his feet against the rough stone and began to climb, hand over hand, the strength in his arms and powerful shoulders hauling his body up the wall. Reaching the top, he slid over the wall and dropped quietly onto the balcony floor.

The balcony was broad, deep and empty. A pair of wide, patio-style doors sat in its centre. The doors, slightly ajar, opened into a room from which a dull light emanated. The partially drawn curtains, fluttered slightly in the icy breeze. Daniel kept his back against the balcony wall and inched forward. Peering through the gap in the curtains, he could see it was a bedroom – Kozlov's bedroom.

To Daniel's left, Sergei Kozlov sat at his desk, with

his back to the patio doors. He was concentrating hard, oblivious to Daniel's presence, reading documents under the light of a single desk lamp which gave the room a soft, warm glow.

Daniel took a breath, drew his knife and prepared to enter the room. There was a knock at the door. Daniel held back.

'Enter,' Kozlov permitted, looking up to his right as the door opened and a small, sandy-haired man entered the room.

Daniel watched and listened.

'Excuse me, Mr Kozlov, I thought you would like to know that all of the security systems have been reset.'

'Very well, thank you, Oleg,' Kozlov nodded curtly.

The small man turned and left, closing the door behind him. Kozlov returned to his papers.

Daniel prepared to move.

As if struck by another thought, Kozlov suddenly stood, strode across the room and disappeared through the door.

Daniel took his chance, opened the patio doors, slipped inside and crossed to where the recess for the interior door protruded several feet into the room. The short walls provided the perfect place to stand unseen.

Not a moment too soon, Daniel stood to the right and pressed his back hard against the wall. The door swung open, doubled all the way back on its hinges, bumped against Daniel's chest, then bounced gently away.

Kozlov slammed his bedroom door closed with a backward sweep of his arm and stomped back across to his desk, deeply irritated by whatever conversation he had just had.

Daniel breathed out in silent relief and waited a moment.

Kozlov settled back to his work.

Daniel crept forward and peered with one eye around the wall. Kozlov was back in deep concentration, his back to the room. Daniel looked at the desk. There were no reflective surfaces. He checked the wooden floor. It looked solid enough and the thick rug would deaden his footsteps. Daniel drew his knife, stepped silently from behind the wall and crossed the bedroom floor. The razor-sharp blade slid under Kozlov's chin, gently grazing against his throat. Daniel stood directly behind.

'Don't move or make a sound,' he said in perfect Russian.

Kozlov froze in his chair.

'Place your hands in front of you, flat on the desk, palms facing up,' Daniel instructed.

Kozlov remained calm and did as instructed.

Daniel unzipped his jacket, pulled the Makarov from his pocket, aimed at Kozlov's head and took two steps back. Carefully, he reached for the door, felt for the key, locked it, then pulled the balaclava from his head.

Kozlov turned slightly in his chair, looking at Daniel sideways.

'Turn around,' Daniel invited, obliging him.

Kozlov turned to face Daniel.

'Bravo,' he said. 'The security system, I assume that was you?'

'Not difficult when you think about it,' Daniel replied.

'Maybe,' Kozlov shrugged. 'Many have tried before. None have succeeded.'

'Maybe they were the wrong people.'

'Maybe they were.'

'You're here to kill me?' Kozlov stated and asked simultaneously.

'Yes and no,' Daniel answered.

Kozlov raised an eyebrow.

'Either way, you're a dead man,' he stated calmly.

'Maybe. Maybe not,' Daniel responded, completely unperturbed by Kozlov's threat.

Kozlov stared at Daniel with black, menacing eyes, his anger obviously boiling beneath their dark surface.

Daniel stared back, emotionless. His piercing blue-green eyes, cold and unwavering, locked on Kozlov's.

Their gaze held for a moment.

Kozlov swallowed involuntarily as a shiver ran run down his spine and he looked away.

'You won't get out alive. You're a dead man,' he stated again, with slightly less conviction.

'So you said,' acknowledged Daniel. 'But maybe I don't want to kill you.'

Kozlov looked confused.

'Meaning?' he asked.

'Meaning I do you a favour, you do me one.'

There was silence for a moment.

Kozlov hesitated then spoke.

'Go on,' he said.

'OK, let's say I was sent here to kill you. Sent by someone you know. But now I'm here, I've changed my mind. I can see alternatives.'

Kozlov paused again.

'Three questions,' he stated. 'If I like the answers, you live. Fair enough?'

'I'm the one holding a gun and a knife. I got in easily enough, I can get out again,' Daniel replied. 'What are the questions?'

'Who sent you?'

'Zoran Durakovic,' Daniel answered.

There was just the slightest flicker of reaction in Kozlov's face.

'Why have you changed your mind?'

'You're Russian. I'm Russian. Durakovic is what? Serbian, Bosnian, Croat, Slovak? I don't know what he is. I don't like him,' Daniel replied. 'You're also an important man. The head man. The chief. I could work for someone like you,' he added.

Kozlov smiled.

'Your loyalty to mother Russia and a compatriot is commendable. You were a solider once upon a time?'

'I was a soldier. A good one, up until six months ago; but things happened, they threw me out.'

'Why would I want someone like you to work for me?'

'Why wouldn't you want me? I got in here. I got past all of your security. I could show you how. I'm a good soldier. I can take orders. I can make things happen. I could make things better for you. I could kill Durakovic.'

Daniel let the last statement hang in the air.

'Who are you? What's your name?'

'Just an old soldier looking for a new cause and some money. My name is Danil, Danil Kuznetsov.'

Kozlov looked like he was thinking again.

'So what do we do now?'

Daniel assessed, made his decision and took the gamble.

'I trust you. You are a man of honour,' he said, almost choking on the words. He placed the gun and knife on Kozlov's desk and stood back.

'What do I tell my men?'

'Be angry – put them on the back foot. Say you arranged for my visit to test your security and it's not very good. Tell them I am being added to your staff,' Daniel explained respectfully, cleverly and subtly turning the tables, putting Kozlov in charge.

Kozlov reached forward, placed his hands on the gun and knife and pushed them back across the desk.

'Take them. You're a brave and resourceful man,' he said.

He stood, brushed past Daniel and opened the bedroom door.

'Come,' he said.

Two enormous security guards stood to attention as the door opened. Kozlov stared at them. The two guards stared at each other, then at Daniel, then back to Kozlov. Kozlov just shook his head and gestured for them to sit.

Daniel followed Kozlov out of the room and along the broad upstairs landing. They descended the massive wooden staircase, crossed the cavernous ground floor entrance hall, continued down a long corridor and entered a large square room. Three men turned in their seats and stared in surprise as Kozlov entered, followed by Daniel. Kozlov glared at the small sandy-haired man Daniel had seen in earlier in Kozlov's bedroom.

'So, Oleg, there's nothing out there?' he questioned, in a growl.

Oleg looked confused. His eyes moved from Kozlov to Daniel, then back to Kozlov.

'No, Sir,' he replied with complete uncertainty.

Kozlov stepped forward and slapped Oleg hard across the face.

'Yes, Oleg, there was. This man was out there,' he bellowed. 'Luckily he was there because I asked him to be. He beat all of the defences, crossed the grounds, climbed the walls and entered my room,' he continued shouting. 'My room,' he roared, emphasising his point. 'He could have killed me,' he raged, angrily slapping Oleg around the head again.

Oleg stared at the floor.

'I, I, I,' he stuttered feebly.

'Stop,' Kozlov commanded. 'Not another word. This is Danil Kuznetsov. He is now on my staff. He reports to me and me alone. Show him the security systems and he will show you how he beat them. Then I want every system changed so that it cannot be done again. Is that clear?'

Daniel smiled to himself and turned to Kozlov.

'It's late. It's been a very busy night. Perhaps it would be better for everyone if we started our review in the morning?' he suggested.

Kozlov's mood calmed slightly and he nodded in agreement.

'Very well,' he conceded, turning back to Oleg. 'Introduce Danil to Taras and find him a room.'

He looked at Daniel. 'Taras is my commander here. He will take care of whatever you need. We will speak again tomorrow.'

With that, Kozlov turned and left.

Daniel looked down at Oleg. The slightly-built man was hurt and confused and his face glowed red from a combination of stress, embarrassment and the heavy slaps from Kozlov. Daniel held out his hand.

'Danil Kuznetsov,' he smiled, introducing himself. 'I am sorry Mr Kozlov reacted that way,' he said, trying to start out on artificially good terms.

Oleg rubbed his face and looked at Daniel.

'It's not your fault. You obviously had a job to do,' he replied in an indifferent tone.

Oleg stood. He was a diminutive man, much shorter than Daniel; the top of his head barely reached Daniel's shoulder.

'Come, I will take you to Taras.'

Oleg led Daniel out of the room, back across the wide open space of the entrance hall and up the staircase. At the top of the second flight of stairs, they turned right, walked down the landing and turned right again, following the corridor past several doors. Oleg stopped at the fourth door on the right, knocked twice and waited respectfully. There was a short delay. Daniel could hear the sound of voices coming from the room – a man and a woman, followed by the sounds of a hand slapping against flesh. He heard the key turn in the lock and the door swung slowly open. A man's face, angry and flushed, greeted them.

'What is it?' the man demanded.

Oleg stepped back slightly, gesturing for Daniel to come forward.

'Taras, this is Danil Kuznetsov. Mr Kozlov has just recruited him. He said I should bring him to you to arrange a room and whatever else he needs,' Oleg explained.

Taras glanced back over his shoulder, then stepped out of the room, leaving the door slightly ajar. Daniel moved a little closer, close enough to look over Taras's shoulder. A young girl lay naked on the bed, her pretty, tear-stained face red and bruised. Daniel looked back at Taras. He was a reasonably large man, maybe six feet tall, broad and muscular. His hair was black, clipped very short and his face was hard and angular. An angry scar ran horizontally across the full width of his upper right cheek, a quarter of an inch below his eye. He appraised Daniel through cold, crystal-blue eyes.

'What was your name again?' he asked, obviously still annoyed that his time with the girl had been disturbed.

'Kuznetsov,' Daniel replied, not bothering to hold out his hand. Taras didn't seem the type to shake it.

'And what are you, Kuznetsov? Why would Mr

Kozlov want to employ a man such as you?' he asked, looking Daniel up and down with disdain.

'I am what Mr Kozlov wants me to be. He employs me because I am very good at what I do,' Daniel answered without answering.

Taras looked at him for a moment, still weighing him up, still pondering Daniel's answer. He half-smiled but didn't ask any further questions.

'Come, I will show you to a room,' he offered.

He led Daniel back to the staircase, up another flight and back down the right hand corridor. They stopped at the fourth door. Taras turned the handle and pushed it open.

'This one will do,' he said, showing Daniel inside.

The bedroom was a good size, approximately fifteen feet square. Inside, there was a sturdy-looking double bed, already made up with clean white sheets and thick, rough woollen blankets. A double wardrobe stood against the right-hand wall and a comfortable-looking chair sat beneath the window set into the far wall.

'This room's directly above mine. There's a bathroom over there. You should be able to find soap and whatever else you need in the cabinet. If there's anything missing, we can sort that out in the morning. Now it's late and I have a girl to fuck,' he stated without humour, turning to leave.

'Are there many girls here?' Daniel asked.

'Why? You want one?'

'No, not yet, later maybe.'

'Girls come, girls go. Take whichever one you want when they're here –except for the ones Kozlov chooses for himself. They have to be exclusive, although they don't last long. He's an animal– likes it rough, likes to force them, likes them to fight.'

'What happens to them afterward?'

'You ask a lot of questions, Kuznetsov.'

'Just curious, that's all. It's no big deal if you don't want to tell me. It's not my business.'

Taras sighed, then answered the question.

'It's pretty straightforward. We bring in the young, fresh girls – only the prettiest ones. We do what we like with them for a few weeks, then when we're done we move them on and sell them. There are always girls here. Like I said, take whichever ones you want, fuck them, do whatever you like to them. It's one of the perks.'

'You sell them?'

'Yeah, we sell them. You sound shocked. What are you, some sort of fucking boy scout?'

'No, just curious. Like I said, I like to know what sort of business I'm working in.'

'It's a very diverse business. A very big business – global, in fact. Mr Kozlov is a very important and very powerful man.'

'I'm sure he is,' Daniel confirmed, deciding not

to ask any further questions. The answers would come soon enough.

Taras left Daniel alone in the room. Daniel took off his coat and boots and lay down on the bed. The mattress was hard but comfortable. He was tired. He closed his eyes and readily drifted into a light sleep. He was in.

*

Daniel was woken by a combination of loud voices, men moving through the grounds below his window and the pale morning sun which now shone through the open curtains of his room.

He sat up and checked his watch. It was 9:00am – time to get started. He quickly showered and shaved, then returned to the security room to find Oleg. There was a loud discussion taking place just the other side of the security room door as Daniel approached. He stopped and listened carefully. An argument raged. Kozlov, Taras and Oleg were in loud debate, their voices easily carrying into the empty corridor.

'Sergei, you don't know who this guy is. He could be anyone. It's a massive risk to our security,' Taras said.

'Security!' Kozlov exclaimed angrily. 'He waltzed straight through the so-called security. He could have killed me, but he didn't. The least we should do is let him show us how he got in.'

'So who sent him? Who would dare send someone against you?'

'Durakovic,' Kozlov replied. 'I should never have trusted that bastard. I knew he was up to something.'

'Durakovic?' Taras questioned. How do you know that?

'He – Kuznetsov – told me.'

Taras frowned.

'It's possible I suppose, but why would Durakovic also tell you he was sending you a gift? Why would he send you the four girls? Why go to the trouble? Answer me that,' he retorted.

'You know why. It's self-serving, isn't it. He plays me, gets me to lower my guard a little – to accept him, to trust him. He kids me along with gifts of women. He knows the sort I like. I also know he wants to punish the English Colonel, the one he blames for killing his wife and kid. He's a bitter man. Two of the girls are the Colonel's daughters; Durakovic wants them to suffer. I have no problem with that; they'll be just like all the rest. We'll use them for a while, then sell them on. Anyway, why would Kuznetsov tell me it was Durakovic? How else would he know the name? What does he have to gain from it?'

Taras considered the questions and the implications for a moment.

'I don't know, Sergei. I just know I don't trust him – not yet. None of us should.'

Kozlov stared into space.

'There was something in his eyes,' he whispered to himself then stated. 'I believe him. There may be more to him than we can see, but I believe him about Durakovic.'

'OK, let's say it was Durakovic. Why now? He has far too much to lose. He can't possibly win. Even if he did manage to kill you, what purpose would it serve? He could never take over – it wouldn't be allowed. He runs a sideshow, nothing more. He would be dead within twenty-four hours; Radimov in Moscow would see to that. He must know what would happen – it just doesn't make sense. We need to check this Kuznetsov guy out before we let him any further into the operation.'

'I don't know why now,' admitted Kozlov. 'Durakovic only exists because I permit him to – he certainly knows that. I also know he doesn't like it. He's ambitious, has ideas above his station – still calls himself commander. But you're right; there is probably more to this than I can see right now. There is something about Kuznetsov, though; something in his eyes. He's a hard man and he's here for a reason.'

'Listen to me, Sergei. Kuznetsov may prove to be someone we want, but let's not be rash or hasty. A few days, maybe a week; we'll find out what we need to know, OK?' Taras advised.

'I agree with Taras, Mr Kozlov. I will get him to show me how he breached the security and get it fixed. But Taras is right, we should not let him do anything else until we check him out,' added Oleg.

Kozlov stood, quietly considering their advice. Taras especially had been with him for a long time. He trusted his guidance and listened to his counsel.

'Very well, Oleg, you work with Kuznetsov. Have him show you how he got in and how to improve our security. Taras, see what you can find out about him. If he's genuine, we could use him. If he's not, kill him. And Taras – I want Durakovic dead.'

Taras and Oleg nodded.

'Agreed,' they said.

Daniel listened carefully. Good, that's it – doubt and uncertainty, he thought. He crept back down to the end of corridor, turned, then walked back toward the security room, ensuring that his footsteps were loud and heavy. He reached the door, knocked once and walked in.

The three men turned and watched him enter.

'Good morning,' Daniel said in a business-like fashion, nodding to each man in turn.

He stood and waited, deliberately putting the onus on Kozlov to speak.

'Oleg will work with you this morning. When

you have finished, find Taras. Come and see me this afternoon,' Kozlov instructed curtly, staring hard at Daniel.

Daniel nodded his agreement.

'Yes, Sir,' he answered respectfully.

Kozlov marched out of the room followed by Taras.

'2:00pm – come and find me,' Taras ordered abruptly.

'2:00pm,' Daniel confirmed without another word.

The door slammed shut.

Daniel turned to Oleg and smiled.

'Where would you like to begin?' he asked cheerfully.

Oleg stared back at him for a moment, obviously trying to assess him. Clearly failing to do so, the diminutive man blinked and shrugged.

'Start at the beginning. Tell me how you got in? Explain how you knew about the systems we deployed, and how you overcame them.'

'Let's go outside. I'll explain as we walk,' Daniel replied.

'Outside? Why?' Oleg asked.

'It will be easier to show you as I explain, plus I need to get my gear.'

'Your gear?' Oleg asked in obvious surprise.

'Yes, I left it in a tree last night,' explained Daniel,

confidently leading Oleg out of the door.

They walked outside. The morning was crisp and bright and a pale, watery sun sat low in the pastel-blue eastern sky. Their breath frosted and floated away in the air like wisps of white smoke as they walked around the house and down the rocky plinth. Crossing the open ground, their feet crunched through the grass, stained white with thick frost and lightly dusted with fresh snow. Reaching the tree line, Daniel ducked under the branches, walked in a few yards and found the tree where he had hung his duffle bag in the branches the night before.

Oleg followed, looking on in disbelief.

Daniel smiled at him.

'How did you get this far before any of the sensors triggered?' Oleg asked.

'Simple. I didn't want them to trigger until I was ready.'

'That doesn't answer my question. You can't decide when the sensors trigger – they just do, it's how the system is designed. And they start much further out – as soon as someone breaks a beam or treads on a pressure sensor, they trigger. It's not a matter of choice,' Oleg stated categorically.

'It is, Oleg. Look around you. What do you see?' Daniel asked.

'Nothing. Why?' Oleg replied, confused by what seemed like a bizarre question.

'Look again. The answers are all around you.'

Oleg turned a full circle, looking in every direction.

'There are just trees. We did look here last night – we searched this exact spot. We searched all over the grounds – every place a sensor was triggered. You weren't here,' he stated with confidence.

Daniel smiled again.

'Imagine you're trying to find someone right now – imagine you're trying to find me, last night. Because I was, Oleg, I was right here.'

Oleg shook his head.

'I don't understand. You couldn't have been – we would have found you.'

He looked at Daniel's face, trying to find some giveaway sign that he was lying.

Daniel stared back, calm, rational and unblinking.

'Your search pattern was wrong, that's all,' Daniel replied.

'Our search pattern? We covered every inch of ground. You weren't here,' Oleg declared again with absolute certainty.

'Exactly,' Daniel replied.

'What do you mean, exactly?' Oleg asked in exasperation, glaring at Daniel in frustration at their cryptic conversation.

'You searched every inch of ground – a typical

two-dimensional search pattern. You looked left and right, forwards and backwards. I watched you do it,' Daniel replied, rolling his eyes upward.

The penny dropped.

'Oh my God, the trees. You used the trees?' Oleg stated and asked at the same time.

'Look how close they are – how big they are. Look how the branches overlap. It's simple – climb above the sensors before they start and bypass them – all of them. Look up Oleg. Anyone above a height of ten feet can't be seen. Not if they're dressed in black; not at night. You'd be lucky to find them with torches in daylight at this time of year.'

Oleg stared at Daniel, still dressed in his black fatigues and shook his head. 'Tell me more,' he said.

'OK, just a moment,' Daniel replied, climbing to retrieve his bag.

Slinging the duffle over his shoulder, he walked back to the edge of the trees.

'This way,' he instructed Oleg nonchalantly.

Oleg followed Daniel along the edge of the open ground until they were almost opposite the blind spot from where Daniel had approached the rear of the castle.

Daniel turned and faced the house, took two sideways steps, then turned to Oleg.

'Stand there.' Daniel pointed. 'Face the castle. What do you see?'

Oleg stood exactly where Daniel had been then turned and faced the house. He looked confused.

'I see the castle,' he said simply.

'Look at it from a security perspective – no, look at it from the perspective of someone who wants to beat the security – to get into the castle,' Daniel advised.

Oleg stood and thought. His eyes ran along the castle walls. Knowing where all the sensors were, he checked each one in turn, then looked across to his left, to the guard standing in front of the main door. His profile was almost side on to Oleg.

Daniel glanced at him. Oleg wasn't the sharpest tool in the box. He was thinking hard, desperately trying to get on to Daniel's wavelength. Daniel decided to help him a little more.

'Think about security at night. What's different to what you can see now?'

Oleg looked again. He looked at the house, the sensors and the guard at the door. What was different? he asked himself. The guard was different; there were always three at night. One at the doors and two patrolling the exterior.

'The guards are different,' he said, sounding pleased with himself.

'And?' Daniel prompted encouragingly.

Oleg sighed and looked again. He looked back up to the guard at the door, then looked at Daniel.

He raised his eyebrows slightly, shuffled a few feet to his right and looked again. Now he could see the balcony to Kozlov's bedroom, but could not the guard at the door. He frowned slightly. What did it mean? He considered it again. If he could not see the guard, the guard could not see him – there was a blind spot.

'There's a blind spot,' he stated. 'You approached from here,' he declared, evidently pleased at his deduction.

Daniel nodded.

Oleg stopped and looked puzzled again.

'None of the sensors triggered,' he said.

'You reset the system, didn't you?' Daniel replied. 'That took at least two minutes.'

Oleg looked up at the castle again and nodded. The puzzled look suddenly returned to his face. There were more questions to ask; more answers to be found.

'How did you get the system to malfunction?' he asked.

'I didn't. I made it work exactly as it was designed.'

Oleg frowned before the second penny dropped.

'It was us, wasn't it? You used me and my men to beat the system. We closed it down just as you wanted us to.'

'Bingo!' said Daniel.

'Tell me everything, please. If this happens again, Kozlov will have me killed, if he doesn't do it himself,' Oleg said, with genuine fear in his eyes.

Daniel saw his opportunity to make an ally and stepped closer to Oleg, placing a huge, friendly arm around his shoulder.

'Don't worry, Oleg. I'm here to help you. By the time I've finished, Mr Kozlov won't believe what's happened. I'm sure you'll get the reward you deserve,' he smiled.

FOURTEEN

The four girls sat huddled on the bed on the far left hand side of the room, talking quietly, their individual stories terrifyingly similar. Each had been abducted without warning, held and then transported to wherever it was they were now.

'There were ten of us brought here this morning from Ukraine. Yana and I are both from Kiev, but there are others from Odessa and Kirovograd and other places. We were held in a horrible house to start with. It was cold and dirty. Some of the girls were raped even before we left to come here. Then a lorry came and we were blindfolded and forced in – herded like cattle – then driven here. It was horrible. Everyone was crying and frightened,' Lesya tearfully explained in her broken English.

Elizabeth and Jennifer nodded as they listened, remembering their own harrowing experiences.

There was a long, drawn-out silence before Elizabeth spoke again.

'They killed Adam,' she said, her voice rising barely above a whisper. The icy edge of her statement sliced through the silence as huge tears rolled down her cheeks and dropped onto her blouse. 'They came into the flat and watched us making love. Adam tried to stop them – they just shot him,' she explained, in a wavering voice. Her senses were seemingly bewildered by her words and recollection.

Jennifer turned slowly, her pale face frozen in shock. She held out her arms.

Elizabeth collapsed into her sister's comforting embrace as the realisation of her boyfriend's death completely sunk in and registered. The impact of her own simplistic statement drove agonisingly through her heart, painfully wrenching at her insides. She cried. She cried until there were no more tears to cry, and her sister, Lesya and Yana cried with her, holding her and each other, bonding together, their lives now physically and emotionally entwined.

Eventually, the girls separated and dried their eyes.

Yana spoke softly to Lesya. She looked sad and confused, not understanding the pain Elizabeth had suffered until it was explained.

'What is to be become of us?' she asked Lesya.

Lesya translated the question into English.

Elizabeth recomposed herself and answered.

'All I know is that Durakovic is sending us to someone else, a man called Kozlov. He said he had selected two other girls. I assume that will be you and Yana. We have been sold into white slavery – sexual slavery,' she explained, her voice faltering once more, struggling to truly comprehend or believe the words she was speaking.

Lesya nodded. 'I have heard of this. There are a lot of girls taken from the Ukraine. They end up working as prostitutes or worse. I never thought it could happen to me. I applied for a job with the promise of being taken to England for a better life – it was just a lie. A man came to my home. He made me show him my body, then forced me to go with him – and now I am here. Yana was taken from her bed by a man she had seen before, in the bar where she worked. He must have followed her home. One morning, just a few days ago, he knocked at her door. When she answered, he and another man forced their way in and just took her.'

'We must get away. Do you understand, Lesya?' Elizabeth asked.

'I understand, but how? These are evil men. They will hurt us if we do not co-operate and do as they say.'

'They will hurt us anyway. They will rape us, abuse us and force drugs on us until we don't know any different; until we depend on them or they are bored with us. And then what?' Elizabeth replied. 'We can't let them. I will not submit to them; not whilst I have breath in my body.'

'I'm so afraid, but I don't know how to get away. Where would we go? We don't even know where we are. There are many men with guns. The doors are locked and the windows are barred. This house is a prison – there are many other girls here.'

'I'm afraid too, but we must try to get away. If we can escape, we can help the others. We have to try, Lesya – we have to,' Elizabeth said, taking Lesya's hands in hers, imploring her to listen.

Lesya smiled through her tears and nodded.

'I will help you.'

Elizabeth nodded in return.

'Tomorrow,' she said. 'We will help each other. We will try tomorrow.'

Familiar heavy footsteps approached the bedroom door. The girls heard the key turning in the lock and waited nervously for the door to swing open.

Damir stepped inside.

'Follow me,' he ordered.

The girls stood one by one, anxious and afraid. Elizabeth bravely led the way, following Damir out of the room, down the stairs and back into the large room where Durakovic was waiting for them.

'Good evening,' he said, with a degree of self-contented maliciousness.

The girls didn't answer. They stood in silence with their heads bowed. Only Elizabeth dared look at Durakovic, her blazing defiance evident in her eyes.

Durakovic stared at her for a moment. He could see the fire that burned deep within her. He wished he could be there when Kozlov and his men violated and broke her. She would fight and scream, scratch and bite. Kozlov would love every degrading minute.

'Eat and sleep tonight. Tomorrow, you will be taken to your new owner, Sergei Kozlov, to do with as he pleases. I am sorry I cannot take you myself, but I have other pressing business here. Goodbye girls,' Durakovic said pointedly, looking at Elizabeth and Jennifer, a sadistic smile spreading slowly across his sallow face.

Damir led the girls away. They crossed the hall and down a wide passageway to a small dining room. The room was dark and depressing and the air chilled and unwelcoming. In its centre, sat a long wooden table, set with eight plain wooden chairs, beneath a low-hanging, black iron chandelier, its six bulbs barely glowing. There was no other decoration – no window to let in further light, nothing to cheer the cold, lifeless room. A simple meal of thick stew, served in wooden bowls, accompanied by hunks of dry, crusty bread and mugs of water had been laid out on the table.

'Eat,' Damir instructed. 'I will be back in half an hour.'

The girls ate in silence, fearful that any conversation would be overheard. The food, despite its simple nature and bland taste, was welcome and they left none.

Damir returned with Mirsad thirty minutes later. Having washed and changed, their appearance and odour was now far less offensive.

Grim-faced, the girls were escorted back through the castle. Locked back in the bedroom, the girls sat huddled together on the bed on the far side of the room, their mood subdued, fearful and quiet.

'My father was a soldier – in the SAS. Have you heard of them?' Elizabeth asked, breaking the morbid silence.

Lesya nodded. 'Yes, I hear of them. They are special soldiers, yes?'

'Yes, they are special soldiers. My father will find us – he will come for us,' Elizabeth explained with unwavering confidence.

Lesya looked at her new friend. She wanted to believe. They all wanted, all needed, to believe, to hold on to the single vestige of hope.

'How will he know where to come?' she asked. It was a simple, obvious question.

Elizabeth's spirits sank and her eyes dropped sadly to the floor.

'I don't know,' she whispered. 'I just know in my heart that he will come.'

They spoke no more. Silence fell along with their spirits. No one knew where they were. No one would come. Each of them thought it, though none of them dared to say it. They were isolated and alone.

They drifted to bed, leaving on one of the bedside lamps. Its dim yellow light glowed softly over the room. Fully clothed, they slept in pairs, wrapped in the thick, rough blankets. The coarse wool and body heat helped to comfort and warm them against the creeping chill of the night.

Elizabeth and Jennifer cuddled together. They slept lightly, woken by every sound and creak that rose eerily through the house. The hours dragged by until their bodies and minds could fight no longer. They closed down, all senses overwhelmed by their mental and physical exhaustion, and they fell into a restless, but deeper sleep.

*

The door to the room opened at exactly 07:00 a.m. and Damir flicked on the main lights. Waking with a start, the girls instinctively gripped their blankets, holding them tightly, as if they were a solid, protective shield.

'Get up,' Damir growled. 'Breakfast will be ready in thirty minutes.'

He turned and closed the door.

The girls listened.

He didn't lock it.

Elizabeth looked at Lesya, waited until his footsteps grew fainter, then crept across to the bedroom door. She gripped the handle, turned it slowly, inched the door open and gazed into the dimly-lit landing. Her hopes were immediately dashed as her eyes fell on Mirsad, who was sat in a large wing-backed chair, watching the door from just a short way down the hall. His ugly, fat, stubble-covered face stared back at her through the gloom.

She closed the door.

'Mirsad,' she said dejectedly.

The girls took it in turns to use the bathroom, quickly washing before walking out of the bedroom, hand in hand.

Mirsad smiled knowingly as they appeared, then stood and escorted them back to the dining room where they had eaten the night before. A cold breakfast of bread, meats and cheese greeted them. The girls picked at the food, their appetites fading as the last remnants of their optimistic mood dissolved away, replaced by a collective, growing sense of fear and foreboding. They were going to Kozlov. They were going to suffer. They were going to die.

FIFTEEN

Daniel left Oleg in the security room and walked back up to his own room. Throwing his duffle on the bed, he stripped out of the black fatigues, took a few short minutes to wash and change into his fresh set of olive green army fatigues, then carefully stood the duffle in the corner.

Leaving the bedroom, he walked slowly, shrugging his coat back on as he went. Moving with a deliberately measured pace through the castle, Daniel took his time, familiarising himself with the layout as he descended through the floors. The castle was cavernous, eerie and cold. Inside and out, its appearance was oppressive and menacing, oozing an atmosphere of pure evil.

Daniel thought about Broughton Hall, the ancestral home of the Temple family. In stark contrast and despite its size, it was a warm and welcoming place. He thought about the many hidden passages and secret hiding places that bygone generations had built into its walls and foundations and wondered how many secrets the castle hid.

He found Taras's room, knocked on the door and waited. There was no response. He knocked again, louder and waited a little longer. There was no response. He tried the door. It was locked. He walked away and continued his inspection, methodically surveying each floor as he descended the huge staircase.

There were five floors, each with two wings; one either side of the enormous central stairway. Each wing held six rooms, making twelve per floor. A total of at least sixty rooms, assuming all of the floors were the same. He thought again, assuming there would also be cellars or rooms even more sinister, buried deep in the foundations. Reaching the ground floor, Daniel stood in the centre of the vast entrance hall and faced the huge double wooden doors that formed the main entrance. The layout on this floor was different. There were four corridors running off the cavernous central space. One to his left, at the end of which was the security room. One to his right, considerably shorter than the other. Two more ran left and right, immediately behind and either side of the staircase. He turned full circle and looked for doors, obvious or otherwise. He counted eight but was certain there must be more. Slowly, he turned again, staring at the walls. They held possibilities, he thought, as he followed them up toward the roof of the castle which towered somewhere above his head, shrouded in the gloom. He refocused on the wall in the corridor leading to the security room.

*

Taras sat talking with Sergei Kozlov in his office on the ground floor of the castle. Apart from Kozlov's personal bedroom, this was the only other room in the castle that had any degree of warmth or homely comfort. The two men sat either side of a magnificent antique desk which stood in the centre of a beautiful, circular oriental rug. The rug was intricately woven with a delicate pattern in wonderful shades of red and gold and dominated the middle of the room. Kozlov sat in a throne-like chair, made of rich, ornately carved dark wood, with a high back and arms upholstered in sumptuous crimson and gold cloth. The desk shone warmly. The mahogany wood was burnished deep reddish-brown, and fine, Russian gold inlays radiated deep brassy-yellow beneath the sparkling light which emanated from a grand crystal and gold chandelier directly above it. A huge fire roared in the great, open fireplace, working valiantly to warm the room as the logs crackled, popped and spat, sending bright orange sparks skipping across the stone hearth.

*

Daniel glanced at his watch. He had five minutes before he was due to find Taras and meet with Kozlov. He turned and stared at the wall to his left, then checked down each corridor. The castle was quiet; there was no one around. Quickly, he crossed the hall and stopped a foot from the stone wall, carefully surveying its surface. The solid grey slabs looked impenetrable, except that the gap between the two central slabs and the remainder of the wall seemed slightly wider. The difference was barely discernible – no more than a few millimetres on the left and right-hand sides and across their top, about six feet up the wall.

*

Taras looked across the desk. Kozlov's face was set firm, his expression severe.

'It's almost time to talk to Kuznetsov,' he said. 'Are you sure you want to go through with this, Sergei?'

'Positive,' confirmed Kozlov. 'What better way for Kuznetsov to prove himself than by killing Durakovic? If he fails, we will kill him *and*

Durakovic. If he succeeds, then maybe we have found someone useful to have around. Either way, we win.'

*

Daniel placed his hands on the wall then ran his fingers across the blocks and along the gaps, feeling the texture of the stone. He moved back and forth along the wall then licked his palm and held it against the slightly wider right-hand gap – it cooled rapidly. There was a draught – a slight, yet unmistakable breath of cold air blew through the narrow crack. He spread his feet wide and pushed hard against the wall but it stood firm. Daniel frowned, took two paces back and surveyed the wall again. There was nothing; no handle to pull, no block to push, no obvious or potential mechanism for opening a secret passage.

*

Taras pondered Kozlov's response.

'We should still check him out. He may be here for other reasons,' he argued.

'What other reasons? If he wanted me dead, he could have killed me last night and be long gone by now. I believe his story. He didn't just make the name Durakovic up, he knows the man. Let's put him to the test. If he was what he says he was, he'll pass easily. If not, he will fail and he will be dead.'

'Anyone can learn to shoot, Sergei,' Taras argued.

'Yes, but not everyone can learn to shoot well. You know the difference, but if it makes you feel better then check him out. Search his room whilst I talk to him in here, OK?'

'Yes, it would make me feel better. I'll go and find him and bring him to you.'

'Bring the rifle back with you. Let's start by seeing if he knows one end of a real gun from the other,' Kozlov said, without a hint of humour.

*

Daniel stared at the wall.

'Come on, Daniel, think,' he whispered.

He checked his watch again. Two minutes gone. Three to go. Taras, Kozlov or both could be with him any second. He examined at the wall. It was dark, grey and cold. None of the slabs looked any different from the others, except for the gaps. He looked at the floor. It was the same.

'Think,' he said again.

His eyes snapped back to the floor. There were gaps between two of the stones. Daniel looked at the wall again, carefully tracing the outline of each stone. Now he could see. At shoulder height, two of the stones were different again. The space was perfect and regular all the way round. He stepped forward and placed his feet on the stones in the floor. Then, spreading his arms wide at shoulder height, he placed his hands on the wall and pushed simultaneously with his hands and feet in four directions. The stones moved smoothly and easily. His feet and hands sank no more than an inch or two as the perfectly balanced, counterweight mechanism rolled the wall smoothly inward, creating a two-foot gap on either side.

Daniel stepped around the wall and entered a short dark passageway. The light from the hall was just bright enough for him to see that it ran twenty feet before a set of narrow stone steps descended into blackness. He walked to the end of the passage and peered down. The steps fell steeply away, but it was too dark to see where they led.

*

Taras stood and walked across the office.

'Be careful, Sergei,' he cautioned, opening the door.

Taras marched down the corridor, his hard-soled, metal-tipped boots clattering loudly against the stone floor. The noise echoed around the great open hall.

Daniel heard the sound and span around.

'Shit,' he said, running back toward the rapidly shrinking opening.

The wall was closing.

Taras turned into the wide expanse of the entrance hall. It was empty. He walked on, his footsteps cracking noisily on the stone.

Daniel listened.

The footsteps grew closer and louder.

He raced to the end of the passage.

The wall closed without a sound.

Daniel stopped dead. Enveloped in the absolute blackness, he listened. The sound of footsteps passed by the secret stone doorway and marched on towards the security room at the far end of the corridor. The office door opened, then slammed closed. The hall was silent again.

Unable to see his hands in front of his face, Daniel fumbled in the dark. The door had to open from the inside as well. He stood in front of the wall, placed his feet and hands as before and pushed hard. Nothing happened.

'Christ, come on,' he whispered, his adrenalin surging and his heart pounding.

He shuffled his feet, adjusted the position of his hands and pushed again. The wall stood firm. He sighed deeply, butted his head against the wall then stood back, taking a deep breath and a moment to think.

*

Taras entered the security room, slamming the door behind him. Oleg sat studying the pages of notes he had made from working with Daniel that morning.

'Have you seen Kuznetsov?' Taras asked.

'He left here about half an hour ago. Said he was going to get changed then come to find you,' Oleg replied, without looking up from his notes.

'What have you got there?'

'Notes I made this morning. He's very good. He showed me exactly how he got in and how to make sure it can't happen again. I think he's on the level, Taras,' Oleg stated confidently.

'Maybe,' Taras answered unconvincingly as he turned the handle and opened the security room door.

*

'Idiot,' Daniel chastised himself.

He stepped forward again, placed his hands at shoulder height and ran his hands slowly across the surface of the wall, blindly feeling his way. In a few seconds he found what he was hoping for; two small indentations – handholds, barely large enough to push his fingers into. He jammed his fingers in as far as they would go and placed his feet on the floor with his toes pressing against the wall, a shoulder-width apart. Simultaneously, he pushed down with his feet and gripping the wall, pulled hard. His feet sank an inch as the stones gave slightly toward him. He stopped, adjusted his grip and pulled again. The door rolled inward.

Daniel stepped sideways, around the widening gap and back into the entrance hall, immediately looking left down the corridor. The door to the security room was open and Taras was stood talking to Oleg with his back to Daniel.

Quickly, Daniel moved away from the opening, stepped a little closer to the security room and stood leaning casually against the wall, blocking the view of the open passage with his body.

Taras seemed to sense his presence and turned to face him.

'You're late,' he snapped.

'No, I was on time, I just couldn't find you – it's a big place,' Daniel countered.

The passage remained open. A cool draft blew softly on Daniel's neck.

Taras turned back to Oleg.

'We'll talk later. You can show me what Kuznetsov told you.'

Daniel remained still.

The secret door stayed open.

Taras closed the door to the security room, turned and walked slowly toward Daniel.

Daniel remained calm, leaning nonchalantly against the wall as he watched Taras advance.

Taras walked by.

'Let's go,' he said.

The stone door slid smoothly and silently back into place.

Daniel followed Taras across the entrance hall, past the staircase, to the far end of the opposite corridor and into Kozlov's office.

Kozlov was sat at the desk facing the door. He looked up as Daniel entered with Taras.

'Kuznetsov,' Taras announced as Daniel followed him through the door.

'Come, sit down,' Kozlov said, gesturing to one of a pair of chairs on the other side of the desk.

Daniel crossed the room and sat calmly in the left hand chair.

Kozlov surveyed him for a moment like he was uncertain, curious, cautious.

'So, tell me a little about yourself. When did you leave the army? What did you do? Where did you serve?' Kozlov asked in a relaxed fashion, gently but openly probing Daniel's story.

Daniel thought for a moment. It was a friendly interrogation, but his answers had to be convincing. He would embellish, but not too much – give irrelevant, superfluous information and pad out his answers as people do when they tell the unrehearsed truth.

'There's not much of a story. I was born and grew up in Kursk. My father worked in a factory; he was a metal worker. We were poor. My father was a miserable man. He liked his vodka and beat me and my mother when he drank. My mother died when I was twelve – I don't know what from. I think it was cancer, but nobody ever said. She just seemed to fade away, like her body had given up. My father became worse after that. When I was fifteen, I had grown bigger and stronger. He came to beat me – I beat him back. I ran away soon after and joined the army. I told them I was sixteen; they didn't ask many questions.'

'Where did you serve?'

Daniel shrugged. 'All over. Small, distant outposts along the Chinese border. At least, I did when I was part of the ground forces. That's where they send all the grunts to start with. I did OK, did as I was told, passed a few courses and showed I could do more than just the basics. Then I got lucky. They needed more fighting men and I was transferred to the Airborne Division – the 106th. I served in Afghanistan and Chechnya, as well as a few other places. Did some real fighting. Life was simple. I went wherever I was ordered to go and did what I was told to do. I was good at it. After that I was moved again, to the 45 Independent Spetznaz where I served for two years. I left six months ago and here I am,' Daniel explained confidently.

'Spetznaz? You were special forces?' Kozlov asked, intrigued.

'Yes,' Daniel stated nonchalantly.

*

Taras quietly entered Daniel's bedroom and stood with his back against the door, carefully surveying the room. There was nothing to see. Everything was neat and tidy. The bed was made and Daniel's only belongings, appeared to be a duffle bag, propped in the far corner. He walked over, grabbed the bag, took it over to the bed, lifted it and spilled the contents across its broad, flat surface. Kuznetsov didn't own much. Some civilian clothes. He checked them. The pockets were empty. A set of dirty black fatigues. He checked the pockets, finding a Makarov pistol, standard Russian military issue, and a knife that wasn't. He continued to look. There was some underwear – clean and dirty. A black woollen balaclava and a pair of old hiking boots. He moved the items around and uncovered some old military insignia, Russian Airborne, a leather wallet and a Russian passport. He opened the wallet, checked it through. There was a small amount of cash. He left it alone, then pulled a plastic ID card from one of the slots. Daniel's unsmiling face stared up at him. Danil Kuznetsov, the name read, Russian Army, 106th Airborne Division. He picked up the passport, compared the name and pictures, then looked at the stamps. A recent one caught his eye – a trip to and from Sarajevo. A trip to and from Durakovic. He frowned. Kuznetsov was genuine. He pushed everything back in to the duffle, stood it back in the corner and left the room, disappointed.

*

Kozlov could not hide his pleasure or interest.

'Tell me more,' he asked, with a broad smile spreading across his usually dour face.

'Not much to tell. I served my country and served it well. They trained me and used me.'

'What skills have you got?'

'I kill people – I'm a sniper. I'm good at it. I would say go and ask someone, but there's no one to tell, if you know what I mean.'

'Why did you leave?'

'I killed someone – someone I shouldn't have. I won't say it was an accident – it was a mistake – wrong guy, wrong place, wrong time. Nobody seemed too disappointed or angry. It was just inconvenient. It was quietly smoothed over and I was invited to leave. I had a good record up till then. A little volatile maybe, but generally a good soldier. I took orders, did what I was told to do. It could have been worse; they could have thrown me in prison. Military prison is not a nice place. I left with the clothes on my back, the few possessions I had and a month's pay. Better than rotting in some cesspit in Siberia,' Daniel shrugged, warming to his character, his confidence growing, his Russian flowing as fluently and naturally as if it were his native tongue.

The door opened and Taras entered the room, carrying what appeared to be a rectangular black attaché case. He placed it on the desk and stood back.

Daniel watched Kozlov, who was looking enquiringly at Taras. Taras nodded, Daniel caught the movement of his head in the corner of his eye. Kozlov looked pleased. The nod had carried so many words. It said, *I've searched, he appears to be clean.* It said, *I'm disappointed, but you might be right. It said go ahead, trust him for now.*

Kozlov nodded and smiled in return. It said one word. *Good.*

Kozlov slid the case toward Daniel.

'Open it,' he said.

Daniel pulled the case forward, flipped the catches, opened the lid and looked at the contents.

'You recognise it?' asked Taras expectantly.

'Of course. It's a VSS Vintorez sniper rifle with built-in silencer and a 4x PSO -1 scope, correct?'

'Correct,' Taras confirmed.

'You know your guns, Kuznetsov, but can you fire one? Accurately, I mean?' Kozlov added.

'Try me,' Daniel said with confidence.

'I intend to, Danil, I intend to. Follow Taras – we have arranged for you to give us a little demonstration. A test of your marksmanship, if you like.'

'Bring the rifle,' Taras snapped, leading the way out of the room.

Daniel closed the case, grabbed the handle and followed him out the door. Kozlov remained in his office.

'We'll talk some more when you return,' he said as Daniel left.

Taras lead Daniel through the house, out of the main doors and around to the opposite side of the house from where Daniel had approached the previous night.

Taras stopped and pointed.

'Down there, just under the first line of trees, there's a dummy propped against the large pine tree. You see it?'

Daniel looked down across the rocky plinth and clear open ground towards the trees.

'I see it,' he confirmed.

'Good. Shoot it. One through the heart, one through the head.'

'That's it?' Daniel questioned.

'That's it,' Taras confirmed. 'Miss and I'll shoot you where you stand,' he added pointing a newly-drawn Glock 17 pistol at Daniel.

Daniel looked at him and narrowed his eyes.

'I'll be lying down,' he replied casually as he dropped to his knees and laid the rifle case on the ground.

He opened the case, pulled the rifle from its moulded compartment then lifted out the relatively short muzzle. He locked it in place, slid the telescopic sight into its mounting and pulled out the ten-round magazine. He tapped it on the ground, slapped it in place and chambered the first 7.62 shell case.

Daniel lay the rifle on the ground, then lay down next it. He looked down at the target and gauged the distance – three hundred and fifty metres, three hundred and eighty-one yards or one thousand, one hundred and forty-four feet – the ground dropping may be thirty feet over the distance. An angled shot. Reasonable distance. A light wind and good light. A piece of cake.

He picked up the rifle, pulled it into his shoulder and laid his cheek gently against the side of the stock. Closing his left eye, he gazed through the telescopic sight.

'I need a shot to get sighted-in,' he said, without moving his position.

'Go ahead,' agreed Taras.

Daniel settled. The ground was frozen solid; it was like being laid out on an ice cube. His hands were cold and, without gloves, his fingers were already going numb. He stared through the sights and focussed on a rounded knot in the centre of the tree trunk, two feet above the dummy's head. He set the rifle to single shot, adjusted the sights, brought the crosshairs dead centre and slowed his breathing. Daniel concentrated, waited for his heart rate to drop, tightened his finger on the trigger and slowly squeezed. The world around him disappeared. There was just him, the rifle and the target. He breathed in, held the breath, breathed out slowly and pulled the trigger.

The gun kicked slightly against his shoulder as the long-stroke, gas-operated piston launched the subsonic, 9mm armour-piercing bullet almost silently from the muzzle. The knot in the tree exploded as the bullet passed through it, slightly high and to the right.

'Sights are off a fraction,' Daniel said, without looking up.

He carefully adjusted the sights.

'One head, one chest, right?' he confirmed.

Taras said nothing.

Daniel pulled the rifle to his shoulder, kept it on single shot and brought the sights to bear. The crosshairs settled on the dummy's chest, slightly left of centre, true and steady. Daniel rehearsed the movement and shots in his head. He settled, then repeated the exercise. He smiled inwardly, totally confident. Time to put on a show. He focussed on the target, closed everything out, took a deep breath and held it for a second.

Taras glared down at him.

'Nice watch,' he said unexpectedly.

Daniel registered the words, but kept his concentration. He breathed out slowly. He fired, adjusted and fired again. Two shots, less than a second apart. Daniel stood up and handed the rifle to Taras with a broad grin on his face.

Taras took the gun, lifted the sight to his eye and looked incredulously at the dummy. There were two holes, one through the heart and one through the head – the dead centre of the head.

'It's a fake. Not bad for six hundred roubles, although I had to pay in dollars. Twenty dollars, can you believe that?' Daniel said shaking his head ruefully as he held up his wrist, flashing the Rolex Submariner at Taras again.

Taras stared at him indignantly, his temper obviously rising, his disappointment even more apparent.

'Let's go,' he said, turning away in irritation.

Daniel followed again. He was in, no doubt about it. He had proven his worth and his ability. Now what were they going to do? He had to get things moving. He *had* to find the girls. Another day was rapidly passing. Another day too long.

SIXTEEN

The long, chopping rotors of the helicopter clattered loudly as it descended slowly out of the grey and rapidly darkening sky. It hovered for a moment before setting gently down on the wide expanse of grass, far enough back from the black gravel to prevent it spitting out a million tiny bullets.

Flanked by Damir and Mirsad, the girls stood, watching with trepidation as it landed. Quiet and withdrawn, they clutched their small, pitiful plastic carrier bags of clothing as they stared anxiously at the monstrous green and black machine.

Elizabeth glanced around. None of them wanted to take this flight. Her eyes darted from girl to girl, to Damir and Mirsad, to their surroundings and back to the helicopter, desperately searching for a place to run, praying for some miracle to happen. She closed her eyes and prayed for her father to appear through the trees; for someone to come, to storm the malevolent house and kill every one of the evil bastards it held within. Nothing happened. There was nowhere to run. No one was coming. All hope had gone.

She opened her eyes and stood silently with the others, shivering against the harsh, bone-chilling cold, desperate to hide her fear. She looked at Jennifer who stood next to her, shaking in the icy wind, tears streaming down her young face. Elizabeth inched closer to her sister. She had to be strong, to hold her nerve, as waves of nausea washed over her and the bile and vomit rose in her throat. Bravely, she swallowed it down and took her sister's hand in hers.

The helicopter settled on the ground and the rotor wash blustered through her hair and stung her face like a biting winter breeze.

The pilot sat passively in his seat and stared out of the windscreen. The twin-turbine engines kept turning over and the rotors chopped lazily round, sweeping in great arcs, like medieval broad swords slicing through the icy air.

Damir and Mirsad stepped forward, gripping a girl's arm in each hand.

Suddenly galvanised, the girls pulled and struggled. Their heels dug into the ground, their arms flailed, their hands slapped and they screamed.

Desperately, they fought with all the strength they could find, but slowly and surely they were dragged toward the helicopter.

Struggling, Yana wrenched herself free from Mirsad's grip, dropped her bag and bolted down the gravel road. She ran hard, tripping and stumbling in her high-heeled shoes. She sprawled to the ground, jumped back to her feet, kicked off her shoes and ran again.

Damir drew his gun.

'Don't fucking move,' he growled at Elizabeth and Lesya.

They stared at the gun and stood, paralysed, their eyes wide with fear, all resistance evaporating.

'Mirsad, give me the other one,' he ordered.

Mirsad threw Jennifer toward him, then set off in pursuit of Yana.

Yana ran for her life. Her bare feet crunched through the sharp gravel, the stones cutting into her feet with every desperate stride.

Mirsad closed her down. His short, muscular legs pumped hard as he sprinted after her. Ten more strides and he was on her. His hand shoved her in the centre of her back.

Yana crashed to the ground, sliding headlong through the gravel, her hands and knees scraping cruelly through the black shale, that tore away her skin.

'No,' she screamed hysterically, her voice loud and shrill, violently piercing the air.

Mirsad grabbed her by the hair, dragging her to her feet.

'No,' she screamed again.

Her arms flailed, striking out with ever-weakening blows.

Mirsad yanked her head back and slapped her hard around the face, splitting her lips.

'Shut up, you whore,' he bellowed.

The girls looked on in horror, helpless, as Mirsad dragged Yana's battered and bloodied body, flopping like a rag doll, to the waiting helicopter. Mirsad slid open the rear door and threw Yana inside before turning back to Damir and waving at him to bring the others.

Damir gestured for them to move.

'Move,' he ordered. 'If anyone runs, I will shoot you all,' he snarled.

Meekly picking up their bags, the girls moved obediently forward.

Mirsad held the door open, waiting for them.

The girls climbed in and submissively took their seats.

Lesya sat next to Yana, gently cradling her as she spoke quietly in their native language. Yana stared up at Lesya and her face took on a demonic appearance. Her wild, bloodshot eyes rolled back as tears mixed with mascara, black and macabre, smeared down her cheeks and mingled with the blood from her battered mouth. Lesya softly stroked Yana's hair as the young girl closed her eyes and slipped into a catatonic trance.

Damir followed Mirsad into the cabin, slid the door across and slammed it shut.

The pilot increased the power and the rotors whined, building to full speed, whirling almost invisibly through the air. Smoothly, the monstrous helicopter lifted from the ground, hovered, turned, then peeled away through the sullen evening sky, leaving Durakovic and his evil house far behind.

Damir left the girls with Mirsad and moved forward to the cockpit.

'What's the flight plan?' he asked the pilot.

'Twelve hours, give or take. We'll keep low, hug the contours and hopefully pass unnoticed. We have several borders to cross and two fuel stops in Bratislava and Kiev before we reach Mr Kozlov's castle,' the pilot explained. 'You best keep those girls in check. We can't afford any disturbance in flight.'

'Don't worry, we'll keep them in order,' Damir said waving his gun in front of the pilot.

'And don't fire that fucking thing either,' the pilot snapped curtly.

Damir grunted and withdrew from the cockpit, returning to sit next to Mirsad.

The passenger area had ten seats. Eight large, comfortable seats, configured as two rows of four, faced the front. Two others, spaced one either side of the compartment, faced the rear. The girls sat together in the rear row, putting as much distance as they could between themselves and Mirsad, who sat angry and agitated, scratching at his scarred face, in one of the seats facing them.

Damir, sat next to him, glared menacingly at the girls, then angrily moved forward. Gun in hand, he leant over the first row of seats.

'I can't use this,' he said showing them the gun. 'But this, I can,' he added, drawing a knife with a wickedly long, curved blade. 'One move, one sound I don't like and I'll slice you open, you understand?'

The girls nodded dumbly, their bodies and minds immobilised by their increasing terror and torment.

Damir nodded and smiled. It was a vile, demonic smile that carried no warmth or humour.

'Good,' he said simply.

*

Daniel strode confidently behind Taras, back into Kozlov's office. The look on Taras's face told the whole story.

Kozlov laughed at his obvious disappointment.

'Come, my friend, sit down, accept the man for what he is,' he said in a loud, almost jovial voice.

Taras sat indignantly, begrudgingly accepting Daniel's presence.

Daniel remained standing, ensuring that his growing confidence didn't spill over into disrespect.

Kozlov looked up at him from his desk.

'You passed the test. Come, sit down. We have things to discuss,' he said, gesturing to the seat opposite Taras.

Daniel sat and waited.

'Was it difficult?' Kozlov asked.

'The test?' Daniel confirmed the intent of the question.

'Yes, a good test of your marksmanship?'

'It was OK. Not difficult, at least not for me. I'm a good shot, I told you.'

'Excellent, excellent,' Kozlov replied, nodding his head in approval.

'Do I have a job?'

Kozlov looked at Taras whose hardened expression barely flickered as he nodded almost imperceptibly.

'You have a job – a very important job. I'm going to take you up on your offer to kill Zoran Durakovic,' he said, as if it were just an everyday statement of fact.

The words were hard and cold – plain, simple and final.

Daniel looked at him impassively. He was going to kill Durakovic anyway, so why not with Kozlov's assistance and approval? It would make it all the easier. Kozlov would even provide the gun.

'When?' Daniel asked.

'You leave tomorrow. We have some new guests arriving early in the morning – some rather special young ladies.'

'Special?'

'The daughters of a British SAS officer will be here for our pleasure,' he smiled wickedly.

The deviant smile turned to a deep rumbling laugh and his black eyes almost shone in sick anticipation.

'There are two others as well. The men will enjoy breaking them in,' Taras added.

'Breaking them in?' Daniel questioned, keeping his voice calm and level as his heart thumped in his chest.

'Fucking them, you thick bastard,' Taras snapped. 'Pump them full of drugs, then make them submit to whatever you want them to do. Oral sex and crack, it's a great combination for getting co-operation. Get them hooked on that stuff and they're desperate for it. They'll do whatever you want them to. They won't mind. They'll even offer themselves. Nothing is too perverse or depraved, just as long as they get their fix.'

Daniel glared at him. It took all his willpower to hold back.

Taras caught the look.

'Don't worry, Kuznetsov, you'll get your go.'

Daniel smirked. 'Just as long I'm not last,' he replied, joining in the sordid conversation, inwardly cursing himself for his minor lapse in character.

Kozlov snapped out of his laughter as quickly as he had started.

'We have serious business to attend to first,' he said abruptly.

Daniel dropped his half-hearted smile and turned to face him.

'Of course, Mr Kozlov,' he responded seriously.

Kozlov grunted in reply, then spoke again.

'Another of my men, Karl Mertz, will arrive by noon tomorrow. He will take you and Taras to our private airfield, about twenty miles from here. From there, he will fly you into Bosnia, to another airfield and then drive you to within a safe distance of Durakovic's house. You'll have to travel the rest of the way on foot. I want you to kill Durakovic. Nothing fancy or complicated – just shoot him and leave. They won't even know you're there. Taras will go with you to make sure the job is done and Karl will wait with the car to bring you back again. Is that clear?'

'Perfectly, Mr Kozlov,' Daniel confirmed.

'Good. No mistakes, Kuznetsov. Do a good a job

and who knows, you might even get paid,' he said, laughing to himself again.

'Yes, Mr Kozlov,' Daniel replied again, respectfully.

'We are done. Leave me now,' Kozlov said brusquely.

Daniel and Taras left the room.

'Take me to the security room. Show me what you showed Oleg this morning,' Taras ordered as they walked back through the castle halls.

Daniel settled into a chair with Taras and Oleg sat either side. Carefully, he studied the plans of the castle and grounds that Oleg had prepared for the session before spending the rest of the afternoon repeatedly going over the information.

'You have wireless movement detectors and pressure sensors around the perimeter, starting fifteen hundred feet out, correct?'

'Yes, fifteen hundred feet,' Oleg confirmed.

'They work and work well, if whoever approaches stays on the ground. The problem is, they miss anything more than a few feet off the floor,' Daniel explained, showing Taras and Oleg how he approached through the trees.

'Once I got in close, it was easy to create confusion, especially when the mind is geared to think in a specific way.'

'What do you mean?' Taras asked.

'Two things. First, you couldn't understand why none of the outer sensors had triggered. Second, when the sensors close in started to alert, you expected to find something or someone – you searched.'

'Standard two-dimensional search pattern,' Oleg added, sounding knowledgeable.

Daniel smiled inwardly. Said nothing.

'You expect multiple targets. You searched and found nothing, creating immediate doubt,' he continued

Taras nodded. 'Go on.'

'Then it was easy. I set all the sensors off – I bet your system went haywire.'

'It did,' Oleg confirmed enthusiastically.

Taras glared at him.

'You searched again and found nothing – creating more doubt,' Daniel repeated. 'I set all the sensors off again. You searched and found nothing. Therefore, you assumed the system was faulty. There was nothing wrong with it. It was doing exactly what it had been designed to do, but because you couldn't explain it, you did just what *I* wanted you to. The cure for 99% of all known computer glitches – you rebooted. You reset the system to fix a malfunction you didn't have.'

Daniel continued to explain and assist for several hours, showing them how to make sure it didn't happen again – how to reconfigure, reposition and recalibrate the sensors. He was happy to do it. It had been a one-time exercise. He couldn't use the same trick again. Not even Taras and Oleg were that dumb, were they?

'Have you got sensors covering the roof?' Daniel asked.

'No,' Oleg answered immediately, without thought or hesitation.

Taras rolled his eyes in frustration, glaring at him again.

'OK, we'll have to look at that later,' Daniel replied.

*

Daniel ate a huge dinner. He had missed lunch and was absolutely ravenous. Kozlov's cook had prepared a selection of hearty dishes for the men at the castle. Most of the men ate in the communal dining room. Daniel joined them, piling his tray with a mountainous plate of chicken, mashed potatoes and vegetables, plus several chunks of bread, some apple pie, a tall glass of water and a steaming mug of tea. He returned to the long wooden dining table but sat slightly apart from the others as he ate, listened and thought.

The men paid him little attention, talking

amongst themselves about girls who were obviously already housed elsewhere in the castle. Which ones were good, which ones still needed breaking in. They talked about duty rotas, the food and pay and about Taras and Kozlov, in between huge mouthfuls of food which they shovelled into their mouths like it was their last ever meal. Those that were off-duty washed their meal down with beer and vodka.

Daniel listened with a tinge of disappointment. There was nothing useful to be gleaned from the inane conversation.

One of the senior guards looked over. He was evidently off-duty, judging by the amount of vodka he was drinking.

'Kuznetsov,' he called.

Daniel glanced toward him. He was a big guy; someone who was once in good shape, but was now no more than a tall frame, carrying slabs of untoned, fat-covered muscle.

'That is your name, isn't it? Kuznetsov?'

Daniel nodded once but remained silent.

'You don't say much. What's the matter with you? You too good for the rest of us?'

Here it comes, Daniel thought. There's always one who has too much to drink and has to prove he's top dog. Daniel looked along the table, cut through him with a withering look, then returned to his meal without a word. It was time to make a necessary example.

The guard looked at his comrades. They stared expectantly. He glanced back toward Daniel, too late to back down. The challenge had been made and accepted. He could take him – the vodka told him so.

The guard stood, walked slowly along the table and, stopping immediately behind Daniel, tapped him on the shoulder. His first basic mistake.

The men at the other end of the table stared in eager anticipation.

Daniel tensed his thighs, relaxed his shoulders and dropped his arms by his side.

The guard tapped his shoulder again, took half a step back and waited for Daniel to stand, turn and face him – to do as expected. His second and final mistake.

'I'm talking to you, Kuz–'

Daniel's elbow fired straight back, connecting with a solid, sickening blow between the guard's legs. Simultaneously, Daniel's legs launched him up and back. The back of his head smashed into the guard's face as his body bent double from the blow to the groin. The combined effect was stunningly brutal.

Pain exploded through the guard's groin a split second before his face imploded. His nose and cheekbones shattered, he fell unconscious to the floor.

Daniel stood over him, then glared down the table.

'Anyone else got anything to say?' he asked icily.

There was no reply. The guards looked on in stunned silence. The message was clear. *Don't fuck with Kuznetsov.*

Daniel left the men to clean up the mess he had made of their friend and returned to his room. He lay down on his bed, stared at the ceiling and took stock. Events were more or less working in his favour. The girls were relatively safe, hopefully unharmed and being brought to him. He would know exactly where they were and who they were with, but their arrival brought the risk that they might inadvertently give him away if they saw him before he could warn them. Added to that, he had just knowingly helped improve the defence and detection systems. Getting the girls out and safely away was going to be harder than ever. The security systems would work as effectively whether someone was approaching or escaping from the castle's perimeter. In successfully executing one part of his plan, he had certainly complicated another. He parked that thought. It was something he would have to address later. He refocused on the here and now, his immediate next steps and a plan for the next twenty-four hours.

He turned his attention back to his room. It had been searched and his duffle had been moved. The handles now faced the opposite way from when he had deliberately placed it in the corner, handles facing outward, into the room. He jumped off the bed and checked the bag. Everything was still there; the Makarov, bullets and spare clip were still intact. He wandered into the bathroom, splashed some cold water onto his face and stared into the mirror. A cold, hard, emotionless face stared back.

Returning to the bedroom, he lay out on the bed, folded his hands behind his head and stared back up at the ceiling. Once the plan kicked into action, there would be no going back. All of their lives would be in immediate danger. He would need to move fast, strike before Kozlov had worked out what was happening and free the girls before he could act. It would all be down to timing. Getting back into, then away from the castle, was the biggest challenge. Doing it alone was feasible. Doing it with two traumatised girls, close to impossible.

*

Daniel woke to the loud clatter of a helicopter reverberating through the night sky. He checked his watch – it was 4:00am. The helicopter was landing close to the castle, in the open ground between the rocky plinth and the trees. He rose from the bed and walked to the window.

The sound of heavy turbines and long rotors chopping through the still night air carried with the flash of landing lights from around the far corner. Daniel's heart pounded, thumping hard against his chest. His mouth went dry as his nerve endings fired a myriad of signals and the synapses sparked in his brain. He stood back from the window, took a slow, deep breath, held it for a few seconds, then slowly released it.

'It's just another mission,' he whispered.

He sat on the floor, crossed his legs and closed his eyes. He breathed, slow and controlled, remaining still and silent for a few moments, then opened his eyes. His mind was clear, his thoughts sharp. He was emotionless, ruthless and ready.

*

The girls looked on with trepidation as the castle came into view. This was a place even worse than the one they had left, its monstrous black walls and sinister features towering above them as the helicopter landed.

Two men, dressed in black, waited as the pilot touched down and killed the engines. They came forward as the rotors lazily wound their way down to a full stop, opened the doors and pulled the girls one by one from the cabin. Mirsad and Damir followed close behind.

In single file, the girls were lead around the castle

to where an opening with narrow stone steps dropped at an acute angle into a tightly enclosed rocky entrance, about six feet square.

The man leading them opened the door.

'This way,' he said, ducking in through the doorway.

The girls followed, pushed and prompted by Damir and Mirsad.

A dark, narrow passageway led away from the door. Inside, the air felt cold and damp. The passage turned right and left, passed other doorways, then opened out into a plain square hall where the air was warmer and drier and the light slightly brighter.

The man leading the way stopped and turned toward them. He was of average height and build. His face, not unattractive, sat beneath an unruly mop of thick blond hair and his emerald-green eyes glinted in the light. He stepped forward and spoke.

'My name is Petr and this is Timur,' he said in a cool, rational voice, pointing to the man accompanying him.

Timur nodded but said nothing.

Petr continued. 'You are at the castle of Sergei Kozlov. Whilst you are here, you will do exactly as you are told. You will call every man Sir and obey every instruction, no matter what it is. Any disobedience will be punished swiftly and severely. Do you understand?'

The girls nodded meekly.

'I said, do you understand?' Petr asked a little more forcefully.

'Yes, Sir,' the girls replied together, their voices weak and quavering.

'Good,' he nodded. 'Myself, Timur and these other men will be looking after you for the next few days or even weeks, depending on how long Mr Kozlov wishes to keep you.'

Elizabeth watched as Damir and Mirsad looked at each other and smiled wicked, knowing smiles.

'You will stay down here tonight and perhaps tomorrow as well. Mr Kozlov will meet you when he's ready. After that, if he is pleased, you will be moved to rooms upstairs, where you will be more comfortable. But that is something you will have to earn,' Petr explained. 'Now follow me.'

The girls glanced around. There were a number of other corridors leading off, left and right, and another set of steps that led up. The castle was as barren and austere as Durakovic's house had been, and their minds filled with fear and frightful anticipation.

Petr lead them a short way down one of the right-hand corridors before arriving at a pair of identical doors, one either side of the corridor. The doors were made of thick steel, with an eye hole placed in their centre.

Timur unlocked the first door and held it open.

Elizabeth held Jennifer's hand as they stood in silent apprehension.

'In,' Petr ordered, holding the first door open.

Elizabeth and Jennifer walked in.

Mirsad went to follow, but Petr threw his arm across the door, blocking his way.

'Tomorrow, my eager friend,' he said.

Mirsad nodded reluctantly as he stared hungrily after Jennifer.

The door clanged shut and a heavy key turned in the lock.

Elizabeth and Jennifer stared at their room. It was a bare cell, eight feet square, with two narrow wooden beds, lumpy mattresses and rough woollen blankets, but they were warm. The girls felt a small wave of welcome relief as they were locked in and left alone.

*

Daniel wandered down the stairs and through to the communal dining room where a number of Kozlov's men sat eating breakfast. Daniel entered the room, conscious of the silence as all eyes watched him, wary of his presence.

'Good morning,' Daniel said confidently, greeting them with an irritating, almost arrogant smile. There was no response.

Oleg walked in to join them.

'Morning, Oleg,' Daniel said handing him a mug of coffee.

'Kuznetsov,' Oleg nodded curtly.

'You need more help today?' Daniel asked, knowing the question would needle him.

'No. Taras said I must do the rest of the work alone. I am not allowed to work with you today.' He looked around carefully before moving closer and speaking quietly. 'Taras doesn't like you.'

'I figured as much,' Daniel replied with just a hint of sarcastic humour.

'He doesn't trust you. You should be careful of him; he's a dangerous man,' Oleg warned.

'So am I,' Daniel replied, with no humour at all.

Taras appeared just outside the door and glared at the two men.

Oleg's eyes fell to the floor and he left without another word, giving Taras a wide berth as he passed.

Taras entered the room.

'We need to prepare. We will leave as soon as possible after Karl arrives,' he advised tersely.

'Fine by me,' Daniel said amiably, ensuring he remained cool. 'What was all the commotion early this morning?' he added as an almost throwaway question.

'Our new guests arrived. The ones Mr Kozlov told you about.'

'When do I get to meet them?' Daniel asked, feigning eager excitement.

'When I say so. You have a job to do first,' Taras replied irritably.

'I'll go get my gear,' Daniel replied with false dejection.

Daniel strode out of the room, back up the stairs and into his bedroom. He grabbed the duffle and removed everything he was going to need. He slid his knife in its sheath on his belt, dropped the Makarov into his inside breast pocket and the spare clip into the opposite outside pocket. Leaving the room he shrugged on his coat and marched through the castle.

'What do we do now?' he asked, meeting Taras at the foot of the staircase.

'Come with me, I will show you the plans of Durakovic's house,' Taras said, leading the way down to the office.

They entered the room. Kozlov was not there. The room was empty, cold and silent. A large map, a hand-drawn plan and a pile of photographs were set out for them to review.

Taras walked around to the other side of the desk.

Daniel stood and looked at the information with contrived interest. He scanned the top photograph. It was a blown-up black and white print of a man, tall but not big or powerful. He had a lithe, athletic build, like someone who kept in shape. It was hard to tell, but the man looked pale. His face was slightly drawn, but his jaw was square and strong. He had long dark hair, starting to grey, flowing down to his shoulders and swept back from his forehead.

'Durakovic,' said Taras handing Daniel the photograph. 'Memorise his face.'

Daniel took the photograph and stared for a few seconds. He knew exactly what Durakovic looked like; his image was already stored permanently in his mind.

'I know what he looks like,' Daniel replied, throwing the photograph onto the desk.

Taras ignored the response and continued working through the material.

'This is Durakovic's house. It's located a few miles outside of Sarajevo. It's well guarded but there's no electronic surveillance. This drawing shows the layout.'

The photographs presented the house just as Daniel remembered it – grey flagstone under a black slate roof. It looked as equally cold, sinister and unwelcoming as Kozlov's castle.

'I've been there, remember? I don't need this shit,' Daniel stated with deliberate irritation. 'You don't believe me?'

Taras didn't answer the question, but continued abruptly.

'If you don't need the photographs, leave them where they are, but listen to what I have to say and perhaps you will get the plan right and we will all come out happy, safe and alive – you got that?'

Daniel smiled. He enjoyed getting under Taras's skin. He shrugged once.

'I've got it,' he stated.

Taras nodded and carried on.

'The house is approached by a single gravel road through dense woodland. We will take two cars. The first will drop you at the junction of the main road and the track. Karl will wait there with the car for your return. The second will be driven by me. You can drop into the trees and approach the house completely undetected through the forest. The tree line ends about four hundred yards before the house. There's an expanse of gravel and then some broad stone steps which lead up to the main entrance.'

'I know the approach. How do we get Durakovic to come out?'

'It's already arranged. He has a meeting scheduled for 9:00am tomorrow. He will come out to greet his guest and walk the grounds.'

'Any chance of the meeting being cancelled or his guest not showing up?'

'No. The meeting is with me,' Taras replied. 'You will shoot as he walks down the steps to greet me. Don't fucking miss.'

'I won't miss,' Daniel assured, fixing Taras with an ice-cold stare. 'What happens after?'

'There's a slight change to the plan Mr Kozlov outlined earlier. I will stay on in Sarajevo for a few days. We are concerned that Durakovic hasn't been as careful as he should have been; we believe he has been conducting unauthorised activities. The authorities may already know that the house has been used to hold women before they are sold and shipped on. I need to ensure the final batch has been cleared and are safely on their way to the UK, pay off the men and close the operation down for Mr Kozlov.'

Excellent, thought Daniel, I don't even need to hide the fact that you don't come home.

'OK,' he said. 'But won't Durakovic's men be concerned that he's just been killed?'

'I doubt it. Apart from Damir and Mirsad, most of them are Kozlov's men. Just think of Durakovic as a franchise owner; a cog in the machine – Kozlov's machine. I will take care of anyone who is unhappy.'

Daniel simply nodded. 'OK,' he said again.

The doors to the office swung open. Kozlov entered, followed by a solid-looking man with short dark hair, dressed in blue jeans, black sweater and black leather jacket.

'Excellent, gentlemen, you are here. Kuznetsov, let me introduce you to Karl Mertz,' Kozlov said as he approached the desk.

Daniel looked up and over Kozlov's shoulder. His eyes met with Mertz's and a fleeting, tantalising look of recognition flashed across his face. Alarm bells crashed through Daniel's head as he stepped confidently forward.

'Mertz,' he said, holding out his hand, acknowledging the man's name.

Karl Mertz took his hand and shook it with a firm grip.

'Kuz-net-sov,' he replied hesitantly, still holding Daniel's hand, appraising him for a second longer.

'You two know each other?' Taras asked, obviously picking up on the suddenly charged atmosphere.

Daniel shook his head.

'No,' he stated categorically.

'No, I don't think so,' Mertz replied with less certainty.

Daniel's heart was in his mouth. He could see Mertz searching through the images in his mind, urgently trying to place Daniel's face, desperately but unsuccessfully trying to hide the thought process. Daniel was doing the same with a little more finesse.

It came to him suddenly. Mertz was ex-German KSK, Kommando SpezialKraefte. Formed in 1995, they were the unified Germany's equivalent of the SAS. Daniel had met the man once, during a five-day combined NATO training exercise. Mertz had been part of the German contingent for sniper and enemy evasion training.

Mertz looked at him, as if he sensed that one of them had completed their mental search.

Daniel's face was impassive, giving away absolutely nothing.

Kozlov's voice cut through the palpable tension, breaking Mertz's concentration for a moment.

'Kuznetsov is ex-Spetznaz,' he said to Mertz.

Mertz nodded.

'He should be adequate for the job then,' he replied.

Kozlov laughed, turning to Daniel.

'Karl is ex-KSK, I assume you know what that is?'

Daniel nodded.

'German special forces, a poor man's SAS,' he added with deliberate calculation and a wry smile.

Kozlov laughed again.

'Good, good, you should both get on very well,' he said.

Daniel breathed a sigh of relief. It was obvious Mertz couldn't place him – at least not yet. Not even with the SAS comment he had intentionally, if riskily thrown in.

'Enough dick comparing, let's go through the plan again before we leave,' Taras irritably cut in.

*

The girls were woken mid-morning. Timur brought them a simple but welcome breakfast of toast, porridge and mugs of hot sweet coffee. After they had eaten, he escorted them from their cells to an open shower room with private toilet cubicles set off to one side.

'Mr Kozlov likes his girls to be clean and attractive,' he said handing each of them a wash bag containing soap, shampoo, make-up, feminine hygiene products and deodorant. 'Undress and throw your old clothes in the bin over there. Shower and dry – there are fresh towels in the cupboard, there,' he added pointing across the room. 'I will bring you new clothes.'

The girls waited for him to leave, then undressed slowly, hesitantly, expecting Timur and the other men to come for them at any moment, but the halls and rooms remained deathly silent.

The showers were hot and powerful. The girls washed and scrubbed themselves clean, then dried, sprayed on their deodorant and waited.

Timur returned, carrying a pile of new clothing. He nodded his approval.

'You look and smell better,' he said, handing over the clothes.

They were better than before.

'You may wear the jeans and warmer clothing,

except when Mr Kozlov wants to see you. Then you will wear one of the other outfits,' he instructed.

The other outfits were much the same as Durakovic had given them – short skirts, skimpy underwear, low-cut tops and sheer blouses. All designed to show off the female body and as much flesh as possible.

'Get dressed,' he ordered.

The girls looked at each other.

Timur stood and waited.

'Don't make me ask again,' he said sharply.

'Yes, Sir,' the girls mumbled weakly, remembering their previous instructions.

The girls dropped their towels to the floor and stood exposed and naked before him.

Timur's eyes hungrily took in their bodies, moving slowly, deliberately, from one girl to the other. He lingered on Jennifer and Yana, their bodies slightly curvier, their breasts fuller. His tongue slowly protruded from his mouth. He licked his lips, his erection rising in his trousers in anticipation of what was to come.

The girls dressed, consciously choosing jeans, baggy T-shirts and heavy jumpers, hiding their bodies, providing themselves with an illusion of comfort and safety.

Timur returned them to their cells.

'Mr Kozlov will see you later. He will choose one

or two of you for himself. The others will be for the men to enjoy,' he said coldly.

*

Daniel and Karl Mertz stood either side of Taras as he walked through the plan one final time.

'Are you both clear?' he asked, looking at each of them in turn.

'Yes,' they confirmed in unison.

Daniel looked at Mertz and their eyes locked.

Mertz looked away, unable to hold Daniel's gaze for more than a few seconds. His dull-brown eyes flicked over Daniel's face one last time before they separated.

'One hour. Be ready to go,' Taras ordered, remaining with Kozlov in the office as the men left the room.

Daniel stopped in the centre of the huge entrance hall and waited, letting Mertz walk on towards the security room.

Daniel was alone. He turned a slow full circle. The castle was quiet and empty once more. The other men were out, completing whatever duties they had been assigned, watching TV or sleeping in their rooms. He crossed quickly to the wall, placed his feet and hands on the appropriate stones and pushed. The door rolled silently open. He stepped inside, waited for the wall to close, then edged his way forward. There was a dull light emanating from the stairway; nothing more than a pale glow, but more than enough to see by. He peered down the stairs. There was no one there. Cautiously he descended, treading lightly, his rubber-soled boots making no sound on the stone steps. Reaching the bottom, he moved quietly into a square hall, stopped, looked and listened carefully.

Corridors led off, left and right and another dead ahead. Men's voices came from somewhere within the labyrinth of corridors, but he couldn't quite place the direction or distance.

He took the first left-hand corridor. The voices faded. The passageway led down to the castle's plant room. A huge, modern generator sat quietly pumping out the power required to run the castle, surrounded by boilers, pipes, monitors, valves and gauges. Daniel backed out of the room and returned to the hall. The voices were still there, eerily echoing through the passageways. He disappeared down the opposite long, dark corridor. The voices faded again. There were doors and rooms left and right. He checked each one. They were storerooms, each piled high with equipment, clothes, bedding, food and provisions; everything Kozlov, his men and any potential guests might need.

Daniel returned to the hall. Time was ticking

away. He moved swiftly down the next passageway. Other corridors ran off from it. He went straight on, coming to two identical doors – metal doors – cell doors, one either side of the passage. He peered through the door on his left. Two young girls sat closely together, talking quietly on one of the beds. They had long dark hair and were dressed in jeans and sweaters. He didn't recognise them and turned away; they weren't his concern. He stepped across to the opposite door and peered through the spyhole. The scene was the same. Two girls sat on a bed, holding hands, talking quietly – Elizabeth and Jennifer.

SEVENTEEN

Karl Mertz entered the security room, greeting Oleg warmly. The two men had worked well together since Karl had joined Kozlov's operation eighteen months earlier.

'What do you know of this Kuznetsov character, Oleg?' Mertz asked.

'Not much. He only arrived a couple of days ago. He beat all of the security systems and ended up in Kozlov's bedroom; could have killed him. Instead, he handed over his weapons and asked for a job. Can you believe that?'

'Kozlov didn't kill him?'

'No. He seemed pretty impressed. Came down here though, ranting and raving. You know how he can be.'

'Yes, I know. You OK?'

'I'm alright. He slapped me around a little – told

me to make sure it never happened again. He was pretty angry, but not like I've seen him before. At least he didn't take a hatchet to my head. He beat a guy to death – Pavel, you remember him? Made a horrible mess; beat his face to a pulp, then stamped on him, cracked his skull wide open.'

'Pavel?' he questioned. 'Yes, I remember him, what did he do?'

'I don't know. I just heard Kozlov ranting about how he had failed him once too often. Next thing they were dragging his body away. I couldn't recognise the face. I only found out it was Pavel when one of the guards told me. They're all scared, you know.'

'I know. What's happened since Kuznetsov arrived?'

'Kozlov initially said Kuznetsov was here by invitation, testing the security. The next morning he admitted what really happened. Taras wasn't very happy. He doesn't like Danil, doesn't trust him.'

'Danil?'

'Yeah, that's Kuznetsov first name. He seems OK to me. He showed me and Taras how he got in and helped me change the systems so it can't happen again. You wouldn't do that if you weren't on the level, would you?'

'Danil,' Mertz said again, thoughtfully. The colour suddenly drained from his face in realisation.

'What's up? You look like you've seen a ghost.'

'No, no ghost. This man is very much alive. Thanks, Oleg. I'll talk to you later, OK?' Mertz said rapidly disappearing out of the door.

*

Daniel peered through the spyhole, relief and compassion washing through his body. The girls were alive and well. They looked pale and drawn; evidence of their harrowing experience etched into their faces, but they seemed to be otherwise unhurt.

The sound of men's voices grew suddenly louder. Heavy footsteps echoed through the underground passageways – footsteps coming Daniel's way. He listened hard. The footsteps drew closer. Time was running out.

He tapped at the door, but the sound barely carried through the thick steel.

The girls stopped talking and looked up at the door, confused and uncertain. None of the men would bother to knock. They sat still and silent. The knock came again. A little louder. A little more urgent.

The voices and footsteps were close now. Four men, two Russian, two Daniel couldn't quite place from their accents. They were coming across the hall, possibly already in the corridor – Daniel's corridor, heading straight for him.

Elizabeth crossed the room.

'Who's there?' she asked hesitantly, her voice barely above a whisper.

There was no reply.

'Hello?' she called again, questioningly.

The key rattled and turned in the lock.

The door opened.

Timur stood angrily in the doorway.

'Who were you talking to?' he demanded.

'No one,' Elizabeth denied.

The blow from Timur was stunning and vicious, sending Elizabeth sprawling across the floor. Blood flowed from her mouth and nose.

Jennifer dropped to her knees from the bed, aiding her sister.

'Don't lie to me and say Sir when you speak,' Timur ranted.

'I was just calling out. I wanted to use the toilet. Please may I use the toilet, Sir?'

*

Daniel moved quickly down the corridor. The footsteps carried on behind him. One man stopped at the cell door he heard the key in the lock. The others continued on. Daniel continued, swiftly and silently, until he ran into a series of washrooms, an open shower area and toilet cubicles. He stopped and looked around. There was nowhere to hide. No way out. The men followed, their footsteps growing louder, in ten seconds, maybe less, they would see him. His eyes darted around the rooms. There was one route left. He ran into the empty passageway. It was dark – much darker than the others. Then the passage stopped, opening into a plain square storage area, lined with solid wooden shelves that were stacked with clothing, towels and wash gear. A dead end.

Daniel looked around the room, urgently searching for another door. The men were still there, still coming. In desperation, he looked up. The ceiling between the passageway and storage room was high. Set at different levels, it rose, ran a short distance, then dropped again, forming a dark recess six feet wide and three feet deep.

Daniel climbed the shelving until his head and shoulders disappeared into the ceiling recess. He ran his hands over the rock; it was cracked and rough.

The footsteps grew louder. The men were seconds from the room.

Daniel gripped the wall, swung his legs in the dark once, twice, three times. His feet hit the ceiling and wedged into place. He pushed out hard with his hands and feet and lay suspended in the darkness, facing down over the entrance.

The men walked in, flicking on a single light. The bare bulb shone dimly in the centre of the room, giving just enough light to see by.

*

Timur stared angrily at Elizabeth.

'There's a bucket in the corner, use that,' he replied unsympathetically as Jennifer helped Elizabeth to her feet.

Elizabeth looked at him with feigned embarrassment.

'Please. I, I have my period. Please let me use the toilet, Sir,' she begged.

Timur paused for a moment and his face softened, he seemed to like Elizabeth's submissive and obedient response. He nodded and stood back from the door.

'Bring what you need, be quick.'

Elizabeth grabbed her wash bag and followed Timur out of the door, leaving Jennifer behind, sitting passively on the bed and staring nervously into the corridor.

*

Mirsad and Damir walked down the rows of shelves, grabbing new clothing – plain fatigues, jeans, sweatshirts, socks and underwear – under Petr's guidance. Kozlov was generous to his men. Durakovic made them buy their own.

Daniel watched them, mentally urging them to go faster. His arms and legs pushed hard against the walls, his muscles straining from holding the suspended weight of his body.

The men looked up and down the shelves, taking their time. It wasn't often they got a free selection of clothing.

Daniel's arms and legs began to shake. The sweat beaded on his forehead, ran down his face and formed droplets on his chin.

Mirsad and Damir stood directly beneath him as, disinterested, Petr walked slowly out of the room.

Daniel lifted his head, desperate to stop the droplets of sweat falling from his face. He breathed hard and pushed harder.

At last, Mirsad and Damir followed Petr. The light went out. The sweat on Daniel's chin fell like the first drops of heavy rain in the dark and plopped onto Damir's back. He walked on, oblivious.

*

Elizabeth stepped into the farthest cubicle from the passageway, next to the open shower area. Keeping her jeans firmly done up, she sat on the toilet.

Timur paced the corridor, his back to the

cubicles. He wasn't at all interested in what she was doing. It was one function of the female body that he had no desire to know any more about.

*

Daniel gripped the cracks in the walls with his fingertips, let his legs swing free, then dropped silently to the floor. He remained crouching, looking back along the dark passageway. Thank God no one ever looks up, he thought.

He moved forward slowly, cautiously making his way back down the passageway. Ahead, the four men were talking. Daniel stopped and listened to the conversation, then crept closer to peer round the end of the wall and across the shower room.

Their conversation over, three of the men walked away, leaving one standing with his back to Daniel. Daniel glanced across to the toilet cubicles, dropped to the floor and looked under to the nearest cubicle. A small pair of feet swished back and forth.

*

Elizabeth sat deep in thought. Someone had knocked the door, why? It wasn't one of the other girls and it sure wasn't one of Kozlov's men. She was thinking hard, her feet sweeping back and forth across the floor. Was someone there, trying to make contact?

Suddenly, a huge hand grabbed her foot from behind. She jumped and squealed before she realised what was happening.

'What are you doing?' Timur shouted.

Elizabeth held her breath for a second as she stared down at the powerful hand still holding her ankle. The hand released its grip and slowly moved a single, cautioning finger from side to side.

'Nothing, sorry, there was a spider,' she called.

'Fucking stupid woman,' Timur growled to himself. 'Hurry up,' he shouted back.

'Yes, Sir, I'm just coming,' she replied, still staring at the hand. Instinct told her this was a friend. 'Hello,' she whispered as loud as she dared, pressing her head against the cubicle wall.

'Elizabeth?'

Tears welled in her eyes.

'Yes, yes, it's Elizabeth,' she replied urgently.

'It's Dan Temple, you OK? Is Jennifer OK?'

Her spirits soared as the tears rolled down her face and she felt a huge smile spread across her face and euphoric relief course through her body.

'Oh my God, Dan, is Daddy with you?'

'No, it's just me. Don't say any more. Be brave, do as you're told. Stay strong; I'll be back, I'm going to get you out, I promise.'

Daniel's hand slipped away.

Timur thumped hard on the door.

'Open the door,' he shouted.

She jumped to her feet, wiped her eyes, flushed the toilet and opened the door.

Timur stared hard at her.

'You were talking again? You've been crying?' he accused and questioned.

'Yes, I'm sorry. The spider made me jump. It frightened me, you frighten me. I was upset, I am upset. I was talking to myself, trying to calm down. I'm sorry, Sir,' she garbled as the words spilled out, her reply full of nervous energy.

She stared at the floor, subserviently avoiding eye contact. Her heart beating hard and fast; the adrenalin coursing through her veins.

Timur looked at her, his face softening for a fleeting moment.

'Back to the room,' he said. 'If you're good, I'll let you out again later.'

'Thank you, Sir,' she replied demurely.

*

Daniel stood back in the shadows and watched Elizabeth being led away. He waited a minute, then followed behind, moving back down the corridor. Passing the cells, he lightly touched the steel door; just hang on, he thought.

Daniel reached the hall, checked the corridors, crossed to the steps and ran up, two at a time. He reached the end of the passage, pressed his ear against the cold, hard stone and listened carefully. Hearing nothing but silence, he placed his feet on the floor stones and his hand in the grooves. He pulled and pushed. The secret door rolled inward and he slipped through the gap and back into the entrance hall.

Daniel stopped in his tracks as he passed the main entrance. Kozlov, Taras and Mertz were engaged in animated conversation just outside the open doorway. Daniel stepped back behind the door and listened.

'Are you sure, Karl?' Kozlov asked.

'Yes, Mr Kozlov, I am totally sure. He's British – SAS.'

'You can't be mistaken, confusing him with someone else maybe?'

'No, I'm certain. I knew I'd seen him before as soon as I met him. I just couldn't place him. It was only when Oleg said that his first name was Danil that it clicked. It's not Danil, its Daniel – Captain Daniel Temple. I saw him a few years ago on a joint NATO exercise.'

'What do you want to do, Sergei?' Taras asked.

'Kill him, what the fuck do you think I want to do? I'm going to take a hatchet to his balls, feed them to him and then cut his fucking head off,' Kozlov growled.

'I think you should wait, Sergei. Let him do what you want done and then kill him. If he fails, Karl and I will kill him. If he succeeds, Karl and I will kill him. Either way he's a dead man, but at least you get Durakovic.' Taras counselled calmly.

There was a lengthy silence.

'I don't think Durakovic sent him. I don't know why he's here. It must be a British undercover operation,' Kozlov replied at last.

'That maybe true, Sergei, but Durakovic messed up anyway. He needs to be taken care of. He's a threat and a liability. You need him out of the way. Let Kuznetsov or Temple or whoever the hell he is do the job. Then we'll kill him, OK?'

'Alright,' Kozlov growled in agreement. 'Bring him back here, though. I want to cut that bastard and watch him bleed, you hear me. I want his blood soaking my hands.'

'Yes, Sergei,' Taras confirmed.

*

Elizabeth sat on the bed next to Jennifer.

'Are you alright?' Jennifer asked.

Elizabeth opened her arms and held her sister close.

'I'm fine,' she whispered. 'Dan Temple is here, it's going to be alright,' she said reassuringly.

Jennifer's body shook convulsively against her sister's as she cried. The same relief and joy washed through her body as it had done with Elizabeth.

'You saw him?' she asked.

'No, but I spoke to him briefly. He promised to come for us.'

'Is Daddy here?' Jennifer asked hopefully.

'No, it's just Daniel. We have to be brave now, Jen. Do as we're told. Daniel will get us out.' Elizabeth said, pulling back and holding her sister's face gently in her hands.

Jennifer nodded. 'OK,' she whispered, wiping her eyes and nose on her sleeve before bursting into tears again.

*

Daniel thrust his hands into his pockets and strode confidently out of the main entrance. Taras saw him appear and whispered something Daniel could not hear as Mertz looked up, watching his approach.

'You ready to go?' Taras asked.

'I'm ready,' Daniel confirmed.

'Excellent,' Kozlov replied, patting Daniel on the shoulder. 'We'll talk more when you return. Happy hunting,' he said with a disingenuous smile.

*

Daniel, Taras and Mertz sat in silence as the car took them from the castle, winding its way down through the dense woodland to the main road. They reached the bottom, turned right and accelerated away.

'You nervous, Kuznetsov?' Taras asked, breaking the heavy silence.

'No, should I be?' Daniel responded.

'Maybe. Nerves can be good for you; they keep you focussed.'

'I am focussed,' Daniel replied with a hard, icy, edge to his voice.

The car fell silent again – an uneasy, tense silence. The sort you can taste, feel and touch. Daniel waited calmly. Mertz had recognised him. Taras and Kozlov knew who he was. Even if he hadn't overheard their earlier conversation, he would have known something was wrong. The atmosphere, the behaviour, the body language had changed – it was all wrong. This was it; a blink test. Daniel sat passively, his determination set hard and fast, his emotions buried deep. Focussed and unfeeling, he would not blink – not now. Not ever.

EIGHTEEN

John Shaw sat at his desk listening intently to the recorded voices over and over again. He considered every word, every phrase; the inflection, the delivery, the two small clicks, then thought back to his last conversation with Daniel. He drummed his fingers slowly on the desk as he listened and stared subconsciously at the telephone.

A man entered the office. He didn't knock. He just entered, anonymously and insipidly oozing in through the door. Shaw registered and ignored his uncharismatic entrance and presence. Joe Gordon, John's recently appointed boss, stood almost transparently, just inside the door. Mr Cellophane, Shaw called him. An intelligent man no doubt, but a pure theorist. Shaw doubted he had ever actively done anything in his life. He had merely evolved his way through levels of management, ticking lists. To-do lists. How-to-do lists. Why-to-do lists and who-should-do lists. John figured he must have ticked a lot of boxes for a lot of people, but not his. His tick boxes were simple and straight forward. There were just three. *Do I like you? Do I trust you? Do I respect you?* Gordon failed on all three counts.

'Shaw,' Gordon said in an uncertain, barely audible voice, his broad Scots accent making the word almost indiscernible.

John shot the man a cursory glance.

Gordon moved forward and stood in front of the desk – grey suit, white shirt, bland tie, with a mop of salt-and-pepper, straw-like hair, badly cut – Mr Cellophane.

John looked straight through him, making no effort to conceal his contempt.

'Shaw,' Gordon said again, just loud enough to break John's concentration.

Shaw exhaled loudly and hit the pause button.

'Sir,' he answered, with complete disdain.

'What are you working on?'

Shaw stared at him for a moment and considered his answer. The truth or a lie?

'A possible case of kidnapping and human trafficking,' he answered. Half a truth; a reasonable compromise.

'Is that something I assigned you?'

'No.'

'No, I didn't think so. I've just been looking at your files. You're still a loose cannon, wouldn't you say?'

'No.'

'I've also been checking on your use of valuable departmental resources – your unaccounted use of valuable resources.'

'What's your point?'

'My point is, Shaw, I'm watching you. I'm not blind to your rule bending or your association with that modern-day lone ranger friend of yours – Temple, isn't it?'

Shaw ignored the question. 'I get things done,' he retorted.

'Maybe, but I can't afford for you to continue being – what's the word?'

'Effective?' Shaw cut in.

'A maverick, I was going to say. Things are changing around here, Shaw. Things will be working my way. *You* will be working my way.'

'I'll be sure to find my pencil sharpener.'

'I don't like your attitude, Shaw. You might have gotten away with it last time, but one more step out of line and you might have to start looking for an alternative career. Do I make myself clear?' Gordon asked.

John stared at him blankly, openly unimpressed.

'Anything else? I am pretty busy,' he said as coolly and irritatingly as he could.

Gordon's face flushed crimson. Annoyed and embarrassed, he turned and left without another word.

John hit play and refocused his thoughts. The recording ended as it always did. Durakovic's chilling words spilled into the room. "They are to be Perdition's Daughters".

Shaw didn't need to listen or think anymore. Angry at his own inaction, he silently berated himself for letting it go this far. But it wasn't too late; he could and would do something now. He reached over the desk, lifted the phone, dialled the number and waited.

'Broughton Hall,' Coleman answered politely.

'Coleman, good morning. It's John Shaw. We need to talk.'

'About Daniel?'

'Yes, Daniel.'

'Do you know where he is? What he's doing?'

'He called me yesterday, on his way to St Petersburg. I assumed you knew what he's doing?'

'No, not in detail. You know how he can be, especially once he's got an idea in his head.'

'Yeah, I know how he is. I know where he is and what he's doing. I should never have let him go; he's not going to make it alone. Whether he knows it or not, whether he wants it or not, he is going to need our help.'

'You had better tell me everything,' Coleman replied gravely.

'I can't tell you over the phone. Will you meet me in London? There's someone else I think we should talk to, once I've explained everything.'

'I'll be there in three hours. Meet me at the Dorchester.'

'Great, thanks, see you there.'

John Shaw hung up the phone, cleared his desk, grabbed his MP3 player and left.

*

The black Jaguar XJ glided silently into the drive of a large, red-brick house, that sat back behind the leaf-strewn lawn, facing the broad, tree-lined suburban avenue. The two men inside exchanged a short glance, a confirmation of their action, before opening the doors and striding purposefully to the front door.

John Shaw rang the doorbell, then stood back, shoulder to shoulder with Coleman, waiting patiently in the chilled early evening air.

Richard Mead opened the door. He stared briefly at the men. His expression fixed and grim, his eyes bloodshot and tired. Their visit came as no surprise.

The men walked through to the lounge and sat in the large, comfortable armchairs, facing across the coffee table to the equally large and well-cushioned sofa.

'Where's Jane?' John Shaw asked with polite interest.

'She's not here – she's gone to stay with her sister for a few days. It's the strain; she can't take the strain. We thought a change of scenery might do her good,' Richard Mead answered. 'Would you like some coffee?'

'No, thanks. You know why we're here.' It was a firm statement of fact, expressed in a blunt but courteous fashion.

'Yes,' Richard Mead confirmed almost apologetically. His whole demeanour seemed unusually nervous and fragile.

'Richard, we know what's happening. We need you to tell us why. We need you to help us, to help Daniel,' John Shaw stated, moving the conversation directly to business.

Richard Mead stared at the two men, blinking hesitantly as he searched for the words. There was nothing he could do to hide the fact that he had betrayed Daniel's friendship – sent him into a death-trap; a deadly spider's web of lies and deceit, in the blind hope of saving his daughters.

'I'm sorry. Daniel was my only hope. I can't leave my girls in the hands of those monsters.'

'Why didn't you go yourself? You're ex-SAS;

you've got the skills, the experience and connections,' Coleman asked.

'I couldn't go. You've heard the tape. Durakovic was quite explicit. It couldn't be me.'

'That's not what the tape said, or meant, is it, Richard?' John Shaw interjected.

Richard Mead sighed heavily and held his head in his hands, staring down at the deep-piled, cream carpet beneath his feet. He said nothing for a long, silent minute.

'No,' he finally whispered, shaking his head.

'Look, Richard, we've known each other a long time. I don't mean to be rude or unsympathetic, but Daniel is out there, risking his life for you. So why don't you stop pissing around and tell us what the fuck is going on,' John Shaw barked, his temper rising.

Richard Mead looked up and stared across the table, his eyes moving slowly from John Shaw to Coleman. His face was drawn and his expression severe. His left hand shakily stroked over his right in a subconsciously comforting gesture. He was a haunted man.

'It's a long story,' he sighed.

'We're not here to judge you, Richard. Whatever it is, we know it must be serious. Whatever we can do to help, we will. But first, we must all help Daniel and your daughters,' Coleman said supportively.

'Yes, yes, you're right. What I am about to tell you will explain everything. Whatever you decide to do thereafter is up to you.'

'Go on,' John encouraged

Richard Mead nodded, drew a long deep breath, let it out slowly and began to talk.

'It all began after I left the army and started Mead Associates with Daniel. The company was immediately in demand and going well –' He stopped speaking and looked vacantly into space, slipping into deep reflective thought, as if he were struggling to recall some piece of information or detail. 'No, sorry, that's not quite correct,' he said after a few moments. 'To be wholly accurate, it all started a short while before I left the army, just before that incident with Daniel and Malik. Actually, it is *the* reason I left.'

'What is Richard?' John asked.

Richard looked back across to the two men, his focus and attention fully restored.

'Parkinson's,' he stated simply, his expression the epitome of sadness.

'Parkinson's?' John queried in surprise.

Richard nodded slowly and spoke quietly.

'I have Parkinson's disease. It was picked up following a routine medical. I complained of a slight tingling sensation and trembling in my left arm. I thought it was a trapped nerve or something. I was sent for some tests and, well, there you have it – they diagnosed Parkinson's. It's at the very early stages still, but it was enough to make me useless to the army, especially the SAS.'

John Shaw shook his head.

'Richard, I am sorry,' he said with genuine compassion. 'But please continue. Tell us what has been going on.'

'Yes, sorry, I'm not looking for sympathy. I thought it would help you to know. It is relevant to the rest of what I have to tell you.'

'OK, please carry on,' Coleman acknowledged

'Well, I left the army but decided not to tell anyone, not even the girls. I still have all my faculties and physically I'm still pretty good. I just get the odd shake every now and then. The doctors say it will take years before I really start to become dysfunctional. Jane and I decided to say that I had decided it was the right time to leave the army and explore new opportunities. I spoke to Daniel, persuaded him into a partnership and started Mead Associates. It was good for both of us; we had Daniel's financial backing and a lot of good contacts, business was pretty easy to pick up. There's always something going on. People, companies, governments – they all need good security advice, or things doing they wouldn't want to do themselves, at least not directly. Daniel wanted to remain pretty much a silent partner, but we used his name and influence with Temple Stamford. The board agreed to use us, or more accurately me, to help with some work in Russia. That's how I came into contact with Sergei Kozlov. We were helping with some work to do with a gas pipeline, part of the Trans-Siberian network. Anyway, Kozlov seemed to like what we did and the way in which we did it. He asked me to undertake some other work on his behalf.'

'You were asked to work for the Russian mafia?' John asked.

'You ask that as if it were some sort of heinous crime. It really isn't that black and white. The Russian mafia aren't that different to many other hugely successful multinational conglomerates or governments; there is an element in pretty much all of them that is far from legal. The only difference is everyone knows that the mafia is organised crime, but at the end of the day, they all make money in every way they can.'

Coleman inclined his head in acknowledgment but said nothing.

'Fuck me, I'm in the wrong job,' John said with a wry smile.

'Carry on, Richard,' Coleman requested.

'The work we did for Kozlov was successful and he asked if we would take on another assignment for one of his regional commanders. The work was extremely lucrative and could easily be passed off as legitimate security advice, so I said yes. What I didn't know, until it was too late, was that the work was for Zoran Durakovic. I only found out when my team and I went to meet Kozlov's man in Sarajevo, and there he was.'

'How did he react when you met?' John asked.

'At first, it was as if he didn't know or didn't acknowledge who I was. We completed the work, again successfully, and he seemed very pleased. As often happens, he then asked us to complete even more work, this time acting directly for him, with Kozlov's blessing – or so we thought.'

'And it wasn't?' John asked.

'No, it wasn't.'

'So what happened?'

'There was a major falling out. Kozlov was very angry; he told me he would never do business with us again. Said if it weren't for the fact that Temple Stamford had introduced us to him and the fact we had completed the previous assignment so well, we would all be buried under the snow in Siberia.'

'And Durakovic?'

'Durakovic revealed his true demonic self. He contacted me and said he knew exactly who I was and what I had done to him and that he would expose me, Mead Associates and the work we had done to the authorities unless I co-operated with him. He asked me to undertake more work. A specific assignment that required specialist skills.'

'He didn't directly mention the death of his family?' John asked.

'No. I think he knows I didn't do that. I think he was angrier about the fact that I pursued, captured and brought him to trial.'

'And the assignment?'

'The assignment was to assassinate Sergei Kozlov. I said no of course. I will remember his response till the day I die. He said I would never be able to rest and that one day I would pay the consequences, unless I agreed.'

'So you told him you had Parkinson's,' David stated.

'Yes, I did. I thought if he knew I was unable to do it, he would find someone else more useful to him.'

'It didn't work.'

'No, it didn't work. He is an evil and vindictive man. He just wouldn't let it go. He said I knew enough people, I could find someone with the right credentials.'

'Daniel, you mean?'

Richard nodded, 'Daniel,' he confirmed. 'I had other men with the right skills, but none of them would actually do it. In an act of war or in the fight against terrorism, yes, but a cold-blooded assassination, no – not even someone as evil as Kozlov.'

'And you think Daniel would?'

'Not directly, no. But when Durakovic took the girls, I knew there was no one else I could or *would* want to turn to. Daniel is the best I've ever come across. I know how close you are to him, Coleman. You watched him grow up. You see a different Daniel to the one I know. When the chips are down, he really can be a totally ruthless, cold-hearted bastard.'

'So you told Daniel half the story and asked him to get Elizabeth and Jennifer back?'

'Yes. I didn't want to lie to Daniel, but what choice did I have?'

'You could have told him the truth. You're right, he can be a ruthless cold-hearted bastard, just like his father was, I know that, I'm not blind. He's also your friend and your partner. He would have gone anyway,' Coleman replied.

John Shaw had heard enough. He stood and offered his hand.

'Thank you, Richard,' he said.

'What are you going to do?' Richard asked with deep concern.

'I'm not going to let my only true friend down. I'm going to help Daniel,' John said. A simple, hard, unequivocal statement of fact. 'You can both do whatever you feel is right.'

NINETEEN

Kozlov paced his office, a distracted and angry man. Temple was going to pay for what he had done. Nobody made a fool out of Sergei Kozlov, nobody. He marched across to his desk, lifted the receiver on the internal phone and pressed a button.

The telephone on the wall next to Petr buzzed loudly.

'Get the girls ready. Bring them to me,' Kozlov ordered.

'Yes, Sir,' Petr responded, turning to the others. 'Time to have some fun,' he grinned.

The four men left their room, walked quickly down the corridor, across the square hall and down to the cells. Petr and Mirsad went to Elizabeth and Jennifer, Timur and Damir to Lesya and Yana.

'Get changed. Mr Kozlov wants to see you now,' they ordered.

The men stood and watched, eager to feast their eyes on the girls' naked bodies, knowing they would soon be able to do more than just look.

The girls slowly removed their clothing.

The men watched, frustrated and tormented, revelling in every second of the sordid, involuntary strip show. Mirsad's eyes fixed unwaveringly on Jennifer's body, watching perversely as she removed her sweater and jeans, then stood trembling in her underwear.

Mirsad stepped forward.

'Everything,' he growled, breathing heavily in his rising excitement.

Jennifer reached behind her back, unhooked her bra and let it drop to the floor. Her breasts stood slightly upturned, large, proud and firm. She stooped and stepped out of her knickers.

Mirsad stood before her, touching distance away. His rough hands reached out, cupping her soft breasts, running down the sides of her body and around her buttocks.

She tried to pull away.

Mirsad grabbed her arm, roughly pulling her back.

'No,' she screamed.

'Leave her,' Petr shouted. 'No one does anything until Mr Kozlov has seen them,' he ordered.

Mirsad grudgingly stepped away.

Jennifer rummaged in her bag. The clothes were all much the same. She started to dress in a tiny g-string and short skirt which barely came to the top of her thighs.

'No bra,' Mirsad ordered.

She looked at Petr.

'Do as he says,' Petr confirmed.

Stay strong, she thought.

'Yes, Sir,' she replied meekly.

She slipped on a white, almost sheer blouse, with a woven floral pattern serving to provide at least some degree of modesty and intrigue.

The other girls dressed in the same fashion.

The men looked on with an air of increasing desire.

Petr led the dressed and made-up girls in single file, their high-heeled shoes clicking and echoing loudly across the stone floor as they crossed the square hall and ascended the stairs. At the end of the passage, the secret door was already open as Oleg and two other security guards waited for them to enter the castle's main hall.

They walked on across the vast, open hall, along another corridor and entered Kozlov's office, following Petr's instructions to line up in front of the waiting man.

Kozlov's intense gaze fell on them, his growing excitement obvious to see. Coldly, he appraised them one at a time. Yana: five feet six, nineteen, with long dark hair, beautiful young body and large full breasts. Lesya: taller, five feet ten, also dark-haired; a lithe, slimmer body, smaller, firm breasts and long, shapely legs. His gaze lingered on her before moving slowly down the line to Jennifer. Similar to Yana, she had a fuller figure, rounded and curvy with long, wavy blond hair which cascaded down over her shoulders, and large, full breasts, partially obscured by her blouse. He nodded his approval before moving on to Elizabeth. She was smaller, slightly built with long brown hair, a slim, athletic body and small breasts. His eyes trailed over them again, then settled back on Yana.

'Her first,' he said before looking along the line to Lesya. 'Save her. She's exclusively mine – and this one,' he ordered looking at Jennifer.

He came back to Elizabeth.

'This one looks supple. The men can have some fun with her,' he said, with a demonic look and humiliating lack of compassion.

Kozlov looked to Petr and nodded.

Petr stepped toward Yana.

She shrank away, her body almost doubling over as she burst into tears, her arms reaching out for Lesya.

Petr gripped her shoulders, pulling her upright and away from the others.

'No, please,' she screamed.

Her body paralysed with fear, too weak to fight.

Petr dragged her across the office.

The girls watched, stunned and terrified.

'Please don't do this,' Elizabeth cried, her words unheard and unheeded.

'Wait,' Kozlov called. 'Which ones are the daughters of the British soldier?'

Damir pointed to Elizabeth and Jennifer.

'Take them, make them watch – let them see what they have in store,' he instructed.

'What about this one?' Timur asked looking over to Lesya.

'Take her to my room, lock her in,' Kozlov replied, briefly appraising Lesya's body again.

Petr half-carried, half-dragged Yana out through the doors, her feet barely touching the floor. He crossed the corridor, stepping directly into another, simply furnished room. In its centre sat a large bed with a plain, uncovered mattress and no sheets. Its presence was there for one purpose and one purpose alone. Petr dragged Yana across the room and sat her on the velvet-padded ottoman that stood at the bottom of the bed.

'Timur, fetch the young lady a cocktail,' Kozlov ordered, an evil grin on his face.

Damir and Mirsad pushed Elizabeth and Jennifer into the room and crowded in after them.

Timur returned carrying a small, ornate wooden box. Its beautifully carved exterior belied its contents. He opened it, gently lifting out the pre-prepared syringe.

Yana looked in terror.

'What's that?' she cried.

Petr held her tightly.

'Just a little something to get you in the mood,' Kozlov said.

Timur grabbed her arm.

She struggled and tried to pull away.

Timur slapped her hard across the face.

Kozlov laughed.

'Don't struggle, my dear, it will ease your afternoon.'

The needle scratched painfully into her arm, pumping in the heroin-based cocktail. The drug surged through her veins; the effects were almost immediate. Yana's head reeled in a sudden state of euphoria. The room span and she sat motionless as the faces of men blurred and distorted around her. Her blouse was torn away, exposing her breasts. Briefly, she came to her senses. She tried to stand, tried to fight. Naked men crowded in, their hands groping and pulling at her body.

She screamed, one word, 'No,' and was gone again.

The drug took her back under its control. Her

short skirt and tiny g-string were ripped from her body. She felt herself being bent backwards over the ottoman at the end of the bed and her legs roughly parted. She opened her eyes. Petr's face swam in and out of focus as he stood between her legs. The other men gathered round, laughing and jeering, naked and aroused, their frenzied, sexual excitement building.

Petr thrust himself forward, penetrating her.

Her hands pushed against his chest as she shook her head and her mouth opened and closed, miming silent screams.

Petr forced himself into her, thrusting hard, again and again.

Yana's cries stuck in her throat as the drugs fooled her body into artificial orgasm.

Petr threw his head back and let out a small, satisfied gasp.

Yana's hands gripped his buttocks, her nails raked his skin, pulling him into her.

Petr withdrew and stepped away.

Kozlov looked to Elizabeth and Jennifer.

'Turn around. Open your eyes,' he roared.

They did as they were ordered.

There was no respite. Timur stepped in to Petr's place. He stared appreciatively down at Yana's body, then stooped, sucking and biting at her erect nipple.

Yana cried in pain.

He gripped her arm and pulled hard, flipped her onto her stomach and spread her legs wide with his own. His hands caressed her buttocks then gripped her hips.

Yana screamed and tried to stand.

Timur pressed his hand into the small of her back, pinning her down. He pushed forward, ramming himself into her body, raping her again.

Yana's body convulsed as she sobbed uncontrollably, semi-conscious, but fully aware of her ordeal.

Damir came next and then Mirsad as she was passed from man to man, raped and violated, over and over. Kozlov watched, savouring every minute of the sick pleasure being drawn from her violent degradation. The last man finished, leaving her young body sprawled naked on the bed.

Kozlov stepped forward, grabbed a handful of her hair and dragged her from the bed.

Yana stood terrified before him. He pushed her down.

'On your knees,' he snarled.

Yana knelt.

Kozlov looked down on her, his fierce erection just inches from her face.

'Please me,' he ordered.

She took him into her mouth.

'Bite me and I'll cut your throat,' he warned.

Her lips closed gently around him. Her head moved back and forth, working him softly with her mouth.

He pushed into her, forcing himself deeper.

She gagged and tried to pull away.

His hands gripped her head and held her tight.

Tears streamed down her face.

Kozlov groaned and released Yana's head.

She slumped to the floor, coughed, choked, then vomited. Yana's eyes stared into space as she lay perfectly still. All of her senses closing down, Yana lay in a waking coma, physically and mentally traumatised. Her young life savagely broken.

'She was good. Shoot her up again, give her something to lift her spirits. Put her in one of the rooms upstairs; we'll work her again tomorrow,' Kozlov said as he dressed.

Elizabeth and Jennifer held each other close, shocked and terrified. They watched the men dress, thankful that their own ordeal was at least delayed. Kozlov approached them. Elizabeth watched him. She loathed and despised him with an intensity she didn't know she possessed. He was the devil incarnate; the only thing missing were his horns. He was a vile, evil and sadistic man. For the first time ever, she wished she could see another human being die.

'Clean up the mess in here. Take these two and

lock them back in the cells. Keep them separated,' Kozlov ordered as he left the room.

'May the men have them?' Petr called after him.

'No – tomorrow, maybe. They deserve some special treatment,' he called spitefully before closing the door to his office.

*

The small, twin-engine aircraft touched down at the private airstrip just outside Sarajevo right on schedule. Daniel waited for the door to open and the steps to be lowered, then followed Taras and Mertz down to the waiting cars. The early morning air was clear, cold and crisp. The weather was bright and the sky a soft powder-blue. A weak winter sun was just starting to shine over the horizon, making the frost sparkle brightly on the ground.

Daniel turned a slow circle, taking in his surroundings. Apart from the long concrete strip, a row of buildings and random scattering of small, dilapidated single-engine planes, the airfield looked deserted. He gazed back to the low-rise, prefabricated structures that age had faded and stained a cross between dull-grey and dirty-brown. At two stories high, the second building in the row stood out above the rest and was topped with a small, hexagonal glass structure. There was no one visible inside. He glanced further along, noting the last building with a faded sign hanging above a single entrance door. He couldn't quite make out the detail of the words and pictures, but he got the idea; it was a parachute club. He wondered how the place operated – or maybe it didn't. Perhaps the signs and advertisements were the only thing left of a business long since closed down.

Mertz called to him in German.

Daniel didn't respond. It was a test; a poor one. The words washed over him as if they were never spoken.

'He doesn't speak German,' Mertz said to Taras, speaking in his mother tongue.

Daniel listened impassively. An expensive education and a degree in languages from Oxford had its advantages.

'Good. Look at him, he's no idea what's coming when he gets back to Kozlov,' Taras replied in very poor German.

Daniel smiled inwardly as Taras blundered his way through the language with a heavy Russian accent. He stared coolly at the two men as they spoke quietly. No, gentlemen, *Kozlov* has no idea what's going to happen to him when I get back, he thought in contradiction.

Taras and Mertz separated and walked to their respective cars.

Daniel let the thought go, breathed in another lungful of cool, fresh air, then slid into the passenger seat next to Mertz. Neither man spoke as they followed Taras's car out of the airfield. The drive was short, and twenty minutes later, Mertz pulled to the side of the road and parked in close behind Taras's Mercedes.

Daniel climbed out of the car.

'You'll be waiting right here – right?' he confirmed.

'I'll be here, ready for you,' Mertz replied, his choice of words flashing an unintentional warning to Daniel.

Daniel walked a few yards to Taras's car, watching Taras observing him carefully in the wing mirror as he approached.

'It's on the back seat,' Taras said through the open window, as Daniel came level with the car.

Daniel opened the rear door, grabbed the small case and slammed the door closed.

'Twenty minutes,' Daniel said. 'Then you can drive up.'

'Twenty minutes,' Taras repeated in confirmation. 'Don't be late.'

Daniel was already on his way, his long stride stretching out across the road. He ducked under the trees and disappeared into the gloom of the forest. He cut left and broke into a long, loping jog that ate up the ground. It was tough going; the ground was steadily rising and the forest floor was covered in small, broken branches, fir cones and rocks. Daniel pressed on, running fluidly over the rough terrain, dodging left and right through the trees, ducking under branches, never breaking stride.

Daniel checked his watch – five minutes to go. He looked ahead; the tree line was breaking, the light becoming brighter. He could see the trees giving way to open ground and he slowed to walk the last few paces, then stopped dead. Dogs were barking – big dogs, close dogs. He recalled the rottweilers, stepped back into the shadows, then crouched down on his haunches.

*

Kozlov sat at his desk, smouldering with anger. His black, unforgiving eyes, set like a like a bitter winters' night. Daniel Temple would soon feel the maelstrom of his fury. He thought about the questions he had asked, ran the answers through his mind, then cursed himself for his slowness of thought. Why was Temple here? He had asked. The answer was stunningly simple and staring him straight in the face: the girls. They were the daughters of an ex SAS officer. Temple is or was an SAS officer. Why else would he be here? He was going to free them, or at least try. He was their knight in shining armour. How very noble. How very British, he laughed to himself.

*

Daniel shuffled forward. Staying low and quiet, he checked the breeze; it was coming from the north. He was down wind; the dogs wouldn't pick up his scent. He checked his watch again – a minute to go. Taras's car was approaching; he could hear the tyres crackling over the loose gravel. He opened the case, pulled out the rifle, assembled and checked it. Tapping the magazine against his boot, he slapped it into place and mounted the sights. Kneeling comfortably against a tree, he pulled the rifle to his shoulder, closed his eyes and imagined the scene. Taras's car would pull to a halt. He would exit the driver's door on the side closest to the house. Durakovic would leave the house, walk down the steps and…

Daniel lined up the sights. The shot was simple – four hundred yards, level ground, excellent light and minimal breeze. He thought back to his test. The double tap on the dummy, chest and head, then thought about the task ahead. He closed his eyes again, rehearsed again; perhaps the shot wasn't that easy after all.

Daniel opened his eyes. Deep pools of blue-green, as cold as the embrace of an arctic ocean, gazed across the clear, open ground.

He watched the car sweep around to the front of the house. Guards appeared from either side, holding huge dogs – rottweilers; two hundred pounds of attitude, muscle and teeth. They barked, snapped and snarled as Taras emerged. He stood and waited.

Durakovic appeared from the main door, walked to the top of the steps, stopped, smiled and held out his arms in an open, welcoming gesture.

Daniel watched him through the scope.

Durakovic stepped forward.

Taras stepped forward.

The two men stood directly in line, their bodies gradually merging into one as Durakovic descended the stone steps.

Daniel lined up the shot and slowed his breathing, closing out the world. Nothing else existed; just him, the rifle and the targets. His finger rested lightly on the trigger. The shots clear in his mind.

'Come on, one more step,' he whispered.

Daniel looked through the telescopic sight. The back of Taras's head came level with Durakovic's chin, their bodies appearing as one. Daniel fired, instantly adjusted and fired again. The rifle kicked. Two armour-piercing bullets accelerated almost silently out of the muzzle at seven hundred and seventy metres, eight hundred and forty two yards, per second. They struck their targets almost simultaneously. The first ripped straight through the centre of Taras's back, snapped his spine, exploded out of his chest, continued on through Durakovic's abdomen, exited through his lower back and slammed into the stone wall of the house. The second took off the top of Durakovic's head as his body started to crumple from the catastrophic impact of the first shot. Then, slightly deflected, it punched through the wooden front door and buried into an interior wall. The two men fell dead as blood pumped from their bodies and ran down the steps.

The guards stood in stunned silence.

Daniel was already moving.

A blur of movement at the tree line caught the guards attention and snapped them into action, unleashing the dogs. The two huge rottweilers bounded across the open ground, growling and snarling, chasing down their quarry as the guards ran behind.

Daniel ducked, dodged and crashed through the trees, all need for stealth removed. A hail of bullets tore after him. Bark splintered and sprayed into the air. Hundreds of missiles fizzed past his head. On he ran.

Snapping, snarling beasts closed rapidly behind him.

Daniel stopped running, span, knelt and raised the rifle in one fluid movement. The first dog was fifty yards out. The second fifty-five; both were closing in fast. Daniel let them come. Forty yards, thirty, twenty, five: the first dog leapt. Daniel calmly levelled the gun and silently fired. The beast recoiled in mid-air, slamming back into a tree.

The second monster closed in and leapt, its jaws wide open and its teeth bared. Daniel rolled on to his back, held the rifle against his shoulder and fired again. The snarling brute somersaulted backwards and fell to the ground, dead.

Daniel was already up and running. The guards were still there, two hundred yards behind, labouring hard through the forest. Daniel approached the main road then stopped abruptly.

He knelt, crawled slowly forward and peered through the rifle's telescopic sights. Mertz was there, exactly where he should have been; waiting. Only Mertz wasn't just waiting; he was stood, leaning across the roof of the car, aiming an identical rifle at the spot where he expected to see Daniel emerge from the trees.

Daniel rolled carefully to his right, way out to Mertz's left, out of his field of vision. Then he stood, moved stealthily down to the road and checked Mertz again. He was still there, in the exact same position, lining up his shot; waiting. Expecting to see Daniel walk or run unsuspectingly from the trees.

Daniel glanced back. The pursuing guards had slowed and stopped. He checked Mertz again – he was still there. Daniel silently crossed the road and dropped off the tarmac into a shallow gulley. He stayed low, working his way back.

Silently, Daniel came up behind Mertz.

Mertz shuffled his feet.

Daniel watched him for a moment. Mertz was getting anxious; Daniel should have been back by now. Daniel removed the magazine from his rifle, slipped it into his pocket and laid the rifle on the ground. Reaching into his coat, he pulled out the Makarov and eased forward.

Mertz was still standing in the exact same position, tiny, shuffling movements of his feet betraying his growing apprehension.

Daniel crept behind him.

Mertz shuffled again, then froze, the Makarov pressed firmly into the back of his skull.

'Nice and easy. Leave the rifle on the roof of the car and step slowly backward. One wrong move and I'll blow your head off. Say yes if you're clear,' Daniel instructed in perfect German, unable to resist adding insult to injury.

'Yes,' Mertz replied.

Daniel stepped away.

Mertz eased slowly backward.

'Turn around,' Daniel instructed.

Mertz turned, a look of shock and amazement fixed on his face.

Daniel smiled.

'Karl Mertz, ex-KSK, you never were very good. I remember you from that NATO exercise. You couldn't find you own arse with two hands and a mirror. Found your level at last?'

'Very clever, Temple, but it's not over yet.'

'It is for you – almost.'

'Almost?'

'I need you to fly me back. Do it and I might just let you live.'

'Why should I?'

'If you don't, I'll kill you – right here, right now.'

'If I agree?'

'You live to see another day. Get me back on time and who knows I might even let you go. You're nothing to me unless you get in the way.'

Daniel waited whilst Mertz thought it through. It was a simple decision.

'OK,' he agreed with a heavy sigh.

'Good choice,' Daniel replied. 'Before we go, reach inside your jacket, left hand, thumb and forefinger and throw out the Glock.'

Mertz reached slowly under his arm, pulled the

gun from his shoulder holster and offered it to Daniel.

'Throw it away, over there,' Daniel nodded to the other side of the road.

Mertz threw the gun. It clattered across the tarmac and disappeared down the bank.

Daniel stepped across to the car, retrieved the rifle from the roof, opened the rear door and dumped it inside. He waved Mertz over to the car.

'You drive,' he said.

Mertz climbed into the driver's seat. Daniel slid into the rear and buckled up.

The Mercedes accelerated away as the two chasing guards spilled out onto the road and stared disbelievingly at the rapidly disappearing car.

*

The airfield was still quiet and deserted.

'Park there, next to the plane,' Daniel instructed.

Mertz parked and switched off the engine.

Daniel opened the rear door and stepped out.

'Get out and open the boot,' he ordered.

Mertz did as instructed.

'Climb in.'

Mertz hesitated, staring into the dark, tight, confines of the boot.

'In,' Daniel insisted, waving the Makarov to enforce the invitation.

Mertz climbed in, bending and squeezing his tall frame into the space.

'Mind your head now,' Daniel said, slamming the lid closed.

Daniel turned and ran across the airfield to the building he'd noted earlier at the end of the row. He tried the door – it was locked. Taking a step back, he launched forward and kicked it hard. The door and frame splintered and gave. He pushed it open and stepped inside.

The business wasn't closed down after all. The door opened into a small office, neat and tidy, its walls covered with posters, pictures of aircraft, people parachuting, single and in tandem. Daniel looked around; there was another door. He crossed the room, entered and took a few moments before finding exactly what he was looking for. He moved quickly, selected what he needed, checked it over, turned and moved toward the exit. Daniel stopped halfway across the office, sat on the edge of the desk, lifted the phone, got a tone and dialled the number. There was no reply.

He clicked the phone, chose another memorised number and dialled. The call was answered on the seventh ring.

'This is John Shaw. I'm afraid I am unable to take your call at the moment. Please leave your name and number and I will get back to you as soon as possible. Thank you.'

Daniel put the phone down. Thoughtfully, he drummed his fingers on the desk then lifted the receiver, dialled the number and waited again. The line hissed and a phone rang, faint and distant. There was no reply.

Daniel dropped the phone.

'Damn it,' he whispered, disappointment seeping into his mind in the chilled gloom of the office.

Whatever he was going to do, he would be doing it alone.

Daniel returned to the car, retrieved the rifle from the rear seat, then released Mertz from the trunk.

'Move,' said Daniel, walking Mertz toward the aircraft.

Mertz regarded Daniel and his gear with a puzzled look.

'Nervous passenger,' Daniel said with a deadpan expression, acknowledging the question on Mertz's face.

Mertz said nothing.

They boarded the aircraft. Mertz span through his pre-flight checks and got the aircraft rolling. Daniel sat behind him, the Makarov held level and steady.

'You're making me nervous with that damned thing,' Mertz said as they taxied to the runway.

'Don't worry, I'm not going to shoot you. I don't

know how to fly,' Daniel replied. 'We ready to go?'

'Yes.'

'Good – stop the aircraft. Now we wait.'

'Wait? Wait for what?'

'Dark!'

*

Lesya hadn't slept at all. Kozlov had returned to his room late, made her strip naked and lay on his bed, stroking herself. It turned him on to watch, but he was distracted and lost interest after just a few minutes. From then, she had lain perfectly still, completely withdrawn, like she wasn't there. Kozlov had paced the room and looked at her from time to time, caressing her with his eyes, but he did nothing more. Eventually, tiredness had overtaken over him and he had lain down on the bed next to her, closed his eyes and slept. She had remained like a corpse, expecting the slightest movement or disturbance to wake him. But he slept a disturbed, restless sleep for the rest of the night. She sensed there was something wrong, as even in his dreams his mind was not at peace, and she was pleased. He was a depraved and evil man.

*

Elizabeth and Jennifer had been placed in separate cells. Initially, they had tried to talk, but were soon shouted into silence. Alone, they had changed back into their jeans and sweaters and tried to sleep, their minds filled and overwhelmed by the terrifying sounds and visions of Yana's sordid abuse.

Jennifer curled into a tight ball and cried, constantly, comfortingly, rubbing her hands over her arms. She no longer needed to imagine what might happen. She had seen it for herself; the disgusting, inhuman cruelty. The physical violation, humiliation and degradation. Thoughts and visions drove her to the edge of insanity. Her mind fought against the vivid, living torment of their nightmare and she mumbled through her tears.

'Daddy, please come, Daddy.'

Isolated from her sister, Elizabeth cried quietly in the dark. She was desperate to stay strong. Daniel was there. He would come; he had promised. She prayed he would be in time.

*

Yana came to, laying naked on a bed. She felt numb and nauseous; her surroundings just a vague tapestry of shape and colour.

In the early afternoon, the men came for her again. There were more men – different men. Each of them wanted their turn. Timur dragged her from the bed, stabbed a needle into her arm, then carried her naked to the same room as before. She didn't fight – it only made it worse. Timur threw her onto the unmade divan and handcuffed her wrists to the bedstead. The men stood in a circle, naked and aroused. They took their time, forcing her to perform, her young body fulfilling every one of their sexual desires. She let them take her in silence, obeying every command and capitulating to every sordid act. Two and three at a time they crawled, straddled and laid on her, like a pack of crazed dogs. Her violation and torment seemed to last an eternity until, at last, they were done with her. She lay defiled and motionless as Timur jacked her full of crack and left her sprawled on the bed. She would entertain the men again tomorrow.

*

The day wore on, growing darker and colder. The weather closed in, bringing the full embrace of winter, and heavy snow began to fall. Lesya watched as it swirled in the wind, dancing in the light which broke through the heavy curtains, as, naked and alone, she stared out of the bedroom window.

Kozlov had taken her clothes and her dignity. Soon he would take whatever else he wanted. She contemplated leaping from the balcony, but she didn't have the courage or the desperation – not yet. She turned away, crossed to the fire and thought of her home. Would she ever see her family again? she wondered as she tried to warm her body. Despite Elizabeth's words of encouragement, she knew no one would come. They were all alone, as hundreds, maybe even thousands, had been before them and would be after them. Maybe, one day, she would go to England, but it would not be the dream she envisaged – not for a better life. It would be as a street girl; a prostitute. A drug-dependent whore, manufactured and sold by men like Kozlov. The tears rolled silently down her face.

The door opened and Kozlov entered, his eyes appraising her, full of desire.

'Lay on the bed,' he ordered.

Slowly, anxiously, she walked to the bed and obediently lay down. She watched him strip. His erection stood out from his belly, large and angry.

'Touch yourself – put on a show for me,' he instructed, his voice rumbling, low and excited.

She stroked herself slowly and delicately. Her hand moved across her breasts, then down, softly along her thighs and lightly through the thin strip of her pubic hair.

Kozlov stood and watched, barely breathing, his eyes following every movement.

'Open your legs,' he growled.

He moved closer and stood at the edge of the bed, stroking himself, becoming more and more aroused.

Lesya closed her eyes.

Kozlov climbed onto the bed and raped her.

TWENTY

The short winter day faded to black. The twin-engine jet accelerated down the concrete runway and lifted into the dark evening sky. Daniel was on his way. He settled into the seat behind and to the right of Mertz, letting him fly the aircraft in silence as he checked Mertz's rifle over; a VSS Vintorez, identical to the one he had used that morning. He pulled the clip, ensuring the magazine was full; ten rounds of nine-millimetre, steel-core, armour-piercing bullets. He set it on the floor then carefully checked the equipment he had taken from the airfield. Satisfied with what he had, he relaxed back in his seat.

It was over an hour before Daniel spoke to Mertz. He was curious. What drove a man to work for someone like Kozlov? To know what he did; to know what happens inside that castle, yet still do it.

'Why Kozlov?'

'What do you mean, why Kozlov?' Mertz questioned irritably.

'Why do you work for him? You know what he does – what sort of man he is? You know what happens in that place, right?'

'He pays well. I keep my mouth shut, do what he asks and he pays – I mean, he pays really well.' Mertz repeated nervously.

'How much?'

'It depends.'

'How much do you make in a year?'

'It depends, half a million maybe.'

'Half a million what? Roubles, euros, dollars?'

'Half a million dollars. He always pays in dollars. Christ, what's it to you?' Mertz snapped apprehensively.

'Just curious. I wanted to know what sort of value you place on those girls' lives and your own.'

'Value?' Mertz answered, then fell silent. He hadn't thought of it in that way before.

Daniel let the question sink in a little further and waited patiently for the full response.

'Look, it's a business, that's all – a business just like any other. I just provide a service – transport, that's it,' Mertz replied in a more defensive tone.

'This thing got autopilot?' Daniel asked, changing the subject.

'What?'

'You heard me. It's a simple enough question.'

'Yes, yes, it has, why?'

'Where's the wind coming from?'

'North, why?' Mertz answered, shaking his head in confusion.

'Set the autopilot to take us on a steady descent to fifteen thousand feet, five miles north of the castle. Then fly in a circle, a holding pattern. There's nothing but open country round the castle, right?'

'Yes, that's right. So we get to the castle and fly in circles. Then what?'

'Then nothing.'

Mertz turned the dials and flicked the switches. Daniel watched over his shoulder.

'That it?'

'That's it, it's all computerised.' Mertz replied then followed with a question. 'I don't understand. Don't you want me to land somewhere? The airstrip we left from, maybe?'

'You don't need to understand, Karl. You just need to do it. That's what you do for Kozlov, isn't it – just do as you're told?'

'I guess.'

'You ever take part?'

'Take part?'

'Yeah, you ever help? What is it they call it, breaking the girls in?'

'No, never. I might work for Kozlov, but I'm not

into that. I'm not a pervert. I just do transport,' he repeated, desperately trying to justify his actions.

'What are you then, exactly, apart from a piss-poor ex-soldier?'

'Like I said, I just do transport. Nothing else. It's all mostly flying these days. The smuggling runs – drugs or arms usually,' Mertz replied, ignoring the jibe.

'You ever transport the girls?'

'Sometimes, but not often. They're mostly taken by land – it's easier. The European borders are wide-open all the way to the UK. It gets a bit harder then, but we get what we need through.'

'We? You sound part of it to me,' Daniel pressed.

'I mean them. They get what they want through. I'm not part of it.'

'Which ports?'

'I don't think I should say anymore; I've said enough already.'

'What have you got to lose? Kozlov's going down. You don't have to be part of anything anymore. You could help. Help me, help yourself.'

'You seem very sure of yourself for one man. Kozlov's a madman. He's got a whole fucking army and he's really pissed at you.'

'You seem to forget, you still need to get out of here alive.'

'No, Temple. You forget. You still need to get on the ground.'

'True, but I think I've got it covered,' Daniel replied confidently. 'I don't need to kill you, though, we've both got options.'

Daniel pulled his double-edged commando knife from its sheath and flashed it across Mertz's face.

'I could just slice bits off,' he said; a cold, calculated and menacing suggestion. 'It would hurt like hell, but you could still fly,' he added, maintaining the emotional and psychological pressure.

'Taras would have reported in by now. You left him behind, remember? You're in a whole world of trouble, Temple.' Mertz hit back, clutching at his final straw.

'Not unless he does it by séance. I left Taras in a pool of blood right next to your pal Durakovic. I don't think he'll be reporting anything. Kozlov won't know or suspect a damn thing – not yet.'

Mertz sighed and rolled his head back.

'Christ,' he sighed. 'If Kozlov finds out I've said anything he will kill me.'

'It's a possibility, but I don't think you need worry about that. I'm not going to tell him. Besides, if you don't tell me, I'm definitely going to kill you.'

Mertz sighed heavily again; he was already on the road to hell. He nodded slowly.

'OK, I'll tell you what I know, but it's not much. Like I said, I don't get involved in that side of the business. I don't need to and I don't want to.'

'Fair enough. Just tell me – how do they get the girls from A to B? Where do they come from? Where do they go?'

'I tell you and you let me go. That's the deal, OK?' Mertz asked nervously.

Daniel inclined his head.

'I'm sitting comfortably, you may begin,' he replied, without answering the question.

'Alright, Kozlov is the head man – I mean, he is *it*. There is no one more senior in the Russian mafia. He spends his time either in Moscow or at the castle just outside St Petersburg; he seems to like it there. He runs the operation via a network of commanders – only men who have earned their stars.'

'Stars?'

'It's a mafia thing – tattoos. Those who have earned the right have stars tattooed on their knees and elsewhere. It signifies their rank and status and means they would never kneel before anyone.'

'Alright, carry on.'

'The commanders are spread throughout the old Soviet block and further down into the Balkan states; Ukraine, Lithuania, Belarus, Serbia, Croatia, Romania, Hungary, Slovakia, Bulgaria, Poland, the Czech Republic. You name it, he has an operation there. They get girls in all sorts of ways; kidnapping, false advertisements, promises of a new or better life, but they all end up the same. They're imprisoned and broken in, as you said – raped, given drugs, violated, and abused over and over, until they just submit. Then they're shipped out and put to work.'

'Shipped where? Shipped how?'

'All over the world. There's demand everywhere. They're the oldest trades in the world, aren't they – sex and slavery.'

'What about the UK?'

'Yes, they get sent there. Several hundred – maybe a thousand a year – and it's growing.'

'Lucrative?'

'Not as much as you might think. It has to work on volume and a percentage of future earnings. A girl sells for between two and ten thousand pounds, depending on the market, what they're wanted for and so on. But then they make maybe a thousand a day and Kozlov takes his cut – a big cut.'

'How do you get them there?'

'Like I said, they're taken over land, then by ferry across the channel, usually through Dover, Felixstowe – sometimes Ramsgate. The European borders are literally wide-open. Kozlov has specially converted transport, trucks and vans with compartments to hide the girls in. They get shipped in small numbers – never more than five at a time. They never get searched – not properly, anyway; a cursory glance at best.'

'Then what?'

'Then they get sold on and distributed all over the country. London, Birmingham, Manchester – all the big cities, and smaller towns too. Kozlov has his own operation as well, run by a commander based in London.'

'And?'

'And nothing. That's it – that's all I know.'

'What about the drugs and arms sales?'

'They're separate – a totally different set-up all together.'

'How?'

'It's a different scale and highly lucrative.'

'How does Kozlov operate that?'

'He uses a network of global contacts. The country commanders manage sales and distribution. He also uses legitimate organisations to get contracts.'

'Legitimate organisations?'

'Weapons companies, security advisors, negotiators – that sort of thing.'

'Security advisors?'

'Yeah, you know – legitimate companies that provide professional security services and personnel. Especially the ones that advise big corporations or governments; they know what's happening and how to get in. There's no shortage of people prepared to work both sides of the equation, especially if the money's right. Everyone has their price, don't they?'

Daniel nodded a brief acknowledgement and stopped asking questions. He'd heard enough – knew all he needed to know – more than he needed to know.

The aircraft shuddered.

'Weather's closing in a little,' Mertz said.

'How long until we get to the castle?'

'Not that long, fifteen minutes maybe. We're on a slow descent now.'

'How's the fuel?'

'Enough for another thirty minutes flying, then we'd better be looking for the airfield,' Mertz answered feeling more relaxed and confident.

He had co-operated and Temple still needed him.

The plane flew on, the computerised autopilot following an exact course.

Daniel sat, calm and relaxed and waited a few moments in silence.

'Tell me when we pass the castle,' he said, shrugging on his coat.

'You cold?' Mertz asked.

'Not yet,' Daniel replied, zipping the jacket up tight.

'The castle is there, down to your left. We're just going into a circular holding pattern now, fifteen thousand feet, like you said.'

Daniel pulled the woollen balaclava from his

pocket, slipped it over his head and gazed out of the cockpit window. From the faint glow emanating from the security lights far below, he could just make out the vague shape of the castle, standing high on its rocky plinth,

'What happens when this thing runs out of fuel? Does the autopilot still work?'

'In a fashion, why?'

'Just wondered,' Daniel shrugged.

He stepped to the back of the cockpit and pulled the Makarov from his inside coat pocket. Mertz turned nervously in his seat, his eyes wide open and fixed on the gun.

'We had a deal, you need me,' he shouted, his voice conveying his sudden anxiety, the pitch changing with a combination of fear and anger.

Daniel aimed.

'I lied,' he stated coldly as he pulled the trigger.

It was a careful, deliberate shot through the neck, designed to debilitate, not immediately kill. The bullet passed straight through the soft flesh, shattered Mertz's vertebrae and severed the spinal cord before slamming into the pilot's high-backed seat. Mertz slumped back, paralysed from the neck down, shocked, bleeding heavily, but fully conscious.

Daniel stood over him and looked down dispassionately.

'Time to go,' he said, slipping his arms through

the parachute straps and fastening the buckle around his waist.

Mertz just stared back, his eyes blinking rapidly.

Daniel slipped the Makarov back inside his jacket, re-sheathed his knife and strapped the rifle to his chest. Leaving the door open, he stepped out of the cockpit. He walked down the fuselage and opened the main cabin door. The icy wind whipped and buffeted around his head. He pulled his goggles down over his eyes and glanced back.

'Happy landings, Mertz,' he called as he stepped out of the aircraft.

The plane flew on.

Daniel pulled the ripcord and the enormous double chute billowed and opened above him. He checked the canopy, manoeuvred the toggles and aimed for the castle.

Daniel controlled the huge tandem parachute perfectly, gliding smoothly through the air as he flew decreasing circles, paragliding in, his dark-blue parachute canopy invisible against the night sky.

The castle loomed up toward him, growing larger and larger through the darkness. Daniel looked down. The roof of the castle was a mathematical puzzle of shapes and angles, tall turrets, sloping roofs and long narrow walkways. He picked his landing spot – a large, flat square of stone in the centre of the castle's roof. Expertly manipulating the parachute toggles, Daniel slowed his descent, hovered in the air and landed as softly as if he were stepping off the pavement.

*

The aircraft flew on, completing its pre-programmed circular course. Mertz sat semi-conscious in the pilot seat, a steady flow of blood running from the wound in his neck. A red light flashed on the instrument panel followed by a loud, audible warning.

'Warning, low fuel,' stated the synthetic voice.

Mertz opened his eyes, his brain screaming at him to move – to take control, to land the aircraft. He sat, paralysed, his eyes blinking in silent terror.

'Warning low fuel,' the voice repeated again and again and again.

The engines roared, stuttered, whined, then faltered again. Finally starved of fuel, they abruptly died. The cockpit was silent except for the sound of the wind rushing through the main cabin door. The aircraft slowed dramatically, then stalled. It hung momentarily in the air, turned nose-down and accelerated, screaming toward the ground. Mertz closed his eyes and waited.

*

Oleg sat in the security room, completing the final reconfiguration of the perimeter sensors. They would be tested first thing in the morning. He switched the system from test mode to live, recalled the men from the grounds and reactivated the outer defences. He glanced over to the master control panel. Everything was green. All was quiet.

*

Daniel reeled in the billowing parachute, unclipped the straps and stuffed the rig beneath a series of wide metal pipes which ran the length of the roof. Crouching low, he surveyed the castle's rooftop. Directly opposite, a door sat squarely in the centre of the tallest tower which continued for another twenty feet above his head.

Daniel unclipped his rifle, pulled it to his shoulder and crossed to the door. He tried the handle; the door was unlocked. Daniel stepped inside, directly onto a narrow stairway, and looked up. The stairs ran a short way, turned, then continued on into the darkness. He looked down. The stairs descended in the same fashion, zigzagging their way through the tower. He listened carefully, then moved forward, cautiously making his way down to the lower floors.

*

It was late and the castle was quiet. Most of the men were relaxing in their quarters or assigned to night security duties.

Kozlov sat in his office, concerned and agitated. Taras should have reported in by now. He had called him on his mobile phone half a dozen times but there was no answer. Something was wrong; he could feel it. But it was catch-22; he couldn't call Durakovic – not directly. He just had to wait. He sat in his ornate, throne-like chair, thoughtfully drumming his fingers on the desk. His mind wandered, brooding and anxious, in need of a comforting distraction. He picked up the internal telephone.

'Prepare the room,' he instructed.

*

Petr put the telephone down and motioned Timur to follow him.

'Kozlov's ready, he wants the room prepared,' he said.

The two men moved out of the lower floor common room, leaving Damir and Mirsad drinking vodka, happily absorbed in a low-budget porn film.

'We'll call down when we're ready for you to

bring the girls. Make sure you're awake,' Petr said as he left.

They strode through the castle to the room opposite Kozlov's office. Petr stopped, turned, knocked on the office door and waited.

'Come,' Kozlov called.

Petr entered, carefully closing the door behind him.

'Good evening, Mr Kozlov.'

'Petr,' Kozlov greeted him in return.

'Please could I just check what equipment you would like in the room this evening?' Petr asked respectfully.

Kozlov thought for a moment.

'Let's have a selection,' he said. 'But the leather straps and bondage gear may be appropriate. I think the one called Elizabeth might be a little feisty to begin with. She might need to be restrained. I think we'll make her watch little sister entertain the men first. Have one of the others give them a little something to help heighten their spirits and cloud their senses. It makes it easier and all the more entertaining.'

'Yes, Sir,' Petr replied.

'Oh, and Petr – make sure the cameras are set up and rolling from the start. We'll send daddy a little DVD of his girls at play,' Kozlov laughed.

*

Daniel reached the bottom of the tower and entered the main landing, still five floors above the open expanse of the vast entrance hall. He stood back in the shadows, listening to the sounds of men moving around in their rooms, TVs, music playing softly and the reverberation of tired men snoring at the end of a long day's shift. He moved on, stepping out onto the broad, central staircase, travelling quickly and quietly to the next floor. Every few steps he stopped, listened and moved again, just a shadow in the darkness. Three more times he repeated the process before stepping silently into the open expanse of the main entrance hall.

Daniel stood in the dark shadows beneath the stairs. Noise and activity carried from the direction of Kozlov's office; the hallway and adjoining corridors were unusually bright. He inched forward and began crossing the great open space. Suddenly, a door to his right opened and men turned into the hall. Daniel was exposed, out in the open. Quickly, he looked right then left. The door to the security office was closed. Swiftly, he moved to the wall, placed his hands and feet against the stones and pushed. The wall rolled silently forward just as the security office door opened. Daniel stepped around the wall and disappeared into the shadows. Laying his rifle on the floor, he drew his knife and waited.

'Good night, Oleg,' yawned the guard, turning into the corridor.

Daniel listened.

The guard walked slowly, making his way down the corridor, leaden footed and exhausted.

Daniel watched.

The guard drew level with the open passage, passed, then stopped dead, as if taking a moment to register the opening.

Daniel waited.

Seemingly confused, the guard stared at the opening, then stepped forward, peering into the gloomy passageway.

Daniel struck like a viper. His left hand shot behind the man's head, yanked him forward and smashed his skull into the wall. His right hand drove the knife straight through his neck. The only sound was a slight rush of air escaping from the guard's severed windpipe, followed by the faint gurgling of blood filling his throat. Daniel dragged the guard into the passage and dumped him on the floor.

The secret door rolled silently closed.

Daniel wiped his knife on the guard's clothes, picked up his rifle and moved on.

A dim light glowed softly from the hall at the bottom of the stone stairway. Daniel walked cautiously down, one silent step at a time, then stopped and listened. A faint sound of groaning and gasping, a man and woman, carried from a corridor further down. Daniel's heart began to pound. He turned right, following the sounds to a door that stood slightly ajar. Pressing his back against the wall, he eased the final few feet down the corridor and peered in. Two men sat on an old sofa, their eyes drunkenly fixed on the TV screen opposite. Daniel glanced at the screen and breathed a soft sigh of relief. An old, low-budget porn film flickered out across the room.

Daniel un-shouldered the rifle, burst through the door and fired twice in quick succession. The bullets tore through each man's chest, slightly left of centre and exploded out of their backs. Blood poured from the ragged holes. Daniel didn't wait to check his work. The men were dead.

Daniel backed out of the room, slung the rifle over his shoulder, turned back to the hall and ran. He reached the cell doors and looked in through the spyhole. Elizabeth was sat in the right-hand room alone. He span on his heels and checked the opposite door. Jennifer was curled into a ball on her bed. Get Elizabeth first, he thought. Then the obvious realisation struck him – no key. He turned and ran back to the room he'd just left. The bodies of Damir and Mirsad lay slumped on the sofa, their lifeless, unseeing eyes staring out into the room. Daniel patted them down. Damir's right-hand trouser pocket clinked as he hit it. He pushed his hand into the pocket and pulled out a small bunch of keys. One was a car key. He ripped it off and threw it away. Two keys were too small; they were discarded. That left two others – one for each cell door, he hoped.

Daniel slipped the key into the lock and threw open the door.

Elizabeth recoiled across her bed and sat fearfully, clasping her knees to her chest. Daniel's huge frame filled the door. He looked down at her, his cold eyes softening as she gasped and flinched. Daniel pulled the balaclava from his face.

'Daniel!' she exclaimed.

'Sshh, come on,' he said, holding out his hand.

Elizabeth took his hand and they span out of the room.

Daniel opened the second cell door and Jennifer mirrored her sister's actions. She sat up on the bed, clasped her knees to her chest and sat shaking her head in panic, quietly repeating a single word, "No", over and over again. Elizabeth dived into the room and threw her arms around her sister.

'It's OK, Jen, it's OK,' she whispered.

Jennifer looked over her sister's shoulder to Daniel who stood blocking the doorway, his familiar face caring and compassionate. She smiled through her tears, unable to speak.

'Time to go, ladies,' Daniel said, prompting them to action.

Elizabeth helped Jennifer to her feet.

Daniel looked at both of them. They were dressed in jeans and sweaters. No shoes, no coats – they would freeze to death in minutes outside.

'You got any other clothes or shoes?' he asked urgently.

'Nothing we'd want you to see us in,' Elizabeth replied.

Jennifer just shook her head.

'Wait here,' Daniel replied.

He turned, ran back to the hall and disappeared down one of the other corridors. Finding the main storeroom, he ran down the length of shelves, grabbing extra clothing, coats, socks and boots, then he turned and ran again.

'Here, put these on. The boots might be a little large. I grabbed the smallest I could see; you can pad them out with extra socks, OK?'

The girls rapidly dressed.

'Ready to go?'

'Yes,' they said.

'No, wait,' Elizabeth said again. 'There are two others; two other girls in the castle. They were brought here with us. Please, Daniel, we must help them,' She implored, pulling at Daniel's arm.

*

Kozlov stepped out of his office and into the room opposite.

'Are we ready, Petr?' he asked enthusiastically.

'Not quite, Mr Kozlov. We're just setting up the cameras now. Ten minutes and we'll be ready,' Petr replied.

'Very well. Call me when the girls are on their way. I want to be ready to direct the action.'

He walked back to his office, poured himself a large measure of neat vodka and relaxed back in his chair.

*

'Where are they?' Daniel asked.

Elizabeth shook her head. 'I don't know. I think Lesya is locked in Kozlov's bedroom. I don't know where Yana is; she could be anywhere.'

'That's sixty rooms, Liz, we don't have time. I have to get you out of here.'

'Please, Daniel, please try. We can't just leave them.'

Daniel frowned. He knew she was right; he had to try.

'Alright. Five minutes. If I can't find them, we have to leave, OK?'

Elizabeth nodded. 'OK,' she agreed.

'Come on,' Daniel said, leading them away from the cells.

They reached the small hall, turned left and ran down the passageway toward the external door. Daniel undid the bolts, turned the lock and opened the door to let an icy wind blow in, carrying a thick flurry of snow.

'A storm's coming,' Daniel snapped, short and anxious. 'Wait here. Huddle down in the corner against the wind, I'll be back in five. If I'm not, you have to leave, do you understand?' He asked, handing his Makarov pistol to Elizabeth.

She looked down at the gun.

Daniel closed his hand around hers, then closed them both around the gun.

'Just point and squeeze,' he said.

'I understand,' Elizabeth confirmed, slowly nodding her head.

'Good. Now listen to me. You run and you keep running – that direction,' Daniel said pointing the way. 'Stay off the roads. Don't stop until you're well away from this place. Find somewhere warm to hide; a farm or something. Wait the night out, then get to town – St Petersburg. Find a telephone in a public place. You know the rest.'

'Yes, thank you, Daniel.'

He was gone, moving back through the dimly-lit

passageways, back up the steps, through the secret doorway and into the castle.

In the main entrance hall, Daniel saw Petr emerge from a room, cross the hallway to Kozlov's office and knock the door. He slammed his back into the wall and waited until Petr disappeared into the office.

Daniel moved on, bounded up the stairs to Kozlov's bedroom and ran down the landing. He stopped suddenly and dropped to his knees. The guard outside Kozlov's room was there, slumped in the large wing-backed chair, fast asleep. Daniel drew his knife and crept forward. The guard slept on. Daniel fell on him from the shadows, clamped his hand over his mouth, drove the knife into his chest, twisted and lifted the blade. The guard made no sound as he slithered out of the chair and slumped to the floor. Daniel dragged him away, down into the gloom of the corridor, then returned to the bedroom, checking his watch. Three minutes gone.

*

Petr entered Kozlov's office.

'Everything is ready, Sir,' he confirmed.

'Excellent, thank you, Petr,' Kozlov replied almost jovially. The vodka going someway to relieving his previously less than favourable mood. 'Come, sit a while, share a drink with me,' he added with deceptive amiability.

'Thank you, Mr Kozlov,' Petr replied, graciously and sensibly accepting the offer.

*

Daniel turned the key in the lock, softly turned the handle, then swiftly entered the bedroom. A girl with long dark hair jumped up from the bed, recoiling away from him as he rushed through the door.

Daniel held up his hands in placatory fashion.

'It's alright, Lesya, I'm not here to hurt you,' he said with a calm, almost soothing authority.

The girl stood perfectly still, her naked body glowing in the firelight.

Daniel quietly closed the door, slowly crossed the room, took a robe from the bathroom and walked slowly toward her.

She stepped back nervously.

'It is Lesya, isn't it?' Daniel enquired gently.

The girl nodded.

'I'm here to help. I have Elizabeth and Jennifer. You must come with me now. Do you understand?' Daniel asked quickly.

Lesya looked confused, fear dulling her thoughts.

Daniel quietly repeated himself in Russian.

Lesya's expression changed as the tears welled in

her eyes. She launched forward, throwing her arms around his neck. Daniel gently draped the robe around her shoulders and pulled her arms away.

'We have to go. Stay right next to me,' he said.

Daniel held her hand as they fled out of the room, along the landing and down the stairs.

Lesya ran with him, then stopped abruptly

'Yana,' she said.

'Sorry, there's no time. I don't know where she is,' Daniel replied, pulling her along as fast as she could go.

'I do. I know where she is.'

Daniel stopped in his tracks.

'Where?'

'Petr's room. She's in Petr's room.'

'Where is it?'

'Third floor, to the right. The third door, I was there earlier – I saw her.'

Daniel pushed Lesya back into the shadows.

'Crouch down behind this chair. I'll be right back, OK?'

Lesya nodded and watched him go.

Daniel bounded back up the stairs. One flight up, he turned right, ran down the corridor and reached the third door. The key was in the lock. He turned it and entered. Another young girl with long dark hair was sprawled naked on the bed, fresh needle marks in her arm. He moved forward. She was semi-conscious but totally incoherent. Wasting no time, Daniel wrapped a sheet around her body, lifted her effortlessly from the bed and carried her from the room.

Lesya saw them coming. She climbed out from behind the chair and followed them down the stairs.

Daniel checked right and left as they reached the bottom.

'Go left,' he whispered.

They turned and ran a short distance.

'Stop,' Daniel instructed.

Lesya looked at the wall.

'Where's the door?' she asked.

She had never seen the secret passage operate. The door had always been open before.

'Put your feet there and there,' Daniel pointed at the stones with his foot. 'That's it. Now place your hands up there. Good. Now push, with your hands and feet together.'

Lesya did as she was told. The door rolled smoothly open.

*

Elizabeth huddled in the corner with one arm wrapped around Jennifer as the snow fell steadily over them and the wind whistled above their heads, whipping across the small rocky opening.

'We have to go, Jen. Five minutes must be up by now.'

She pulled Jennifer to her feet.

'Hold my hand. Stay right by me. Run as fast as you can to the trees.'

Jennifer nodded silently.

The two girls stood and prepared themselves. Elizabeth stood at the bottom of the steps and held her sister's hand, then suddenly turned in fright as the outer door burst open.

Lesya flew through it, straight into Elizabeth's stunned embrace.

Daniel stood behind her with Yana held in his arms. He set her down on the freezing ground.

'Liz, come with me. The rest of you wait here,' he said urgently.

Elizabeth took Daniel's hand as he dragged her running through the passageways to the storeroom.

'Find them some clothes and get them dressed. I just need to do one more thing,' he said turning out of the room.

'Where are you going?' she turned to ask nervously.

Daniel was gone, running down the dark passages and back up the steps to the hall, moving like a phantom in the darkness.

*

Kozlov drained his glass, containing his third large measure of vodka, in a single gulp.

'Come, Petr, let us entertain the English ladies,' he said, an evil grin spreading across his face, flushed red with vodka.

Petr stood. 'I'll have them brought up, Mr Kozlov,' he replied, lifting the telephone on the desk.

He pressed the button, dialled the internal number and waited. There was no answer. He hung up, dialled and waited again. There was no answer.

Kozlov looked at him.

'Damir and Mirsad are down there, probably drunk and asleep,' Petr said by way of explanation.

'Send Timur down to get them,' Kozlov snapped.

*

Daniel pressed his ear against the security room door. There were no voices, just the regular clicking sound of someone lightly tapping at a computer keyboard. Daniel pictured the room in his mind. Whoever was in there must have their back to the door. Carefully, he turned the handle and opened it an inch. Oleg was sat at one of the computers, working on his security improvements. Daniel looked at him. He was a small, slightly-built man, hunched over a computer terminal. His thinning sandy hair tousled and uncombed. Daniel thought for a moment. Oleg was, in any other life, a harmless individual, but he had chosen, in one way or another, to be there, and he was in the way. Daniel stepped silently into the room, his compassion no more than a fleeting thought. Oleg was too busy, too focussed, to notice anything. Daniel closed the gap between them and struck with awesome speed. Clamping one hand on Oleg's head and the other around his chin, he turned his hands rapidly in opposing directions. Oleg's head span savagely with them, snapping his neck in an instant. Daniel let him go and he flopped forward onto the desk, dead.

Daniel scanned the master control panel, then flicked his finger across a row of green glowing buttons, switching off all of the security systems. Satisfied he could do no more, he turned and left, carefully closing the door behind him. He ran back to the passageway and slipped through the gap as the door rolled smoothly back into place.

The girls were waiting, ready to go. Elizabeth tried to stand Yana but she flopped and sagged like a rag doll, gazing at her with vacant eyes.

'What's wrong with her?' she asked.

'Drugs – she's been pumped full of them. It's part of the process,' Daniel answered. He looked around. 'Everyone ready?' he checked.

They all nodded. 'Yes,' they said.

Daniel crept up the stone steps, looking for the patrolling guards. They would need to let the first guard pass, then go quickly, using the short time gap, dark night and worsening weather to cover their escape.

Daniel ducked back into the shadows as a guard approached. He watched him pass, walking slowly, hunched into his coat. His thick, fur-lined hat, pulled down tightly over his head. His eyes partially closed against the biting, raw wind and blustering snow. Daniel let him go, then dropped back to the bottom of the steps.

'Let's go,' he said.

'What about Yana?' Elizabeth asked.

'Just concentrate on yourselves. Head for the trees and stay close. I'll bring Yana,' Daniel replied lifting her easily into his powerful arms.

He lined the girls up in front of him – Elizabeth, Jennifer, then Lesya. He closed the outer door and placed his foot on the second step.

'Go, go, go,' he said, pausing a second to let them clear.

One by one, the girls emerged from the small rocky opening and ran hard across the open ground.

Daniel paused a beat, then pushed off the step, launching himself up and out into the snowy night air.

The biting icy wind and snow swirled around

them as they struck out across the open ground, aiming for the cover of the trees. Elizabeth led the way, followed closely by the others. Daniel brought up the rear, urging them on, carrying Yana in his arms.

*

Timur wandered out of the prepared room toward the secret door, mumbling obscenities to himself. Damir and Mirsad were a waste of space, he thought as he went.

He opened the door and stepped into the darkened passageway, tripping as he walked. His eyes, still adjusting to the darkness, gazed down at the shape before him. He dropped to his haunches, squatted over the body lying in the passage, then jumped to his feet in realisation. Turning, he ran back through the opening and headed into the security room to find Oleg asleep, slumped across his desk.

'Oleg, wake up! There's something wrong! Oleg? Oleg?'

He moved to the desk and tried to shake the man awake. Oleg's open eyes stared back at Timur, dull and lifeless. Timur stared in disbelief, then looked at the security panel. The lights glowed red; all of the systems were off. He span on his heels, raced across the room and hit the panic button. The external floodlights flared, bathing the grounds in brilliant white light as the sirens began to wail.

TWENTY-ONE

Daniel pushed them hard, running ahead and leading the girls on. They plunged through the tree line as the external lights flashed and the ground behind them was lit a bright fluorescent white.

'Move,' Daniel shouted urgently.

The girls ran as fast as they could, stumbling and tripping in the darkness. The trees crowded in and the low branches scratched and tore at their faces and bodies as they fled blindly through the forest.

*

Kozlov stormed out of his office, leaving Petr trailing in his turbulent wake. Guards ran from their rooms and swarmed down the great open staircase, gathering en masse in the centre of the enormous entrance hall. Timur ran from the security room, shouting down the corridor.

'There's someone here. Oleg is dead. All of the systems are off. There's another dead guard in the passage – Yakov, I think,' he reported in breathless panic.

'Temple,' Kozlov exploded, his face turning crimson with rage. 'Find him. Get the girls, kill them, but I want Temple alive,' he ranted.

*

Daniel urged the girls on. The wind dropped and the snow ceased under the dense cover of the trees, but it was cold, bitterly cold and the frozen ground was solid and slippery beneath their feet. They ran hard, crashing through the trees, desperate to create distance between themselves, the castle, and their inevitable pursuers.

With Daniel leading the way, they cleared the outer perimeter and the security sensors. Elizabeth ran close behind him, twisting and turning, following Daniel's every move. She ducked under a branch and stumbled, her feet slipping on the hard, unforgiving ground. Her right foot slid into a rocky crevice and she fell forwards and sideways, screaming as she tumbled down the steep incline and thudded onto her back in a broad forest hollow. Winded and gasping with pain, she clutched her right ankle, trying to catch her breath.

Jennifer and Lesya tumbled down the bank and dropped to their knees beside her, breathing hard, concern etched on their faces.

Daniel laid Yana gently on the ground and turned to Lesya.

'Try to get her up. Get her moving,' he instructed in Russian.

Lesya nodded and slid across the forest floor to her friend.

Daniel knelt beside Elizabeth.

'Let me see,' he said.

He undid her boot but didn't remove it, knowing that if the ankle was bad she'd never get the boot back on. He held the ankle in both hands and moved it gently.

Elizabeth gasped in pain.

'It's not broken, just badly twisted,' he said, feeling the swelling.

He removed his own boots, took off one pair of socks and formed a tight strapping around her ankle. Putting his own boots back on, he re-tied Elizabeth's and pulled her to her feet.

'This is going to hurt, sorry,' he said. 'Put your foot down.'

Elizabeth stood, placed her foot on the ground and took a couple of paces, wincing as the pain shot through her ankle.

'I'll be fine,' she said, bravely forcing a smile.

'Good girl,' Daniel nodded.

Lesya had Yana on her feet and was gently slapping her face.

'Come on, Yana, wake up.'

Yana's eyes slowly fluttered opened.

'That's it, Yana, come on – it's Lesya.'

'Lesya,' Yana mumbled semi-coherently.

'Yes, that's it, talk to me, Yana,' Lesya repeated, holding Yana's hands, patting and rubbing them, urgently trying to bring her to a full state of consciousness.

*

A dozen guards, led by Timur, poured down the secret inner passages. They divided at the bottom of the steps. Four went left with Timur to the cells. Four went right, running toward the common room, and four went straight on to check the external door.

Timur could see the cell doors were open well before he reached them. He turned around. There was no point in looking – the girls were gone. He ran back to the small inner hall. A guard appeared from the right-hand passageway.

'Damir and Mirsad are dead,' he called urgently as he ran. 'Sweep all the corridors down here. Check all the rooms – make sure they're not hiding somewhere.'

Another guard came running from the exit corridor.

'The external door is unlocked. There are footprints in the snow leading out to the forest,' he shouted.

Timur ran up the steps, back into the castle and down to Kozlov's office. 'They've escaped, Mr Kozlov,' he panted. 'Max reported footprints in the snow leading out eastward to the forest, but they're disappearing fast in the storm.'

Kozlov angrily slammed his fist on the desk.

'Get the men ready, go after them. Petr, you lead them. Timur, Petr is in command, go with him. Don't come back unless you have them.'

'Yes, Sir,' the two men confirmed leaving the room.

'Timur, get twenty men. Be out front in five minutes. I'm going to change,' Petr ordered.

'Yes, Petr,' Timur nodded, before running back down the corridor to assemble his men.

*

'We've got to find somewhere to hide out for the night. We can't get far with both you and Yana,' Daniel said, stating straightforward, obvious facts.

'I'll be OK. Yana is coming round slowly – we can make it,' Elizabeth replied, with optimistic encouragement.

Daniel smiled. 'We're definitely going to make it,

but you still need to rest that ankle, and we need Yana capable of running on her own,' he responded confidently, despite his inward reservations. 'Can you go on a little further?'

'I'll run all night if I have to,' she confirmed.

Daniel turned to Lesya.

'How's Yana?' he asked.

'She can walk.'

'How you doing, Jen?'

'I'm OK. I'll help Liz, we'll be fine. We best get moving, hadn't we?' she asked. Her voice and face reflected every ounce of her fear and concern.

'Sure, we're going again now. OK, ready to move?' Daniel checked.

The girls didn't reply. They were already up, bravely hobbling, stumbling and dragging their feet forward.

The girls moved as quickly as they could, hand in hand, quietly supporting each other. Daniel strode along beside them, tall and strong, encouraging and cajoling, not giving any of them the opportunity to drop the pace or think anything but positive thoughts.

Daniel called the girls to a halt and listened hard. Sounds of their pursuers' noisy progress carried through the darkness. Stealth not a consideration, Kozlov's men were spread in a wide arc and right on their trail.

'Move,' Daniel whispered harshly, urgency in his voice.

The girls got the message and picked up the pace as best they could. Daniel glanced over to Elizabeth. She was drawn and pale. The agony of every step cut deep into her face. They needed somewhere to hide. They needed it fast.

Daniel led the way, turned south and urged them on.

Elizabeth stumbled and fell again, her face contorting in agony as she mouthed a silent scream, bravely fighting the pain.

Daniel stood beside her, slid to the rifle around to his chest, lifted her to her feet and crouched down, offering her his back.

'Jump on,' he said. 'Time for a ride.'

She didn't argue. She scrambled onto his back and wrapped her arms loosely around his neck.

'Come on,' he said as he took off, bounding through the trees.

The girls strode out after him, Lesya dragging Yana by the hand as she stumbled on like a tired, bedraggled toddler.

Their pace quickened, just about maintaining the gap between themselves and their trackers. Daniel's long, loping strides, ate up the ground, pulling them along relentlessly. Staying beneath the trees, out of sight and the worst of the weather, he led them around the treeline, running parallel to the St Petersburg road.

The men behind came on, their pace unrelenting, closing the net slowly but surely. Daniel glanced back. There was no way they were going to outrun their pursuers. He glanced left and right. The brilliant arced line of their torches danced and swept through the trees, cutting them off. The bright circles and probing beams of their lights inched ever nearer.

Suddenly, the road ahead of them lit up and a strange roaring sound filled their ears. Daniel slowed and dropped Elizabeth gently to the ground.

'Wait here. Stay low, out of sight,' he said.

Moving back along the tree line, Daniel edged closer to the road. The wind howled, whipped and billowed the snow, driving it into thick, high banks and heavy drifts on either side of the road.

He crouched low. The lights grew closer and closer and the roar of heavy diesel engines labouring hard over ice-packed roads filled his ears. Then the snow shone a brilliant white as headlights cleared the first in a series of bends and illuminated the road ahead.

A huge snow plough pushed on, throwing out a bow wave of snow, ten feet high. It was followed by a small convoy of trucks, battling their way through to St Petersburg.

Daniel knew it was their only chance. He turned, ran back and collected the girls.

'Follow me,' he called, pulling Elizabeth onto his back and getting the others to their feet.

Staying just inside the tree line they ran to the road and stumbled along the bank, their pace keeping them marginally ahead of the convoy.

The snow plough slowed, blasting its air horns as the convoy approached the final bend before the road straightened again.

Daniel let the first truck crawl by, selecting the last truck in the convoy as his target.

The men behind were closing fast. Bright lights waved and searched through the trees. It wouldn't be long – time was running out.

The second truck approached – a logging concession, its massive trailer piled high with thirty foot tree trunks.

Daniel let it pass, checked urgently left and right and moved the girls slowly along.

The men drew closer.

Daniel pulled them to a stop and turned them to face the road, looking down over the slow-moving convoy, now just a few feet below.

The final truck approached.

'Wait until I say, then jump. Don't hesitate. Don't think about it – just jump. Clear?'

They looked at each other, then at Daniel, all of them nodding nervously.

'When you hit the truck, crawl to the far edge

and slide under the cover where it's flapping loose – you see it?' he asked, pointing across.

They nodded again.

The lights on the bank were almost on them. A few more seconds and the powerful beams would find and hold them like rabbits in headlights. The chase would be up. There would be no escape and no mercy.

The final truck pulled level, its long trailer covered by a thick tarpaulin that sagged lazily in its centre, and the surface rippled in the wind like waves on the water. Daniel waited another second, praying that whatever lay beneath the cover was going to be forgiving. Landing on a pile of scrap iron, pointed spikes and sharp edges sure as hell wouldn't be pleasant, but it was a risk they were just going to have to take.

The lights grew larger and brighter. The searching beams broke through the last few trees and they were just ten seconds from discovery.

'Jump,' Daniel urged as loudly as he dared.

Jennifer leapt, kicking her legs in the air as she cleared the bank.

Lesya didn't wait for her to land. She kicked off the bank and was in the air just as Jennifer landed in the centre of the truck with a jarring thud.

Yana stood wavering on the edge of the bank; she couldn't move.

Daniel looked down at the truck. It seemed to be flashing past at a speed which belied its previously snail-like crawl. It was picking up speed. There was no time left.

'Not your day, is it,' Daniel stated, lifting Elizabeth over his head.

She looked at him anxiously, but there was no time to ask the obvious question. Daniel threw her from the bank. She flew through the air and slammed into the canvas-covered sand, sending pain shooting from her ankle to her hip and through her back.

Jennifer and Lesya rolled together, lifted the edge of the tarpaulin and ducked underneath, dropping two feet into the wet sand.

Lights broke onto the bank. Voices were shouting; their words drowned out by the wind and roar of the trucks.

Daniel lifted the fear-paralysed Yana into his arms, took three steps back, ran hard and launched into the air.

'Oh shit,' he said quietly.

The rear of the truck rapidly approached – they were going to miss.

Daniel turned his body in the air, lifted Yana and threw her as hard as he could. She landed, thumping into the canvas with two feet to spare. Daniel's momentum kept him going. His body crashed into and off the back of the trailer and he fell.

Elizabeth gasped in horror as she watched Yana land and Daniel fall. She looked up at the trees. Lights swept along the bank and reached the position from where they had jumped; it was still a desperate race. She slid across the canvas, grabbed Yana's hand and pulled with all her strength, fearsome determination and adrenalin dulling the pain in her leg.

*

The men on the bank stopped dead; the trail had abruptly ended. Their lights swept along the bank, left and right, then onto the road, flashing across the final truck as it disappeared around the bend in the road.

Petr looked at his men.

'Where are they?'

'The trail just stops, right here,' one of the men answered, shining his torch at the ground, right at the spot from where Daniel had jumped.

'Have they crossed the road?'

'There are no tracks leading down the bank, Petr.'

Petr frowned, his expression changing from confusion, to anger, to enlightenment as the thought struck him.

'It's a trick. Look up in the trees,' he said, shining

his torch up through the branches of the closest tree. 'Search the trees – they must have climbed them to hide in the branches,' he stated with certainty.

*

Elizabeth pushed Yana beneath the tarpaulin and slid in after her, landing softly in the wet sand next to her sister. They lay on their backs, breathing heavily, staring at one another in disbelief through the darkness. Lesya suddenly burst out laughing; a spontaneous act of nervous excitement as she threw her arms around Elizabeth's body, thanking her for saving them.

Jennifer glanced around.

'Where's Daniel?' she asked nervously.

Elizabeth pushed Lesya's arms away and shook her head.

'He fell saving Yana,' she said. 'I saw him jump with Yana in his arms. He could see they were going to miss the truck. He threw Yana – I saw him fall,' she explained, the tears welling up in her eyes.

Lesya's nervous laughter stopped abruptly. Daniel, the man that had saved her – the man that had saved them all, was gone. He had given his life to save Yana, a girl he didn't even know. She looked at Elizabeth and shook her head, her optimistic energy replaced by numbing shock. What were they going to do? The flirtingly brief hope and belief had just been shattered.

'He just fell,' Elizabeth said again, her face creasing in sorrow as she realised the enormity of their loss.

The girls lay in stunned silence.

'What are we going to do?' Jennifer asked, the returning fear evident in her voice.

'We do what Daniel instructed. We get to town, go somewhere public, find a telephone and call for help,' Elizabeth replied, with as much conviction as she could find.

*

At the last possible moment, Daniel caught, one-handed, the length of rope which trailed from the tarpaulin down the rear of the truck. His feet hit the ice covered road, bounced once into the air, then dragged into the snow. Grimly, he held on, then kicked his legs and turned his body as his feet scrambled along the road in a despairing attempt to find his balance.

Desperately, Daniel held onto the rope as his body dragged along the road's icy surface. Winding the rope around his hand, he pulled hard, scrambled to his feet and turned his body to face the rear of the truck. Gaining balance, he reeled in the length of rope, placed both feet flat on the ice and crouched low, skiing on his boots behind the truck.

Hauling himself closer to the truck, Daniel pulled hard on the rope and, turning his feet, he swerved out, wide of the truck, and looked down the length of the trailer. The ribbed metal sides were wet and slippery. Along the top, protruded metal loops, designed to take the tarpaulin rope sat at regular intervals, but lower down there was nothing.

He turned his knees, swung back in and pulled himself closer to the rear. Winding the rope around his arm, he held it taught, bent his knees and jumped. His feet swung up and planted firmly against the rear of the trailer. Shortening the rope, Daniel climbed, hand over hand, keeping the rope tight as he moved. He reached the top and slid his body over the edge and onto the tarpaulin.

The wind billowed in, rippling the canvas, as Daniel ducked his head under the tarpaulin cover.

'How are we all doing?' he asked easily, dropping down onto the sand.

'Daniel!' Elizabeth exclaimed with delight. 'I thought you were – I saw you fall. We thought you were dead.'

Daniel smiled. He could see the tension and fear in their faces.

'I'm fine. It wouldn't do for your knight in shining armour to fall off his horse now, would it?'

he said, trying to put them at ease. 'We should be clear now, at least for a little while. We'll be in St Petersburg soon. We'll have to keep moving and stay out of sight as much as possible. Kozlov won't be far behind us and I'm pretty sure he'll have men in town by the time we get there.'

'What are we going to do?' Elizabeth asked.

'We're going to do what the old advert said, and let the train take the strain,' he answered, with an encouragingly confident grin.

The girls stared at him, their faces a mixture of growing confidence and confusion.

'We'll go to the station and take the next train to Helsinki. We can't risk going to any of the authorities here. Chances are that the local police would hold us and hand us straight back to Kozlov – for a handsome reward, no doubt. We must get across the border and out of Russia. Help will be there. By the time Kozlov realises, if he realises, where we have gone, it will be too late,' Daniel explained, trying to sound as confident and convincing as possible. 'Rest now. We will be on the move again before too long.'

*

The men swept along the bank, searching through the trees as Petr stood and watched the taillights of the convoy slowly disappear from view.

'There's no sign, Petr,' Timur called as he returned. 'We would have found them by now. They must have crossed the road.'

Petr looked thoughtfully again at the fading taillights.

'Maybe,' he said. 'Timur, take ten men and sweep the other side of the road. I will take the rest of the men back to the castle, load up the vehicles and head into St Petersburg. That has to be where they're running. If you don't find anything, follow the road to town. We'll pick you up, OK?'

'Yes, Petr,' Timur confirmed.

*

Petr stepped in through the castle doors, stamped the snow off his boots, crossed the hall and headed down to Kozlov's office. Kozlov stood, pensively staring into the roaring log fire, his hands clasped tightly behind his back.

'Well?' he demanded, turning at the sound of Petr's approaching footsteps.

Petr shook his head. 'We lost them.'

'You lost them?' Kozlov echoed incredulously. 'Twenty men and you lost them,' he added angrily.

'Temporarily,' Petr replied nervously. 'We are sure they are heading into St Petersburg. Timur is still searching, following the road to the city. I came back to get the vehicles. We will find them again,' he continued, trying to sound assured and confident.

'You'd better,' Kozlov stated menacingly.

'Yes, Sir,' Petr acknowledged, almost bowing as he turned away, relieved to be leaving still in one piece.

Petr worked quickly, dividing his ten men into five pairs, each of them loaded into a big Toyota 4x4. They roared away from the castle, snow, mud and gravel spitting out from heavy-treaded winter tyres as they careered down the icy road to re-join the hunt.

TWENTY-TWO

The massive snow plough rumbled on, determinedly clearing the way as the convoy followed in its wide tracks, steadily making its way into St Petersburg.

Daniel peered out through the gap between the metal sides and canvas tarpaulin. The city was inching closer and he recognised houses and buildings he had passed just a few days before. The roads began to clear and the giant plough stopped, lifting its massive, angled blade before pulling off the road to the let the convoy pass. The trucks drove on, flashing their lights and blasting their horns in thanks.

Rolling through the outskirts of the city the convoy separated, the trucks steadily turning away, taking different roads south and east to Moscow, Minsk, Latvia and Belarus. Daniel watched them leave one by one until only the truck they were in remained, rumbling its way through the streets.

Daniel checked the street signs, peering through the gap in the tarpaulin, watching every turn. They were heading for the commercial rail terminal at the seaport, taking a route through the south of the city. Luck was still on their side. He glanced at his watch under the illuminated city lights. It was 2:00am; they would have at least four hours, maybe longer, before the early train left for Helsinki.

'We need to get out of here,' Daniel said to the girls. 'Get ready. When the truck stops next, we'll jump out over the side, OK?'

The girls nodded and moved along the side of the truck, loosening the tarpaulin, easing it away so that they could slip easily through the widened gap.

'Jennifer, you and Lesya help Yana – I'll lower Elizabeth down.'

The huge truck rolled to a stop at the next set of traffic lights. Lesya and Jennifer held Yana's arms and lowered her over the side as far as they could before dropping her to the ground and jumping out after her. Daniel followed suit. Leaning as far over the side as he could, he gently lowered Elizabeth. Jennifer stood with her arms raised, helping to support Elizabeth's weight as her feet met the ground.

The lights flicked to green. The great diesel engine roared as the driver crunched into first gear and slowly accelerated away. Daniel threw his legs over the side, hung for a second, then dropped to the road a few yards away from the girls.

'Off the road,' he called, waving them over to the dark shadows of a narrow alleyway set between two old office buildings.

'Where are we?' Elizabeth asked.

'Southern edge of town – not too far from the centre of the city, I think,' Daniel said, looking around. 'How's that ankle holding up?'

'It's OK.'

'Liar,' Daniel smiled.

He turned to look at the others. Jennifer and Lesya were cold and frightened but otherwise holding up pretty well. Yana was a mess, still enveloped in a drug-induced haze; it would be a while yet before she came out of it. He looked at her face. It was pale and haunted. She had been the first, he deduced; subjected to unbelievable, abhorrent abuse. It would take a great deal of professional care before she had any sort of life again.

Daniel kept them sitting for a moment longer, calming them down and focussing their minds, explaining what they had to do.

'We have to get to the Finlyandsky rail terminal to get the train that runs to Helsinki. We'll move slow and cautious. Watch the roads carefully and stay out of sight as much as possible. The weather will help. If you see any traffic or any people, get out of sight and hide until they've passed. Whatever you do, stay together. If we do somehow get separated, just keep heading for the station. It's north and slightly west of us on the other side of the city, on the other side of the Neva river – that way,' he said, pointing up to his left.

'How will we find it if we lose you?' Elizabeth asked.

'See that road sign? That says station. Find one that looks just like that. It will say Finlyandsky Vokzal; keep following it. Lesya can read the signs for you. The rail terminal is a large white building with lots of square pillars and a clock tower on top. There's a big statue of Lenin right in front of it.'

They moved out with the heavy snow swirling around them as the lazy, ice-laden wind whistled through the deserted streets, cutting through them, numbing their faces and freezing them to the bone. Daniel led the way, his arm wrapped around Elizabeth, supporting her weight as she hobbled one excruciating step at a time. Lesya and Jennifer followed, each of them holding one of Yana's hands as they walked behind, their eyes nervously scanning the road ahead.

*

Petr's 4x4 convoy caught up with Timur and his men

as they marched down the centre of the road, following in the snow plough's tracks. Petr slowed his vehicle, then braked to a stop alongside Timur.

'Anything?' he asked.

'No, nothing. They may have found a way past us, but we can't find any tracks. There must be something we missed.'

'The trucks we saw earlier – they must have managed to get onto one of them. Anything else and we would have found it. Climb in, spread the men out in the other vehicles. Let's go; they'll be in the city by now.'

'Yes, Petr,' Timur answered, following Petr's instructions.

The men moved quickly down the line, climbing gratefully into the warm interior of the Toyotas. Petr accelerated away, the heavy 4x4 snaking its way down the road before straightening out and settling into the centre of the path left by the snow plough. The others followed in disciplined, evenly-spaced order.

The line of Toyotas entered the city and divided as Petr instructed each of the drivers by radio to form a search grid. They drove with care, slowly working their way through the streets towards the city centre. Five vehicles, each with four pairs of eyes, watched every street, scanned every alleyway and surveyed every inch of city pavement.

Petr's Toyota cruised through the streets,

splashing through the icy, snow-slushed roads, following the course of the river through and around the northern fringe of the city, toward Finlyandsky Station.

Timur drove around and into the city from the south whilst the three other vehicles spread themselves in a line, north to south, driving the roads west to east across the heart of the city. Every vehicle instructed to converge on the Peter and Paul fortress on the northern bank of the river – working the grid, closing the net.

'Anything yet?' Petr asked over the radio.

'Nothing,' Timur replied.

The others followed suit. The streets were cold and lifeless.

'Drop two men out of each car – cover the streets on foot. Scour the alleys and side streets – check everywhere. We have to find them,' Petr ordered.

The cars slowed and men climbed reluctantly out. The search intensified.

*

The streets of the city were deathly quiet and desolate. Only the insane ventured outside this late in these temperatures.

Daniel pulled his balaclava down to cover his face. The girls stopped holding hands and pulled the sleeves of their sweaters down, wrapping the cuffs around their hands before ramming them deep into their coat pockets. Their collars were turned up and their heads bowed low against the freezing wind, but nothing kept out the gnawing cold as they trudged on in shivering, frozen silence.

Daniel kept the girls marching, ducking through alleys, small side streets, across back lots and car parks, staying off the wide, main thoroughfares, zigzagging his way across the city. They reached his first checkpoint, Baltiysky Station and Obvodny canal bridge. Daniel checked the roads. They were clear and quiet. He lifted Elizabeth off her feet, waved the girls forward, then ran across the bridge. Safely reaching the far side, he turned and ran down the steps onto the footpath, running the length of the canal and out of sight.

As they reached the bottom of the steep set of steps, Daniel set Elizabeth gently on the ground, supporting her weight as they walked, slowly making their way down the narrow, snow-covered path. On either side of the frosted-glass canal, the banks rose high, providing a degree of shelter from the wind and limiting their chances of being observed from the road. It was a long way round, but Daniel knew it was their best chance of being able to travel undetected.

Elizabeth hobbled gamely along, keeping pace as best she could; every step was becoming harder and slower. Her badly swollen ankle had seized completely; every movement sent jarring pain from her foot to her hip, contorting her face with pain. Daniel saw she could walk no further. They needed to rest and get out of the weather. They needed transport. He called the girls to a stop beneath a narrow footbridge and ushered them back to sit off the path where a clump of small trees and concrete supports formed a small wall on either side.

Set back in the shadows, the small space provided a three-sided shelter where they could hide, obscured from the road and sheltered from the worst of the weather. Huddled together for warmth, the girls sat with teeth chattering, noses and cheeks glowing red and their frosted breath pluming in the air.

Daniel dipped his hand inside his jacket, pulled out the Makarov and handed it to Elizabeth.

'Just in case,' he nodded.

'Where are you going?' she asked fearfully.

'We need transport. You can't keep going on that ankle, especially in this weather.'

He thought again, reached into his pocket and handed Elizabeth a handful of scrunched-up roubles.

'If I don't get back to you, buy four tickets to Vyborg, not Helsinki. If you ask for Helsinki, they'll want your passports.'

'Vyborg – got it,' she replied nodding. 'Then what?'

'When the train gets into Vyborg station, get off with all of the other passengers and mingle with the crowd, but don't get separated – stick together. Get out and away from the station as fast as you can. Find a telephone, call your father and tell him to call John Shaw or Coleman – tell him what has happened. He will arrange to get you over the border and into Helsinki. You'll be safe then. They'll arrange to have men waiting to get you home.'

'Won't there be someone in Vyborg?'

'No, I'm sorry. No one knows where we are. We're still on our own, Liz.'

She looked at him, the concern reflected in her frozen face.

Daniel stared intently into her eyes.

'I will get you home, I promise.'

Elizabeth stared back, the tears welling in her eyes. She threw her arms around his neck and kissed him on the cheek.

'Home,' was all she could say.

He held her face in his hands.

'Wait here. Keep out of sight. Keep together and keep warm. I'll be back as fast as I can.'

Daniel stood, turned and bound away, rapidly disappearing from view.

He ran back down the path, crossed the canal and headed back toward the large car park they had passed, between Baltiysky and Varshavsky station.

*

Two men watched as a man crossed the empty street, his size, appearance and activity immediately catching their attention. He was a big guy – someone who didn't fit. Someone who didn't want to be seen, but had little choice about crossing the road. He gradually moved out of the shadows and looked left and right, scrutinising his surroundings, cautious and careful. It was Temple.

They stood back, watched him come, then let him pass, standing silently in the dark shadows of the deep recess of the office building doorway. He hadn't seen them – that was obvious. They let him run by, then radioed in.

Timur was closest. He braked hard and span the big Toyota round, sending it sliding across the road. Then, hitting the accelerator, he straightened up and drove fast.

*

Daniel heard the high-revving engine from blocks away; not the sound he wanted to hear. He stopped dead and listened hard, gauging the direction, speed and distance – all were bad – coming towards him, fast and very close.

A black 4x4 skidded in a wide arc around the corner behind him, fifty yards away. He didn't need any more information. He took off, ran fast and ducked into the first alley on his left. He could hear the car behind him, its engine roaring, accelerating hard and glanced back over his shoulder. There were two men, he hadn't seen before, running just twenty yards back, the sounds of their footsteps masked by the chasing 4x4. Immediately behind them, a big Toyota swung into the alley, its headlights blazing, bathing the entire length of the narrow cut-through in brilliant white light. Daniel sprinted, pumping his legs hard and fast in huge, ground-eating strides. The two men fell behind and were overtaken by the 4x4 as it squeezed its bulk down the alley. Daniel glanced back again. The two men leapt into a door recess as the 4x4 caught and passed them, its door handles and flared wheel arches sending sparks darting and screeching into the air as they scraped down the walls. The Toyota roared closer, smashing through boxes and crates, exploding fragmented cardboard and wood into the air as it crashed through them in reckless pursuit.

*

The girls huddled together, shivering under the dark, frozen niche of the bridge. Elizabeth whispered to the girls, hoping that the conversation would take their minds off their situation and distract her from the nagging pain in her ankle.

'It's so cold,' Jennifer complained through chattering teeth.

'I know. It won't be for much longer; Daniel will be back soon. Then we'll be moving again.'

'He will come back, won't he?' Lesya asked.

'Yes, he will,' Elizabeth confirmed with absolute certainty. 'He's a friend of my father's. He was a special soldier too. He won't ever let us down, I promise.'

The sound of a large car slowing down on the road above cut their conversation dead. The car stopped. The girls listened intently, anxious looks on their faces.

'Shhh,' Elizabeth cautioned raising a single finger to her lips.

Doors opened and slammed closed. The sound of heavy footsteps reverberated over the metal footpath of the bridge directly above their heads.

The girls held their breath.

Men's voices carried across the canal.

'Search the footpath. Follow it round to Nevsky Prospect – we'll pick you up there.'

The footsteps came closer, crossed the bridge and walked on around the pavement toward the steps, a hundred yards further down the path.

'We have to move, quickly,' Elizabeth urged.

'Jennifer, help me. Lesya, you take Yana.'

'You have a gun,' Lesya said.

'So do they!' Elizabeth replied. 'Now move while we still can,' she ordered.

The girls slid down the icy slope, moving back onto the path, quickly and quietly.

The men reached the steps and walked slowly down, shining their torches into the dark corners of each and every hiding place.

The girls hustled down the narrow path. Elizabeth gritted her teeth and bore the pain, moving as quickly, if not as easily, as everyone else.

The men reached the bottom of the steps and turned onto the path. The bright beams of their torches shone ahead of them as they marched on, checking the banks on either side, closing on the narrow footbridge.

*

Daniel hit the end of the alley. Ahead of him, a steep embankment swept down toward the railroad and the gaping black opening of the first long, dark tunnel out of the city. Daniel vaulted the low wire fence, tumbled down the steep incline, regained his feet and bound onto the tracks.

The Toyota skidded to a halt and waited for the

two men on foot. Reaching the 4x4, they wasted no more time, jumping onto the running boards either side of the car. They gripped the roof rails and held on tight as the vehicle accelerated in hard pursuit and snow sprayed from the car's deep-treaded winter tyres.

The road veered away before sweeping back round on a flatter course. Coming back in, closer to the track, the big 4x4 flew side-on around the last bend, tyres struggling to grip on the ice-laden road as the driver tried to make up lost ground.

Daniel drove himself on, a hundred yards clear, leading them away from the city. Dead ahead, the tunnel opening loomed and the huge black arch sucked him in like a monstrous, gaping mouth.

The black Toyota accelerated again, crashed through the fence and hurled down the bank onto the track.

Daniel plunged into the absolute blackness of the tunnel, ran hard for a distance, then stopped dead. The track beneath his feet rumbled and vibrated as the first, faint sound of a locomotive entering the far end of the curving, mile-long tunnel registered. Daniel glanced back over his shoulder. The Toyota was closing in fast. He turned, dropped to his knees and snatched the rifle from his back. Pulling it tight into his shoulder, he took a deep breath, levelled the sights and fired. The man riding the right-hand side of the Toyota catapulted backwards through the air. Daniel swung left and fired again. The second man slipped from the running boards, his legs momentarily dragging over the rough, stone-covered ground before he fell away and Daniel watched him tumble along the track, unable to hold his own body weight against the drag of the earth.

*

The men moved quickly down the path, closing the gap between themselves and the girls.

The girls hurried on. The next set of steps, leading up and away from the path, lay another hundred yards ahead.

The men approached the footbridge and the bright light of their torches filled the shadows of the small recess where the girls had been. There was nothing there. They paused, instinct or intuition telling them they were close. The strong beams of light flashed down the path and thick snow swirled and dazzled before them as, just out of their reach, the girls passed under the final bridge and mounted the steps.

*

The sound of the locomotive filled Daniel's ears. The

lights from the Toyota filled his eyes. Both were travelling fast down the tunnel, mercilessly bearing down on him.

Illuminated and blinded in the bright xenon headlights, Daniel remained composed, calmly assessing the centre of the left-hand side windscreen. Smoothly, he levelled the rifle, paused, then fired. There was a moment's delay.

The Toyota came straight on, still accelerating.

Daniel rolled from the track and pressed his back hard against the wall. The big 4x4 swept past him, a faceless corpse at the wheel. Suddenly it turned hard left, flipped, crashed and rolled horizontally down the track. Shattered and broken, it came to a stop, upside down, thirty yards further into the tunnel. The engine revved then faded to a low diesel tick over. The tunnel was enveloped in darkness once more.

*

The girls reached the steps and started to climb. Nearing the top, Elizabeth stayed low and, crouching on the second to last step, peered over the concrete, checking the street. They were at a crossroads, where four of the main thoroughfares traversing the city formed a wide square. Elizabeth glanced left and right, then focused on the centre of the road, where steam rose from a large manhole cover, keeping it clear of snow. She eyed it carefully.

'Come on,' she said, standing to lead the way.

Bright torch beams suddenly cut through the darkness and lit their bodies, silhouetting them against the black night sky.

'Run,' Elizabeth cried. 'There,' she pointed to the manhole cover.

The girls ran fast.

The heavy, snow-dulled footsteps of the chasing men carried ominously behind them and merged with the growling noise of a 4x4 accelerating toward them just a street, maybe two, away.

They reached the cover and dropped to their knees, their fingers scrabbling and scratching against the wet, slippery metal. Desperately, Elizabeth pulled hard and the cover gave an inch. Jennifer and Lesya rammed their fingers through the gap, tearing the skin from their knuckles. Together, they heaved with all their strength.

The men were on the steps, climbing fast.

The cover slid open.

Elizabeth shoved Yana through the opening onto the ladder, sending her tumbling unceremoniously to the bottom, where she landed in a crumpled heap on the wet concrete floor of the tunnel. Elizabeth clambered after her, followed by Jennifer, then Lesya. In the dark confines of the pipe, none of them stood on ceremony. They bumped, squashed and trod on each other as they frantically scrambled down the ladder with one shared objective – safety.

The men hit the top of the steps as the black SUV flew into the centre of the square and skidded to a stop. Beneath it, the heavy manhole cover closed with the slightest of clunks.

*

Daniel moved cautiously toward the inverted Toyota. Inside he could see the last man remained trapped upside down in the Toyota's passenger seat, stunned and disorientated.

Daniel stopped, waited and listened.

The sound of the approaching locomotive abruptly registered. A circle of light appeared in the darkness. It grew larger and drew nearer. Massive airhorns blasted.

Daniel watched the man's hands scrabble and tear at his seat belt.

The train roared on, oblivious to the shattered Toyota's presence.

Daniel turned away and began to run.

Blinding light and deafening sound washed over the stricken Toyota and down the tunnel. The heavy, rumbling sound of the locomotive combined with the terrified, tortuous screams of the man.

Daniel ran hard.

Brutally, the sound changed. Metal slammed and crunched into metal. The Toyota exploded, sending shattered fragments of metal, glass and human remains blasting down the passage. Searing flame roared after it.

The train came on.

Daniel ran harder.

The train's brakes bit hard. Sparks and ear-piercing metallic screeches screamed through the tunnel as giant metal wheels locked onto slick, cold rails. Heavily-laden carriages bucked and kicked, then slewed from the track as the train derailed from the centre, back.

Daniel glanced behind.

The front end of the train slid towards him faster than the tunnel's entrance ahead. With brakes on full and its wheels biting into the track, the massive engines' momentum kept it coming. The carriages behind decoupled and slammed into the walls of the tunnel. Empty, lighter carriages kicked, span and cartwheeled into the air, crashing down onto the others with devastating force. Smoke and debris blasted through the tunnel.

Daniel pumped his legs harder, willing every ounce of energy, every yard of speed from his body.

Still, the train closed.

The front of the locomotive towered over him,

its single, high-mounted spotlight, illuminating Daniel like a great cycloptic eye. He looked up. The entrance was never going to come soon enough; there was no way out. He glanced either side – the walls of the tunnel were flat, blackened brick – no recesses. No shelter. He felt his body slow. His legs could give no more. He wasn't Superman; he couldn't outrun a locomotive.

The train closed in.

He made the decision; his only chance. Desperately, he threw himself forward, his arms outstretched in front of him. He hit the ground hard, thumped into the stone-covered sleepers, buried his face into the dirt and held his breath.

The front of the train swallowed him.

He felt a rush of air as the engine and front carriages poured over him; huge wheel axles passing an inch above his head. Then another and another, and another. Carriage after carriage rumbled over him, sending bright orange sparks cascading over his body as huge metal wheels sliced either side of his body.

Then it was over.

The train finally groaned and squealed to a halt. Daniel listened to the sound of feet dropping to the ground and crunching up the track on either side of the train. He waited for them to pass, rolled out between the wheels and looked up the tunnel. Men were running back towards what was left of the rear of the train and the mangled wreckage of the smouldering Toyota.

A loud hissing sound filled the tunnel.

'Oh shit,' Daniel said.

He shouted after the men. They couldn't hear. He let them go, jumped to his feet and ran hard again.

The massive explosion boomed down the tunnel and a searing ball of fire shrouded in billowing, thick, black smoke roared after it. The fireball tore down the tight, enclosed space, consuming everything in its path.

The mouth of the tunnel was just yards away. Daniel dived forward and left.

The ball of fire and smoke enveloped him.

Daniel blasted through the entrance, hit the ground with a shuddering impact and rolled through the thick, snow-covered grass. Beating out the flames with his hands, he pulled the smouldering balaclava from his face and lay still and silent. His heart pounding in his chest, he looked back at the tunnel, then up to his right. It wasn't over yet.

Two more black Toyotas sat side-on at the top of the bank, their engines idling as men sat inside and out, surveying the scene below.

Daniel scanned each one in turn. He recognised most, but some of the faces were new. Neither Petr or Timur were amongst them. Perhaps he'd gotten lucky. Maybe one or both were now scattered and burned in the wreckage of the tunnel behind him. He rolled left, further away from the track, and came up behind a tall stack of thick wooden sleepers. Kneeling in the dark, he watched the men carefully.

Blown out through the tunnel, engulfed in ball of fire and plumes of thick black smoke, it was obvious they hadn't seen him, as their attention was still firmly fixed on the entrance to the devastated tunnel and burning locomotive.

He checked his rifle and the did the math. There were seven rounds, plus six in the spare mag – thirteen shots. Eight men at close range; more than enough. He calculated again. The men would scatter after the first, or if he was lucky, second shot. They would return fire. They had automatic weapons and undoubtedly more ammunition – not a good equation. It was the wrong time and place to get caught in a firefight, especially one he couldn't win. He sat tight and waited. The men would move soon, that was certain.

Time ticked slowly by and a small grumble of anxiety crept in. He needed to be moving – needed to get back. The girls would be nervous. They were cold, alone and frightened. They would be thinking and making bad decisions – a recipe for disaster.

Daniel peered round the wall of sleepers and listened hard.

'Come on,' he whispered impatiently.

Then he heard them, faint and distant, but definitely coming. The wailing sound of sirens punctured the cold night air, growing stronger and more insistent.

'That's it, come on,' he said again.

At the top of the bank, the men started to move. Reluctantly dispersing, they climbed casually back into their 4x4's and drove slowly away.

Daniel watched them go, paused just a few more seconds, then moved. Keeping low, he crept up the steady incline of the bank, lay flat on the ground and cautiously peered over the top to the streets above. The road was clear. Warily, he made his way across the strip of black tarmac, into the small side street directly opposite the railway embankment, then cut onto a narrow path between two buildings.

Kozlov's men hadn't gone far. They were driving a slow circuit, no more than four blocks square. Daniel stood back in the shadows and watched them pass. The sounds of engines, screeching tyres and sirens grew louder as emergency service vehicles descended on the scene of devastation.

Daniel headed back toward the stations and the car park, travelling slower and more cautiously than before. He had miscalculated; he hadn't thought they would deploy men on foot – not in this weather. He wouldn't make the same mistake again. He moved from recessed doorway to dark shadow, from dim alleyway to narrow cut-through, checking every turn as he went.

The car park lay dead ahead. He surveyed it carefully from the darkness of an unlit alleyway, his eyes scanning slowly from building to building, doorway to doorway, side street to side street. There was no one there. He listened hard. There were sounds of distant traffic and of wailing sirens, but nothing close.

Cars, vans and trucks were scattered widely over the open tarmac lot. His eyes ran down each row until he picked out the vehicle he wanted, an old Sherpa-style van, about the same size as a Ford Transit, with sliding side windows in the driver and passenger doors. He checked the street again, then ran directly for it. It took less than twenty seconds to force the window, slide it open, reach in and unlock the door. Thirty seconds after that, the van was hotwired and moving.

Daniel drove with caution through the ice-laden streets, heading back across the canal. In the wide square, adjacent to the small footbridge he parked the van and surveyed the streets through the windows. There was no one in sight. He checked the mirrors and back down both sides of the street. The tail lights of what he thought looked like a Toyota SUV disappeared round a left-hand turn before he could be sure. He checked forward again. He saw them now; two men coming out of a narrow alley, moving quickly, searching urgently – out of place. He watched them go, running until they disappeared down another side street and out of view. With one final check, Daniel jumped out of the van, ran down the steps and ducked under the bridge to the girls. They were gone.

TWENTY-THREE

Shaking with nervous energy, the girls anxiously held their breath as they waited silently at the bottom of the sewer shaft. Fearfully, Elizabeth stared at the manhole cover, listening intently to the rumble of the Toyota's engine parked directly above.

The scream in Jennifer's throat stuck as Lesya clamped her hand firmly over her mouth and her eyes flashed, warning her to absolute silence as the rats scratched and scurried around their feet.

'Where are they?' called a man's voice from above.

'They were here – we were right behind them. Didn't you see them?'

'We didn't see anyone. You sure it was them?'

'Positive.'

'They can't have gone far. They must be hiding somewhere. Search the square. We'll drive a slow circuit in case they try to make another run for it.'

The girls moved off slowly, tentatively picking their way through the small furry bodies that scampered and crawled around their feet in the darkness. Elizabeth led them on, following the wide underground tunnel that ran beneath the city, joining with other pipes, tunnels and shafts, forming the criss-cross maze of a permanent twilight underworld.

Relieved to be out of sight, away from the snow and biting, icy wind, Elizabeth took them, as best she could determine, northward, through what appeared to be a main tunnel with other small tunnels and shafts sporadically leading off left, right and up, back to street level. Their progress was slow, hindered by Elizabeth's ankle, so they walked with care, allowing her to limp painfully along at her own pace.

Feet splashing through the inch of water, grime and filth that coated the bottom of the old brick tunnel, they made their way through the eerie subterranean system, gasping occasionally as the rats scurried over their feet, or at the almost overwhelming stench which emanated from the ageing, rusting iron pipes.

The tunnel wound on until, at last it ended, feeding into a large square bunker. It was dimly lit and warmer than the tunnel had been, heated by the collection of steam and hot water pipes that fed the city's buildings high above.

A short way into the bunker, the girls stopped moving, suddenly aware that they were no longer alone. Their eyes, now more accustomed to the dark, peered through the gloom, gradually picking out shadows and silhouettes. Small frail bodies of children lay strewn over the concrete shelves, ledges and widest pipes that lined and crossed the room. Dozens of eyes stared back at the girls, nervously blinking at the strange figures who had unexpectedly invaded the sanctum of their underground world.

Disbelievingly, Elizabeth stood with Lesya, surveying the small, dirty and bedraggled figures; the eldest she could pick out was no more than twelve. They were the street kids. The city's orphans, abandoned waifs and strays. They lived in the sewers, making their living begging or stealing in the train stations, or thieving on the busy shopping streets during the day. They sheltered by night in the relative warmth and safety of the labyrinthine world beneath the city. They looked anxious and frightened, their pitiful, grimy faces watching and waiting.

'Speak to them, Lesya; tell them we won't hurt them,' whispered Elizabeth, sensing their fear.

Lesya nodded and spoke softly, telling them not to be afraid. They weren't there to hurt them or to tell anyone about them. She told them they needed help too, and asked if they could stay, just for a little while.

A boy stood at the back of the room – the leader. He was tall, taller than the others, and painfully thin.

'Are you orphans too?' he asked in a soft, clear voice.

'No, we just need somewhere warm to stay. There are men, bad men, chasing us,' Lesya replied. 'Please can we wait here?'

'They won't come here, will they?' the boy asked nervously, his dark eyes opening wide with apprehension.

'No, they won't come here,' Lesya reassured him.

'The police come here sometimes. They drive us out of the tunnels and beat whoever they find, but we have nowhere else to go,' the boy replied sadly.

'We won't tell the police, I promise.'

The little boy nodded slowly.

'You can stay,' he permitted, pulling his ragged old grey blanket around his shoulders and settling back against the warm pipe which ran along the length of his wide concrete ledge.

None of the other children spoke. They accepted the boy's ruling and settled quietly back down to sleep, the girls' presence no longer of interest or concern.

*

Daniel stared in disbelief at the empty space. He

thought for a moment. There were only two possibilities. They had been recaptured or they had to move and were on the run again. Either way he had to find out, and fast. He thought again. The two men searching. The look of urgency. They had to be Kozlov's men. The girls were definitely running. He turned back onto the path, ran hard, bounded back up the steps, darted across the street and into the cover of a shop doorway. The low rumble of the 4x4 he'd seen moments earlier carried from just a few roads away. It was cruising slowly, searching the main streets, whilst the two men on foot covered the alleys and side streets. Daniel took off after them, running quickly and quietly. Reaching the side street, he stopped and peered round the corner. Seeing no one, he ran on.

The two men appeared just a short distance ahead, moving to the next alley. Daniel waited for them to turn, then ran again. The alley was a wide thoroughfare, split all the way down its centre by a tall wooden fence mounted in concrete pillars. Set on a low concrete wall, it divided the ground and parking spaces between two different apartment buildings. The men separated; one either side of the fence. They walked on, moving slowly down the length of the alley, shining their torches into cars, door recesses, refuse bays and dark shadows, carefully searching every hiding place.

Daniel snatched the balaclava from his pocket and pulled it down over his head and face. Walking slowly and silently, he slid down the left-hand side of the fence, checking the ground ahead for anything that might sound and give him away. The road was clear. Drawing his knife, he crept forward, no more than a black-swathed shadow.

Ahead, the man stopped, nervous, uncomfortable and alone in the dark. He turned slowly to his left and flashed his torch across a line of parked cars.

Daniel ducked behind the last in the line and crept closer.

The man walked on.

Out of sight, Daniel stayed low and ran down the line of cars, light on his feet.

The man and Daniel came to a narrow gap where another small path ran horizontally across the alley. They both crossed to another line of cars.

The man went right.

Daniel ducked left.

There were eight cars and a small truck parked nose to tail. Daniel crouched low, ran, overtook the man and waited.

The man walked slowly, edging closer to the front of the parked row – closer to Daniel.

Daniel dug into the snow, picked up a handful of stones and threw them high and away to his right.

They fell to the ground, a series of light clicks on the concrete.

The man stopped and turned, warily flashing the torch in the direction of the sound.

'You OK, Kiril?' asked a voice from the other side of the fence.

'Yes, fine. I thought I heard something,' the man replied, with evident unease.

'Mind the bogey man doesn't get you,' his partner laughed, sensing his discomfort.

Kiril turned back, coming face to face with Daniel, his black hooded face punctuated by two hardened, unforgiving eyes.

Daniel's hand clamped across Kiril's mouth and drove his head back hard against the side of the truck. His knife sliced straight through Kiril's windpipe, vertebrae and spinal cord with unbelievable speed and force. Daniel kept hold of Kiril's jacket as he gently dropped him to the ground and rifled through his pockets. He found Kiril's gun, emptied it, then threw the clip in one trash can and the empty gun in another. He checked his wallet, took the cash, threw the wallet on the ground and left the body where it lay; just another violent city mugging.

Daniel ran silently to the end of the alley, stopped and listened. The second man was still some way back, searching purposefully. Daniel rested his back against the fence and waited.

'Kiril,' the man called.

There was no answer.

'Kiril?' he called again.

Daniel put his hand over his mouth.

'Coming,' he replied in a slightly muffled voice.

They both approached the end of the fence.

'Is that you, Kiril?'

Daniel span round the end of the fence.

'No, the bogey man!' he said, driving his knife into the man's chest, clamping his left hand over his mouth and pushing him backward to the ground.

The man's face contorted in shock as he hit the ground hard, his head thudding into the snow-covered concrete. Daniel pulled the knife and knelt over him, his hand clamped like a vice around the man's throat.

The man shook his head pleadingly. Blood trickled from the corner of his mouth and his hands grasped Daniel's arm, trying in vain to pull him away, trying to cry out. Daniel's hand remained firm, letting out no more than a muffled whimper.

'Where are the girls?' Daniel asked, relaxing his grip just a little.

The man shook his head again.

'I don't know. We couldn't find them.'

Daniel pressed his knee into the man's stomach.

'You sure?'

The man gasped and nodded. 'Yes, yes, I'm sure.'

Daniel stared down at him, no mercy in his eyes – no compassion in his thoughts. His knife plunged back through the man's heart and his hands fell limply to the floor. Daniel wiped the knife clean, took the gun and the man's money, threw the gun in the trash and the money in his pocket. At least the train fare to Helsinki was no longer a problem.

Daniel dragged the body further back into the alley and shoved it under an old abandoned car. It would be frozen within the hour and found later rather than sooner.

*

The girls sat warming themselves on one of the broad pipes which ran across the width of the squared room. Elizabeth assessed the tunnels leading off from the bunker; she had no idea which way to go. The main tunnel from which they had exited didn't appear to continue. Instead, there were now four smaller tunnels. One to their right, one to their left and two straight ahead. Which one? she wondered. They were temporarily safe, but lost and alone, and she wished that Daniel had never left them. She wished he were with them, leading the way, calm and confident – in charge, in control and indestructible. She looked at her companions. Jennifer, her sister, so very afraid. She was on the very edge of rationality, unable to cope with the extraordinary mental and physical pressure. Lesya, strong and determined, just as she was. And then there was Yana. She doubted Yana would ever be the same again. The drugs had worn off now and she had totally withdrawn, her mind closed down, shutting out the horrific trauma of the abuse she had suffered at the hands of Kozlov and his men. She sat in a world of her own, barely functioning, staring into space, occasionally rocking back and forth or mumbling softly to herself.

Elizabeth spoke quietly to Lesya.

'Ask the boy. We need his help to find our way out to Finlyandsky station. Theses tunnels must lead all over the city. One of them must take us there.'

Lesya nodded. 'I'll ask him to show us the way.'

Lesya crossed the bunker, quietly picking her way through the small huddled bodies, careful not to wake the children that slept all around. She climbed onto the boy's ledge. He looked so young, breathing softly, sleeping peacefully and she hoped his dreams were more pleasant than the reality of his pitiful life. She watched him a moment longer, then gently shook him awake.

He woke with a start and Lesya gently soothed his brow with the softest of touches.

'It's alright,' she whispered. 'My name is Lesya, I have a little brother just like you,' she added warmly.

'What's your name?' she asked.

'Pasha, my name is Pasha,' he answered quietly and self-consciously, unused to any show of adult warmth or affection.

'How long have you been here?'

His eyes blinked rapidly. 'I don't know. Two years, maybe – a long time.'

'Where are your parents?'

'I don't know. I grew up in an orphanage in the city, but I ran away; they were horrible to me there. It's better here, safer and warmer, and I have friends,' he explained.

'Those are my friends over there,' Lesya said, pointing across the bunker. 'That's Elizabeth and Jennifer and Yana. We were in a horrible place, too. We ran away just like you, but we need some help now. Will you help us, Pasha?' she asked.

The little boy looked at the three girls and then back to Lesya.

'What sort of help?' he asked, appearing suddenly more serious and grown up.

'Well, we need to find Finlyandsky station, but there are men chasing us. They want to hurt us. Will you show us the way through the tunnels?'

Pasha stared into her face and then around at the children sleeping.

'We are all very hungry. Will you pay if I show you?'

Everything on the streets has a price. Nothing comes for free.

'We don't have any money, but I can get you some later. I'll also promise not tell anyone where you are, if you show us the way,' Lesya replied in negotiation.

Pasha nodded; he knew that Lesya's silence was worth more than a day's food for all of them. It seemed they had reached a compromise. He nodded his agreement.

'I'll show you the way,' he confirmed.

'Thank you, Pasha,' Lesya smiled.

*

Daniel had little choice; he couldn't spend the entire night scouring the streets. If the girls had been sensible and followed his instructions, they would be heading for the station. That's where he had to hope he would find them. He watched the street and listened. The big 4x4 was close by. He waited, listened to it approach the bottom of the alley, then turned and ran in the opposite direction, heading back to where he had left the stolen van. He crossed back through the side roads and alleys, checking the junctions and more brightly-lit main streets carefully, before emerging from the shadows. Gradually, he worked his way back to the canal, found the van and jumped into the driver's seat, breathing a small sigh of relief not to have encountered any more of Kozlov's men. He started the van, pulled out into the road and drove cautiously through the city toward the Nerva River and the numerous bridges which crossed into the northern half of the city.

Reaching the Dvortsovaya embankment, Daniel stopped; the bridge was drawn and closed for the night.

'Shit,' he said, pulling over to read the notice.

All the bridges would be the same. The city was effectively cut in half until 5:15am. He checked his watch – it was just 4:00am. There was nothing else for it; he would have to wait. He locked the front doors, climbed over the passenger seat and laid out in the half-empty length of the cargo area.

*

The girls were woken by the rumbling sound of heavy thunder rolling through the tunnels. They looked at each other nervously as the walls around them trembled and reverberated. Pasha laughed as he spoke to Lesya.

'It's five o'clock,' he said above the noise. 'It's the first subway train of the morning. The tunnel is just down there at the end of that pipe,' he added, pointing across to their right. 'Come, I'll take you now.'

'To Finlyandsky?'

'Yes, Finlyandsky. Come, this way,' he said enthusiastically as he scurried off down the right-hand tunnel of the two that lay directly ahead of them.

Lesya helped Elizabeth to her feet, then pulled Yana along with her as the four girls set off in pursuit of Pasha.

The small boy moved quickly and confidently through the underground labyrinth, turning left and right, crossing pipes and switching tunnels without a second's thought or hesitation. The tunnels filled with thunder again. The morning trains rumbled through just yards away, on the other side of old thick walls, which seemed to shake to their foundations as the trains clattered past. Then there were more sounds, of traffic and of feet, thousands of feet, walking and running, clicking and stamping. The city was waking. The station was filling. Another hectic working day had started.

The girls peered up through thick metal grills as they passed beneath, watching the early morning rush swing into action.

'This way,' Pasha called, confident that his voice would never carry above the chaotic sounds above.

*

Daniel woke from his light sleep to the sound of a horn blaring. The bridge was reopening. Climbing back into the driver's seat, he started the engine and switched the heater to full. Then he waited, watching as the bridge lowered and the barriers swung away, re-opening access to the northern half of the city. Daniel checked his mirror and pulled out into the flow of traffic already queuing to cross.

*

Petr pulled his Toyota to the side of the road and waited for the other three remaining drivers to call in from their vehicles. It had not been a good night. Timur and his team were certainly dead. Olaf had lost two of his men, and despite their search, they had been unable to find any trace of them. Most concerning of all, there had been no further sightings of either Temple or the girls. He sat nervously drumming his fingers on the steering wheel. They had to be here somewhere. They had to be planning to get out of the city. He looked in his rear-view mirror at the crowds thronging around the station, then glanced up at the huge clock, reading it backwards. It was 5:15am, busy and getting busier; the perfect place to disappear, he thought. That's what he would do. He would wait until the city and the stations were busy, melt into to the crowd and take the first train out and away. But which station? A train to where? He wondered. He looked across to the tall statue of Lenin, mentally working his way through the city stations. Moskovksy – they wouldn't go there, it didn't make sense, the trains would take them further into Russia. Vitebsk – that was a possibility. Trains from there headed south and west into Belarus, a possible escape route. Baltiksy was unlikely. They were mostly short distance commuter trains. Ladozhsky was outside of the city centre and served the cities to the north, up to Murmansk. They wouldn't go there. That left Finlyandsky and the trains to Helsinki, just five hours away. This was the one. This is where they would come, right here. He radioed his men.

'Get here fast. Cover the entrances. I will be inside. Stay in radio contact. Call me as soon as you see them,' he ordered.

He jumped out of the car, deployed his men and ran toward the main entrance.

*

Daniel caught sight of Petr and tracked him towards the station through the windscreen of his van as he pulled into the station. He sat, waited and watched. Two more of the big black Toyotas pulled in and parked, the men dispersing toward the numerous entrances and exits of the station.

Daniel sat for a while and thought it through. There were too many doors for the men to fully cover, but they would be vigilant. Getting by unseen was going to be tough. Petr had been smart in deducing their most likely escape would be by train and even smarter selecting this station as the most obvious point of departure. Daniel needed to be clever too. He climbed back into the rear of the van and rummaged through the contents. There were two large canvas tool bags with an assortment of building and decorating tools in reasonably good condition, two pairs of overalls, both white with the odd spattering of paint, and a plastic hardhat, also white. Daniel emptied one of the tool bags, dismantled the rifle and dropped it inside with his balaclava. He grabbed a pair of overalls. They were large, very large. He took off his coat, pulled the overalls easily on over his fatigues, then slipped his coat back on. Popping the hard hat on his head, he pulled the peak down at a low angle and jumped out of the rear of the van. With his bag over his shoulder, he walked calmly toward the main entrance, whistling as he strolled casually along.

The station was unbelievably crowded. People rushed in and out of the doors, bumping and jostling as they went. Daniel moved with the rest of them, just another worker heading for his day's labour. The men watched him amble through the entrance. He was a big man, but it wasn't Temple; the wrong clothes, too fat and too slow. He registered for a fleeting moment, then melted away, another face in the crowd.

*

Pasha led the girls directly beneath the station and then away, scampering down a small tunnel that angled off to their left. Bent almost double, they moved in single file, steadying themselves with their hands on either side of the damp tunnel walls as it shrank lower and narrower.

'Where are we going?' Lesya asked.

'This way. You can't get out of the tunnels in the station and the first shafts are too close; people will see you. You have to climb out down here, then walk back. It's the only way,' Pasha advised.

Seconds later, the boy stopped and pointed up.

'Here,' he said smiling.

The girls gathered round, huddled next to an old rusting ladder that was fixed precariously into the crumbling concrete of a narrow tube that led up to the surface.

'I will look,' Pasha said.

Lesya nodded. 'Thank you.'

Pasha shot up the ladder. Easing the round metal cover open a fraction, he peered out, checking as far as he could see in every direction. It was a task he performed almost every day. The manhole cover was partially obscured by a clump of small, scrubby bushes. It sat on the far edge of a broad area of open ground, part grass, part broken concrete and rubble, covered in a thin layer of frozen snow. The ground lay in front of what was once going to be a new building, before the money ran out and the construction work had stopped. Seeing no one close enough to spot him, Pasha wriggled out, then ducked his head back into the hole.

'Come on,' he called, before rolling away to the cover of the nearest bush.

Lesya pushed Elizabeth to the ladder.

'You go first, then Jennifer. I'll bring Yana with me.'

Elizabeth eased her way up the ladder, using her one good leg to push herself up one step at a time. She scrambled out of the small opening, rolled away to the bushes and lay still behind Pasha.

Jennifer climbed fast, hand over hand, pushing and pulling her way to the top as quickly as she could. She burst out of the hole and rolled in next to her sister.

'Come on, Yana, up we go,' Lesya said encouragingly, helping Yana to climb.

She stayed right behind her every step of the way, whispering gentle words of encouragement until

Yana's head broke the surface and she crawled free on her own. Lesya followed her out and lay next to Pasha on the hard, ice-cold ground.

She smiled at him.

'Thank you, Pasha,' she said, kissing him gently on the forehead.

The little boy smiled back, his eyes growing large and watery at the small display of affection.

'The station has a small, rear entrance over there – it hardly gets used,' Pasha said, pointing across the wide expanse of waste ground. 'You can get closer to it without being seen by going through the building there.'

He pointed again, to the partially-built steel and concrete framework of the now-derelict construction. The wing of the never-to-be building ran away behind them, then turned at a right angle back towards the far side of the train station.

'You will come out over there,' he said, indicating the far end of the structure. 'Very close to the entrance. I will show you the way,' he smiled, warming to his new-found companions, particularly the lady who had kissed his head.

*

Daniel casually ambled his way through the station, looking up at the information boards. The train they needed, the Repin, would be leaving at 8:00am; a little over two hours. Standing in line at ticket window nine, he waited patiently, discretely scanning the terminal as the queue shuffled slowly forward. Kozlov's men were posted in pairs at the larger entrances and the doors that weren't directly covered could easily be seen from the others. Even if the girls made it this far, they would never get in unnoticed. He glanced at the clock again; it had just turned 6:00am. Time was slowly but surely running out. He had to find them, and fast.

*

Pasha jumped to his feet and quickly led the girls away from the terminal, into the old shell of the building. The building was dim and damp. Water ran down the walls and dripped into large, icy puddles that covered much of the cracked, uneven concrete floor.

'Follow me carefully, it's dangerous,' he advised, pointing to a cavernous black opening that loomed unannounced in the middle of the floor.

A ragged hole, edged by the cut-off, razor-sharp steel endings of the reinforced concrete opened before them. Lesya peered down into the darkness, unable to see the bottom. The hole just fell away; an infinite, black empty space. She walked on slowly, following Pasha's footsteps exactly, as the small boy picked his route with care.

'What is this place?' Lesya asked, looking at the floor which was littered with empty shell cases, discarded used syringes and other unsavoury items.

Pasha shrugged. 'I don't know. Just a building. There are places like this all over the city,' he explained. 'It's OK during the day, mostly, but at night no one comes here, except drug addicts and pushers or worse.'

'You don't come here?' Lesya asked.

'No,' Pasha replied shaking his head. 'It's too dangerous and I can't afford drugs. A lot of the kids sniff glue; it makes them weird. I tried it; it made me very sick. I didn't like it. I save my money. One day I will get away from here,' he continued, his sorrowful words suddenly adding years to his young face.

'I'm sure you will, Pasha,' she said, running her hand softly through his hair.

*

Daniel purchased five second-class tickets to Vyborg with money to spare and slid them into his pocket. He turned slowly and strolled out to the platforms, wandering past the iconic steam locomotive #293, the train which bore Lenin, disguised as a railway worker, from Finland into the city at the start of the 1917 October revolution.

The platforms ran long and straight, then sloped gradually down toward the track away to his right. To his left, the tracks ended at the buffers and numbered gates. Daniel held up his hand and shielded his eyes from the bright, early morning sun which set the frost sparkling like millions of tiny diamonds scattered over the ground. There was another way in, well out of sight of the terminal, where the tracks were clear and easily accessible as they ran away from the station, turning and winding their way out through the northern part of the city, before rolling into the open countryside and the long run north.

Daniel checked again. Despite the crowd, no one was watching; no one was interested. Casually, he strolled the length of the platform, down the gentle gradient of the slope toward the track, crossed to the low wire fence and hopped over.

Disappearing from view between two small brick huts, he leant with his back against the wall and peered around the corner toward the road at the rear of the station. It was quiet and unguarded. Petr had gambled on covering the main entrances only.

Daniel surveyed the ground, looking across the wide expanse of grass, broken concrete and rubble toward a large, part-built, L-shaped, four-storey building. He watched the building for a moment. It was obviously just another underfunded Russian project now left to crumble. The structure was dark, and the grey concrete and rusting steel framework looked drab, cold and sombre. He was about to turn away when the slightest hint of movement caught his eye; figures in the shadows – Petr's men?

Daniel crouched down, using the shadowy space between the huts to hide his huge frame. He watched carefully as the figures moved from concrete pillar to concrete pillar, cautiously approaching the end of the building. Daniel could make them out more clearly now. They were just street kids. The city was full of them; nothing to worry about. He turned his attention back to the road and the rear of the station. It was still clear. He looked back to the small-framed figures still moving slowly toward the end of the building, noticing the slight, athletic figure of the girl limping slowly behind and to the left of the others. She stepped warily in and out of the shadows. Daniel watched her with growing interest. At last she came clearly into view. It was Elizabeth. He breathed a huge sigh of relief, stood and walked slowly out from between the buildings, taking off his white hard hat.

*

In the shadows of the building, the small group stopped in their tracks and huddled in closer together as the tall figure emerged from the side of the rail tracks. The girls looked on apprehensively. The figure edged closer, his features masked by the glare of the sun. Anxiously, they stepped slowly backward, half-turning, ready to run.

'What's wrong?' asked Pasha.

'That man, coming this way. He might be one of the men we told you about,' Lesya replied with deep concern.

Jennifer raised her hand over her eyes, stared intently, then gasped out loud as the man removed his hat and waved it twice over his head.

'It's Daniel!' she exclaimed. 'Oh thank god, we've found him, it's Daniel!' she repeated excitedly.

The girls waved back excitedly until Daniel gestured urgently for them to stop. He ran across the open ground.

Pasha stood back, nervously hiding behind Lesya.

'It's alright, Pasha, he's our friend. He won't hurt you,' Lesya said, placing a reassuring arm around his shoulder.

Daniel pulled the girls back into the shadows.

'What happened?' he asked.

'We had to run. Men came down the canal path looking for us. We only just got away. We climbed down into the sewers and Pasha here helped us,' Elizabeth explained.

'Good thinking,' Daniel nodded, before dropping

down onto his haunches and gently holding the boy by his shoulders.

'Thank you, Pasha, you're a brave young man. I am very grateful to you,' he said in perfect Russian.

Pasha looked in awe at Daniel as a broad smile beamed across his face at the praise.

Daniel checked his watch.

'It's six thirty. The train leaves at eight. I've already got the tickets, so I suggest we wait here, out of sight, until the very last minute, then make a dash for the train. We'll enter the station the same way I came out, run back along the track and jump onboard just as the train is leaving. With any luck, Petr and his men will miss us completely. They're not watching the platforms; only the front doors.'

*

Petr patrolled up and down the great expanse of the main terminal, prowling with the nervous energy of a caged tiger. His eyes darted from one tall man to the next, to every small group of women and back to the doors in rapid succession. There was no sign and his nervousness grew with each passing minute. Returning to Kozlov without Temple and the girls just wasn't an option – not if he wanted to live. Once more, he checked the train times. The 8:00 am train to Helsinki was the one he had guessed they would aim for, if indeed they came at all, and they'd better. He was betting his life on it.

The clock ticked slowly round. Trains came and went. Crowds of people swarmed through the station and Petr stalked the station floor, becoming more and more agitated and anxious, but still there was no sign.

The loud public address system announced the departure of the 8:00am train to Helsinki. Petr's eyes darted around the terminal, looking for unusual movement. Anxiously, he scanned every person, moved urgently from door to door and frantically called his men. One sighting, just one glimpse was all he needed. Still there was nothing.

*

Daniel glanced at his watch, then knelt and lifted Elizabeth effortlessly into his arms.

'Let's go,' he said, striding out across the wasteland.

Jennifer, Lesya and Yana ran close behind.

'Stay with me,' he called to them, lengthening his stride.

The girls jogged beside him as Pasha watched them go, gratefully clutching the handful of roubles Daniel had given him. It was more money than he would make from a month of begging on the streets.

They crossed the open ground as quickly as possible. Daniel ducked in between the two small brick huts, crossed the track and struck back towards the sloping platform edge.

'Move in front of me. Get on the train and stay out of sight,' Daniel called to the girls.

*

Petr's pulse was racing. Whistles were blowing and doors were clunking shut. The train was leaving. He stood in the centre of the terminal and turned full circle, his eyes darting and head swirling. The horrific, sickening thought struck him – the platforms, they must have made the platforms. He remembered Daniel's words at the castle. "People always use two-dimensional search patterns". He had covered the doors, the main entrances and the exits, those coming in and those going out. What if they had already been in the station? What if they were already on the platform? Already on the train? He turned and ran.

Petr burst out of the doors and onto the long stretch of platform. The train was already rolling slowly. He looked down the long length of carriages. All the doors were closed – all except one, the first door of the furthest carriage, right at the far end of the platform. It swayed open as a tall man, wearing a white hard hat, stepped up from the platform, carrying the small, athletic frame of a young woman in his arms.

Petr stared and swallowed hard as reality dawned.

TWENTY-FOUR

Petr stood momentarily transfixed, the fleeting, incredulous scene taking one, thumping heartbeat to register. Then he responded – a snap judgement call. It was a natural, automated, knee-jerk reaction. A decision nine out of ten people would make – the wrong decision. His eyes took in the movement and the people. His brain processed the information and confirmed the recognition. The name Temple screamed through his mind and his untrained reactions took over. He turned and ran toward the target, straight down the length of the platform. The train began to accelerate alongside him, rolling steadily out of the station. Too late, he realised his mistake. He should have chosen the immediate point of entry – the door which had been directly in front of him on the platform. He grasped for the next and thumped the button hard. The door remained closed. The train was leaving, the door was locked – they were all locked. He continued to run, dodging past passengers, leaping over luggage and careering down the platform. The train accelerated out of reach, but still he ran.

At last, Petr's brain confirmed it was a futile effort. His pace slowed and his head rolled back in despair. Easing down to a leaden-footed, beaten walk, he stood at the end of the platform and roared his frustration.

*

'It's OK, you can stand up now,' Daniel said to the girls as they crouched below the window line in the centre of the last carriage.

The girls climbed to their feet and followed Daniel through to the next, near-empty carriage. Finding a group of seats, they sat in silence, letting the adrenalin surge and nervous energy drain from their bodies.

'Thank you, Daniel,' Elizabeth said.

They all nodded. 'Thank you, Daniel,' they said in turn, believing that they were now free and safe.

Daniel brought them crashing back to reality.

'We're not home yet,' he said sternly. 'Not until we cross the border.'

'They won't find us now, will they?' Elizabeth asked nervously.

'All I'm saying is that we have to stay alert. They were at the station. Petr's not stupid; he knew we'd be there. We were lucky he didn't think to cover the platforms. If they think we made it this far, there's nothing to stop them getting ahead and boarding the train later, assuming they're not onboard already.'

The girls looked around anxiously as the dread came flooding back.

'Please don't let them find us and take us again,' Jennifer pleaded fearfully, tears welling up in her eyes.

Yana sat silently back in her seat and pulled her knees up to her chest. Wrapping her arms around her legs, she rested her head against the window and stared vacantly out at the passing cityscape, singing gently to herself.

Daniel looked at her sympathetically. She was in a bad way. Her mind, far more than her body, had been shattered. The slightest hint of a return to her ordeal caused her to mentally close down, firmly shutting out the world and everything around her.

Lesya placed her hand gently on Yana's knee.

'Don't worry, we're safe now. I won't let anything else happen to you, I promise,' she whispered, glaring at Daniel.

Daniel listened to her words and stared hard at her in return. He said nothing. It wasn't the time or place. They were far from safe and he knew it. Lesya was making promises, and however well intentioned, they were promises she could never keep.

'Who's hungry?' he asked cheerfully, changing the subject and trying to lift their mood.

They all nodded, forcing half-smiles, except Yana.

'Great, I'm ravenous. I suggest sandwiches and snacks rather than the full buffet car. It's better that we stay here and attract as little attention as possible. The fewer people that see us, the fewer traces we leave, OK?'

The girls nodded again with a little more enthusiasm.

'One gourmet picnic coming up,' Daniel smiled. 'Wait here, I'll be right back.'

Daniel wandered down through the train, using the excuse of getting food to carefully search the carriages. If Petr and his men were aboard, Daniel wanted to see them before they saw him. He walked slowly, checking each carriage thoroughly before entering and moving on. They had done well. Their luck was still holding. There was no sign of Kozlov's men; the train was clear. He relaxed just a little. The next two and half hours to Vyborg would be safe. He wandered back to the buffet car and spent the remaining money on a selection of hot rolls, pastries, coffee and chocolate.

*

Petr ran back into the station, calling in his men over the radio as he went. The men gathered round.

'We missed them,' he growled, his face flushed crimson, with anger rather than exertion.

The men looked at him and then at each other in disbelief.

'How?' they asked almost as one.

'I made a mistake, a wrong assumption; the wrong search pattern,' Petr replied, ruefully shaking his head. 'Olaf, find out where that train stops.'

'Yes, Petr,' Olaf confirmed, running to the ticket counter.

He returned moments later, handing Peter the information he wanted. The men stood back and waited whilst Petr rapidly scanned the train timetable.

'Vyborg. They don't have any passports – they will have to get off at Vyborg,' he said with conviction.

Petr looked at the men.

'Get the cars. Olaf, radio ahead – get the chopper ready,' he ordered.

The big, black Toyotas accelerated away from the station, screeched around the city streets and out onto the Sestroretsk road.

The big Mil Mi-8 helicopter was already sat with

its engines idling, the huge rotors turning lazily as the pilot waited for Petr and the men to arrive. The 4x4's skidded to a halt in front of the castle. The men jumped out and ran across the open lawn to the waiting chopper. Petr was the last to climb aboard. Dejectedly, he slumped into his seat and slid the door closed.

'Let's go,' he said.

The noise inside the cabin changed as the pilot increased the power and the rotors rapidly transformed from a slow and lazy whomp-whomp, to a fast, loud and heavy whack-whack-whack. The great machine lifted into the sky. Rising vertically, it cleared the height of the trees, pirouetted ninety degrees, climbed and accelerated north.

Sergei Kozlov turned in his seat next to the pilot and faced Petr, his expression dark and his brow deeply furrowed.

'You missed them?' he asked with thinly disguised anger.

Petr stared for a moment, not realising that Kozlov would be on board, unable to hide the look of shock on his face. He nodded slowly, reluctantly admitting his failure.

'We missed them – just,' he added quickly.

'You know where they are now?'

'The train. They're on the Repin, Mr Kozlov. They can't get off until they reach Vyborg. We'll be there ahead of them. We won't miss them again.'

'A second failure would be most unfortunate. There would be consequences – unfortunate consequences,' Kozlov acknowledged menacingly.

Petr knew exactly what he meant.

'Yes, Sir,' he replied sombrely.

*

Daniel returned to the girls with the selection of food and they all ate hungrily. Aided by the warmth of the carriage and the steady rocking motion of the train, one by one, they drifted into exhausted sleep.

The train left the remnants of the city behind, entering the snow-covered fields of the open countryside. Daniel sat alone. He stared out of the window, deep in thought, and evaluated their next objective, calculating the possibilities and alternatives. He took the optimistic possibility first. They would reach Vyborg in two hours. If by some miracle Kozlov and his men had either miscalculated their route or simply given up the chase, they would leave the train and call for help. After that, they would hide out and wait to be taken over the border to Finland and safety. He thought about the odds, smiled to himself and discounted his optimism without any further consideration.

Option two; the most likely scenario. Kozlov and

his men would be waiting in Vyborg. Four, maybe five men would be posted in the station – on the platform this time. The rest would be dispersed outside, just in case they somehow slipped through for a second time. Daniel mulled it over. He had no idea what Vyborg or the station would be like. It was the main stop for the customs checks. Therefore, it stood to reason that the place was pretty large. There would be police, government officials and other more clandestine security personnel in significant numbers. Usually that might be a good thing, but not in Russia. Not under these circumstances.

Option three; the final choice. He ran it through in his mind. There was no alternative. He had hoped for a clean getaway, but he knew that had been overly optimistic; a more drastic and unexpected course was their only chance of escape and survival. He looked over to the girls. All but Yana were sleeping. Yana stared unblinking at the white, frozen landscape as it rolled past her window.

*

The Lynx helicopter flew low and fast. The men inside stared solemnly at one another.

'What time does the train reach Vyborg?'
'10:30am.'
'Are you sure that's where they'll be?'

'They're on the Repin. The girls won't have passports; they'll have to get off there.'

'And then what?'

'Call for aid and either hide or strike out for the border.'

'Call who?'

Two of the men shrugged.

'Guess we'd better be on time then,' the dark-haired man said simply, glancing at his watch, then at the two men sitting adjacent to him. 'It's going to be tight. I don't like this; I don't like at all.'

The two men nodded and remained grim faced. There was nothing else to say.

*

Daniel pulled the spare magazine for the rifle from his coat pocket, then opened the canvas workbag and checked the ammunition already with the gun. There were thirteen rounds; he had no need to count, but it was a time-served routine – check and double check – any good soldier knew you could never be too prepared. He clicked three rounds from one magazine. Loaded them into the other, leaving him with one full ten-round mag and three spare bullets. He dropped the full magazine into the bag and placed the three spare bullets into his pocket. Next, he took out the Makarov he had retrieved from

Elizabeth and checked it over. He had two full clips – ten rounds in each. He slipped the gun and spare clip into the opposite pocket. He was good to go.

Daniel looked out of the window as the heavy sound of rotor blades clattered overhead and a big Russian Mi-8 helicopter turned and swooped in low over the ground, cruising the length of the train.

Elizabeth opened her eyes, gasped and watched in horror as the enormous black and green machine flew in close, banked steeply and rose away again.

'It's them,' she exclaimed, the fear palpable in her voice.

'I know,' Daniel stated calmly. 'Time to go.'

'Go?'

Daniel looked down at her, his face calm and resolute. There was no time for discussion or explanation.

'Get them up and ready, I'll be back in a second.'

Elizabeth roused the others.

'We have to go,' she said as they stretched the stiffness from their limbs and rubbed the sleep from their eyes.

'Go? Are we at the station?' Jennifer asked.

'No, not quite, it's not far. There was... There was a helicopter,' Elizabeth explained hesitantly. 'It flew over a minute ago. It's them – they're still out there.'

Elizabeth watched as Jennifer's returning hope and optimism crumbled before her eyes.

'What are we going to do? Daniel can't beat them all. They're going to catch us and take us back,' she cried.

Elizabeth gripped her sister's shoulders.

'We're going to do exactly what Daniel tells us. He got us out and he's got us this far; now come on,' she demanded assertively, snapping the words at her sister.

Daniel returned to the carriage, the assembled rifle strapped to his back. He looked at Elizabeth and briefly nodded his approval.

'Let's go. Lesya, bring Yana,' he instructed, leading them out into the space between the last two carriages.

'The train will be slowing down in a minute. Once the speed has dropped enough we're going to jump. Kozlov's men are at the station. It will take them a little while to realise that the train is late, a little longer to find out we're not on it, and even longer to find our trail.'

The girls looked out of the window. The countryside flashed past at an alarming rate. They looked nervously back at Daniel. He looked focussed and confident.

'Ready to go?' he asked.

The girls nodded dumbly.

'Good. When I say, jump. Push off hard and watch where you're landing. The snow's pretty thick; we'll be alright.'

He stepped back into the carriage, smashed his elbow through the glass-covered case and pulled the handle hard. The emergency brakes clamped on with full force. The wheels locked and bit into the tracks. Sparks and ear-piercing metal screeches filled the air. The train's speed halved in seconds, sending passengers and luggage tumbling through the carriages.

Daniel hit the button. The door hissed open, the emergency brake automatically releasing the locks on all doors. Frozen air poured in and blustered around them as Daniel pushed Yana and Lesya toward the opening.

'Go,' he said.

Lesya held Yana in front of her. She looked out of the door and down. The ground still seemed to be rushing beneath her feet. There were no tracks to clear. It was a jump straight out onto a narrow, snow-covered bank which dropped steeply away to the open fields below.

'Go,' Daniel called again.

Lesya gulped in a breath, held it a second, pushed Yana hard, then jumped after her. They thumped into the ground, rolled and kept on rolling, momentum carrying them at speed down the bank. They slithered to a stop at the bottom of the incline, wrapped in the thick, soft blanket of snow.

Jennifer moved hesitantly toward to the open

door, the knuckles on her hands whitening as she gripped the sides hard.

'Let's go, Jennifer,' Daniel ordered with no time for pleasantries.

Jennifer pushed her head out of the door and anxiously watched the ground. Fearfully, she swayed back and forth in the opening like a ski jumper waiting at the gate.

'Come on, Jen, I'm right behind you. You can do it,' Elizabeth urged.

Daniel stood in behind her, placed his hand in the centre of her back and shoved hard. Jennifer screamed as she was launched out of the doorway, her arms turning frantic circles in the air. Then she was down, tumbling through the snow toward the bottom of the bank.

Daniel scooped Elizabeth into his arms.

'It's really just not your day, is it!' he quipped, launching himself through the door, taking Elizabeth with him before his comment could register.

Daniel released Elizabeth in mid-air.

'Sorry, this is going to hurt,' he said as he let her go.

They landed a few yards apart. Daniel rolled twice on the levelling ground, controlled his movement and came easily to his feet. Elizabeth thudded side-on into the snow and rolled further down the bank, painfully jarring her ankle as she slithered to a stop.

The train careered on.

Daniel wasted no time. He got the girls up and moving, putting as much distance as possible between themselves and the soon-to-be stationary train.

The going was hard and the fresh snow soft and deep. Their feet sank with every step, slowing their progress to a crawl. Elizabeth struggled bravely, desperate to keep pace, but with every agonising step she fell further behind.

'Keep going,' Daniel called as he turned and headed back.

He stopped in front of Elizabeth, stooped and offered the broad expanse of his back.

'Climb on,' he ordered.

She didn't argue; she could walk no further. She threw her arms around Daniel's neck and clambered gratefully onto his back.

Daniel picked up the pace, marching out in front of the girls, urging them to keep up as he headed for the cover of a thickly-wooded area on the far side of the snow-covered fields.

TWENTY-FIVE

The pilot hovered steadily over the ground, then set the massive helicopter gently down, sending a thick cloud of snow swirling into the air. Ducking his head low, Kozlov stepped out of cockpit and walked clear of the whirling rotors to the collection of waiting cars. The men followed.

'Get back-up – track the train into the station. We'll drive in the rest of the way,' Petr called to the pilot as he left.

The helicopter rose into the air once more and turned back south, following the course of the rail tracks. Petr watched its dark shape hover momentarily, then turn on its axis and fly away.

Moments later, the pilot's voice sounded clearly over Petr's radio.

'Petr, the train has stopped two miles down the track. It's stopped dead.'

Petr swallowed hard; Kozlov had heard the message too. He could feel his eyes boring into the back of his head as Petr stood close to panic. He thought hard and fast.

'Stay up – search the immediate area from the air. We're on our way. Call in if you see anything – anything at all,' he ordered.

Petr turned and ran to the line of waiting 4x4's. He jumped into the lead vehicle and instructed the driver as they accelerated away, skidding and sliding through the snow-packed roads, moving in rapid convoy through the outskirts of the town.

'Denya, this is Petr. Anything yet?' Petr radioed to the pilot.

'Nothing, no. Wait, yes – I have them – half a mile from the track, heading west across the fields.'

*

Daniel looked up as the sound of the helicopter grew louder, sweeping in low from the east.

'Shit, come on girls, let's move,' he called, urging them to pick up the pace once more.

The helicopter passed directly above them, flying low, stirring up a billowing cloud of snow as it clattered noisily overhead.

The girls responded immediately, fear-stricken panic driving them forward, floundering through the heavy, energy-sapping blanket of snow towards the cover of the trees.

Daniel breathed hard and doubled his efforts, forcing his legs up and through the snow at an unbelievable rate.

*

'They heading for the forest, south-west of your position, Petr,' Denya reported. 'I'll stay overhead and guide you in.'

'We have you in sight now, Denya.'

Denya increased the helicopter's elevation until he could see the road over the dense expanse of forest.

'Roger that, Petr. I can see your convoy now. You're approaching the end of the road. It comes to a dead stop at the tree line as you clear the next bend, a quarter of a mile ahead. You'll have to be on foot from there.'

'Do you still have them in sight?'

'Yes, for a few more seconds. They'll be under the trees soon. I'll lose them, but they'll be heading straight toward you.'

'Understood, Denya. Land the chopper. Come in on foot behind them.'

'OK, Petr, landing now. Denya out.'

*

Daniel reached the tree line first and ducked in under the branches. Immediately,

the ground cleared and the thick snow was replaced by a frozen forest floor, covered with pine needles and a thick layer of frost. He stopped, lowered Elizabeth gently to the ground and checked on the other girls.

'Everyone alright?'

The girls nodded breathlessly, exhaustion and fear etched on their cold, pink faces.

'They're going to find us, aren't they?' Jennifer asked.

Daniel ignored the question.

'Go and help your sister,' he said turning away.

He walked back to the edge of the trees and watched the massive black and green helicopter turn, hover, then land two hundred yards from where they stood. The sound of the whirling rotors faded and died.

From behind the broad trunk of a large pine tree, Daniel observed it carefully. A lone pilot climbed down from the cockpit and scanned the tree line through a pair of binoculars. The pilot took his time, sweeping his field glasses along the trees either side of the tracks left by Daniel and the girls. Seeing nothing, he moved forward slowly, following the deep footprints in the snow. Daniel watched him come as he carefully pulled the rifle from his back. Lesya appeared at his shoulder, shuffling forward to kneel just behind him.

'What is it?' she asked quietly.

'Nothing to worry about,' Daniel replied.

Kneeling next to her, he pulled the rifle into his shoulder.

'Is it them? Are they coming?'

Daniel didn't answer; he merely gestured with his chin in the general direction of the pilot who was now walking directly in their footprints.

'He's going to find us,' she said anxiously.

Daniel didn't respond. There was just him, the rifle and the target. The rifle gave the slightest of sounds – a small metallic twang as it kicked into his shoulder. The pilot's head exploded, sending a plume of red spraying into the air. He was dead before his body thumped into the snow. Daniel re-shouldered the rifle, ran out to the body, grabbed the radio and earpiece from the dead man's belt and ran back to the trees.

'Let's go,' he said, getting the girls to their feet. 'Lesya, you and Jennifer carry Elizabeth. Yana, just stay with us,' he instructed, his voice blunt and cold.

He moved out, shoving the radio into his top pocket and pushing the earpiece into his ear. Pulling the rifle from his back, he held it loosely to his shoulder, sweeping it in slow, controlled arcs over the ground ahead as, ready to fire, he led them cautiously through the forest.

The forest floor was as hard as concrete, the air crisp and frosty. The light was dim and murky, intermittently lit by shafts of sunlight which occasionally found a break in the thick cover of trees and beamed brilliant white rays on the ground.

Daniel stayed in the dark, never once crossing or entering the beams of light.

'Denya, come in,' Petr's voice crackled in Daniel's ear.

'Denya, we're coming in north-east of you. Do you have them yet?'

Denya didn't reply.

Daniel stopped. Petr and his men were closing in directly ahead – fifteen, maybe twenty well-armed men. The firefight wouldn't last long; not on this ground. Not in the trees. There were too many men, and with this much cover they could move freely and get too close. He knew he would be overwhelmed by the numbers and sheer firepower. He turned west, back to open ground. They were all on foot now. With open ground and a little distance between them, he could level the odds.

Daniel led the girls back into the fields, pushing them on at a fast, unrelenting pace, aiming to put as much space between them, their pursuers and the tree line as he could. Before long, the ground began to slope upwards, then levelled off again. Ahead of them stood a small crop of buildings – a farm – the shape of the buildings standing as black silhouettes against the pale-blue winter sky and snow-covered fields.

'Denya, come in,' Petr's voice called more urgently. 'We're approaching the tree line, north-east of your last reported position, come in.'

There was no reply.

Daniel stopped. 'Keep going,' he instructed the girls.

'What are you doing?' Elizabeth asked.

Daniel removed his black jacket, revealing a pair of white, paint-spattered overalls.

'Evening the odds,' he smiled. 'Now get going. Hide in the barn and wait for me.'

The girls moved on, glancing back once to see Daniel dropping his coat and balaclava. He marched forward a few strides then lay down on the frozen ground, all but disappearing as his white-clad body moulded into the snow.

Daniel worked quickly, pushing a mound of snow up in front of him before gouging out a small, half-moon shaped space. Then, placing the three spare bullets in front of him, he lay perfectly still.

Totally invisible, Daniel waited.

Dressed in black, the men emerged from the

trees. One by one, they stepped confidently out from the shadows of the forest.

Daniel stared down at them, assuming Petr to be the man in the centre, leading the way, directing the men and picking out the obvious deep imprints in the snow. With a wave of his arm, he dispersed the men in a well-spaced line across the open field and co-ordinated their advance. Black against white, standing out like the ebony keys on a piano they came slowly forward. Daniel counted them. Nine men: fewer than expected, but more than enough to contend with.

*

The girls moved cautiously to the front of the barn, then looked across the yard to the large farmhouse and collection of shabby-looking outbuildings. The windows on the front of the house were boarded over. There were no animals in the yard and nothing but snow in the fields. The buildings looked run-down and deserted, like they were only inhabited in the warmer spring and summer months.

Lesya swung the broad double barn doors open and stepped inside. It was a large, dark, empty and eerily quiet space. The wooden floor was bare, apart from a light scattering of old straw and a few remaining bales stacked against the left-hand wall.

On the walls, old tools hung rusting and unused, and the pale winter light and wind came through the myriad of holes and cracks in the planking.

Jennifer helped Elizabeth over to the straw bales and eased her down as Yana trailed forlornly behind them. Cold and afraid, they huddled together in silence, listening and waiting.

*

Daniel let the men advance, waiting for them to reach the centre of the field. He could see Petr in the centre of the line speak into his radio, but there was no voice in his ear. Whoever he was trying to raise, it wasn't Denya; nothing could raise Denya again.

Calmly, Daniel levelled the rifle and brought the sights to bear on the first target. The man on his far right was adjacent to where his line of sight ended, and the only man who had any chance of making immediate cover once he started to fire.

He rehearsed his movements. If he was lucky, he would get two shots off before the men scattered or hit the ground. Even then he would have the edge. The men were exposed, out in the open and well out of the effective range of their own weapons.

Daniel slowed his breathing and focussed, staring unblinking through the telescopic sight, he lowered the crosshairs and centred them on the man's chest. His finger resting lightly on the trigger, he closed out his surroundings, took a large, smooth breath in, held it, then let it out, slowly and evenly. Perfectly relaxed, he fired, moved and fired again. Two men down.

The man in the centre looked left along the line of men, as first one man then another fell. A cloud of red mist floated in the air as their bodies jolted back, struck by some strange invisible force and the snow around them turned a bright shade of reddish pink as their blood poured into the snow.

The man in the centre was signalling urgently, gesturing wildly with his arm, but it was already too late for the third man in line. The bullet span him around, tore through the upper right side of his chest, shattered his shoulder blade and punched a gaping hole in his back as it exited. Three men down.

The men dived forward and lay flat in the snow. Daniel stopped firing and watched with cold calculation. The man in the centre signalled to his men, directing the four men who remained to his right further around to the right flank.

Daniel glanced left. He could see what Petr was trying to do. The slope and curve of the ground meant that he couldn't see the far side of the hill. The men to Petr's right started to move, rolling away through the snow. Daniel turned his body and stared down through his sights. The men were rolling away fast. Daniel aimed at the man furthest from Petr. The crosshairs levelled on the centre of his back and tracked him as he rolled. Daniel waited, then fired with unerring accuracy as the man's chest fleeting presented itself in mid-turn. Four men down.

Daniel smoothly realigned his aim, stared through the sights, tracked the next target and fired again. Five shots. Five men down.

Daniel watched as the men immediately stopped rolling and lay perfectly still. The men were confused and afraid; should they stick or twist? Every silent shot had found its target, moving or not.

Daniel concentrated and fired; no compassion, no mercy. The men had put themselves in harm's way and harm was there to meet them. Daniel watched as the panic set in. The men were up now, on their feet and running hard, running blind; desperately they clambered through the snow in an anxious attempt to evade the sniper fire. Three men ran, desperate to reach the cover behind the hill. Daniel took the leading man first; like a fairground shooting gallery, he swept the gun ahead of the line, waited for each man in turn to cross into the sights, fired and watched them fall into the blood-stained snow.

Daniel stared down at Petr. He was running next to one of his men. Daniel brought the rifle to bear, slowed his heart rate and took his time. Levelling the sights in the centre of the Petr's chest, he fired. Petr went down. Daniel snatched the magazine from the rifle and snapped in his last three bullets.

The last man scrambled across the snow, his terrified, erratic movements making the shot that much harder as he ran side-on to Daniel. Carefully, Daniel levelled the sights and focussed on the man's black-covered head, tracking his run towards the safety of the far side of the hill. Gently, he squeezed the trigger.

The man stumbled and fell, sprawling face down in the snow.

Daniel relaxed and waited.

The man hauled himself up onto his hands and knees, breathing hard, his frosty breath billowing out from beneath his mask.

Daniel watched him, detached and emotionless.

The man clambered to his feet.

Daniel fired. Nine men down.

Daniel rolled onto his back and stared straight up into the barrel of a Glock-17 pistol. A black-hooded man stared down at him through dispassionate, emerald-green eyes. With bitter realisation, Daniel closed his eyes, then opened them slowly. Petr was not down in the field. Petr was stood over him, flanked by four other men and pointing a Glock at his face.

Petr pulled the balaclava from his head.

'Not as smart as you thought you were,' Petr said,

with a self-satisfied grin. 'Get up, Mr Temple, leave the rifle on the ground.'

Daniel rose slowly to his feet.

'Put your hands behind your head,' Petr ordered.

'May I get my coat? It's getting a little chilly out here,' Daniel responded. 'Dmitri, get his coat. Empty the pockets first.'

'Thanks,' Daniel nodded as his coat was handed to him.

He shrugged it on.

'What now?'

'Now we wait for, Mr Kozlov. He won't be long. He's very keen to talk to you.'

Daniel followed as Petr lead him into the wall-enclosed farmyard. Behind him, one of the men shoved him forward, regularly digging hard into his ribs with the barrel of his gun. Daniel looked straight ahead as he passed the barn, not daring to give it the slightest of glances.

*

Inside the barn, the girls listened to the sound of muffled footsteps. Lesya jumped to her feet, ran to the door and stared out through a small crack in the wooden boards. She gasped, then clamped her hand over her mouth to keep the sound in as she stepped slowly back from the doors.

'It's them, they have Daniel,' she whispered harshly, her voice conveying nothing but abject fear.

The girls stared at her in disbelief.

'What are we going to do? Can you see him? Can you see Daniel?' Elizabeth asked, rising to her feet and shuffling halfway across the barn toward Lesya.

Lesya gathered her nerve and stepped cautiously back toward the door.

'Yes, it's Petr and some other men. They have Daniel at gunpoint – they've caught him.'

'Oh God, what are we going to do?' Elizabeth asked again.

'Run, we have to run,' Lesya replied.

'I can't run. I can barely stand. Go without me.'

'No,' exclaimed Jennifer. 'We're not leaving you here to go back to that monster.'

'You must. You have no other choice.'

'No, Liz, I'm not leaving you.'

Lesya looked at the sisters for a moment, then at Yana. She was going nowhere either. She just sat staring into space, her mind closing down once more.

Lesya nodded slowly. 'OK. We stay – stay here, stay together,' she said nervously.

'We can hide at least. They might not find us,' Elizabeth said with faint optimism.

'Where can we hide?' Jennifer asked.

From the centre of the barn, they looked around

urgently, seeing nothing but bare empty space.

'There's a loft. We could hide up there?' Jennifer added.

'No, wait, look – down here,' Elizabeth whispered, pointing at the floor, exactly where she was standing. 'Is that what I think it is?'

Lesya moved back to the centre of the barn floor and smiled.

'It's a trapdoor.'

'Down there, quickly – no, just a minute,' Elizabeth said changing her mind. 'Help me move these bales.'

'To where? What are you doing?' Jennifer asked.

'Stack the bales round the trapdoor, with one balanced so that when the trapdoor closes again, it will fall on top, covering it,' Elizabeth explained. 'They might miss the door if they only take a quick look in here. We didn't see it when we came in and it wasn't covered over then.'

They worked quickly and quietly, dragging the bales across the floor, positioning them around the small trapdoor in the floor.

*

Daniel stood perfectly still and silent, waiting and watching, coiled and alert. There were five men and he was unarmed – tough odds, but not insurmountable. He glanced back to Petr as he looked around the yard. The old farmhouse was dark, still and quiet. The windows were covered with thick boards; the doors undoubtedly locked. It would be too much aggravation to break in. He looked across to the barn. The doors were not fully closed and swayed slightly in the breeze. The central wooden bar to hold them shut had been removed. He turned to Daniel and raised an enquiring eyebrow. Daniel stared coldly back, his face expressionless, blank and hard.

'The barn, take him in the barn,' Petr ordered, leading the way.

Two men followed Petr.

Daniel moved forward, escorted by the other two men, one to his right, the other close behind, constantly prodding him in the back with his gun. They approached the doors. Petr swung them open, stepped inside and surveyed the empty barn with disappointment.

Daniel breathed a sigh of relief. The girls had either left or were hiding.

The man dug Daniel in the ribs.

'Inside,' he ordered.

One more time, just one more time, thought Daniel, as he deliberately slowed his pace.

Petr and the two leading guards stood with their backs to Daniel, scrutinising the gloomy interior of the barn. The third guard walked slightly ahead. Daniel slowed again. The guard behind him stepped forward, pulled his arm back one more time and rammed the gun forward. Daniel was ready. He span with lightning speed, grabbing the gun with both hands and pulling hard. The guard lurched toward him as Daniel simultaneously pushed hard from his knees, accelerated his bodyweight and snapped his head forward. His forehead exploded with bone-crunching force into the guard's face and dropped him unconscious to the ground. Daniel held onto the gun as the guard to his left reacted, turning and firing at the spot where Daniel had been stood. Daniel wasn't there; he was already diving and rolling away. The guard turned, following Daniel's movement, trying to adjust his aim. Daniel came up smoothly to his knees and cut him down with a short, controlled burst of fire.

Inside the barn, Petr and the two remaining guards dived for cover, either side of the wide-open doors.

Daniel didn't wait for their return of fire. He moved again, rolling out of sight of the main doors and coming to his feet on the right-hand side of the barn.

*

The girls huddled together beneath the trapdoor, shaking with trepidation. Yana's body and mind could take no more and she collapsed to the floor as her legs buckled beneath her. Lesya knelt beside her and gently cradled her head in her hands. There were no words of comfort she could give.

Trembling in silence, in the pitch-black space beneath the barn, they listened intently. Short bursts of gunfire erupted, then ceased. There were no voices; no other sounds. The barn fell still and quiet. Jennifer and Elizabeth held each other close and waited for the trapdoor to open.

'What do we do? They must have killed Daniel,' Jennifer whispered tearfully.

'Stay quiet. Find a way out – quickly,' Elizabeth replied.

The girls turned and tried to see their way in the all-consuming blackness. Carefully, Elizabeth limped forward, her arms outstretched, feeling her way.

*

Daniel moved silently around to the rear of the barn. The ground rose higher along the back wall, meeting a single-storey wooden extension halfway up its eight-foot wall. Daniel climbed onto the roof and stared down through a gap in the wooden slats. Petr and the guards were knelt inside the barn doors, directly ahead. Daniel looked up, then climbed again, crossing the gradually sloping roof of the upper tier of the barn. Reaching the dormer-style opening of the hayloft, he eased open the wooden shutters and stepped silently down onto the dust-covered floor of the loft.

*

Elizabeth slowly felt her way forward. Finding the right-hand wall of the blackened room, she eased her way down its length. Lesya turned and copied her movements, making her way slowly toward the left-hand wall. In a mirror image, she worked her way down the opposite side of the room.

Jennifer pulled Yana to her feet and eased her silently away from the trapdoor opening. In the centre of the cold black space, they stood and waited as Elizabeth and Lesya blindly worked their way down each of the walls.

Elizabeth crabbed sideways, moving hand over hand, remaining in constant contact with the walls that were made of rough wooden planks, cold and damp to the touch. Suddenly, the wall disappeared and she fell forward, sprawling headlong into an unseen opening, gasping as she fell. She hit the earthen floor with a dull thud and the girls froze like statues, holding their breath.

*

The two guards looked at each other, then across to Petr. The muted thud appeared to come from behind them. Petr held up his hand, signalling them to silence, and the three men knelt, listening carefully.

Daniel eased forward and watched the men carefully. He looked down on them, his interest drawn by their sudden change of focus. They had heard something. What was it? It wasn't him. Petr signalled the guards again. They were going to circle the barn. Petr would go right and the other two left, meeting at the single door at the rear. Daniel watched them. Perhaps it was the girls. Were they moving, trying to make good their escape? Where were they? He hadn't heard or seen anything. They weren't outside; not behind the barn.

The guards and Petr moved, slowly and carefully easing their way out through the doors and around the sides of the building. Daniel waited, then looked down again, scanning the barn floor. There was nothing there; just a pile of straw bales in its centre and a trail of straw that ran from the wall to his left.

'Clever,' he whispered to himself, as Petr and the guards disappeared from the barn.

Daniel eyed a thick rope that hung from an old, rusting pulley suspended from the centre of the main roof beam. Quietly, he leant out, pulled the rope in and tugged it once. It held firm. The pulley was locked. Daniel wrapped one leg and one arm around the rope, then, holding the Uzi 9mm machine pistol in his right hand, he stepped off the mezzanine loft floor, letting the rope slide smoothly through his arm and leg as he dropped quickly and silently.

*

The girls shuffled quickly towards the sound of Elizabeth's whispering voice.

'Come on, this way,' she called, urgently guiding them towards her. 'There's a passage here.'

The narrow passage was pitch-black. Holding hands the girls moved forward in single file, walking blindly through the blackened tunnel. Elizabeth lead the way, limping heavily, with one arm outstretched. Lesya followed, pulling Yana stumbling along behind her as Jennifer brought up the rear, whispering loudly, urging her sister on, desperate to get away.

*

The sounds of vehicles sweeping into the yard spurred Daniel back into action. The immediate fight was over; it was time to run again. He leapt to his feet, ran to the doors and pulled them closed. Returning to the straw bales he jumped over the first row and lifted the centre bale, revealing the small, wooden trapdoor set in the barn floor.

'Clever girls,' he said again.

Slinging the machine pistol over his shoulder and the Glock into his pocket, he opened the trap door. Climbing halfway down the ladder, he set the centre bale exactly how the girls had done, then eased himself down the rest of the way. The trapdoor closed above his head and the straw bale fell back into place.

Daniel moved cautiously through the darkness until he found a wall and began to feel his way along. If the girls had been down here, they had found a way out. His hand slipped off the end of the wall into a narrow passage. He moved blindly forward, following what appeared to be a straight, narrow passage. Gaining in confidence, he walked faster; the darkness held no fear.

*

Elizabeth stumbled into and up a set of steep wooden stairs. She climbed using her hands and feet until her head bumped into what felt like a plain wooden door. Her hands fumbled in the dark until she found a large round handle to her left. She turned it and pushed. The door held firm. Anxiously, she felt her way across the door, searching for bolts or a lock.

Footsteps sounded faintly through the sheer black passageway behind them.

'They're coming,' Jennifer said, her terrified voice frantically spitting out the words.

Elizabeth's hands moved with even greater urgency, frantically feeling their way over the door. She found the handle again, feeling every inch of surrounding wood until her fingers scrambled over a small key nestled directly beneath the bulbous handle. Simultaneously, she turned the key and handle and pushed hard. The door swung inward and she spilled through the door, falling into the gloom of the farmhouse kitchen.

*

The small convoy of vehicles swept into the farmyard and skidded to an abrupt halt. Sergei Kozlov stepped out of his car and surveyed the scene as his heavily armed men dispersed. He turned as Petr approached. The man looked pale and afraid, like a man who had failed again, and Kozlov's face reddened in anticipation, his anger building, like the first ground-breaking tremors of an erupting volcano.

'Temple?' Kozlov growled.

'No,' Petr shook his head.

Kozlov's open hand swept harshly across Petr's

face; the hard but not stunningly brutal blow, whipped Petr's head round and made his cheek glow fiercely.

'The girls?' Kozlov growled again.

'No,' Petr repeated, shaking his head again, preparing himself for another assault. It didn't come. Kozlov turned his back and glanced around the yard, taking in the dead guards lying outside the barn door.

'How many men?'

'Ten, twelve – I'm not sure.'

'You're not sure?'

'No, I took a small team around the hill and came in behind Temple whilst the others came across the field, following their tracks. Temple caught them out in the open. He still had the sniper rifle.'

'So what happened?'

'He killed them – all of them. They never stood a chance.'

'What about you?'

'I had him, Mr Kozlov. I crept in behind him and caught him cold.'

'You didn't kill him?'

'No, you said you wanted him alive. We brought him up here to the barn. There was no sign of the girls. I think he told them to keep running. They can't have gone far.'

'What about Temple?'

Petr looked shocked as he recalled what had happened.

'He moved so fast. One second he was walking under guard into the barn and the next he was rolling away, firing. We dived for cover and fired back, but he vanished like a ghost.'

'He's not a ghost, Petr; not yet. I can assure you he is still very real and he has to be here. Now find him, or I will personally gouge out your eyes with my thumbs,' Kozlov stated angrily.

*

The girls quietly closed the kitchen door, turned and waited anxiously. The footsteps grew louder. The handle on the kitchen door turned ominously slowly. In their haste, they had left the key on the other side. Fearfully, they backed away. Lesya turned, her shaking hand reaching for a large frying pan that hung from a row of hooks along the wall. Elizabeth followed suit, drawing the largest knife she could find from the block that sat on the kitchen dresser. The door inched open. Jennifer and Yana cowered back into the room, hiding behind the other two girls.

A huge man stepped cautiously into the room. Lesya sprang forward as soon as the man emerged from the darkness. She swung the heavy frying pan, aiming for his head. Her swing stopped in mid-air;

her wrist held in a vice-like grip. The man span her round, pulled her in close and locked a long, well-muscled arm around her slender neck. Elizabeth didn't hesitate. She bravely stepped forward, stabbing the knife hard toward the man's torso. The knife sliced through the air, then stopped abruptly as the man parried her blow and twisted her wrist upwards and outwards, sending the knife spinning to the floor.

'You two getting lunch?' Daniel asked nonchalantly.

'Daniel!' the girls exclaimed as they were released from his grip, elation and relief washing over them.

'Shhh,' Daniel warned. 'We've got company,' he said, pointing toward the yard.

The girls swept through the kitchen and into the broad inner hallway of the large farmhouse. Lesya ran to the front window and peered through a small gap in the closed shutters into the yard.

'Kozlov,' she said, in a hoarse, urgent whisper.

'What do we do?' Elizabeth asked.

'There are lots of men. Kozlov is speaking to someone. I can't quite see who it is,' Lesya said, still staring out of the narrow window next to the front door.

'They can't know we're in here – not yet,' Elizabeth replied.

'Sit tight for the minute. If we move now, there's

a good chance we'll be seen. Let's just sit tight and watch,' Daniel advised, his voice calm and relaxed.

*

Three men observed from the cover of the tree line that crested the top of the hill, as the small convoy of black vehicles swept into the yard and disappeared behind the farmhouse.

'Is he down there?'

'According to this he is,' replied the dark-haired man, holding up a small hand-held GPS tracking device.

'Prognosis?' asked the older, silver-haired man.

'He's fucked,' the dark-haired man replied.

'Prognosis?' the older man sighed and asked again.

'Let's move closer and get a better look. I can't see how many men are down there,' the dark-haired man replied more constructively.

'I agree. We're not much use up here whatever happens,' stated the third man, running his hand through his greying, brown wavy hair.

'OK, we'll move closer. But listen carefully, both of you. We're not much use to anyone dead. Let's be careful and stay out of sight. Don't move until we absolutely have to. Remember, devious is best,' he said, with half a grin and a steely glint in his eye.

*

Petr gathered the men around him in a tight circle.

'OK, listen up. Temple is here somewhere and so are the girls. They're on foot, so they won't be moving very fast. We know they're not south of us, so forget that direction. It's unlikely they've gone east; that would lead them back in the direction you came in. I think you would have seen them. That leaves the farm, the open ground to the west, and the forested ground to the north. Spread out and search for tracks. The snow is deep; it shouldn't be too hard to pick up their trail. If you find anything, anything at all, report straight back to me. One last thing – Temple is armed and very dangerous. You've seen what he's capable of, so be careful. And remember, Mr Kozlov wants him taken alive – the girls too.'

The men nodded their understanding, then formed into three teams of four men. The first and second teams headed out, scouring the open country west and north of the farm. The third team stayed close, fanning out to search through the outer farm buildings.

'What about the house?' Kozlov asked, looking over to the darkened farmhouse.

'We haven't checked it yet. I don't think they made it that far before we arrived. Temple certainly didn't. He was down there, overlooking the open fields, between here and the trees.'

'Send a couple of men over to check it. The girls may have found a way in.'

'Yes, Sir.'

The third team searched the small outbuildings dotted around the farm, then returned to the yard.

'Nothing, Petr,' their leader confirmed.

Petr nodded dejectedly. 'Very well. One of you come with me to check the house – let's see if there's any sign of forced entry. Send the rest of the men to join the other teams. Tell them not to search too far. If they can't find any tracks, it means there aren't any.'

'Yes, Petr,' the leader acknowledged, dividing his men as instructed.

The men dispersed, movingly quickly to their newly-assigned tasks. Petr moved forward and walked side by side with one other man towards the small gate that led into the narrow strip of garden fronting the farmhouse.

*

Lesya stepped nervously back from the shuttered window as the gate squeaked open and the men walked purposefully toward the front of the house.

'They're coming,' she said fearfully.

Daniel walked calmly forward, pressed his back

tight against the wall and peered through the narrow gap. Petr and the guard approached. Daniel turned to the girls.

'Get in the kitchen, lay down on the floor and keep very still and quiet,' he instructed.

The girls moved quickly, crawling on their hands and knees into the kitchen. They lay face down beneath the large table which sat in the centre of the room.

*

'Check the back,' Petr instructed, walking up the narrow path towards the front door. The guard turned away, crossed the snow-covered grass and disappeared around the side of the house.

Petr reached the front door and tried the handle; it was securely locked. He looked right and left. The windows of the house were shuttered, both inside and out. He stepped right, approached the first window, pressed his head against the wooden boards and peered in through the narrow gap, trying to see through the gloom of the unlit room. Unable to discern anything, he pulled away and walked to the other side of the path and repeated the exercise.

The guard reappeared. 'Nothing, it's all locked up – there's no sign of anyone. No sign of forced entry,' he reported.

'Good. Let's go,' Petr said, turning back towards the open yard.

*

Daniel watched Petr and the guard leave and breathed a small sigh of relief.

'It's OK, you can come out now, but stay away from the windows as you move,' he said, calling quietly to the girls.

The girls emerged looking pale and afraid.

'Go through to the sitting room and get comfortable; it looks like we might be here a while,' Daniel instructed, directing them to the door on the opposite side of the hall.

The girls walked through to the sitting room. It was a dull, square room filled with old, solid looking furniture. It felt cold and damp, but at least they were indoors and out of the biting cold wind. They sat on the sofa and huddled together, anxious and exhausted.

Daniel entered the room.

'It'll be dark soon. We'll lay low in here for a few hours, wait until nightfall, then sneak out of the back. With any luck, it will be morning before they find our tracks again.'

'What if they find the passage under the barn?' Elizabeth asked.

Daniel shrugged his shoulders. 'Then we'll be moving sooner than we planned. Try to get some rest now. I'll keep watch and wake you if we need to do anything.'

The girls spread themselves out on the old sofa and armchairs. Daniel briefly left the room, returning moments later with four thick blankets.

'Here,' he said. 'These should keep you warm.'

The girls smiled weakly as they wrapped themselves in the blankets and settled as comfortably as they could.

Daniel stepped back into the kitchen, locked the door to the passage, then pulled a plain, hard chair away from the table and set it by the window to keep watch.

The afternoon light began to fade and the sky dissolved from brilliant-blue to an abstract canvas of pale-grey, layered by thickening charcoal cloud and splashed with subtle shades of pink and orange, as the weak winter sun began to sink away to the west.

*

Sergei Kozlov stepped from the warmth of his car and listened to the reports. The men had found nothing and his dark eyes narrowed as his scheming evil mind drew the obvious conclusion.

'They're still here,' he said in low, rumbling, growl to Petr.

'Yes, Sir,' Petr replied, his gaze roving over the collection of farm buildings before coming back to rest on the barn doors.

He stared at the closed doors for several seconds as the realisation hit. Who had closed the doors? Temple and the girls had been outside, hadn't they? And neither he or his men had been back inside the barn since Kozlov arrived.

'We should check the barn again, Sir. We may have missed something in the speed of our earlier search,' he said, directing two of the vehicles to swing around.

The cars pulled up close, their full beam headlights shining through the doors as Petr pulled them open to survey the now brightly lit interior. He ushered two men forward.

'Check the loft,' he ordered, stepping further into the barn.

His eyes carefully scrutinised the bare wooden space. Apart from the single door at the rear, there was no other way in or out. Slowly, he scanned the walls. They held nothing more than a collection of old, rusting farm implements. He stood and thought. His men had checked and searched the entire perimeter and the tracks around the farm; there was no sign of anyone or anything. Whoever came in here, must still be in here. He stared at the small stack of straw bales sat in the centre of the floor, then at the trail of straw leading from the left-hand wall. The bales had been moved, but why? He walked across and sat down on them, lightly drumming his fingers on the hard-packed straw as he thought. He could think of no reason, but there was an obvious response – move them back. He called to his men.

*

Daniel watched the vehicles swing around the yard, shining their headlights onto the barn doors as Petr hauled them open and stepped inside. There was a brief pause, then men were moving, being called inside. It was time to go.

Stepping quickly back through the hall and into the lounge, Daniel roused the girls with a firm shake, his finger pressed to his lips, warning them to silence.

'We have to go. I think they found the passage. It won't take them too long to either follow it or work out where it leads.'

The girls were up and ready before Daniel completed his sentence, a new wave of fear and adrenalin surging through their bodies as they prepared to bolt from cover like antelope fleeing from a hunting pride of lions.

'Lesya, watch the front. I'm going to check our

exit,' Daniel said, disappearing through the door.

Lesya moved to the front window and watched the flurry of brightly-lit activity in the yard with nervous interest.

Daniel ran upstairs to get a better look at the land to the rear of the house. The garden was wide and deep, ending at a low stone wall, that dropped to the narrow road behind. There was no gate. Beyond the road, a series of open fields rose steadily to higher ground and rolling, thickly-forested hills beyond. Daniel scanned the garden, along the wall as far as he could see, then out across the fields. In the dim twilight, he could just make out the turning into the farm entrance and the short lane which ran directly down to the farmyard to his left. There was a large, black 4x4 parked across the entrance. He assumed it was occupied, despite its outwardly dark and cold appearance. With the exception of the car, there were no other signs of Kozlov's men.

*

Petr directed the men into the barn and watched as they moved the straw bales, leaving a thin layer of straw and dust covering the sturdy wooden floor. He stepped forward, his head bent, his vision fixed just an inch or two in front of his feet. Suddenly, he stopped, dropped to his haunches and swept away the dust with his hand. Remaining perfectly still, he stared at the trapdoor in disbelief.

'Fuck,' he whispered before standing.

He turned to run back to the yard, but there was no need. Kozlov was stood directly behind him, his hands shoved deep into the pockets of his long winter coat and his collar turned high against the rapidly falling temperature. His face was turning a brighter shade of red beneath his close-cropped, greying, black hair as he glowered at Petr.

'A way out?' Kozlov asked menacingly.

'Possibly,' Petr replied.

'Open it. Get men down there – now,' Kozlov barked.

Petr was moving before Kozlov finished the order, organising the men.

'Bring torches. Get the trapdoor open and see what's down there – quickly,' he shouted.

The men fetched the lights and ran back into the barn. Four men opened the trapdoor, then dropped rapidly through the opening to search the earthen-floored room below.

'There's a passageway,' one of the men called.

'Follow it. See where it leads,' Petr answered.

'Wait,' Kozlov shouted. 'Which way does it lead?'

Petr peered down into the room. The man pointed. Petr pointed.

'North,' he advised.

'Towards the house?' Kozlov asked.

Petr looked up, checked his bearings and swallowed hard.

'Yes,' he confirmed, realising the enormity of the single word.

'Send two men down the passage. Get the rest of the men to surround the house. They've been in there all the time. Temple is making us look like fools,' Kozlov bellowed, his anger boiling over into rage.

*

The girls were lined up in the hall, ready to go as Daniel bounced down the stairs. Unlocking the back door he eased it quietly open and peered out. Carefully he checked their route again – it looked clear.

'All set, ladies?' he asked confidently.

The girls nodded nervously.

'Right, listen carefully. Run to the end of the garden, but don't jump the wall. It appears short, but the drop on the other side is much deeper. Climb over and lower yourselves down. Run across the road, hop over the fence, then cut sharp right and aim to get to the woods as quickly as possible. Get into the trees, then run straight up the hill. Don't stop for anything. Whatever happens, just keep running, OK?'

The girls nodded again.

'Liz, I'll carry you. There's no way you'll keep up on that ankle.'

Liz nodded and smiled weakly.

Daniel pushed open the door.

'Let's go,' he said. 'Lesya, lead them on – keep Yana with you.'

Lesya stepped out of the door and ran hard, dragging Yana along beside her.

'Run, Yana,' she urged, as Jennifer caught and overtook them.

Daniel waited for them to reach the wall, then scooped Elizabeth into his arms and bounded after them.

Three men watched them go.

Daniel reached the wall, eased Elizabeth over the edge and dropped her gently to the ground. Urgently, he turned, hearing sounds of men running through the front garden. Petr was shouting orders.

'You men take the front. You take the back.'

Daniel didn't wait. Throwing his legs over the wall, he dropped to the ground and scooped Elizabeth back into his arms. He ran on, then stopped, dropping heavily to the ground as Kozlov's men spilled noisily into the back garden, encircling the house.

Ahead, Lesya, Yana and Jennifer ran on. They cleared the fence, crouched low and skirted the edge of the field toward the trees. Daniel watched them go; vague, shadowy figures, disappearing rapidly into the darkness. He rolled to his side and pulled Elizabeth close into the lee of the wall.

'We'll wait until they enter the house, then move,' he whispered.

Muted sounds of gunfire rose from the house and the sound of Petr shouting his orders carried to where they lay in in the darkness.

'Ready?' Daniel asked lifting Elizabeth back into his arms. He ran toward the fence, vaulted over, then pushed on. They were almost clear when the lights on the 4x4 parked in the farm entrance flared and they flashed for a brief, but crucial, second through the light.

'Shit,' Daniel cursed. 'Let's hope they didn't see us,' he added, vanishing into the darkness and out of range.

*

The sound of gunfire died, replaced by the sound of a car horn blaring repeatedly. Petr ran to the garden wall, leant over and waved the car forward. It accelerated the short distance down the road and slid to a halt, the window already open.

'The field,' the guard said pointing.

'To me,' Petr called, rallying his men.

Kozlov stood back and let Petr work and reorganise the men. One team and one vehicle with Sergei Kozlov at the farm. One team and one vehicle accelerated down the road, heading for the gated forest track a mile to the east. The remaining men went on foot, following Petr over the fence and into the field as the chase began again.

TWENTY-SIX

The sound of the blaring car horn filled Daniel's ears.

'They saw us,' he said, with resigned sarcasm, as his pace increased.

Reaching the edge of the forest, he turned and watched as one of the vehicles flew down the narrow country road, its lights ablaze.

'There must be another road somewhere nearby,' he said, turning away and running up the steadily rising ground.

Daniel glanced over his shoulder; his assessment wasn't good. Petr was leading eight men across the field, jogging at a constant, ground-eating pace, following the tracks in the snow, under the glare of their bright torch beams.

Daniel drove himself on, pumping his legs hard, forcing just a little more speed. He caught up with the other girls.

'Run,' he demanded, glancing once more over his shoulder.

Behind him, the men had reached the first line of trees. They slowed their pace a little to confirm the direction of their quarry, then started to run again.

Daniel stepped out in front and ran hard, carrying Elizabeth in his arms. They crested the first ridge and ran down the slope, picking up pace as the ground slanted steadily away.

Lesya stumbled and fell, sprawling head-first down the hill. Daniel didn't have time for sympathy; he could see she wasn't hurt.

'Up, Lesya, come on,' he urged.

She hauled herself to her feet and ran on, catching up with the group as they started to climb once more.

Again, Daniel glanced back. Lights swept over the brow of the hill behind them. The men were still chasing; the distance was closing.

The girls were exhausted. Their bodies were failing; they had nothing left to give. Adrenalin, nervous energy and absolute terror kept their legs going, one flagging stride after another.

'Come on, we're out-running them,' Daniel lied encouragingly.

Daniel was thinking hard; he knew they couldn't outrun their pursuers – not for much longer.

Their pace slowed even further as they reached the top of the second hill and hauled their bodies through the trees, willing the steep incline to come to an end.

At last, the hill levelled off, then dropped steeply away again. Daniel looked down. Ahead of them, the ground at the bottom of the hill was open and level and a collection of wooden huts sat gathered in a small, fenced-in compound. Around the huts, huge piles of roughly-prepared logs stood in neat rows beneath yellow fluorescent lamps, giving the snow a bright, golden glow. Several large vehicles, lorries and pickup trucks sat parked in an avenue between the logs and huts. It was a logging camp.

'There,' Daniel called. 'Run for the trucks. See if you can get one started,' he instructed, setting Elizabeth down. 'Jennifer, help your sister.'

She had no time to answer. Daniel turned and disappeared into the darkness, moving swiftly and silently back towards Petr and his men.

The girls ran on, tripping, falling and rolling over the hard, frozen ground in their desperate pursuit of safety.

Daniel saw the lights dancing and swaying through the trees as Petr and his men approached. Petr had spread out his men with care; some were beneath the trees, others a short way out from the tree line, covering any attempt Daniel and the girls might make to cut across the open field.

Daniel knelt in the darkness, close to a large pine tree, pulled his balaclava down over his face, unslung the Uzi 9mm from his shoulder and waited for the range between him and Petr's men to close.

*

The girls reached the compound and ran directly for the row of parked trucks, their optimism cruelly dashed as they approached. The trucks were old and rusting, their tyres bald and flat – they hadn't moved in years.

'Oh, please, no,' Elizabeth cried, as she hobbled in behind the others.

The sound of a car driving fast along the forest track filled their ears and headlights flared in the road away to their right. Horrified, the girls looked at each other in rapid succession as their panic rose.

'The huts,' Elizabeth shouted above the sound of gunfire which had erupted from the trees high above them.

The girls ran. Elizabeth gritted her teeth and forced her legs to run through the pain. They crashed through the door of the first hut, slammed it closed and peered anxiously through the small window.

A black 4x4 cleared the bend, swept into the compound and skidded to a halt.

Nothing happened.

The men inside just parked, sat and waited.

*

Daniel waited calmly in the darkness, letting the men approach steadily through the trees. The first of Petr's men appeared off to his left. He ducked beneath a branch and stepped in toward Daniel.

Daniel turned and fired; a short, controlled burst, centre mass. The man fell. Daniel rolled away as the trees around him exploded in a rapid return of fire. He stayed low and moved right.

Petr's men advanced, leap-frogging one another through the trees, their torches off and laying down covering fire as each man in turn moved forward, uncertain of Daniel's position.

The forest was deathly black. Daniel came up to his knees. Holding the Uzi in a light, double-handed grip, he closed his eyes and listened hard.

To his right, the forest floor crackled.

Smoothly he turned, fired and found a target.

Orange flame flared in the blackness from the returned fire, and bullets spewed through the tress. Wood erupted all around as the trunk above his head splintered into a million pieces.

Daniel rolled away again as sound and movement registered from every direction. There were too many men, too close.

Daniel stood, turned and ran.

*

The girls sat in the darkness of the small wooden cabin, breathing hard and listening harder. The 4x4 had stopped in the compound some minutes ago and there was still no movement. The sound of gunfire echoed from the hills above and they looked at one another nervously.

'Lesya, check the window. Jennifer, see if you can find another way out,' Elizabeth said, trying to keep the girls focussed.

Lesya crept back to the window and peered into the compound. The black car was there, still and quiet. Jennifer stood and looked around the cold, bare cabin; there were just two rooms. She moved into the second room – there was nothing to see. The only door was the one they'd come through and the only two windows, one in each room, faced the front. There was no way out.

*

The firing stopped. Daniel kept running, opening the

distance between himself and Petr's men. At the edge of the trees he stopped, moved forward more cautiously, then knelt and waited again. Ahead, two men were moving warily through the field toward him, a short way out in the open ground, their black shadows standing out against the snow. Daniel stood, fired two short bursts and emptied his clip. The men fell.

Immediately behind, the trees erupted again. Bullets fizzed around Daniel's head and sharp splinters exploded into his face as round after round blasted into the trunks.

Momentarily stunned, Daniel fell backwards. His left cheek burned like hell and blood flowed down his face from a series of slashing wounds. Shaking his head,

he jumped to his feet, ducking low under a hail of bullets as he ran again.

Without breaking stride, Daniel determinedly pulled the empty clip from his Uzi and slapped in a replacement. Suddenly, he broke from the trees and ran hard into the open field.

The report of a rifle shot cracked through the freezing night air and Daniel fell face-first into the snow with blood pouring from his wound. Grimacing with pain, he instinctively reached down to feel the gash in his leg. The bullet had sliced through the muscle of his thigh; a painful, debilitating wound. Gritting his teeth, he drew a deep breath, clambered to his feet and ran on, firing the Uzi blindly behind him.

The rifle cracked again.

The Uzi span away. Daniel stumbled and fell, his right arm outstretched and his left arm tucked beneath his body. Blood trickled into the snow. He stayed down.

Daniel felt a sharp kick to his ribs and his body moved slightly. He made no sound. No response. A man stood by his body, then dropped to his haunches and rolled him over. Daniel fired the Glock left-handed into the guards face at point blank range and the back of the guard's head exploded. Petr kicked the gun from Daniel's hand as the butt of a rifle crashed into the side of Daniel's head. He blacked out.

The chase was over.

*

Lesya stepped back, away from the window, with tears streaming down her face.

'They have Daniel,' she whispered solemnly.

Elizabeth looked at her, then moved to the window. She stared in shock at the men stood around Daniel's prostrate body as he lay bleeding in the snow. She moved back into the centre of the room as the girls came together and silently held hands.

*

Dazed and in pain, Daniel felt himself being hauled back to his feet and marched down the hill. Feigning near unconsciousness, his eyes scanned the logging compound as his vision cleared.

A single black 4x4 was parked outside one of the huts and another came roaring into view on the single forest track. It braked, skidding to a stop close to the other, and four men stepped out.

Sandwiched between several guards, Daniel looked straight ahead, ignoring the four sets of footprints in the snow, as they reached the bottom of the hill and passed the cabins. In front of him, the hulking, bear-like figure of Sergei Kozlov, flanked by his two bodyguards, lumbered forward, wrapped in his long black coat.

Kozlov stepped in close and Daniel could see the anger and hatred boiling behind his black, pitiless eyes. Daniel held his gaze, his piercing blue-green eyes equally as cold, hard and unforgiving.

Kozlov looked away as if remembering the night, not so long ago, when he first met Temple and what he saw in Daniel's eyes – no fear.

Kozlov looked at Petr and nodded. It was as close

as he came to saying, "well done".

'On your knees, Temple,' Petr ordered.

Daniel didn't move. He stood, feet apart and arms up, with his hands clasped behind his head and blood running from the wounds in his thigh and shoulder.

'On your knees, I said,' Petr raged, kicking the back of Daniel's knee.

Daniel buckled slightly from the blow, regained his balance and stood firm.

The butt of a rifle crashed between Daniel's shoulders as Petr simultaneously kicked into the back of his knee again. He had no choice; the power of the blows forced him down and he knelt on one knee.

'That's better,' Kozlov laughed a deep rumbling laugh as he stared down at Daniel.

'You're going to die now, Mr Temple, very painfully, I'm afraid, but first I need to know – what have you done with my property?'

Daniel stared back at Kozlov, his eyes conveying far more than any words could say.

'You'd like to kill me, wouldn't you, Temple? Perhaps you should have when you had the chance. Now, I'm afraid, the game is over,' Kozlov said.

He reached into his inner coat pocket and pulled out a small stainless steel hatchet. The brilliant, razor-sharp blade, glinted brightly under the fluorescent light.

Daniel's expression remained firm. His emotionless eyes bored into Kozlov's, then flicked past him as the doors to the other black 4x4 slowly opened. Three more of Kozlov's men climbed out, dressed identically to the others, their black balaclavas pulled down over their faces, hiding their features. They walked slowly towards the group of men.

With Petr stood behind him and two men flanking either side, Daniel knelt on the cold, hard ground and watched them approach. The men stopped and stood respectfully still and silent behind Kozlov and his bodyguards.

They all waited.

Kozlov turned his attention back to Daniel.

'Tell me what I want to know and I promise not to take too long in killing you. Where are the girls?'

Daniel knelt in silence. He was never going to answer that question. He wouldn't dignify Kozlov's questions with an answer of any description. His eyes darted around the group of men, desperately searching for the one small opportunity he needed. His hands were free. If he could just take one man out, he stood a chance. A slim one, but a chance nonetheless.

Petr would be the man. He was stood directly behind Daniel and way too close to react in time. Daniel thought it through. Despite his wounds, he could launch himself up and backward, straight into Petr. His men wouldn't fire, not immediately; they would hit their own man. It was his only chance. He tensed his body, ran the movement through in his mind and waited for the moment.

Kozlov sighed heavily. 'A hero to the last, Mr Temple? We'll find them anyway, but have it your way. I'm going to enjoy killing you. Goodbye, Mr Temple.'

Kozlov raised the hatchet slowly, then froze like a statue. His arm held perfectly still as a Sig-Sauer pistol pressed firmly into the base of his skull. Kozlov's bodyguards stood equally as motionless, pistols pressed equally firmly into the exact same spot at the backs of their heads.

'I believe what we have here is a Mexican stand-off,' said the smooth, crystal-clear English accent. 'Stand up, Daniel.'

Daniel rose to his feet, unable to believe his ears or the sound of the familiar voice behind the mask.

'Drop the axe. Tell your men to drop their weapons and stand back.'

Kozlov thought for a moment.

'Take a look around, my friend. You're still out-numbered and out-gunned. I think you have made a very big mistake. You won't get away from here alive,' he said calmly.

'Maybe not, but then you won't be alive to see it,

whatever happens. Now tell your men to drop their weapons or I'll put a bullet through your head,' the voice said with calm authority, jabbing the gun harder into Kozlov's skull to enforce the point.

'Step away, Daniel,' the voice added.

Daniel took the Glock from Petr's hand and stepped back from the group.

Kozlov sighed heavily again and dropped the hatchet to the ground.

'Drop your weapons,' he ordered.

The guns thudded one by one into the snow as the men dropped them to the ground and stood back.

'Tell your men to leave – that way,' the man said pointing back towards the open fields.

Kozlov nodded to Petr and the men. 'Go,' he said.

The bodyguards moved to join the other men, obeying Kozlov's order. They walked slowly backwards, keeping Daniel and the three mystery men firmly in view until they reached the end of the compound. There, they turned, walked up the snow-covered hill and disappeared from sight.

The three men stood back and Kozlov turned slowly to face his opponent.

His eyes narrowed.

'Who are you?'

'A fair enough question,' the man said pulling the balaclava from his head.

The two men with him mirrored the movement and stared at Kozlov, their gaze hard and unforgiving.

Kozlov looked at the man stood before him and recognition slowly dawned.

'You?' he said blinking, unable to rationalise why the silver-haired man was there. Then full realisation hit and his expression changed. He knew he was a beaten man. 'I should have known. Daniel Temple, as in Temple Stamford. Sir David was your father?'

Daniel nodded. 'He was,' he replied simply.

'You're the silent partner in Mead Associates?'

'I am.'

Daniel looked at the two men either side of Coleman. John Shaw smiled, winked and nodded.

'Daniel,' he said, by way of a greeting.

Colonel Richard Mead looked toward him, concern and question in his eyes.

'They're safe,' Daniel said. 'They're in the cabin,' he gestured with his head toward the small wooden hut.

Richard Mead nodded. The second question hung invisibly in the air. Daniel registered it and responded.

'They're alright,' he added.

The weight of the world lifted instantly from Mead's shoulders and he turned his full attention and anger back to Kozlov.

'You evil son of a bitch,' he said raising his gun. 'What were you going to do with my daughters? You sick fucking bastard.'

Kozlov swallowed hard. He had no answer. He closed his eyes.

Richard Mead fired.

Kozlov's body thumped into the snow, dead.

*

The shot boomed and echoed around the open compound and tore into the black silence of the cabin.

'Oh my God, no, Daniel,' Elizabeth cried.

The girls cried inconsolably. Daniel was dead; executed by Kozlov and his men. There was no hope for them now. They moved together and held each other tight. It offered little comfort.

The sound of footsteps heading toward the cabin cut harshly through their grief, forcing their breath to catch in their throats. Elizabeth wiped her eyes and tried to look again for a way out, but there was nothing. No window, no door, no hidden exit. They were trapped.

The footsteps grew closer and louder. The handle turned and the door burst open. Yana fainted, falling in a crumpled heap. Golden fluorescent light spilled into the cabin and the three pale, tear-stained faces, stared at the huge figure filling the doorway.

Daniel beamed a broad smile back at them.

'It's OK, you're safe now.'

'Daniel,' Elizabeth cried. 'We thought you were dead.'

Daniel didn't comment. 'Come on, there's someone here who is rather anxious to see you.'

The girls walked hesitantly out of the cabin into the snow-covered compound.

'Daddy,' Jennifer screamed, joy, relief and excitement washing over her in equal measure.

She ran into her father's arms, closely followed by her sister.

Richard Mead pulled them in and held them tight.

Daniel stepped into the cabin, followed by John Shaw.

Shaw gently lifted Yana from the floor as Daniel offered Lesya the crook of his arm and the two men took the girls to the warmth and safety of one of the 4x4's.

Placing Yana gently on the rear seat of the car, John and Daniel left Lesya to comfort her.

'Thank you, Daniel,' Richard Mead said as he released his girls and walked over to shake Daniel's hand.

Daniel nodded frostily, then wandered across the compound, to where John now sat with Coleman on a low stack of logs.

'What the hell are you doing here – thank god. How did you know?'

'How did we know what?' Coleman asked, glancing at John Shaw.

'How did you know we needed help or where to find us?'

'Your watch,' John answered simply.

'My watch?'

'I got it fixed for you, remember?'

'Yeah I know, so?'

John Shaw sarcastically rolled his eyes.

'Christ, Dan, for someone as intelligent as you are, you're being very bloody slow. I added an extra little feature – a tracker. The same one we put in all the diplomatic watches. I always knew exactly where you were. I didn't like leaving you to go it alone. I listened to that tape over and over and liked it even less. I knew I had to do something. Kozlov was a nasty bastard, but an organised and resourceful one. So is Durakovic. I know how good you are, Dan, but you would never have made it alone. So I spoke with Coleman and Richard yesterday and here we are.'

'Was. Durakovic is dead,' Daniel replied.

'God almighty! I understand why you did this, Daniel, but it was very misguided. Richard should never have asked you – the odds were just too high,' Coleman said, shaking his head.

'Richard lied to me,' Daniel said in a low angry voice.

'Yes,' Coleman confirmed. 'But I think it best you hold that temper of yours in check until you've heard the whole story. You're going to need to do some thinking; this goes far deeper than any of you realise.'

Daniel nodded in agreement as another thought struck him. 'You knew Kozlov.' It was a statement, not a question.

'Our paths crossed once or twice. Years ago, when I worked for your father,' Coleman acknowledged. 'But now is not the time or place for explanations. We need to get out of here.'

Richard Mead led his daughters towards one of the two vehicles. They walked slowly, hand in hand, as Elizabeth limped awkwardly along.

'Who are they?' John asked, gesturing with his chin as he tended Daniel's wounds.

'The tall one is Lesya. The other one is Yana. They were locked up with Elizabeth and Jennifer. I couldn't exactly leave them behind.'

'What's wrong with the smaller one?'

'Kozlov and his men took her first. She's going to need a lot of help and care. Mentally, she's shot to pieces. We'd better get out of here. I don't suppose it will take long for Kozlov's men to regroup and come back. Let's get everyone into the cars; we can sort out what needs to be done later. Coleman, could you have Andrew Campbell meet us at the airport. He can take care of any legal requirements. Let's go home,' Daniel said, patting John on the shoulder.

Daniel stood and walked with Coleman and John Shaw to the second of the cars.

'It's not over, is it?' Daniel simultaneously stated and asked.

'No, I wouldn't think so,' Coleman confirmed, with a slow, sorry shake of his head.

TWENTY-SEVEN

The two black 4x4's accelerated out of the logging compound. From high on the hill, Petr watched them go. He had remained close with the men, ready to respond as soon as Kozlov gave the word. The word never came.

He watched as one of the men angrily confronted Kozlov, shooting him through the head without a second's warning. His thoughts and emotions were strangely mixed. A combination of detached, macabre fascination, loyal frustration, relief and revenge blended and blurred as Kozlov, the man he had served and feared above all else fell into the snow, dead.

The men looked to him now. In the absence of Taras, Petr was in charge. He wouldn't be for long – he knew that. The short struggle for power would soon begin. The successor would be Vladimir

Radimov, Kozlov's commander in Moscow. There was no one more powerful left in the organisation. Radimov held the power base and would act swiftly to seize control and take revenge.

*

Daniel sat next to Coleman and stared thoughtfully out of the window as John Shaw drove.

'We'll be with the chopper in ten minutes,' John confirmed, without turning round.

'So what's the story? Why did Richard lie to me?' Daniel asked.

'I think it's best if Richard explains that to you himself. What's more important is what we are going to do now,' replied Coleman.

'He didn't need to lie to me, whatever the reasons. I was his friend and his partner – I would have gone anyway. I wouldn't have left Elizabeth and Jennifer with those guys. He must know that.'

'He does know that. Take it easy with him, Daniel. You'll understand once you've had a chance to listen and talk.'

'So what now?'

'Now we plan. Whoever replaces Kozlov will be hard on our trail sooner rather than later. The Russian mafia aren't used to this. They won't be letting it go. They'll want an eye for an eye.'

'Great,' John Shaw chipped in from the front seat. 'Now I'll have someone else after my arse.'

'It won't be you, John. It'll be Richard and Daniel that have the dubious honour of being top of their hit list. Once we know who the new head man is, we can start the negotiations.'

'Negotiations? I'm not running any more. Let them come,' Daniel stated.

'You still don't get it, do you, Daniel? This is a war you should never have entered and sure as hell one you can't win. These aren't some small-time, backstreet hoodlums. This is a major organised crime operation. They are hard, ruthless and resourceful. They live by a code and will never stop coming. Not now, not ever –' Coleman took a deep breath. 'Not unless we or you negotiate a settlement.'

'A settlement?' Daniel questioned.

'They'll want revenge at first. Honour must be served. However, they're not stupid. They'll know who you are and who your father was. Temple Stamford pumps billions of dollars every year into the Russian economy. For every deal done, every dollar of profit made, the mafia takes its cut, a substantial cut – it's just the price of doing business. It's high time you got to grips with this, Daniel. If you really want a different life, to run that business of yours successfully, not just as a sleeping partner, you have to take on more of your father's mantle.'

'I'm not my father and I'm not trying to be. What are you suggesting? You pay them more? Buy them off? What sort of business is that?'

'Grow up, Daniel, for God's sake. Stop being so bloody naive,' Coleman snapped. 'What you did for Richard was very admirable. I'm very proud of you. Your father would have been proud of you, but you can't spend your whole life being some sort of lone ranger.'

John Shaw laughed out loud. 'That's the second time you've been called that this week!'

Coleman frowned. 'What I mean is, this is a very serious business. The sooner you two realise that, the better. You can't just approach it like some overgrown boy scout. You have to accept, whether you like it or not, that there are some battles you can't fight, with guns, knives and fists – no matter how good at it you might be.'

'So we just cower away and pay up, is that it?'

Coleman glared at the man he had seen grow from a boy.

It was a look Daniel hadn't seen for years.

'Who said anything about cowering away?'

'But I thought you said –'

'You didn't hear me say anything of the sort. I haven't told you what we're going to do,' Coleman cut across him angrily. 'Now just listen.'

*

The small private jet touched down at the isolated airstrip just outside St Petersburg twelve hours after the call had been made by Petr. Vladimir Radimov stepped onto the tarmac. He was a tall man, immaculately dressed in a perfectly-tailored, navy Armani suit. His handsome features were set firm and his thick, neatly-groomed, fair hair fluttered slightly in the light, chilling breeze. His crystal-blue eyes scanned across the men waiting by the row of three cars. He nodded once.

'Petr,' he said in greeting.

Petr guided him to the waiting limousine parked in the centre of the row.

'What happened here?' Radimov asked as the cars pulled away.

Petr sat nervously beside him and explained the story, or at least as much as he knew. Radimov nodded and listened, asked questions and prompted for further detail, as Petr recounted everything he possibly could.

'The strange thing is, I'm sure Kozlov knew the older man, but I'd never seen him before. He definitely had some important connection to Temple, though.'

'Thank you, Petr. You have done well,' Radimov assured.

*

The Bell 430 helicopter flew low and fast, swept across the Russian border with Finland and swooped in to land at the small deserted airstrip. The Temple Stamford jet was already waiting. The four men and four girls ran up the steps as the aircraft began to roll. The door slammed closed. The jet accelerated down the runway and lifted into the cold, 4:00am sky.

Inside, the four girls remained together, talking quietly, the relief evident in their pale faces as the jet climbed and the full realisation of safety dawned.

John Shaw reclined his chair, closed his eyes and fell asleep, seemingly without a care in the world, before the plane levelled off at its cruising altitude.

Daniel sat one row in front of John, his forehead pressed against the window, looking out at the dark-blue emptiness of the still-darkened sky. He felt strangely depressed. The was no euphoria of bringing the girls to safety; no sweet taste of victory. Nothing to savour in the deaths of Zoran Durakovic, Sergei Kozlov or their men. Just the thought of betrayal and of the fight still to come.

He sat up, suddenly aware of Richard's gaze, and turned to cut him a short, disappointed look before letting his head rest back against the window.

Richard Mead moved, sat next to him and spoke quietly.

'I'm not sure what Coleman or John told you, or even what you may have worked out for yourself, but would you at least allow me to explain things for myself?'

Daniel stared at him for a moment, his eyes cold and hard. It wasn't a look of understanding or friendship.

'I'm not sure I want to hear it, Richard. You lied to me, plain and simple. I risked my life for you, to get Elizabeth and Jennifer back, and you lied. You didn't need to do that, Richard. What did you think would happen? Did you think I wouldn't go? Did you think you needed to fabricate a story, is that it? You can say what you like, Richard; I thought we were friends and partners. I thought you knew me better than that. Well, we're not and you don't. I really don't see the point in saying anymore. Go back to your family, Richard. They're safe enough for now. We'll work out what to do with the company later.' He cut the conversation dead and stared back out of the window.

Richard Mead returned quietly to his seat.

John Shaw opened his eyes, raised his chair and sat forward behind Daniel, whispering over the back of the seat.

'I don't often say this, but you're wrong, Daniel. He didn't deserve that. You go back a long way – give the man a chance. Despite what's happened, you owe him that.'

Daniel didn't reply, but John's words had registered loud and clear. Despite his tendency for inappropriate comments and witty quips, when John spoke seriously, he was logical, insightful and accurate.

Daniel sat and mulled over Coleman's and John's words. A few minutes later, he left the main cabin and disappeared into the small, private office. He had work to do.

*

The small convoy of vehicles roared up the long drive toward Kozlov's castle, swept into the wide expanse of gravel and skidded to a halt in front of the main doors.

Radimov stepped from the car, crunched across the gravel and strode confidently through the entrance. Petr followed in his wake, hurrying along behind, trying to keep pace as he entered Kozlov's office.

'This place is freezing. Get it warmed up,' he ordered, sitting in Kozlov's throne-like chair.

'Yes, Sir,' Petr nodded.

'Don't call me, Sir, Petr. I don't like it – Mr Radimov will do.'

'Yes, Mr Radimov,' Petr acknowledged.

'When you take command of this region, I want

you to find somewhere else to operate from. I can't stand this godforsaken place. I assume you do want to command, Petr?'

'Yes, Mr Radimov. Thank you, it would be an honour,' Petr responded.

'Good. I don't think Kozlov made the best of you. It's unfortunate what has happened here, but Kozlov brought it on himself; it's not your fault, it should never have happened. Nonetheless, we cannot let it go unpunished; our enemies will think us weak. You're a smart man, Petr, I definitely want you working for me. Come and sit – let us work out how and when we shall strike back at these men, Mead and Temple. I have no further interest in the girls.'

*

An hour later, Daniel opened the door to the small private office and called to Richard and Coleman.

'Richard, Coleman, I need to talk to you both,' he said gravely.

The two men made their way back through the aircraft and disappeared behind the closed office door. It was some minutes before the office door reopened.

'I'll make the arrangements, Daniel,' Coleman said in a calm and business-like fashion, closing the office door once more.

Daniel nodded, his face betraying no emotion as he led a shocked, pale and drawn-looking Richard back to his seat to spend the remainder of the flight in deep thoughtful silence.

*

Radimov scanned Petr's face from across the wide, ornate desk. His emerald-green eyes sparkled with drive and energy.

'We are agreed then, Petr. You will leave tonight. We will fly you in as far as Paris, then smuggle you across the channel in one of the usual transports. There will be no trace of your entry into the UK. Take two of your very best men with you; our team in London will supply you with weapons. Temple will be your first target, he presents the most danger. Once he is out of the way, you can move on to Mead and his family. Then it stops. The message will be clear enough. No one crosses this organisation. Now go – earn your stars.'

'Yes, Mr Radimov. I will leave as soon as I am ready.'

Radimov nodded his approval, but said no more as Petr left the room and closed the door behind him.

*

Coleman emerged from the small office as the jet lined up for its final approach to Stansted airport.

'OK, Daniel, I've made the arrangements. Andrew Campbell will be waiting for us when we land. The formal preliminaries have already been taken care of. We won't need to worry about passports or customs. We should be on our way pretty much as soon as we land. John will escort Lesya and Yana to a safe house where further arrangements for them can be made. A medical team will be standing by to take proper care of your wounds, Daniel.' Coleman explained, then turned to Richard.

'Daniel asked me to contact Jane – she'll be at Broughton Hall when we get there.'

Richard Mead nodded. 'Very well, thank you,' he acknowledged quietly.

'John, it's up to you whether you come to Broughton after you have left Lesya and Yana, or whether you just want to go home.'

'Home, I think. I'd better show up in the office tomorrow, or this new guy will be issuing divorce proceedings.'

Two and a half hours after take-off, the aircraft touched down and taxied into the Temple Stamford hangar. Andrew Campbell, the medical team and numerous suited officials waited. Coleman led the way out of the aircraft, followed closely by John Shaw and Richard Mead. Daniel brought up the rear, escorting the girls one final time, down the steps and across to the waiting cars.

Daniel stepped into the rear of an ambulance, turned, sat and watched as John Shaw climbed into another car and was driven away. Coleman stood with Richard Mead, signing the documents Andrew Campbell had prepared for their arrival.

Richard returned Andrew's pen, then turned to Coleman.

'Thank you, Coleman,' he said, sweat breaking out on his forehead, his face turning ashen grey.

'Are you alright, Richard?' Coleman asked.

Richard didn't answer. He slumped forward into Coleman's arms. Coleman lowered him gently to the ground.

'Help me here,' he called.

The medical team tending Daniel left him, running to Richard's aid. Daniel followed them slowly.

Richard Mead lay on his back, his breathing low and shallow. The doctor assessed him quickly.

'Heart attack,' he stated.

The girls ran from the car.

'Daddy,' Jennifer cried.

Richard Mead lay on the hangar floor, the medical team working frantically over him.

Daniel pulled the girls away.

'Let them work,' he said.

With his contorted face covered by an oxygen mask, Richard was taken on a stretcher into the back of the ambulance as the doctor urgently pumped his chest.

'Coleman, take the girls home. I'll go with Richard. They need to finish patching me up, anyway. I'll call as soon as I have any news. Send a car for me in the morning,' Daniel instructed.

Coleman ushered Jennifer and Elizabeth away as gently as he could.

'Come on, your father is in the best of hands. We'll arrange for you to visit the hospital after you've seen your mother. Daniel will call with any news.'

Tears streaming down their faces, the two girls climbed reluctantly into the back of the car and watched the ambulance pull away as, with blue lights flashing, it faded into the distance.

*

Concealed in the rear of the apparently half-loaded articulated lorry, Petr and his two men sat encased in the small steel cell as it drove onto a ferry bound for Dover.

A brief check of its manifest and shipping documentation and the lorry cleared customs, drove through the dock gates and headed for London. A short while later, the lorry pulled to a stop, its airbrakes hissing loudly as the driver parked anonymously in the vast lorry park. The door to the cell clicked open and Petr stepped forward, followed by his men. He walked confidently through the half-empty trailer, jumped down from the rear and crossed to the waiting car.

*

Daniel sat perfectly still as the nurse stitched and dressed the wounds in his leg and shoulder and cleaned up his face.

'There you go, Mr Temple. Try not to put any strain on the stitches for at least a week,' said the male nurse as he left.

'I won't, thanks,' Daniel acknowledged.

He stood and dressed, then pulled back the curtain to his cubicle and wandered back to the A&E reception.

'Mr Mead?' he asked.

'Are you a relative?' the receptionist asked.

'No, I came in with him, though. I'm a close friend – his family are away. Could you tell me how he is, please?'

'I'm sorry, sir. Perhaps if you could wait over there, I'll see if one of the doctors will speak to you,' the receptionist replied, gesturing to the row of seats in the waiting area.

Daniel took a seat and tried to relax as he waited. He thought back to the brief conversation on the plane and regretted what he had said. John had been right; he should have given Richard the chance.

The doctor approached.

'Mr Temple?' he enquired, stony faced.

'Yes.'

'Please could we step into the consulting room for a moment?'

Daniel stepped into the room and watched as the doctor thoughtfully closed the door.

'I understand you are a close friend of Mr Mead?'

'Colonel Mead, yes,' Daniel said correcting the doctor, giving Richard his proper title.

'Sorry, Colonel Mead. I also understand Colonel Mead's family are away?'

'Yes, that's right.'

'Do you know if they are contactable?'

'No, no they're not. They will be away for some time. I may be able to contact them later.'

'I see,' said the doctor, mulling over the options, visibly coming to a conclusion.

'In that case, Mr Temple, I do have some very bad news. I am afraid Colonel Mead passed away a few minutes ago. I'm very sorry.'

'Were you with him?'

'No, I wasn't. The private medical team that brought you in were trying to resuscitate him, but I am the senior registrar – it falls to me to convey the news. I know they did everything they could – I am very sorry.'

'That's fine, thank you, doctor,' Daniel nodded as he walked out of the door, out of the hospital and across to the pay phone.

Coleman hung up the telephone, bowed his head and wandered solemnly back into the drawing room where Jane, Elizabeth and Jennifer sat, anxiously waiting for news.

Jane watched Coleman as he came through the door, expecting the worst. One look at Coleman's face confirmed her fears.

'Oh my God, please, no,' she said tearfully.

'I'm sorry, Jane, girls, Richard died a few moments ago. The doctors did everything they could. I really am very sorry.'

Coleman left the room, giving Richard's family their moment of private grief.

TWENTY-EIGHT

Daniel ordered a taxi then left the telephone box and walked around to the main entrance of the hospital to wait. A short while later, he was booked into a local hotel room, where he fell into a restless sleep.

Daniel woke early, showered and waited for his car and change of clothes to arrive. Thirty minutes later, he had dressed, checked out and was sat in the car as it pulled into the heavy morning traffic.

'Broughton Hall, is that correct, Sir?' asked the driver, a cheerful tone to his voice.

'Yes, thank you,' Daniel confirmed, sitting back and closing his eyes.

The weather was dull and grey, the thick cloud threatening rain. Daniel dozed as the car slowly wove its way through congested roads. He woke as the car swept through the gates of Broughton Hall and crackled up the long gravel drive.

'Thank you,' Daniel said, climbing out of the rear seat.

Slowly, he walked up the wide stone steps. The front door opened as he approached.

'Morning, Coleman,' Daniel greeted the silver-haired man solemnly. 'How are Jane and the girls?'

'Devastated,' Coleman replied. 'We need to talk. I've been up all night, but I have the information you wanted. There are things to discuss. Things to do, quickly.'

Daniel looked at Coleman. He looked tired and drawn. His face was pale, behind its covering of grey whiskers. He nodded.

'As soon as I've spoken to Jane and the girls,' he confirmed.

'OK. They're in the drawing room,' Coleman replied.

Daniel turned left and wandered down the warm, wood-panelled hallway, to the drawing room. The room was beautifully and comfortably furnished, but despite the warm fire burning brightly in the grate, it conveyed a sad and sombre mood. Daniel crossed the room, bent and kissed Jane Mead lightly on the cheek, followed by Elizabeth and Jennifer.

'I'm very sorry,' he said quietly, not wishing to reignite their grief.

Jane nodded. 'Thank you, Daniel. Thank you for

everything you have done. I know Richard would have been immeasurably grateful.'

Daniel just nodded.

An awkward silence fell. Daniel shuffled on his feet.

'I have to talk to Coleman. There are things we need to get resolved. I'll be back shortly,' he said, excusing himself.

Daniel joined Coleman in the study. They stood together, shoulder to shoulder, in front of the huge, arched window, staring out across the grounds.

'We have to act quickly, Daniel, if we're to see your plan through. Kozlov has already been replaced. A man called Radimov – I know who he is,' Coleman said, looking at Daniel.

Daniel raised an eyebrow and went to speak.

'Don't ask; just accept that I know what's going on. I still have contacts and ways of getting information. I may be retired but I still function.'

Daniel nodded. 'I know. I thought we'd have more time, but here's what I propose do.'

Coleman nodded. 'This has to work, Daniel. If it doesn't, you face an all-out war with the Russian mafia, and trust me, that's something you really don't want.'

'Agreed. I'll make the calls, then we'll talk to Jane and the girls.'

*

The telephone on Kozlov's desk rang loudly. Vladimir Radimov answered it on the fourth ring.

'Radimov,' he stated clearly and confidently.

'I cannot help you if you cannot help me,' the voice said in perfect Russian.

'I'm sorry, who is this?'

'You don't know me, but Kozlov did. Kozlov knew and feared my name, just as you will.'

'Fear you?' Radimov queried incredulously. 'Why should I fear you? Who are you?'

'Because I can burn you. Kozlov knew that. He was a sensible man – a man who negotiated.'

'Who are you?'

'Temple.'

'Temple, you're a dead man.'

'No, Radimov, I'm very much alive and I'm ready to go to war.'

Daniel waited and listened to the static silence and sensed the change.

Radimov's memory had sparked. He knew the name and made the connection. Sir David Temple would have been a name Kozlov mentioned regularly. A name he respected. A name he had feared.

'What can I do for you, Mr Temple?' Radimov asked more respectfully.

'We have a little business that needs bringing to a conclusion.'

'I'm not sure I understand.'

'Don't fuck with me, Radimov,' Daniel snapped, sure that he had the upper hand. 'Call off your dogs and do it now.'

'And if I don't?'

'If you don't, the millions of dollars your organisation creams off the Temple Stamford gas pipeline contracts will evaporate overnight, and that's an awful lot of money.'

'You need me as much as I need you, Temple. Your company can't operate here without me – you wouldn't do it,' Radimov stated confidently.

'These are people's lives we're talking about – people very close to me. You just watch me. You also forget, Temple Stamford controls a significant number of newspapers and news agencies around the world. I could make you and your friends the most photographed and written-about people on the planet. One call is all it would take. Influential people would abandon you. Your money would dry up and your faces would appear on the front page of every newspaper from San Francisco to Sydney.'

'And if I agree?'

'Then your organisation keeps the money rolling in and stays out of the press.'

'What about Mead? Someone has to be seen to

pay. I need to set an example.'

'Colonel Mead died a few hours ago.'

'Died? How?'

'Heart attack; he wasn't a well man. Kozlov knew that, so did his friend Durakovic.'

'How do I know this isn't a trick?'

'Check the obituaries, he'll be in them.'

'Obituaries appear in newspapers, newspapers you control.'

'I don't control all of them and I certainly don't control the signing of death certificates.'

'Very well, I'll check, but that still doesn't satisfy my need for an example, Mr Temple.'

'It does. Nobody has to know Colonel Mead's death was a natural one. There's nothing to stop you saying you had him killed, assassinated, poisoned. There's no one to deny it. I'll even run stories to that effect in my newspapers. The world loves a good conspiracy theory. You can still have your example and our business would be concluded.'

The telephone went silent.

'Very well, Mr Temple, I agree to your proposal – almost. I can't call off my men, it's too late – so here's my offer. If my men fail, I will send no more. You and your friends will live. I will claim the assassination of Colonel Mead and we will call the matter closed. Do we have a deal?'

'We have a deal,' Daniel said grimly, ending the call.

TWENTY-NINE

Daniel and Coleman entered the drawing room. Jane Mead sat with her daughters. They looked pale, afraid and heartbroken.

Daniel looked at them sympathetically, but had no words of comfort. No small talk.

'I'm sorry to get straight to business, Jane, but time really is against us. I have to explain some of the background to what has happened, how Richard was being blackmailed and by whom. You have to understand, we still have things to do to safeguard your future.'

Jane Mead looked at him tearfully and nodded slowly. She understood.

'It's alright, Daniel. Please continue.'

Daniel explained his plan.

Jane and girls nodded and cried.

Daniel remained passive, unemotional and focussed.

'You all agree?' Daniel asked.

Jane nodded. 'Yes, we understand,' she confirmed, her voice low and weak.

'We have to move fast. Radimov is already acting; he wants his revenge. Everything we do now will be done with the utmost speed and secrecy. Every transaction will be untraceable, at least not to you. Your new life starts right now –today,' Daniel explained, speaking directly to Jane.

Jane nodded again. She looked sad and bewildered by the speed and enormity of what was unfolding.

'You are now Jane, Elizabeth and Jennifer Edison. Your new passports will be here within the next twenty-four hours. Your entire life history, every computer record, every detail, will be replaced. Everything that was, will have gone. Once the work has been completed, everything about your previous lives will have been erased – permanently. The Mead family no longer exists. Your house in Tunbridge Wells will be purchased by a development subsidiary of Temple Stamford at full market price. Your personal effects will be removed and shipped to a storage warehouse, where they will be theoretically lost before being shipped again, untraceably. Your flight to Vancouver leaves tomorrow evening. Mead Associates has been wholly purchased by Temple Stamford. Bank accounts in your new name have been opened in your local branch of a Canadian bank. Another subsidiary of Temple Stamford has deposited the sum of just over $6 million Canadian dollars. The transaction will be unconnected and untraceable to any of us. The money equates to the value of your house, Richard's share of Mead Associates at today's exchange rate, plus a parting gift from me. Andrew Campbell, our company solicitor, will take care of all of the details.'

'What about Lesya and Yana?' Elizabeth asked.

'Don't worry about them. Andrew and an interpreter are talking with them now. My people have already been in contact with the Poppy Project, who offer support, counselling and accommodation for victims of human trafficking. I also have people trying to contact their families. I think they would both like to go home as soon as we can make it happen. Whatever happens, I can assure you they will be safe and well taken care of,' Daniel said reassuringly.

*

Petr took little interest in the passing countryside as the car sped through the narrow country lanes. He sat with his men, checking the weapons and talking quietly. It was to be a quick hit. Nothing fancy. Nothing elaborate. Just in and out, using as much firepower as necessary. His orders were plain and simple – kill Daniel Temple.

*

Coleman turned to Daniel.

'Walk with me a while, Daniel, let's leave Jane and the girls to have some time to themselves,' he said placing his hand on Daniel's shoulder.

Daniel and Coleman walked through the house and out into the cold, grey and damp afternoon.

'Something's still bothering you, Daniel,' Coleman stated intuitively.

Daniel nodded. 'They're still coming – coming for me, coming for them. I really thought we might have a little more time. This guy, Radimov, took control immediately. He knew what was expected and sounds as equally shrewd and hard as Kozlov ever was.'

Daniel stopped walking, his mind clicking up a gear, alarm bells sounding in his head.

'They're here already,' he stated.

'Are you sure?'

'Radimov said he couldn't stop them. It was too late. They must be here – out of contact.'

'You should all be safe here, at least for another twenty-four hours. After that Jane and girls will be gone. Lesya and Yana are safe. That's the point.

They'll go for me first – I'm sure of it. They won't come here.'

'Oh my god. The farm – Mrs Hall, Daniel, I'm so sorry, I didn't think.'

'No, it's OK, neither did I. I was too wrapped up in everything else.'

'You'd better get going. Take the Range Rover – take my gun from the safe in the study, you know where it is.'

Daniel left Coleman, jogged stiffly across the grounds and through the house. Grabbing the gun and car keys he sprinted to the garage. Leaping in to the Range Rover, he started the engine, snapped it into gear and floored it. The tyres squealed, wheel-spinning across the smooth concrete floor as the big 4x4 shot through the opening and onto the drive, sending gravel spitting in all directions. Daniel raced down the drive, simultaneously pressing the buttons on the steering wheel for the hands-free phone.

*

Petr's car drove slowly past the entrance to Temple Farm, turned at the road junction and doubled back to pull to a stop opposite the open-gated track. The three men climbed out and walked up the narrow, rutted lane towards the large, walled yard of the farmhouse. The car pulled away. For safety, Petr had arranged for their collection to be initiated by a telephone call after the job was done. No call – no collection.

Petr watched the house carefully as the three men approached. The afternoon light was fading rapidly and a thick blanket of dark-iron cloud hung low as the winter evening came closing in. Heavy drops of rain began to spot on the ground.

At Petr's signal, the three men stopped, waited and watched as a stout middle-aged woman walked past the downstairs windows, flicking switches and sending light spilling a short way across the darkening yard.

Petr moved them forward.

'Don't harm the woman, we may need her,' he ordered as they approached the door.

Petr stepped ahead, holding his Glock pistol one-handed behind his back. He reached forward and rang the doorbell.

The three men waited in silence as the rain began to fall.

The door opened and a jovial-looking, grey-haired lady stood before them.

'Good evening. May I help you?' she asked, politely and cheerfully.

The telephone began to ring.

'Excuse me a moment,' she said, turning her back on the door, heading for the wall-mounted telephone in the hallway.

Petr burst through the door, followed by his men.

'Temple Fa-'

Petr's hand slammed down the receiver.

*

Daniel listened as the telephone rang.

'Come on, Mrs H, pick up,' he said anxiously as he drove.

'Temple Fa-' he heard her familiar voice start, then abruptly cut off.

'Mrs H?' Daniel called. There was nothing.

The phone went dead.

'Shit,' Daniel said, pressing the accelerator to the floor.

*

Petr followed his men as they bundled Mrs Hall into the lounge and threw her down onto the sofa. She was breathing hard, her eyes wide open with terror.

'Where is Daniel Temple?' Petr asked.

Mrs Hall shook her head. 'He's not here,' she replied, her eyes nervously darting from one man to the other.

Petr nodded to the other men. 'Check the house,' he ordered.

The two men left the room and closed the door.

Petr looked back down at the woman on the sofa.

'Who are you?' he asked in a heavily-accented voice.

'I'm, I'm just the housekeeper,' she fearfully stammered.

'Where is he?'

'I, I don't know, he's been away. I'm not sure when he'll be back. I don't even know if he's in the country.'

'He's here, which means he'll be back. Are there any guns in the house?'

Mrs Hall shook her head. 'I don't know, I don't think so,' she answered.

'This is a farm, isn't it? He must have a shotgun or something?'

'No, I don't know, I'm just his housekeeper,' she repeated.

Petr nodded slowly. 'Very well, housekeeper, we'll just wait.'

*

It was raining hard. Daniel drove at breakneck speed, his heart thumping in his chest. He hurled the Range Rover through the narrow country lanes. The big V8 engine growled and roared as Daniel pushed the stability and traction control systems to their limit.

Daniel entered the last quarter of a mile, slowed the car and killed the lights as he cruised by the gated drive. There was no one there – the road dark and quiet. He turned at the road junction, doubled back and pulled the Range Rover across the gateway, blocking the drive. Climbing out of the car, he stepped in to the torrential rain, chambered a round in the Sig-Sauer and clicked on the safety.

Daniel stepped off the track, carefully made his way through the adjacent field and into the orchard, approaching the yard under the cover of the trees and large stone wall. He reached the small door in the centre of the orchard wall, eased it open an inch and looked across to the house. Lights shone in the windows. He checked each window in turn.

Seeing no one, Daniel stayed inside the orchard, followed the wall until he was level with the rear of the house and climbed over. He dropped silently into the shadows at the end of the garden and moved forward, keeping his eyes firmly fixed on the house.

Staying out of the light, he crept in low, just close enough to see into the house. The lights in his study were off. The rear corner of the house was dark. He moved forward, slowly and cautiously and peered in through the window. The thick curtains separating the study from the lounge were open. Mrs Hall sat with her back to him on the sofa. Petr was sat on a dining chair facing her. There appeared to be no conversation.

'How many?' he whispered questioningly.

He moved again, round to the front of the house, and ducked beneath the lounge window. He rose slowly with his forefinger pressed against his lips. Mrs Hall gave a small start as Daniel's distorted, rain-soaked face appeared at the window behind Petr. Daniel saw her reaction and ducked away.

Petr span. 'What is it?'

'Nothing, sorry, heartburn,' Mrs Hall answered. 'I always get it when I'm nervous.'

Petr sat back on the chair, drumming his fingers on his thigh.

The men returned to the room.

'The house is clear, Petr.'

'Good, now we just wait. Find some food and make some coffee,' he ordered.

'Yes, Petr,' the men acknowledged.

'I could make you something?' Mrs Hall offered.

The men looked momentarily relieved.

'No, I want you right here with me,' Petr snapped. 'Get some coffee,' he ordered again, turning back to the men.

'Yes, Petr,' they said, moving out of the room and back down the hall to the kitchen.

Mrs Hall looked as casually as she could over Petr's shoulder, as, with her heart in her mouth, she waited for Daniel's face to reappear.

Once more, Daniel rose slowly beneath the window, like a crocodile raising its eyes from the water. He checked Petr's location, then eased a little higher. Mrs Hall stared at him. Daniel stared calmly back, then slowly moved his finger from his mouth to his eyes. He pointed at each eye, then held up one questioning finger.

Mrs Hall understood. She coughed slightly and inclined her head, rubbing three fingers across her chest.

'Sorry,' she said. 'I've got a tickly throat. Please could I have some water?'

Daniel watched the silent performance through the window.

'You're a star, Mrs H,' he whispered and ducked away.

Daniel cleared the house, turned and jogged the short distance to his newly-converted barn and offices. Finding the key box, he entered the code, took the key, unlocked the door and slipped inside.

Daniel stepped into the office and grabbed the spare house keys from his desk. Dropping Coleman's gun in the drawer, he hit the button beneath the desk and one section of the floor-to-ceiling bookshelves slid away, exposing a narrow stainless steel door. He walked forward, punched the six-digit code into the electronic lock and waited for the solid metallic click before pushing the door open.

The steel-walled room was lined with gun racks and an array of high-quality, high-tech military equipment. Daniel grabbed what he needed; his own SIG-Sauer, silencer and a pair of night vision goggles, then closed and locked the doors. He slipped back out of the barn, splashing lightly across the yard toward the house.

Ducking back beneath the sitting room window, Daniel slowly raised his head. Mrs Hall was still sat on the sofa, facing the window, sipping a tall glass of water.

Daniel waited an agonising moment for her to see him.

'That's it, now please get this,' he said, as her eyes opened slightly, acknowledging his presence.

Daniel pointed at Mrs Hall, then pointed upwards.

'Come on, go upstairs, out of the way, Mrs H.'

Mrs Hall stared for a second, coughed and nodded again. She took another sip of water, then spoke to Petr.

'I'd like to use the bathroom please,' she said, placing her glass on the small table next to the sofa.

'Where is it?'

'Upstairs, but don't worry, I'm not going to leap out of a window and run away. Where do you think an old woman like me would go?'

Petr nodded. 'Very well, but don't take too long.'

Mrs Hall rose to her feet, glanced once at the window, then left the room.

Daniel moved round the house, ducked beneath the kitchen window and waited.

The men in the kitchen lifted mugs and plates from the kitchen table and walked back toward the lounge, carrying their coffee and sandwiches.

Daniel slipped the key silently into the lock and turned it slowly. The door opened with the faintest of clicks. He inched it open, slipped inside, found the main fuse box and flicked the master switch off.

The house plunged into darkness.

Daniel pulled the night vision goggles over his eyes and stepped into the hall, his SIG-Sauer raised in a double-handed grip.

Two men emerged at the end of the hall.

Daniel watched, cold and detached as their bodies, bathed in shades of green light, moved slowly forward.

Daniel dropped to his knees and fired, two double taps – head and heart. Both men went down.

Suddenly, bullets sprayed down the hall. Dust and fragments exploded in the confined space as walls and doors disintegrated and a solitary bullet found its target.

Daniel rolled forward, dived into the dining room and slammed his back into the wall, leaving a brilliant red smear of blood daubed across the paintwork. He lifted his hand to his arm. It was graze, nothing more. He sat and listened. Petr was moving, stumbling up the blackened staircase.

'Fuck,' Daniel exclaimed.

He rolled out of the dining room, came to his feet, ran the short distance to the stairs and peered around the wall.

Petr was waiting.

A burst of bright orange flame flared from his Uzi machine pistol as he fired at the sound, ripping plaster from the walls and blasting debris down the hall.

Daniel pulled back and waited. The firing stopped. He inched forward, glanced round the corner, stepped out and fired.

Petr was gone.

Daniel listened carefully. The sound of Petr slapping in a fresh clip was followed by slow cautious footsteps. Petr was moving down the landing, searching for Mrs Hall.

Daniel reached the top of the stairs, stood still and silent, then slowly peered around the corner.

Petr was busy. He was at the second door, a door to his left – the bathroom door. He leant forward and turned the handle. The door was locked. He stepped back, fired a short controlled burst, and the handle dropped to the floor.

Mrs Hall gasped loudly as the bullets tore through the flimsy wooden barrier.

Daniel stepped round the corner.

Petr span and fired.

Daniel dropped to his knees, aimed and fired in one fluid movement.

Petr fell and thumped hard into the floor, dead.

Daniel walked slowly down the landing, stopped and listened at the door.

Mrs Hall cried softly in the bathroom.

He knocked politely.

'Don't forget to flush, Mrs H,' he said with a cruel injection of humour.

Mrs Hall opened the door and fell into his arms.

'It's OK, Mrs H, it's all over now.'

THIRTY

John Shaw entered his office and slumped dejectedly into his chair. Flicking on his computer, he checked his calendar. His first meeting of the day, 9:00am, was Joe Gordon. He glanced up at the clock – it was 9:15.

'Great,' he said.

He leaned back in his seat and took a large gulp of his coffee as the man himself appeared, a dull-grey apparition oozing through his office door.

'You're late, Shaw. Where have you been?'

'Out,' John replied abruptly.

'Out where? You know, I really don't like your attitude.'

John glared at him. 'You know, I really don't care,' he answered, as he stood and started to empty the drawers of his desk.

Gordon stared in disbelief, dumbstruck by the response. He stood, unable to respond as John dropped his few personal possessions into a small cardboard box and walked across the office.

'You know what it is I like about you, Gordon?'

'What's that, Shaw?'

'Absolutely nothing,' John said cuttingly. 'I'll be back for the rest of my things later.'

*

The British Airways flight to Vancouver touched down on time. Jane, Elizabeth and Jennifer Edison cleared passport control, collected their small amount of baggage and headed for the exit.

In the bright, open concourse, Jane stopped with the girls by her side and scanned the large, crowded space, looking for the driver Daniel had promised would meet them.

From behind her she heard a man ask, 'Mrs Edison?' She turned.

A tall man with greying, brown wavy hair stood with his face partially hidden behind the name sign. "Edison" it read in large, black, handwritten letters.

Jane nodded, 'Yes,' she confirmed.

The man dropped the sign to his side and she gasped.

A brilliant smile beamed across the man's face.

'Daddy,' the girls cried, flying into their father's arms.

He held them tight as Jane joined them with tears of joy flowing down her smiling face.

'How?' she asked. 'I thought you were dead. We weren't even able to say goodbye. Daniel had us whisked out of the country,' she said through happy tears.

'I know. I'm sorry. It was Daniel's plan which he executed perfectly. We're safe now.'

*

Daniel drove sedately through the congested London streets and pulled in at the kerb outside the Benjamin Hotel. He stepped out of the car and bound up the marble steps into the foyer.

The dark-haired receptionist watched him approach. He looked battered and bruised, but still wonderfully handsome.

'Hello, Daniel,' she beamed.

'Hello, Teresa. I'm here to collect three things,' he said smoothly and confidently.

'Three things? You only have two bags in store,' she replied questioningly.

'I know,' he replied, with an easy smile.

'What else have you come to collect?' she asked, her golden-brown eyes sparkling.

'You,' he replied, pulling her close.

He kissed her hard, let her go and stared intently into her eyes.

She stepped back and smiled.

'I'll be ready at five. Come back and get me,' she said breathlessly.

'I will,' he said, turning and bouncing back out of the door.

*

John Shaw was waiting outside the Vauxhall Cross building as Daniel pulled in.

'Have you thought about my offer?' Daniel asked.

'I have,' John replied grimly.

'The answer's no?' Daniel asked, taking in John's expression.

John flashed a jubilant smile. 'Are you kidding? Just give me a hand for five minutes, will you?'

The two men cleared security, crossed to the elevators and headed up to John's office. Joe Gordon was still there, rummaging through John's things.

'I haven't left yet,' John growled as he entered.

Joe Gordon stood back, a look of surprise and embarrassment on his face as he looked at the huge man next to Shaw.

'Oh, I'm sorry, Dan. This is the arsehole I was telling you about.'

Gordon looked Daniel up and down.

'You must be Temple,' he said with disdain.

Daniel nodded. 'Hello, arsehole,' he replied, without offering his hand.

Gordon stood in stunned silence as the two men each lifted a box from the desk and walked calmly from the office. They rode the elevator down and crossed the marble reception area. John dropped his ID tag onto the desk as he passed.

'Bye, guys,' he said with a smile.

They walked shoulder to shoulder out of the doors.

'You know, Temple-Shaw sounds really great. It would never have worked with you taking a more active role with Richard. Temple-Mead sounds like a fucking train station,' he added, bursting into laughter.

Daniel laughed with him. 'Let's go get a drink. Then there's someone I really have to go and meet.'